I0572335

"Without a doubt, the good ship Earth
on which we all travel has problems."
Carlos Cortés

"Only when the last tree has been cut down,
the last fish been caught,
and the last stream poisoned,
will we realise we cannot eat money."
North American Native Proverb

Paradise in Limbo

Novel

T.S. Aguilar

Disclaimer: This is a work of fiction.
Any resemblance of the characters described herein with persons living or dead is unintentional, purely coincidental and couldn't be avoided.

PARADISE IN LIMBO
A T.S. Aguilar book
First edition: 2022

ISBN: 978-0-9687711-9-8

An Unpleasant Incident

The dimly glowing digits of the radio alarm clock on the bedside table in the hotel room show the time of 03:58 o'clock. Anabelle Bouchard, thirty-one-year-old society news photojournalist of an international publication headquartered in Switzerland wakes up and suddenly sits bolt upright in bed.

It is quiet all around as one should expect at this early hour of the morning in a five-star hotel. There is barely a sound, except the faintly muffled roar of a car passing by the hotel.

She wonders what caused her to be wide awake so early in the morning. Then she remembers the long flight from Madrid to San José in Costa Rica and the difference of seven time zones between Europe and Central America. It is jet lag that keeps her from getting her usual rest. Her internal clock is already chiming midday.

She turns on the bedside lamp, gets up, and walks over to the little fridge to get a bottle of mineral water. She stops at a small round table standing by the window. A folding card says breakfast is served from six in the morning. The grumbling of her stomach is going to get worse during the next two hours.

Turning to the window, she pushes up a slat of the jalousie and peers down at the still dark Avenida Central, the city's narrow main street lined with shops and hotels.

She spots a ragged boy sitting behind a stack of newspapers in the glare of a single streetlight on the corner of a side street. He can't be more than ten years old. His head sinks onto his chest exhausted from his nightly watch to secure the lucrative spot for selling the Sunday rag. His head snaps back, he yawns, stretches, and leans on the bundles of newsprint for another snooze.

Anabelle looks into a wall mirror to her left and notes the paleness of her face and trim body down to her feet. She hopes to get a tan during her short stay of only five days. The weather is supposed to be pleasant with lots of sunshine in July.

Remembering a chat with a Costa Rican in Zurich who said this time of year is called *veranito* - little summer – that makes it the only country in the world claiming to have five seasons - summer from January to March, winter from April to June, veranito in July, and autumn from August to November that isn't much different from spring in December. Instead of the usual sequence of winter, spring, summer, autumn, here it is summer, winter, little summer, autumn, and spring. Oh well, anything will do to be different.

She gets a bottle of carbonated water out of the small fridge, unscrews the top, takes a big gulp, lets out a hearty burp, and wanders off to the bathroom to take a shower.

Feeling a bit better, she dresses 'properly', as her late father, who was a naturalist himself, would have said. She puts on off-white twilled cotton shirt, shorts and sturdy shoes that will be just right for trudging along sandy and muddy paths on her round trip.

She packs all her belongings into her backpack except two cameras, a small digital voice recorder and her handbag, and is ready to leave and have breakfast, but the radio alarm clock shows only 04:35 o'clock. Why is the time passing so slowly? She is eager to get out of the big city and go in search of her first destination, the mansion of an American film star near Bahía Potrero on the Pacific coast.

She sits down on the bed, picks up her handbag and takes out the roadmap and the tourism brochures she was given upon her arrival at the airport last night. Thanks to the detailed map index, she finds the five locations of the luxurious homes of celebrities and tycoons she is supposed to interview and take photos of interior and exterior of their abodes for her exclusive report.

When she asked her editor if all the foreigners on her list would be in Costa Rica at the same time in July, he assured her in one of his best Churchillian imitations, "Oh, yes, yes, yes, yes, they will all be there!" He claimed to have received that information from a 'reliable' source at the Costa Rican embassy in Bern. Still in doubt about meeting all five inhabitants of these homes, she contemplates alternatives like taking photos of the pompous estates of national leaders, businessmen and women and interviewing some of them.

Folding up the map and tucking it into her handbag, she looks at the brochures. 'Costa Rica - Land of Peace' announces the first one of the *Instituto Costarricense de Turismo*, the national tourist board based in Miami, Florida, USA, according to the imprint. Presented is a list of key dates such as '1989 - 100 years of democracy', '1948 - abolition of the armed forces', and so on.

Hard to believe, Anabelle reckons. Outside of Costa Rica barely anyone knows anything about these dates. Not mentioned is the historic fact that Costa Rica was the last country in the world officially still at war with Germany 48 years after the end of World War II, although the Nazis' Third Reich had ceased to exist in 1945.

Costa Rica is probably the 'Country of Peace' because it dozed through the wars, just as it obviously slept through and forgot to repeal the declaration of war. This must have come to an end when some government officials in San José were woken up by the noisy celebration of West and East Germany's unification in 1991.

'Costa Rica - Land of Eternal Spring' claims the next pamphlet. That can be filed under 'assumptions' based on the five seasons as well as the very cold wind that whistled around her ears as she stepped out of the airport building to get into the car she had rented last night.

'Costa Rica - Land of Pristine Nature' trumpets the opening of the third booklet. Anabelle is now convinced that the Ticos, as the Costa Ricans call themselves, are not very frugal with self-praise. She reads with a mixture of scepticism and happy expectation that the country has more than 30 national parks with flora and fauna unique in the world, wonderfully clean, babbling mountain streams found everywhere, and rivers and lakes ideal for fishing. The whole country is claimed to be just one paradise.

Although all these national parks and flora and fauna are not really of interest to her, she expects to have a wonderful time if only half the points listed are not outright boasts and lies.
***
The first light of the approaching day floods over the layers of mist nestled in Costa Rica's central valley. Clouds of pink and grey stand in stark contrast to the dark blue tones of the western horizon. The cones of three volcanoes stand threateningly at the northern edge of the valley. They appear to watch over the sleepy towns and villages in the early Sunday morning stillness. The southern flank of the valley's mountain range still lies in murky darkness.

The dark figure of a hulking man strides hastily uphill across a pasture on the slope of Mount Pico Verde. He wears a wide-brimmed black hat pulled low over his forehead. A dark cape billows with every step, lending this somewhat bulky, muscular figure a certain elegance. His chunky boots gleam like patent leather walking through the wet grass. Sheltered by some bougainvillea bushes near a small coffee plantation, he stops abruptly, looks around and listens to the sounds of the early morning.

There is silence in the valley, almost oppressive and certainly irritating for a city dweller. Apart from the distant call of a rooster, all the man hears is his rattling breath. He's not used to the thin mountain air at an altitude of 1,800 meters above sea level. Angered, he suppresses a coughing fit by slamming his fist on the sternum. He spits out a glob of brown phlegm, leans with his elbows on his knees, and waits in this crouched position for his pulse to settle and the ringing in his ears to subside.

He has no eyes for the beauty of the angel's trumpet blossoms or orchids as he hurries on. In a wide arc, he trudges past houses and farmsteads of the mountain village of San Antonio, avoiding the paths where an early riser might run into him. He has only one object in mind - a detached, simple wooden house on the hillside above the village.

***

Was it a sound or the force of habit that woke Felipe Suárez from his deep sleep? As a bus driver and courier he is used to getting up early. Dazed, he looks up over his left shoulder at the window without a pane. One shutter is open. Hadn't he closed both of them last night? He grunts, stretches, and grimaces at the image of the graciously smiling Madonna in luminous paint at the foot of the bed. He's waiting for his morning erection to subside to go for a piss. He imagines how nice it would be if his bride Olga were lying next to him and would take advantage of his genital offerings. Often, she used to do that before he woke up. When he lay there and was awakened by her gentle bonking, he could calmly await the things that were to come and came. It was the most marvellous way to start a new day. With a deep sigh, Felipe rolls onto his side.

***

Startled by Felipe's sudden movement, the man in the cape hastily ducked and retreated from the window. He is moving silently and close to the wall. Here, he knows, the floorboards of the porch around the whole house don't creak. He sneaks along in his socks with his heavy boots taken off and tied with their shoelaces to the belt of his trousers. Under his breath he curses the shutter hinges he had oiled two days ago. Greasing them hadn't helped one bit. Although those damn things don't squeak any longer, they emit an audible cracking sound instead.

4

***

Felipe is unhappy that Olga still had to get her parents agreement for their planned marriage and the wedding. She had assured him to get back to his house late in the afternoon with hopefully positive news. So, he can spend a very quiet day. The next morning, Monday, he is scheduled for the early shift driving his bus from San Antonio to San José and accordingly would have to go to bed early. With a disappointed look, he swings his legs out of bed, fishes with his feet for the leather slippers, gets up, and staggers across the rough floorboards to the toilet.

***

The man in the cape is trying hard to organise his thoughts. He will have to come up with a new plan in a hurry. He can't execute this job as he wished, considers various possibilities of a fake suicide, and discards them all. He did not bring a pistol or any other paraphernalia that he might leave behind to fool criminal investigators.

Leaning against the east wall of the house, at a spot without windows, he pauses. He rubs his chin with his calloused fingers and racks his brain. To his great irritation, he is separated from Felipe only by the thin wooden wall and hears that guy splashing loudly while relieving himself and softly singing a popular tune. For that thought interruption alone, the man feels like killing Felipe and rising anger starts to blur his vision.

***

The sweet, acrid smell of his urine stinging Felipe's nostrils somehow reminds him of last night's meal in Rafaelo's Linda Vista restaurant of ill repute. He ate chickpeas with pork and downed a few glasses of *guaro*, the cane liquor demonised by Padre Alfonso.

When Olga prepared this meal and he washed it down with a few glasses of *guaro*, his piss didn't smell that bad the next morning. Perhaps there is something to the rumour of Rafaelo stretching the meat portion of the *garbanzos catalanes* with the regularly disappearing stray dogs of San Antonio. One should put El Fisgón Caledon, the local gumshoe on his trail to snoop on him.

Felipe shuffles into the dark kitchen and wonders if he should have breakfast now. He opens the backdoor of the house facing the mountainside to let in light and fresh air. But to the south it is not very light yet and there is no breeze. The mountain ridges only stand out faintly against the false dawn.

Outside the door at the tub filled with rainwater Felipe undergoes a brief, superficial wash of eyes, nose, ears, and armpits. He dries his face with a dishtowel and slaps his wet hair back with one hand. That's sufficient.

At the kitchen table, he lifts the cheese bell and cuts a thick strip off a chunk of Turrialba cheese. He sprinkles a bit of salt on it, wraps it into a small, soft tortilla, and bites off half the *cartucho*, the bullet as he calls his pre-breakfast snack.

Munching his food, he walks through the living room, unlocks the front door, and steps out onto the porch. With one hand he holds onto the plank on top of the railing.

The old, shrivelled lacquer paint crackles softly as it splinters under the pressure of his strong hand. He shoves the remaining snack into his mouth, licks thumb and forefinger, grunts satisfied, and leaning with his elbows on the railing, he watches the wonderful spectacle of sunrise.

The fog in the valley dissolves in the first strong rays of the sun. The rusty corrugated iron roofs of the old houses in the city of San José and the glittering steel and glass facades of the new office towers come hesitantly to light. The cities of Cartago, San Pedro, San José, Heredia, and Alajuela line the Central Valley from east to west like pearls on a string. The Irazú, Barva, and Poás volcanic cones are now bathed in a pale blue light and stand out prominently against the purplish blue of the northern horizon.

The trade wind is pushing thick clouds over the Atlantic depression Llano de Tortuguero. In an hour, when the cities come awake, the clouds on top of the mountains will resemble nightcaps or hats that will fritter away by midday.

Felipe loves to watch this early morning spectacle whenever he can. Although he wears only shorts and a grubby T-shirt, he hardly feels the damp cold of the early morning. He is a mountain man, born here and again living in this place since his return six years ago. He suffers in the stifling heat of the towns in the valley and is grateful for every hour he can escape the choking stench of exhaust fumes in the metropolis San José.

He shifts his weight from one plank of the porch to one that gives a little. The main entrance door behind him shuts silently. He shifts his weight back to the other plank and the door opens up with an agonised squeal. Slowly he moves to and fro and enjoys this game. He has fooled many a visitor to his house with this trick and used it to lend credibility to his ghost stories, which are well known in the village. It reinforced his reputation of being the *Ángel Negro*, the Dark Angel with magical powers.

It hasn't bothered him since his return to his birthplace to be seen by the villagers as the Dark Angel. He accepted never to be considered as a fellow citizen, a member of the village community, due to his somewhat mysterious origins and some incidents of many years ago. He was and is an outsider of this society that is stuck and firmly anchored in manners and idioms of Miguel de Cervantes' times of the 16th century. It suits him fine to be left alone. Lost in thought, he shifts his weight again and once more the door closes and then opens up again with its agonised cry for some grease.

***

The man in the cape stands frozen in the kitchen with bated breath. He looks into the living room when the door closes quietly. Then it opens with a hideous squeal that rings in his ears. He is unable to move and expects to see Felipe enter. But nobody enters the house and not a breeze can be felt. What's going on here? Where is Felipe? He dreads a direct encounter here in the house with this fellow who is reputed to be as strong as a bear. He would lose a face-to-face confrontation with him.

Is it possible that ghosts have a hand in play after all? What a load of rubbish! There are no ghosts! Still confused, he looks around and silently retreats out of the house through the backdoor.

From time to time, he peeks around the doorpost into the kitchen until he remembers a conversation between two villagers he overheard in the Linda Vista restaurant. Those two guys were arguing whether ghosts exist or not. One insisted that ghosts do exist and mentioned Felipe's house and the door that opened and closed magically. The other laughed at him and talked about the two loose planks in the porch that Felipe used for this trick. He should know, he claimed, because he built the porch and forgot to properly secure the two planks in question. Everybody within earshot had laughed at the superstitious man and mocked him, although every one of the amused men and women gave ghost stories more credence than the thundering sermons of the local priest.

The man in the cape concludes that Felipe must stand to the left of the front door. He returns to the kitchen and takes a heavy, over one-meter long machete hanging on the wall. The blade looks dull but when the man tests its sharpness with his thumb, he nicks the skin on its razor-sharp cutting edge. He licks the drop of blood oozing from the little cut and moves on.

Slowly, calculatingly, and cold-bloodedly, he strides silently through the living room. With his right hand he raises the machete and waits for the front door to open with its loud squeal.

***

Right after their honeymoon in Spain, Felipe and Olga will renovate, improve, and extend the house. That is his firm resolve. The house will have to be extended for Olga to move in and to have sufficient space for their eventual offspring. It is their fervent wish to have a family of perhaps two or three children even if they cannot get married in church and their offspring will be denied baptism. All that religious stuff is of no consequence to him.

His beliefs, after years of conditioning, came to an end when the local priest cursed him to roast in hell and suffer the most excruciating punishments at the hands of Satan because he was a bad boy guilty of all sorts of indescribable sins like fornication and slapping the behind of the mayor's wife, calling her 'a horny wench' and inviting her to his place for a 'good, orgasmic fuck' to which she succumbed and wasn't seen again for a whole week.

When he surmised that Satan had to be a good guy, better even than the grand master on cloud number seven, for punishing all the bad guys, the priest became infuriated and spat out that Satan is a really bad egg, the worst. He fornicates with lewd witches and dishes out a lot suffering to all sinners.

Felipe gave it some thought and then said it doesn't make any sense that Satan would punish all those who emulate him. Wouldn't he welcome them, invite them to partake in delicious meals of stolen food and never-ending orgies with lubricious wenches like the mayor's wife? After all, Satan and the sinners were cut from the same cloth, weren't they?

Felipe smiles briefly remembering how the speechless priest flapped his jaw before he ran away and denounced him as a spawn of the devil who wasn't even baptised and was successful, against all laws of society, because of dubious business dealings and thus enjoyed a shameful life.

He thinks of his upcoming wedding at a registrar's office in San José. There they wouldn't have to bother with approval of the church or appeasing Olga's parents who were determined to prevent their bond of matrimony. It would be a good turn of events with both of these parties out of the picture.

The reasons for the priest's irrational outbursts remained hidden from Felipe. He suspected it had something to do with his affair with the mayor's wife, who later got a divorce and made a living as a porn film star in the United States. A few dark hints from his aunt Maruja were also a clue, although he didn't pay any heed to them.

The reasons for the nagging of Olga's family on the other hand were clear. Her parents belonged to one of those fanatical religious sects from the wealthy countries of the Americas up north, the USA and Canada. They would never consent to their daughter marrying an infidel, even though Olga had split from the sect some time ago and was labelled a heretic.

Felipe understands why she is afraid and a bit sad that she will not have the support of her family and be excluded from the circles of the community once they are married.

Many times he and Olga discussed this sore point when she shared her fears with him. Usually he could put her mind at rest with his life's story. He grew up without relatives in a strange family and achieved something in life without the help of friends or members of the community. She would quickly adjust to her new situation and could count on his affection, support, and love. Soon, when their children's laughter echoed through the house, their little world would be perfectly all right.

The door behind him opens with its familiar squeal. Still deep in thought, Felipe hears the faint sound of somebody's heavy breathing. He straightens up and turns his head, a little surprised. The flash of his heavy long machete's blade against a black background is the last thing he sees in his life.

***

The man in the cape wields the machete with all his force. The slash is perfect. Felipe's head separates from the torso between the fifth and sixth cervical vertebrae of the neck, flies in a slight arc to the left into the garden, rolls down the slope, bounces like a ball over a stony surface, and comes to rest in a clump of tall margaritas. The broken eyes stare up at the porch.

The assassin is obviously familiar with this type of 'wet' job. In the moment of landing the blow, he quickly leaned against the doorpost and pushed his victim's upper body over the railing with one foot. The blood pumping out of the stump of the neck splashes over the bushes, flowers, and gras below. Unmoved, he observes the last convulsions of the body and waits in this position until the blood flow peters out. Then he lets the limp body slide to the floor and turns away muttering, "That's the fate of people who know too much stuff they're not supposed to know."

He breathes very calmly now, goes into the kitchen, washes the blood off the blade, hangs the machete back on the nail in its place. The first part of his task has been successfully completed.

The man slips on gloves and begins a systematic search of the house. Without haste he looks into every pot and box on the rough, wooden shelves and puts everything back in its place where he found it.

He doesn't find anything in the living room either and sighs with a hint of helplessness. Should he still have to search the bedroom? But there is hardly any hiding place, only an open wardrobe, the bed, a chair, and an open bedside table. He lifts the mattress. Nothing. An old worn leather jacket hangs behind the door. Whose garment might it be? It seems to be too small for Felipe. Judging by the cut, it's an old-fashioned women's jacket. He reaches into the inside pockets. They're empty. Paper crackles in the torn lining. He pulls out a bulging and sealed rectangular brown envelope.

The man weighs the envelope in his hand and examines it for signs of opening. He rips it open, pulls out dollar bills and a key to a safe deposit box that he puts into his wallet. It takes him a while to count the hundred and twenty thousand dollars. It is not the documents he had expected to find but a nice bonus for his work.

Having finished his search, he leaves the house through the back door. He looks around cautiously. No one is in sight. Who would come up here so early on a Sunday morning? He walks close to a hedge in Felipe's shoes until he gets to the trail that leads to the summit of Pico Verde. He sits down on a ledge, takes off cape and hat and rolls them up. The rope intended for the hanging of Felipe and slung over his shoulder and chest is discarded in the bushes. So are Felipe's shoes. He unbuckles a nylon backpack from around his waist, takes out a pair of running shoes, puts them on, and stuffs everything else inside the bag, including the heavy boots, hat, cape, and the money in its envelope. He looks at his watch. 05:46 o'clock. That means with a little over an hour's hike to the village of Aserri, he can catch the bus that will deliver him almost to the door of his abode in San José before 08:00 o'clock.

Cheerful, the man swings the backpack over a shoulder and follows the direction to Aserri as indicated on a signpost. Whistling a merry tune, he notices that his breath has stopped rattling. It doesn't surprise him. His doctor was right when he said that physical ailments are mostly of psychosomatic origin. With his job well done, he can now breathe easily.

***

At 06:45 o'clock, Anabelle is sitting at her table in the hotel's arcade café, waiting impatiently for her bill. She was surprised when the waitress informed her breakfast was not included in her room bill. The manageress was summoned and confirmed it because only a room with a bath had been requested in her booking that had been prepaid from overseas. Her objection that the hotel's advertisements showed all rooms to include breakfast was dismissed and the manageress even threatened to call the police if she refused to pay for the breakfast. Anabelle gave up, settled the bill and was glad to leave this run-down dump still advertised as a luxury grand hotel.

She picks up her cameras, voice recorder and handbag and is ready to leave when a young man formally dressed in suit, stiff collar and tie comes to her table, introduces himself as the press officer Hernan Galindo of the national tourism institute and sits down without being invited to do so. He welcomes her to the country with the usual *"Bienvenida a Costa Rica"* and enquires whether she has information material and a travel itinerary.

Anabelle is confused. She asks him how he found out that she is in the country, since hardly all tourists are greeted like that. He is calling on her, he explains, because she is a journalist. Her suspicions aroused, she asks how he found out and why she is given this attention? Is her visit monitored? Is it his intention to control her with an official 'tour guide'? She hopes to cut him off with her questions, because she wants to get going and be on her way to the coast. The argument about breakfast has already wasted too much of her time and she still has to retrieve her rental car from a public parking lot, since the receptionist had claimed that the hotel garage was full.

Galindo notices her impatience. She has the straps of her two cameras and the handbag already over her shoulder and a hand on her backpack. He orders a coffee and quickly explains that he only found out about her presence due of the manageress' attention. She should definitely get to know this lovely lady, Doña Marilena. She can tell her where to buy the best precious stones and the famous native gold jewellery at the best prices. Anabelle thanks him for the tip, is not interested in the purchase of touristic junk and adds that she got to know the manageress, that arrogant bitch, well enough and more than she would have liked.

He is taken aback by the hotel's manageress being called an 'arrogant bitch', and hands her a thick folder of information for journalists. She tries to reject it saying that she has sufficient information for the purpose of her trip, but he insists that she should at least have a look at the brochures that highlight everything worth visiting and will confirm Costa Rica's reputation as a gem of environmental protection and conservation.

Anabelle leafs through a brochure and wonders what Galindo actually wants to achieve with his verbiage. On the one hand he has obviously come because she is a journalist, and on the other, he makes suggestions as if she were a tourist who wants to offset the cost of her trip with the purchase of dubious cheap gems. It makes her even more suspicious that Doña Marilena had sicked this representative of the tourism institute on her after she had torn up her reservation upon her arrival last night and claimed the hotel was fully occupied until the press pass was shoved under her nose. She wants to question him but thinks of her task of having to deliver photos and interviews for an exclusive report and her limited time and does not bother to pursue this matter.

She mentions that her trip is fully planned and the exact destinations are marked on her map. Still, she'd like to know more about the much-touted conservation program because she's been sceptical about the information she gleaned from the brochures so far and asks if it is true that more than twelve percent of the national territory is totally protected with over thirty national parks and nature reserves. That just seems incredible in view of the documented information about Brazil, Ecuador, Bolivia, and neighbouring Nicaragua. The other thing that puzzles her is the lack of information about crime and tips for precautionary measures, as is common in other Latin American countries.

Galindo beams a big smile and assures her that it was a good to address these points precisely. He is proud to tell her that crime is practically unknown in Costa Rica, with the exception of some burglaries. She can feel completely safe. In this respect as well is Costa Rica the land of peace and friendship, a small paradise of tranquillity amidst the turbulences of the rest of the world.

Her information regarding the conservation programs is correct. There are even 45 protected forest areas that cover a total of more than 10,000 square kilometres of land equivalent to twenty percent of the national territory. These areas include national parks, biological and wildlife sanctuaries, and recreational areas. Everywhere in the country she will not only find untouched nature, but also the cleanest beaches, rivers, and lakes in the world. Nowhere would she discover even a trace of pollution of the waters or destruction of nature. Costa Rica is the country with the largest conservation program per capita of any country in the world.

Galindo proves his tourism expert skills. With half-truths, embellishments, and blatant exaggerations, he offloads a pack of lies into Anabelle's pannier. He knows, like all his clever colleagues, that visitors, tourists, only see what they want to see of what is shown. Galindo dishes up everything beautiful and withholds the ugly truths on the assumption that she's just another village idiot.

That's what tourism is all about besides unhealthy, overpriced food, loads of alcohol, and hoping the morons go home with a memorable sunburn. Once this journalist has seen a few beautiful sites and survived her stay with life and limb unscathed, she will almost certainly write a report in jubilant tones. It is his job to achieve this goal.

Happy to have evidently landed in a true paradise as presented by Galindo and documented in the information folder, Anabelle grabs her backpack, bids farewell and walks briskly in the glorious sunshine across the small square in front of the neoclassical building of the National Theatre. In the guarded public parking lot, she climbs into her rental car and drives out of town towards the Pacific coast along the almost empty streets of an early Sunday morning.

***

An old rattling bus serves the route Alajuela to San José. It starts with a wheeze from the transmission and then gets moving in first gear while emitting a thundering fart and a massive cloud of black smoke from its exhaust before the driver manages to hammer the gear shift into second.

An old man on a rusty bicycle overtakes the bus with ease. The bus driver looks surprised at first and shouts at 'the old bitch', as he calls his vehicle, to get moving while rocking to and fro in his seat.

It is quite a spectacle and amuses the few passengers in the front. They join in the driver's shouting, but the bus can't catch up with the cyclist on the slightly inclining road despite all the verbal encouragement and abuse that ends in uproarious laughter when the bus takes a right turn and finally picks up some speed on a downhill stretch of road.

Olga sits in the back of the bus in one of the seats of the last row. She looks deeply troubled and wants to be alone with her thoughts and the awful memories of the meeting with her parents.

It was supposed to be a beautiful day. She had only wanted to talk to her mother who had been so encouraging on the phone yesterday. The hope of getting at least her consent to marry Felipe was shattered when her father intervened and the family visit last night turned into a nightmare. Instead of open arms and a conciliatory conversation, she was met with her father's distrust and suspicion that escalated into an unbelievable climax. Her father's words that she couldn't marry Felipe, not only because the family didn't agree, but because Felipe was her brother, are still ringing in her ears. His spiteful laughter sounded diabolical. She would never forget him almost bursting with venom when he foretold her never to find peace even after death. She had committed an original sin! Incest! With her brother! She was a slut, a whore, a piece of dirt! In the hellfire of eternal damnation she would roast!

Olga had been so mesmerised by his outburst that she didn't pay any attention to her mother who sat opposite her on the sofa with her hands in her lap, rolling her eyes mockingly and snickering while listening to her husband. Stunned, Olga heard his tirades, unable and unwilling to believe his words, yet unable to maintain the necessary distance to stand up and turn her back on this religious zealot forever. After all, it was her father who demonised her. She couldn't imagine him shying away from the worst of lies in order to bring her back into the sect to which the family belonged and that she had escaped some time ago.

At that moment she simply lacked the human experience to recognise that his words had nothing to do with Felipe or the family. It was just his power game. He tried desperately to maintain his status as head of the family and resorted to the dirtiest tricks to do so. It was his only way to compensate for the lifelong humiliation he had endured because of his sexual impotence. He was not the begetter of any of his children to whom he had nevertheless tried to be a good father. He made up for his failure in the matrimonial bed with an iron fist towards the entire family.

That way he maintained a minimum of self-respect and saw every attempt of his children, who all had different fathers, as an attack on his authority as head of the family when they wanted to go their own way.

Olga should have noticed something fishy about his shouting. When her three-year older brother José was dragged in as 'evidence' and the birthmark on his abdomen was presented, she noticed that it was very similar to Felipe's. Thus, Olga fell for the claim that Felipe's mother had been a cheap whore who had a leg-over with any man in San Antonio for a few drinks, also with Olga's father. Allegedly, it provided proof of her blood relationship with Felipe.

With tears streaming down her cheeks, she rushed out of the house, ran away from the cult camp and only wanted to be with Felipe for some comfort and reassurance as quickly as possible and talk to him about everything. But it was too late for the last bus, and she could not locate a taxi.

She found shelter for the night in a cheap hotel in Alajuela and set out early in the morning on her trip to San Antonio.

Olga's separation from her family was sealed. The chasm had become unbridgeable. She wondered how it could have happened that her father, who had never cared about religion for most of his life, turned into a religious fanatic? It was the story of thousands of families in Latin America who are inveigled to join one of these sects run by ruthless North American profiteers that operate under the guise of religiosity and promise eternal peace of mind.

Seven years earlier, when Olga's father, as finance manager of the town of Bagaces, was caught with his hands up to his armpits in the municipal treasury, the entire family had been expelled from the town in disgrace. Three years later they ran into the 'missionaries' of the 'Church of Divine Enlightenment'. All family members were persuaded to quickly join the sect, which had become active in Costa Rica only recently. Father became finance manager, mother ran the community kitchen, brothers Juan and José were allowed to swing a hammer building the camp, Diego, the good-for-nothing, had become a preacher, and Sister Martina sat in the reception room and delighted the missionaries with the sight of the cleavage of her barely covered humongous breasts.

Only Olga didn't really want to participate. She understood what was going on. The newly won 'lambs' moved into one of the new houses in the barbed-wire enclosed camp, were dressed in uniforms, given a job and regular meals, and had to sign all their worldly possessions over to the sect in exchange for peace of mind. Within two years, the religious community had become one of the largest real estate owners in the country. In order to avoid ending up with the hated reputation of being a *terrateniente*, a big landowner, the acquired hectares of farmland, pasture and forests were auctioned off and millions of dollars were made.

Olga wanted to break away from the sect as soon as she realised that the zeal demanded and displayed had nothing to do with the propagated religiosity. Praying five times a day, penance and choral lessons served to keep the 'lambs' from coming to their senses. It didn't surprise her one bit. Had these poor people come to their senses and realised that as a result of gifting their property to the sect they now owned nothing, there would have been a revolt. All the 'gifts' of interest to speculators would go under the hammer at auction. When a large profit had been achieved, the sect's 'world leader' would visit and give laudable speeches in an American accent that not even those sect members who spoke good English could understand. The young women of the sect were driven to the airport on such occasions, where they cheered the 'leader' on command when he got out of or into his private jet.

Once more taken to the airport to cheer the 'Divine Messenger' for the fourth time in six months, Olga seized the opportunity amidst the chaos when the big boss rattled down his jet's gangway totally shitfaced and kissed the runway with his bleeding snout. She slipped away and asked a bus driver in front of the airport building if he would take her to San José without paying the fare because she had no money. He agreed, said he seemed to remember her and asked if she had lived in San Antonio. Yes, but that was more than four years ago and only for a year, although her parents were from that village but had moved around a lot. At the terminus in San José, the driver invited her for a meal and a cup of coffee, and she shared her story with him. He offered her shelter at his house, but she preferred to visit a girlfriend who could provide housing and work. Olga had promised the nice guy, who introduced himself as Felipe Suárez, that she would visit him soon in San Antonio. She had kept her promise, fell in love, and was now on the run to him.

The bus rumbles into the terminal station. Hastily Olga jumps out of the bus through the back door and runs down Calle 6 and Avenida 5. She twists a foot on the uneven pumice blocks of the

16

pavement. She hardly notices and hurries on. Breathless. From a distance she sees the bus to San Antonio. The few passengers on this Sunday morning have boarded the bus and it is ready to depart. Olga runs in the middle of the street and waves with both hands.

The bus driver sees her in the rear-view mirror and waits until she gets on, out of breath. She sits down on the front bench, and he winks at her. She knows him as Felipe's colleague but cannot remember his name. He stares at her heaving bosom until she warns him to keep his eyes on the road. He laughs and claims the old vehicle has an automatic pilot.

His remarks and her replies result in an amusing play on words. Olga almost forgets her grief. In a good mood, she gets off the bus in San Antonio.

It has started to rain. The water droplets are so fine that the precipitation feels like dense fog. People on the way to church don't even bother to open their umbrellas. Despite all protective measures, the wetness standing in the air settles in hair and clothing and moisturises exposed skin.

Olga takes a shortcut across a pasture from the bus station to Felipe's house. The path through the damp grass is arduous but shorter than the road that winds its way over several hairpin bends up the mountain. On the narrow bridge over a rivulet that is already called Río Grande at this point, she passes Bernal, the mentally retarded son of the local police captain. He doesn't look at her and babbles incomprehensible stuff. People say he's the born politician because he talks all the time and nobody understands him, does nothing and yet lives better than anyone else in town.

Arriving at the lower garden fence, Olga looks up the steep slope to the house and sees through the slats of the porch railing what looks like a bundle of rags. The front door is open, and she has the impression that Felipe, in a sudden rush of cleanliness, must have decided to tidy the house. She wants to sneak up the side stairs, approach Felipe on tiptoe in the house and surprise him from behind. She climbs over the waist-high garden fence with a tingling feeling of excitement.

She creeps towards the house and stops. Everything is so quiet. Something is wrong here. She can feel it. He must have noticed her already and is now preparing a surprise of his own. She peeks out from behind a bush and sees Felipe peering out of a tall bunch of margaritas. That looks so weird. He looks up with a serious expression and doesn't respond to her calls.

Amused, she walks along the slope, carefully watching where she steps on this steep terrain. Arriving above the flower bed, she notices that Felipe hasn't moved yet. Distracted, she slips up, falls onto her hip, slides down the slope, and tries to grab hold of the damp grass. A red-brown liquid oozes through her fingers. Disgusted she lets go and her slide comes to an abrupt end in the patch of flowers. Where is Felipe? She looks down and finds herself sitting on his head, the bloody stump of the neck pointing up.

It takes a moment for her to grasp the situation. Gently she touches the head. She feels it isn't a papier-mâché dummy Felipe had put there as a practical joke. It is his actual head.

She lets out a bloodcurdling scream, falls over, picks up the head and hugs it, shrieks, cries, then drops it again. The mental suffering drives her insane, she screams out her pain with her mouth wide open. She gasps for air and belts out one piercing scream after another. They go unheard. She falls into a trance-like state of shock, turns the head to look at the face and cradles it in her arms.

Her sobbing subsides. She gets up with difficulty, climbs along the slope and up the stairs to the porch. She takes one look at the body stretched out there and descends again.

Olga leaves the property through the garden gate. Not noticing the few people coming towards her scrambling to get out of her way because of the head in her arms and the blood smeared dress and arms. She walks along the mountain road into the village to the police station.
***

Eduardo, in the rank of Auxiliary Policeman, is proud of his uniform. It was issued to him when he was invited to join the rural police force after the elected President of the Republic took office fourteen months ago. His tireless campaigning for the party that governs the country, qualified him for the position of policeman despite being barely able to read and write or add two and two together. His sudden elevation from butcher's assistant to a man of authority follows the tradition in Costa Rica, as in most Latin American countries, to replace all personnel in the police, customs and other public offices after a change of government.

These jobs are called *chorizos*, pork sausages, that are distributed to party members and supporters who helped to win the election. So it can happen that one meets yesterday's shoeshiner or ambulant banana vendor today as policeman, customs officer or clerk in the passport office, while a former accountant of the state bank may stand on one of the streetcorners of the capital as a black-market currency dealer attracting tourists with his wailing cry, "*Dolares, colones, Señores, cambio, change!*" Qualifications of any kind are conveniently overlooked, as are the enormous costs, losses, and corruption accompanying this ludicrous and indiscriminate turnover of personnel.

Eduardo stands in front of the San Antonio police station in his shiny boots and khaki-brown uniform decorated with all sorts of cords, tassels and martial badges. All day long he stares out from under the peaked cap pulled down to his eyebrows and enjoys the sight of the señoritas stumbling past on stiletto heels. He may hold the door open for important people who wish to enter the station's inner sanctum but denies access to community-known bellyachers who, in his opinion, have no reason to come to the police station. Occasionally he slaps the thick end of his American baton into the left hand to show passers-by that he is ready for action. This is the life he's always wanted, yes, Sir, standing around and being respected.

He sees a dirty young woman approaching the police station with a bundle in her arms. Dirty as she is, he won't let her enter. She should go wash herself first, though she has quite a passable figure. If she were clean he would like to have some fun with her in one of the holding cells, like the captain has with the village slags when teaching them a lesson in civility.

***

Olga stops in front of the policeman who keeps her at a distance with his baton. He asks harshly what she wants. She lifts the bundle a little and murmurs she needs to speak to the captain. He grins, knowing that the captain doesn't wish to be disturbed during Sunday's televised Italian league football game. He pokes her in the ribs with the thick end of the baton, grunts that the captain is very busy and that she should piss off. But she won't move.

He hisses that she's a persistent little slut and raises the baton ready to hit. Before he can bring it down on her head or shoulder, she presses the filthy bundle on his chest, his clean uniform! Horrified, he jumps back, slams into the door that opens, and lets out a scream. It's a head, a human head, that she pressed on him! He blows all his fuses, lashes out and hits Olga several times before she falls to the ground. Howling loudly he runs away once he has recognised the head. It is that of Felipe Suárez, the *Ángel Negro,* the much-feared Dark Angel.

The noise at the entrance startles the policemen inside the station who are engrossed in football shop talk. A sergeant rushes to the door, but instead of any expected revolution proclaimers, a young woman lies bleeding on the steps.

The sergeant rants about the mess and his curses lure his colleagues to the door. Seeing the severed head the woman is holding by the hair, they pull back. The sergeant remarks that it is the head of the *Ángel Negro.* The other cops nod in agreement and are at a loss for words.

Finally, the craggy faced captain Edwin Rodríguez shifts his bulky figure into the crowd, has a look at Olga and chimes in, "Holy shit! This is really an unpleasant incident. Now we can forget about the rest of the football game. Damn it, just when it got interesting."

Olga's Confession

Detective Inspector Rico Ramírez, a quiet, thirty-year-old career criminalist, sits at the kitchen table with an almost finished breakfast on a plate in front of him. He sips his coffee and reads a report in the Sunday newspaper. It's about the kidnapping of a member of parliament's two children, the case he had solved two days before. The abduction of the kids had turned out to be a set-up by the father, the MP, to extract ransom money from his wife's rich family.

"It's disgusting," grumbles Rico. "A few facts mixed in with speculation and hypotheses. Is that supposed to be objective reporting? It's amazing what these inkpissers pass off as sound journalism. Truly unbelievable!"

His wife Martha, pregnant in the seventh month, gets up from the table, casts him a resigned look, holds out a dish of rice and black beans, and asks if he would like some more of the *gallo pinto*. Politely he declines and voices his preference for marinated chili peppers stuffed with cottage cheese. It is his favourite snack of a Sunday breakfast because it lets 'fresh air whistle through his noggin'. But his wife knows that the snack makes him as horny as a tom cat in May. She denies him his treat with the jocular remark that he will have to go without it for at least the next three months.

The telephone is ringing. Rico gets up from the kitchen table, goes into the living room, picks up the phone after the fourth ring and says: "Yes? Talk to me!"

Gustávo "Gus" Goicoechea, Rico's older colleague of the OIJ, the *Organisación de Investigaciones Judiciales*, the crime investigation organisation is on the phone.

"Hello Rico. It's me, Gus. You've got to bail me out. I'm alone at headquarters. All our colleagues on Sunday duty are busy in the field with other cases. It's this: the police captain of San Antonio called. He has arrested a woman who sawed off her boyfriend's head, he said. It's probably a jealousy drama or domestic violence like the couple in San Ramón last Friday. The woman has confessed but refuses to sign the confession."

"Gus, you squawk like an old maid who sat down on her ball of yarn. What do I have to do with this case? Seems to have been solved already."

"No, it hasn't been solved at all, Rico. She refuses to sign. There is something fishy about it. Please, help me. I'd go but have to deal with eight other cases already. Five alleged suicides, two unidentifiable corpses in Río Súcio, and a child beaten to death by its drug addled mother. That is enough to get excited, isn't it?"

"Listen, there's no need to get excited. The cases you listed sound like a perfectly normal Sunday morning. And now you want me to go to San Antonio, me, who is off duty."

"I know you're off duty and I'm sorry to bother you, but I'm not asking for much. Drive over to San Antonio, inspect the crime scene, collect evidence, see the pathologist who will be checking the corpse, and talk to the alleged killer, the woman who refuses to sign her confession. You're most efficient dealing with such a case and should be done within a couple of hours. What do you say?"

"What I say? You're messing up my holy Sunday, Gus. As a special favour and only if you promise to buy me a couple of beers, I'll go. But if I have to spend more than two hours of my valuable time on this case, I'll squash your balls with a steam iron."

"Yes, yes, Rico, always your empty promises. I'll get you a couple of beers and more if you want. Thank you, hombre. Did you hear? I, the proud descendant of proud Basques, thanked you."

Rico hangs up the phone, strolls deep in thought back into the kitchen and looks at Martha. A shrug, raised eyebrows, and she knows what's up. He takes his jacket off the hook, puts his arm around her shoulders, strokes her long black hair, gives her a gentle hug and kisses her forehead. "See you soon."
***

The San Antonio police station's bare holding cell reeks of disinfectant. Rico squats in front of Olga. She is crouching in a corner. A constant stream of tears washed tracks on her cheeks. She cries silently and makes barely a sound.

He wonders if a cold-blooded murderess goes into severe shock and weeps in deep sorrow as is evidently the case with this young woman. He shouldn't ask himself such a question to prevent the inclination of getting emotionally involved with the suspect.

He is holding the confession in his hand, reads it once more and asks in a calm voice whether she, Olga Miranda Cisneros, confessed voluntarily to have committed the murder. When she doesn't answer, he wants to know why she is refusing to sign the confession.

Again, he receives no answer. He knows that he won't get a word out of her. She needs medical attention urgently.

He gets up, goes into the guard room, and demands that the captain call a doctor immediately to provide medical care for the suspect. Then he adds that he wants to inspect the scene of the crime and asks for a policeman to accompany him there.

Edwin ignores the demand of medical care for the woman he arrested and refuses to provide a police escort for Rico. He states that all the cops are busy looking for the murder weapon, which a witness claimed to have seen the woman throw away somewhere along the mountain road. Rico just needs to drive along that road, where the policemen are looking. The scene of the crime is the last house on the slope above the village. A guard should stand in front and the pathologist is there.

Rico is surprised. "The pathologist? Why the pathologist? Isn't the inspection of the murder victim completed?"

"No, it's only just begun. The pathologist arrived about ten minutes before you did."

"Really? That's very odd. Your report states that the cause of death was the victim's decapitation. His head was sawn off with a bone saw, you claim. How did you come to that bold conclusion without any pathological findings?"

Edwin puffs up his chest. "I'm an experienced butcher. After looking at the cut of the neck, I knew right away that you can only make such a smooth cut with one of the finest bone saws. Yes, I know my stuff and the tools of my trade."

Rico would laugh at this windbag if it weren't such a serious matter. He asks him, "Is that so? In your career as a butcher, have you ever persuaded a live animal to keep still while you were sawing off its head?"

"What? Of course not! That's impossible!"

"Indeed? But it works with a human?"

Edwin looks caught with his hand in the cookie jar. "Uh... not if he's still awake. She drugged him beforehand. Yes, that's how she did it. You know how wenches are, don't you?"

"No, I don't. Also, I didn't see it mentioned in your report."

"That's because Olga lied. Typical woman. Yes, yes, that will be the reason why she refuses to sign her confession."

"And? Did the suspect confess of her own will? No problems?"

Edwin blushes and looks down at the tips of his boots. "Now, uh, well, one could say so."

A constable standing in the corridor leading to the holding cell grins broadly. Rico looks at him and continues to question Edwin, "May I assume that the young woman suffered her injuries on head, collarbone, forearm and ankle by walking into a revolving door?"

The constable roars with laughter. Edwin snaps angrily, "Shut up, Sánchez! Control yourself! Listen, Sir, I haven't killed anyone! You're interrogating me as if I'm the suspect. The little slut in the cell is the murderess! That's beyond any doubt as far as I'm concerned. She was very stubborn during the interrogation, and I helped to loosen her tongue a little. One can drive a pig to slaughter only by using a big stick."

"You describe your interrogation method very vividly, captain. How long have you been in the police service?"

"Fourteen months. Why do you ask?"

Rico just nods in response. He knows now that the captain received his appointment to the local police force as a *chorizo* and got only rudimentary police training, if any.

Rico leaves the station and after a short drive stops at the murder victim's house, looks around and murmurs: "This is a gorgeous location. What a view! Incredible."

A bored corporal of the local police stands at the garden gate. Rico shows him his identification and enters the house through the backdoor. He takes a quick look around the kitchen, the toilet and shower niche next to it, goes into the living room, looks into the bedroom and walks through the open front door onto the covered veranda. A man, his back turned, is busy examining the decapitated corpse. Rico asks if he is the pathologist.

Without turning, the man rasps, "Hello, Ramírez, you queer fish. I was expecting you. I heard you are supposed to close this case. That won't happen any time soon."

"Doctor Bustamante! I am glad Goicoechea called you to come here. Why do you say this case will not be concluded any time soon? What can you tell me?"

"We can dismiss the suspicions and allegations in the police report. It's complete nonsense the captain pulled out of his arse. First of all, the time of death is two to three hours ago. There is no sign of a fight or poisoning of the victim. I assume the victim was beheaded with a smooth, very sharp weapon from behind by a man

24

of enormous strength. From the location of the body, it's certain the perpetrator is a right-handed master of his craft, a professional killer, because a surgeon could not have done it any better."

"Could a bone saw have been used as the murder weapon?"

"What? A bone saw? No, Ramírez! You shouldn't believe anything written in the police report. As I said, the beheading was carried out with a very sharp, smooth-bladed weapon, something like a Japanese Samurai sword."

"It's unlikely anyone in our country would come walking up here with a Samurai sword to behead a man. How about a machete? Is it feasible a machete was used?"

"That's possible if it is a long one in excellent condition and superbly sharpened. One of those machetes used for poking around in the garden is out of the question. Why do you ask?"

"I've seen something of interest in the kitchen. Could I have a pair of your surgical gloves and a large plastic bag?"

"Sure. But why? Have you found a machete in the house?"

"That's correct," says Rico, puts on the latex gloves and goes into the house. In the kitchen, he takes the long machete with the clean blade off the wall and checks the cutting edge. He puts it in the plastic bag and returns to the porch. He shows it to Doctor Bustamante who takes one look and sucks air through his teeth.

"Oh yes, Ramírez, that could be the murder weapon if it is very sharp. Have you tested it?"

"No, but I had a close look at the cutting edge. It appears to be honed to perfection, doesn't have a single nick."

"Good, good. I'll send it to the forensic lab with all the other stuff I will have gathered."

"I have a couple more questions, doctor."

"Go ahead."

"Is it possible the decapitation did not take place in this house and the corpse was only dumped on the porch?"

"Out of the question. No, there's blood spilled all over the garden and it looks as if the head had ended up in the flower patch where the accused woman found it and picked it up. Also, the small splinters of lacquer paint on the inside of the victim's hands and elbows appear to be identical to the paint on the balustrade. It may mean the victim was holding on to the railing and possibly resting with his elbows on it."

"I see. Is it possible more than one person was involved and the victim was decapitated while he was held to the balustrade?"

"I doubt it very much. Just look at the corpse's muscles. That guy was as strong as an ox. It would have taken more than one person to hold him down with the executioner swinging the weapon. Impossible. No, I presume it was a surprise attack from behind while the victim was standing at the railing."

"Okay. You seem to have a clear picture of what happened here. When the corpse is picked up for transfer to the morgue, tell the driver to stop at the police station to pick up the victim's head. I have to go back to the station for another word with the captain."

"Good luck, Ramírez. Tell him that the woman is innocent. She couldn't possibly have done it."

"I will, doctor. And thank you for your excellent work."

Rico drives back to the station where people are queuing up. As he finds out, they are all residents of San Antonio who 'volunteered' to provide 'witness statements' in support of the captain's allegation of Olga having killed the Dark Angel. Every one of the men and women has been briefed by the captain and are supposed to confirm his report in the hope that the evidence found at the scene of the crime will be so meagre that one convincing witness testimony will clear the path for Olga's conviction.

Rico settles in Edwin's swivel chair and interrogates one 'witness' after another, embroiling them in contradictions with his questions. Thus, he can tear up one statement after another and throw it in the wastebasket. They are all conjectures or amount to slander of Felipe Suárez and Olga Miranda Cisneros. Only one woman insists that her testimony is a statement of truth. Rico asks her if she is willing to repeat it under oath in court. When she confirms it, he mentions casually that perjury carries a penalty of at least five years in prison and promptly she retracts her statement.

Edwin finds Rico's method of interrogation simply disgusting. His whole day is spoiled. Instead of watching football on TV, he sees his house of cards collapsing. He doesn't understand the detective at all. Why is he making life so difficult for himself?

Everything was so neatly arranged - deed, victim, suspect - simple and spicy, like pork sausages. His boys would keep looking and surely find a whole pile of murder weapons. The scene of the crime could have been prepared with two buckets of ox blood in such a way that even the most hardened reporters of the yellow press would have puked. The pathologist could probably have been persuaded to make a statement that fits his police report with enough bundled cash or, in the worst case, a trip to Miami including a visit to a brothel. Olga, the little slut, belongs in jail, basta!

But how can he persuade the detective to see his point of view? After all, he can't tell him that he called his contact in the governing party who urged him to close this case by hook or by crook. Even less can he tell this detective that it is an excellent and perhaps last opportunity for him to settle a score with Olga's father.

He just couldn't forgive the ignominy of the old Miranda having bequeathed his family with that retard Bernal. It was a drawn-out drama that had started with Edwin screwing Miranda's wife twice a week in the back of his butcher shop in return for brisket, steaks, and pork chops. The result was the healthy boy, Diego. When his wife had found him out, she threatened him with divorce to forego a discovery of her long-standing affair with the priest from Aserri. The result of her dalliance was Bernal. It prevented her from going through with the divorce. So, she claimed the old Miranda had put the bun in her oven. And what a bun Bernal had turned out to be - a total failure not even fit for police duty! Edwin had had to nibble on that bun ever since.

While he paces up and down, deep in thought, the van of the San José morgue stops in front of the station. The driver enters the guard room and says that he is supposed to pick up a severed head. Absentmindedly Edwin points to a large waste bin in the corner. The driver takes a look and starts to berate the captain of this station for the desecration of human remains, which amounts to a criminal offence. Ripped out of his thoughts, Edwin shrugs and mutters that he didn't have better storage for that filthy head full of blood and mud. The driver should just get the head out of the bin and piss off. An argument ensues that goes on until the driver has managed to put the head into a plastic bag and leaves.

The severed head incident distracts Edwin so much that he does not notice his rumbling stomach or Jorge Alfaro, Felipe's colleague, who entered the station with three other bus drivers in tow. The four men make their statements, sign them, swear that they would also repeat their statements under oath in court, and disappear again. Only once they have left and he listens to Rico calling a colleague on the phone does he feel relieved of the nightmare of having no answer to his problems with Olga and her family. What he hears in the one half of the phone call spoken by Rico seems to indicate a different path of getting the conviction he seeks for Olga.

The captain hears Rico say the character witness statements made by Jorge Alfaro and his three colleagues seem to indicate that the murder victim had business dealings with the drug mafia, in particular a capo named Federico Poscietti living as a pensionado in Bahía Potrero. It raises the possibility of a revenge murder.

Furthermore, Olga is said to belong to a fanatical religious sect that could have an interest in Felipe's death, since she is allegedly the sole heir to Felipe's considerable assets, which would ultimately flow into the sect's coffers as a so-called 'gift'. Rico also mentions the mysterious aunt Maruja in Sardinal, Guanacaste, who was Felipe's confidante and allegedly is informed of all the details of his work and dealings. She could turn out to be a source of background information and provide leads to identify and capture the murderer and solve this case.

He will have to investigate if there is any substance to the potential motives for the crime - revenge murder by the drug mafia or enriching a religious sect via the detour of Olga's inheritance. He will also have to figure out how he can contact and interview the aunt in Sardinal about her relationship with Felipe and his collaborators, friends and acquaintances says Rico and ends the conversation.

Edwin rubs his hands and confronts Rico, "I told you so, didn't I? The little bitch has something to do with the murder."

A man with a black satchel enters the station and messes up his speech. He introduces himself as Doctor Vicente Gallego, who had been called by Doctor Bustamante to provide a medical exam and give first aid to a young lady in this police station.

He wants to know where he can find the lady and is told she is in a holding cell. He pulls back and asks if she is under arrest. If she is, he can't examine her. Only doctors assigned to the crime investigation organisation can do that.

Edwin starts to gloat and quickly says, "Oh yes, she is under arrest on suspicion of having committed the brutal murder of her boyfriend and..."

Rico raises a hand to stop his flow of words and interjects, "No, she is not under arrest. Matter of fact, she is illegally detained. Go ahead, Doctor Gallego, examine her."

The doctor looks at the station's police captain, then that guy in civilian clothes sitting at the desk and asks him, "Who are you?"

Rico shows him his OIJ identification and points to the corridor leading to the holding cell.

The doctor wants to follow Rico's directive but is held back by the captain. His head appears ready to explode when he barks, "Just now you said on the phone that the little whore in the holding cell is involved in a revenge murder, has dealings with the drug mafia, and motivated a religious sect to have Felipe Suárez killed. So, the arrest of that slag is fully justified, and she should be detained."

Calmly, Rico lets him finish his outburst and responds, "No, I didn't say that. I stated to my colleague that the murder victim may have had dealings with the drug mafia and a religious sect may have an interest in taking possession of the victim's estate assets. The evidence obtained so far proves the woman is not involved in any of these schemes and has to be presumed innocent. You twist and falsify what you hear to suit your hypotheses and assumptions. It appears to be your specialty. Your scribbled police report is bullshit and Olga Miranda Cisneros' confession was either obtained under duress or is a figment of your imagination. Let the doctor pass or I will put you under arrest. Do you understand me?"

Turning a bit pale, the captain takes his hand off the doctor's chest and lets him pass.

Rico rummages the desk for an envelope, finds one for the police report and Olga's 'confession' and tucks it into his jacket pocket.

"What are you doing?" protests the captain. "Those are my documents. You have no right to take them."

"Yes, I do have the right to confiscate documents needed for an enquiry into your conduct and activity as a rural police officer."

"Enquiry? I've only done my duty to the best of my ability."

"Precisely. Your ability. It appears to be influenced by an unfathomable hatred of the woman you accuse to be a suspect in the murder. That's enough reason to launch an enquiry and get to the bottom of why you refer to her as a bitch, slag, slut, and whore. Is it possibly a case of your advances having been rejected by her?"

"That's ridiculous! You don't know what's going on in this community and how Felipe and Olga were regarded here. They were not welcome and everybody wished they'd leave."

"But Olga didn't live here. She was only visiting."

"Yes, but she and her family used to live here."

"Really? That's interesting. Should I presume then that your hatred of her has something to do with her family?"

"Well, uh... uh, no. I don't hate her."

"Hard to believe. You scolded an irreproachable and attractive woman with a select choice of expletives that amount to slander."

"I never did! I never did!"

"Of course, you did, and several of your underlings are witnesses. So, I have a good reason to have you investigated and subjected to an enquiry."

Just when the captain wants to plead with Rico not to have him investigated, a distraught looking Doctor Gallego comes back from the holding cell, grabs the telephone, and calls an ambulance service to pick up a patient urgently and have her transferred to a hospital for treatment and observation. He turns to Rico and explains that he gave the young woman a sedative but couldn't do much for her except patching up her most obvious wounds. She suffers from severe shock and appears to have been beaten with a truncheon. The ulna of her right forearm is possibly fractured.

The flashing lights of an ambulance stopping in front of the station brings the doctor's lengthy account of the medical exam to an end. Two paramedics enter with a stretcher, are directed to the holding cell where they pick up Olga and carry her out. Rico asks them to hold it and steps up to the stretcher.

He looks at Olga, holds her left hand, and says, "You'll be all right now. I'll see to it that you will get the best of care and be protected."

Vaguely she appears to smile and nod before she is carried out, loaded into the ambulance, and driven away to the Hospital México in the company of Doctor Gallego.

Rico turns to the captain. "That's the devastating result of your interrogation methods, Capitán. You must have mistaken the young woman for a pig you were driving to slaughter."

"I didn't do that! I didn't do that!" barks the captain and whines, "I don't even have a truncheon!"

"Is that so?" asks Rico and suppresses an urge to laugh about the captain almost going down on the knees in front of him. "Well, Capitán, implicating your subordinates in the beating of an innocent woman with a truncheon causing severe bruises, a fractured forearm and serious psychological trauma makes it worse. I will initiate the interrogation of you and all your staff and the investigation of all the station records. That has been overdue for at least the past fourteen months."

He passes the folder with the witness statements to the captain with the words, "I leave this folder with you for safekeeping until

an OIJ courier will pick it up. If you lose, misuse or falsify the information, you will do so at your peril. Goodbye, Capitán."
***
Rico has to take it easy while he drives home on account of all the distracting thoughts racing through his mind. He stops in front of his townhouse in Montes de Oca and pauses for a moment to decide what to do next.

When he enters the house, Martha sees the signs of distress on his face. She knows her husband well enough to steer clear of silly remarks or empty questions and just gives him a hug. He appreciates it and holds her in an embrace until she lets go of him.

Rico goes to the guest room he uses as his home office, takes a small voice recorder from a shelf, switches it on, and speaks his entire detailed account of what he found out in San Antonio into it. He adds some of his assumptions of who might be behind that grisly murder and have ordered it. He intends to use a transcript of the recording for his initial case report.

His assumptions of who might have ordered the murder reach quite far back into the history of the allegedly paradisical country to put the details he conveys in the proper perspective. It concerns mainly the country's Rapid Reaction Force, the guarantor of the oligarchy's encroachments not coming to light. The RRF is called upon to 'disappear' people who might have gained an insight into dirty business and corruption. One cannot entrust such a delicate job to the often unqualified and poorly trained members of the rural, urban, border and harbour police, whose members are traditionally exchanged after each presidential election won by the opposition, which is practically every four years. Only the OIJ is exempt from this cyclical exchange of personnel at the level of investigating inspectors due to pressure from international police organs. As a consequence, the OIJ's activity is limited to investigating capital crimes and searching evidence. Establishing potential links to the oligarchs in this process are hindered and effectively denied.

Rico calls Gus and tells him about his encounter with the police station's captain in San Antonio. It turned out the suspect's confession was obtained under duress and Olga Miranda Cisneros was possibly tortured. The evidence collected at the crime scene and the pathologist's investigation provide proof that she could not have committed the murder. Gus can read all the details in his interim report he will deliver tomorrow. He mentions that the San

Antonio police station's captain and all records have to be investigated for malfeasance. Also, the four statements of character witnesses about the murder victim's link to the drug mafia need to be verified. He is not surprised to hear Gus explain drug mafia connections will be impossible to verify. Access to the central computer system has once again been blocked. The security code for access to the electronically stored data has been moved up to ministerial level.

It means Rico would have to beg for information from the Minister for Public Security through the official channel of submissions and applications just to find out whether the statements of the bus driver Jorge Alfaro and his three colleagues are assumptions and rumours or facts. Any request specifying Felipe Suárez's alleged dealings with the drug mafia, in particular a capo living as a pensionado in Bahía Potrero, and Olga's membership in a fanatical religious sect would be checked at the ministerial level. If confirmed, then his information requests will be denied.

Rico is frustrated by this state of affairs. He will have to take the initiative by starting a direct investigation with a visit of the alleged drug mafia capo in Bahía Potrero since Olga cannot be questioned for at least the next three days, according to Doctor Gallego. Rico tells Gus he will drive to the Pacific coast to follow up on that lead. He ends his call asking his colleague to assure observation of and strict safety measures for Olga Miranda Cisneros, who was admitted to the Hospital México. She could be the key witness in the murder enquiry. She should be completely isolated pending detailed questioning and protected against an assassination attempt.

Once he hangs up the phone, Rico is quite certain that the conversation with his colleague was recorded and will be passed on to the higher-ups in due course. He will have to prepare his interim report with a transcript of his recording to prevent any dubious interpretation of what was said during the phone call.

Before he starts typing his report on his laptop computer, he tries to estimate how much time it will take to locate and interview the capo. Together with the time needed to drive to Bahía Potrero, it will probably take between six and seven hours or longer. It is just past 10:00 o'clock. His return trip would start very late in the day. It might be a good idea to stay for the night on the coast and return early on Monday morning.

He asks Martha who prepares lunch in the kitchen to accompany him for a chance of breathing the fresh air of the sea and having a quiet night in one of the hotels. After humming and hawing about midday approaching, she agrees and will pack some items for the trip while he types his report.

Rico finishes his task within half an hour, saves the file, shuts the laptop and is surprised to see Martha waiting for him with two suitcases and several stuffed plastic bags.

Amused he asks her, "Do you plan to go on an extended vacation?"

Waving his question aside and with fists akimbo, she says, "Men will never understand women."

"Did you pack something for me?"

"Of course! Your toothbrush is in that bag," she says with a mocking smile and points to the smallest bag.

"Okay, I guess that's all I need. Shall we go?"

He grabs the two suitcases and takes them outside to stow in the trunk of the car.

She asks, "Don't you want to eat something before we go?"

"No, if we leave right away, we will have time for a snack along to way and arrive in Potrero in time for a dip in the ocean."

"Where do you want to have a snack along the way? Surely not in one of those shitholes in Esparza?"

"No! What are you thinking? Only twenty kilometres down the road is a much better dump where *chicharrones* are freshly made."

"*Chicharrones*?" Martha looks at her husband with disgust. "You want to serve your pregnant wife a plate of pork rind fried in rancid fat? No, thank you, I think I'll stay home."

He shuts the trunk and says mischievously, "Too late, my dear. But calm down. They also serve *empanadas*, *chorizos*, fried yucca and *platanos*, everything a criminalist's heart desires. For pregnant women's strange cravings they have chocolate cake garnished with marinated fish. So, hop in the car while I lock the house."

She sits in the car and mutters with a smile, "Impossible, that guy, simply impossible."

He rushes back into the house, opens the fridge, takes a plastic bag out of the back of the freezer compartment, his 'private bank', counts out thirty thousand colones, the national currency, and returns the rest of his savings to the freezer. In the bedroom he gets a box of twenty-four bullets out of the depth of the wardrobe, pockets it, and leaves the house. After checking the steel bars at the windows briefly, he locks the front door, shuts the steel grate in front of it, secures it with two padlocks, and is ready to leave.

They drive through San José's north-western suburb Cinco Esquinas and the small town of Santo Domingo de Herédia on their way to the motorway.

The glorious midday sunshine bathes the landscape in a diffuse light. In the shimmering heat the mountains seem close enough to touch, coffee plantations simulate the wave movements of a green sea, and the reflection of the whitewashed houses contrasts with the light pink to dark violet colour cascades of the bougainvillea bushes that seem to pour into the street.

Martha asks why hardly any people can be seen on the streets and in the parks on this glorious day.

It triggers Rico into one of his long monologues about everybody indulging in the new popular activity of TV masochism. Friends and families fall out over a football game penalty not granted. Chubby moms grieve over the sexual attractiveness of lithe soap opera beauties from around the world and console themselves by stuffing their faces with yet more fattening junk food. The old traditions of the weekly communal dance and singing were replaced with disco brawls and drunks bawling in the street. An overturned bus in Pang Yang Ho, wherever that may be, is being hyped up as the major newsworthy item on TV while one's neighbour hangs himself out of despair over his loneliness. The flood of manslaughter and murder, war and other disasters pouring out of the boob tube has become commonplace and many viewers feel left behind because nothing newsworthy like that ever happens in their nook of the woods. The social media platforms with their virtual 'friends and followers' do nothing to overcome social isolation despite being pushed by the mainstream media as the guarantors of social adhesion. It leads to expressions of hatred, humiliation, and denigration that none of the senders would ever have the courage to say to the face of the recipients. Out of sheer boredom and a lack of prospects in a society that is splitting into the smallest cells, people are only too willing to resort to violent behaviour or become drug users and dealers. That is the sad reality of what is praised as progress around the world and, of course, also in the 'land of peace and friendship'.

He continues mentioning the experience of his investigation in San Antonio without revealing details. "It's really perverse, isn't it, as if a human life wiped out in the most brutal way isn't enough, the fellow creatures of the victim try to drag phantasms of Hollywood psychopaths into the realm of reality and accuse those affected, be it the victim or friends and family, as guilty of the crime. The fine line between reality and fantasy is becoming increasingly blurred."

Suddenly he can't get rid of the thought that the suggestion of Felipe Suárez' dealings with the drug mafia was only intended to put him on the wrong track. He pulls over, brakes sharply, and wonders if continuing the investigation on the Pacific coast on his own initiative was really a good idea.

Martha interrupts his train of thought. "What's wrong? Did you forget something?"

He looks at her as if surprised to see her. "No, I'm just thinking about the case. Nothing fits together. It seems to me that the crime will have a wider impact, far wider than the actual deed suggests. I have some vague notions but can't find a starting point."

"Can I help you? Just tell me what's bothering you."

"Okay, your female intuition has helped me several times in the past. Perhaps you have an answer to one of the key questions. If a woman kills or has her lover killed in a most brutal fashion to satisfy her greed, do you think she would go into severe shock?"

Martha pulls the corners of her mouth down for a moment and thinks out loud. "Your question contains various contradictions. A woman goes to bed with a partner out of love or greed. Both together do not work, since either the partner's love or money and possessions are the object of her desire. Killing a lover, in the literal sense of that word, out of greed you can cross out. She wouldn't kill a lover brutally either. Why would she, if she can see her loved one kick the bucket also in a very gentle way. Most definitely she would not have her partner killed. If it really is her lover, she personally would like to see his spirits depart and wouldn't suffer a severe shock. If the victim was killed in a most brutal way, then the woman is not the perpetrator. If she saw the partner just as a meal ticket and finds out after the killing that the object of her desire, money or goods, is not available, she may experience a minute shock. If she is a gifted actress or mentally deranged, she could feign a severe shock, but a good doctor could quickly unmask it based on her pulse alone. However, since the woman suffered a severe shock, she did not kill the man or have him killed but became emotionally unhinged by his death and the brutal nature of the murder."

"Wow, what would I do without you," mumbles Rico. He looks at his wife thoughtfully. A first-class criminal psychologist has been lost on her. The motive of the fanatical religious sect using Olga for its enrichment was wiped like breadcrumbs off the table by her with just a few sentences. He will no longer need to investigate that possibility. He is sure of that and thanks Martha for her analysis.

He resumes driving along the motorway and thinks about the captain in San Antonio. Olga's alleged confession is the infamous product of a village policeman's obscure obsession. What could have been the captain's motive? Immediately after his return to San José, he will have to investigate the butcher of San Antonio very intensively. Who knows, he might even turn out to be the murderer.

But first, he will have to investigate the claim of the murder victim's connection to the drug mafia and interview Federico Poscietti. Not much may come of it, but any clue as to Felipe Suárez's personal background could help shed some light on the case. Then there is this mysterious Maruja, mentioned by Jorge Alfaro, one of Felipe's aunts who lives near Bahía Potrero. If he can find her, she will surely have quite a bit to tell him.

The Storyteller

The evening sun approaches the horizon and seems to dip into the Pacific. A flock of screeching green parrots takes its final flight of the day. Their wings wildly flapping, they rush into the crown of a mighty mango tree, where these wretched aviators seem to congratulate each other on their successful landings, croaking loudly like a group of crash pilots. Unfazed by the noise above, a grey fox stalks through the undergrowth towards its den. Fat iguanas lie on a cliff above the Pacific beach. They blink and nod in the brilliant glow of the sunset. Their hunt for hatched sea turtles will soon begin for them. These very small turtles crawl from their clutches at the high tide line across the wide sandy beach as fast as their fin-like arms move them forward to escape to the sea so far away for them. Pelicans sit on a cliff in the surf of the rising tide that is heralded by increasingly large waves. These majestic birds preen themselves and prepare for their night's rest.

The sun's glowing fireball is halfway below the horizon. In a matter of minutes, Bahía Potrero will plunge into darkness and nocturnal stillness, broken only by the glare of lights and wisps of noise emanating from the monstrous hotels across the bay.

A young man in jeans and a fluttering short-sleeved shirt trudges barefoot through the still-warm sand of the beach. He heads toward the lights of the cantina at the north end of the bay. He carries his polished cowboy boots, held together with a cord, over his shoulder. The last light of day lets his face appear to be cast in bronze. An amulet made of sun-baked clay, turquoise enamelled and decorated with a frog, the carved image of the Chorotega natives' god of fertility, dangles from a thin leather strap on his chest. Two brown balls made of clay are strung on the leather strap to the left and right of the amulet. Even for the most near-sighted *gringa*, as the female tourists are called in Costa Rica, his talisman has the obvious shape of an enormous penis with testicles. The amulet does not fail to have its intended effect. The nickname given by the native Chorotegas to the young man is *Montañero*, Mountain Conqueror, on account of his reputation of climbing every Mons Venus to the greatest satisfaction of the respective women who go astray with him. At least, that's the legend spun around this rent boy.

"Monty, what's the news?" calls out the cantina's proprietor, the fat Chavez, who goes by the ironic nickname *Flaco* for Slim, when he recognises the young man in the dim light of the coloured lightbulbs above the terrace.

Only two women in the company of a man are the guests populating the cantina's terrasse this Sunday evening. All the tables and chairs are back in their usual places and cover the dance floor where last night villagers and a few high-spirited tourists stuck their sweating bodies together to the pounding rhythms of salsa, soca, merengue and lambada.

The young man wipes sand off his feet, puts on his boots, goes to the bar, turns his pockets inside out, and casts a worried look at the keeper of the cantina. "I am fried, Flaco. My wife took all my money. I don't have a *centimo* on me. Will you give me a beer on credit for now? How about it? I pay you when I've made some money with my service."

"Make money? Here? On a Sunday? Monty don't be stupid. You want to make real money? Go to Playa Flamingo. There are plenty of desperate gringas in the hotels longing for your service."

"Forget it, Flaco. I've been banned from entering those houses after three gringas got into a fight over me and destroyed a bar."

"In that case you should think about getting a proper job with regular income and not get drunk on credit."

"What are you suggesting, Flaco? Get a proper job here? I have to feed and clothe a wife and four children. How am I supposed to do that with the meagre wages of a *peón* working in the fields or helping a fisherman? Just look at these creeps that followed your advice. They have barely enough to get drunk once a week and then go home to beat up their wives and children. That's not the life I want to live. No, I'll stick to my way of earning a living. I make more money by fulfilling a gringa's wet dreams and the romance of a tropical night than a *peón* earns in a week."

"Sure, but that isn't a safe bet, is it? You know how fidgety most gringas are. When I crack a resounding fart, they mistake it for machinegun fire and take off like a flock of chickens. Then they spread rumours back home and the Yankees cancel their bookings for a vacation in our country. Do you remember the American troops stationed here? We had hardly any income because the tourists didn't show. As a *peón* you'd be better off in the long run."

"Ah, don't tell me about times long gone. The American troops are gone as are the Sandinistas next door. It is useless to grapple with the past. I have to look forward in the direction of my amulet. So, tell me what the local market has to offer."

"Have a beer, Monty," says Chavez, opens a bottle, and pushes it across the counter. "The stout Californian and her two girlfriends left this morning. They were pissed off when they heard that you preferred to service that Italian redhead. I think the three gringas had hoped to have another quartet with you."

"Thank goodness I escaped that battle. Three quartets a week were too much for me. Even my amulet started to go flaccid. The Italian was of much better quality. But she left this morning as well to return to Milan and the loving arms of her husband. Pity."

Chavez looks pensively at Monty and sighs. The guy's right. One cannot earn a living to feed a family in this locality with a day's work as a *peón*, a labourer. He takes a deep breath and the toothpick out of his mouth, and points to the table where the two women and the man are sitting. "Try your luck with those folks. They arrived today. The couple is from San José and the woman is a journalist from Europe. She speaks Castilian."

"Castilian? You mean, she's Spanish?" Monty asks, a little taken aback. "Forget it. Most Spanish women complain a lot and don't want to pay. The few who try to lure me with a bundle of cash are so frazzled that even a fiery bull gets limp horns."

Chavez laughs. "You're unbelievable, Monty. The woman is not a Spaniard. I don't know where she's from. So, get to work but don't scare her off with your dirty jokes."

Monty meanders over to the three guests with an impish smile, asks if the fourth chair is free, plonks his bottle of beer on the table, and sits down before he is invited to sit down and join them.

Two small, dark-brown hands grab into the chicken wire that stretches around the terrace between the corrugated iron roof and the parapet to prevent deadbeats from escaping. A small face with inquisitive big eyes, a snub nose and framed by frizzy black hair tied with bright red bows into pigtails appears between the hands and grins at Monty.

He barks at the little girl clinging to the chicken wire behind the woman who speaks Spanish, "Get lost! Only adults talk here!"

The little girl ducks and runs away giggling softly.

The woman is astonished. "That's a strange greeting," she says to Monty and adds, "Are all the locals here that friendly?"

Monty looks at her innocently. He recognised her as the woman from Europe by her lisped Spanish pronunciation and says, "I was talking to that little spy behind you."

She looks around, sees only a few dim lights in the dark of the night and in the faint light of the rising moon the silvery gleaming crests of waves rolling into the bay.

Monty is amused about the woman's puzzled face and turns to the man to his left: "The little spies are pretty quick. If you don't scare them off, they babble everything they heard in a completely twisted manner to their parents and other children in the village and in the end one gets a bad reputation."

The man smiles and asks Monty with a tinge of sarcasm, "Then... you have a good reputation to uphold?"

"Oh yes, hombre," boasts Monty. "I have an excellent reputation from Canada to Italy. Even in Japan I'm well known and loved."

"And what do you do for a living to have such a reputation and be loved in Japan?" asks the man curiously.

"I, uh... I'm a solo entertainer," mumbles Monty blushing a bit while he studies the wooden grain of the tabletop.

The man looks at the amulet and grins mischievously. He asks Monty, "Are you a local? Do you live here?"

"Oh yes, born and raised not too far from here."

"You must travel a lot with so many fans around the world."

"No, I have never travelled much. The women, uh, I mean my fans come here where I entertain them."

"Aha... What's your name?"

"My name? I'm Juan Antonio Castro but I'm better known by my artist's name Montañero, Monty for short."

"Pleasure to meet you, Monty. I'm Rico Ramírez." He points with an open hand to his left, "This is my wife, Martha," and turning his open hand to the woman next to Monty, "And this is Anabelle Bouchard, a journalist from Europe."

Inquisitively, Monty turns to Anabelle, "So, you're from Europe. Are you Spanish? You speak Castilian like a native."

"That may be so, but I'm not Spanish. I'm French. My mother is from Andorra and my father from France. I grew up in Switzerland, speak Spanish, French, German, and Italian," explains Anabelle.

"Impressive!" responds Monty. "Four languages! That must come in handy being journalist. So, uh... where's your watchdog?"

"My watchdog? What do you mean?"

"You're a journalist, aren't you? You're not allowed to travel around without a watchdog who assures you see only what you're supposed to see and write glorious reports about our little paradise."

"What are you getting at?"

Monty leans back and takes sip of beer. "Well, let me tell you what's going on. The tourism institute became very cautious when a couple of reporters and photojournalists of a major German news magazine slipped into the country unannounced and unnoticed a few years ago and published a sensational report about foreign criminals who live here. It portrayed Costa Rica quite correctly as a safe haven for major villains wanted around the world. The report caused one hell of a racket and has not been forgotten. Migration officials and hoteliers were instructed to report without delay the arrival of foreign journalists who are screened and, unless they turn out to be just social news junkies, are provided with an escort who will dictate which path has to be followed.

"At all costs it must be avoided that more skeletons of this clean country are dragged out of its dark abyss into public view. Until now everything could fairly effectively be concealed under the cloak of democracy, demilitarisation, and conservation of nature.

"The nearly 1,000 citizens who disappear every year, the rate of sex crimes and robberies, not to mention murder and manslaughter that match those of the cities notorious as centres of these crimes in the Americas, Asia, Africa, and Europe on a per capita basis, are kept secret and under wraps. The same is applied to environmental destruction with the world's highest per capita rate per year, the pollution of our rivers with tons of untreated sewage being dumped into them every day as well as the uncontrolled use of thousands of tons of highly toxic pesticides on our farmland that turns rivers, lakes, and long stretches of our coastline into open sewers.

"Naturally, in view of the government's massive denials and the publication of official statistics, the facts of the looming disaster of turning the entire country into a wasteland are hardly given attention or credence. Everything we need most to survive, clean air and water, fertile soil, and intact nature, is systematically polluted and destroyed. Although Costa Rica serves as a prime example, it is not the exception in this regard to the rest of the world."

Monty takes another sip from his bottle, looks at Anabelle, and asks, "All clear what I'm getting at? So, where's your watchdog? Or are you one of those social news junkies that can safely be let loose to roam the country?"

Anabelle looks hurt. She has a degree in journalism and regards herself as a proper news reporter not a social news junky. But now she is very hesitant to speak about her assignment of reporting celebrities' social news.

Martha can see how Anabelle hums and haws and turns to Monty, "You are very eloquent and very well informed. Where and how do you get your information?"

"Ha, I'm an autodidact. I read everything with great interest to learn about our country. Sometimes a news magazine, a scientific report, or a book is left behind and occasionally it's just a friendly chat with one of my fans after my entertainment. We don't get any real information in these parts from the official news channels. But let me ask you, how you got together? You're a Costa Rican couple and you, Anabelle, are a journalist from Europe. Are you old friends together on vacation?"

"No," says Rico. "We met by chance when Anabelle asked us where the mansion of an American film star is located."

"An American film star?" Monty laughs at Anabelle. "Don't tell me you fell for that old canard. Listen, Anabelle, neither Liz Taylor nor John Wayne were ever here when they were still alive, and no other famous actor resides anywhere in Costa Rica. That was a lie of a contractor who put up a few miserable houses near here to attract buyers. There's only one pompous mansion on a cliff of Playa Flamingo. Belongs to an architect. But it's locked because the owner is in hospital in a coma. He slipped and fell down the cliff."

He empties his bottle in one long draft and chuckles.

Anabelle gives him a dirty look. She feels repulsed by this *bocón*, this big mouth, although she is also strangely attracted to him. She tries to set the record straight when she says, "I received information from a very reliable source of a luxurious mansion in the vicinity of Bahía Potrero that belongs to and is occupied by a famous American diva whose name I can't reveal. You are probably misinformed. After all, you would hardly know how prominent people behave or find a secret hideaway somewhere to retreat from the fuss they face on a daily basis. Anyway, I'll get into the mansion and do my photo report. On that you can rely."

Monty grins unmoved by her sarcastic tone aimed at him. "Reliable source? Who was that then? Some tourism institute official? That would explain your misinformation."

A bit miffed she asks, "Can I speak to the contractor who built the other houses here? He should know where the celebrities' mansions are located."

He shakes his head and retorts sharply, "No, you can't talk to him. He's on the Caribbean coast and rages because he's not permitted to clearcut his forest."

Rico gives his wife a worried look about the increasingly hostile tone between Anabelle and Monty and intervenes, "How so? Why isn't he allowed to do that? It's his forest, isn't it? Or is there a dispute about the legal ownership?"

Before Monty can answer, Rico claps his hands and gestures to Chavez to bring a round of drinks to the table. He says, "My wife and I haven't eaten. May I invite you? I'd like to see the menu."

Monty is amused. "A menu? Here? You kidding? Here you eat whatever comes on the table. All that woman in the kitchen ever served me was fat lip and cold shoulder."

Chavez waddles over holding the drinks in his sausage fingers. He is happy about the laughter and puts the drinks on the table. "Everyone enjoying the evening? Fine, fine, I like that."

"Yes, you beanstalk, and we are hungry," says Monty. "We had a laugh about your menu. What can you serve for the four of us?"

Chavez casts briefly a thoughtful look into the night sky, clutches his belly and warbles in the direction of the kitchen, "Linda, my beauty, did Carlos sell his catch of the day to the beach hotel or has he still got it?"

With the distinct sound of nylon stockings rubbing against each other, Linda shuffles through the fly curtain made of wooden bead chains in the kitchen doorway, places her massive figure on flat feet in front of the bar, adjusts a tiny cap on her piled up black hair with the grace of a little finger spread away, looks cross-eyed at her beloved husband and yells, "Carlos!? Are you still sitting on your fish, or have you already sold it to that drunk Pablo!?"

Shocked by the attack on her eardrum, Martha chokes on her drink. Anabelle, who was taking notes, breaks the tip of her pencil. Monty laughs when he sees Rico crouching and covering his ears.

A moment later, the fisherman Carlos walks onto the terrasse with a heavy red snapper balanced on his left hand. Chavez waves him over to the table and, with a light bow, transforms himself into a slobbering head waiter. "Ladies and gentlemen, red snapper fresh from the sea like you won't have it anywhere else. May I suggest red snapper fillets in a white sauce, à la maison?"

"I didn't know you spoke French," comments Monty. "Doesn't à la maison mean that the guests who complain about your food get a knock on the head with the big ladle? Surely you don't want to disappoint our visitors, Flaco. *Pescado entero* is Linda's speciality. Now go on and let her do her magic."

"But Monty, you know..." Chavez starts to protest when he sees Rico nodding eagerly and giving him the thumbs up. Reluctantly he tells Carlos to take the fish to the kitchen for Linda to clean it out and fry the seventy-centimetre-long fish in its entirety in olive oil. Thus, Chavez will not even get the tiniest piece of this delectable catch. In a last attempt of changing his guests' mind in his favour, he mutters, "But that will take at least thirty minutes to an hour."

"That's fine," says Monty. "We have a bit more to talk about, don't we, Rico? Here's my answer to your question why the contractor isn't allowed to clearcut his forest. He came to Bahía Potrero and bought some hundred hectares of land with the intention of building something like a resort for rich Americans. He failed in the sands of our Pacific Ocean beach. His real estate agent suggested to buy rainforest, raze it to the ground for the export and sale of tropical timber, and recoup the millions he had lost. He was one of nine Americans who bought a total of 30,000 hectares rain forest. But before they could cut down the first tree, the government suddenly remembered that in accordance with cabinet resolution 5,904 of 11th March 1976 the native reservation *Cabécar la Estrella* was intended to be set up on that land and expropriated it. The contractor refused to abide by the expropriation and still fights for his parcel of rainforest tooth and nail although he was offered a compensation of $1,000 per hectare, which is equivalent to the price he paid for it. He argues that the amount offered will only compensate him for the basic purchase price but not for the couple of million he had to pay in bribes to gain possession of the protected rain forest acreage.

"Since the government cannot bring itself to publicly rule out the 'eventual exploitation of the timber' and thus declare the area an 'absolute protection zone', which would deny the government itself access to the natural treasures of this area, the developer insists on compensation that corresponds to the 'commercial value' of about $2,000 per cubic meter of tropical trees growing there. The case has made waves as far away as Washington and the US Government even considered economic sanctions against Costa Rica forthwith if the American owners are denied 'economic exploitation' of the rainforest."

Rico remembers to have read about it in the press and says, "But this case has been going on for years. How was it even possible to purchase a piece of rainforest that was per cabinet resolution declared to be protected?"

Monty shrugs, "I wouldn't know. But think of the thousands of poorly paid government employees who'd be happy to sell you their beloved grandmother for the right amount of cash. Those gringos probably got possession of ancient property documents that were issued per decree by the Spanish king in the 1600s. Paying the appropriate bribes, they had them transcribed into new cadastral documents by a bureaucrat familiar with that procedure. That way all obstacles were removed for the initial purchase of the land."

Anabelle laughs uproariously in response to his explanation, takes a pamphlet she received as part of information package for journalists out of her handbag and pipes up, "That is not possible, and you know that very well. Look here: according to the laws of this country, the protected areas are public property and cannot be sold at all! You are only a *cuentista*, a storyteller and dish out your wild stories to show off and appear informed. You don't seem to know anything about the laws of your country and not even where to find the diva's mansion! Ha! What do you actually know?"

With his fire of unbridled anger rising, Monty can hardly control himself but manages to calmly ask her, "Since when are you in our country? Two days ago, or just one? And you talk already like one of our ambassadors who in all likelihood was the reliable source of information you think is the undeniable truth. What do you know about the enforcement of laws in our democratic country and the sale of protected land and forests? If your mind is shut to learn about those facts, you should at least keep your ears open and listen when I give you a brief history of our land."

"Oh yes, of course," jeers Anabelle. "Another story, a brief history this time. Go on then and bore me to death."

"I will," retorts Monty. "Are your ears unbuttoned? Yes? Then listen and listen well. After the bloody coup in 1948 to overthrow a fascist government that refused to step down when it had lost the election, the military was abolished and replaced by public police forces. What looked so pacifist was just a smart political move at the time. It prevented a US military intervention against the junta's slightly socialist program. Instead of defending itself like the other countries of the isthmus with poorly equipped and unmotivated armed forces against an invasion of the USA, which have been common for more than one hundred years as a reaction to any social development in Central America, the junta was defenceless, guaranteed democratic conditions, and relied on protective treaties with the members of the Organisation of American States. It worked because the vast holdings of North American fruit companies were not touched or challenged. As a result, the authorities governing this country could calmly do as they saw fit in what became known as a 'forgotten paradise'. The lesson learned was that under the cloak of democracy and peace one can indulge in anything for which one's neighbours are condemned and attacked because of their use of the force of arms against their own people.

"Just to probe your knowledge a little, Anabelle. Do you know that in this little paradise of ours, from 1950 to 1984, the area of rainforest was reduced from 28,200 to less than 14,000 square kilometres and that since then several hundred square kilometres were deforested year after year in our country, which is only about 51,100 square kilometres in size? No? That's what I thought. Well, you're an educated woman and I'm just a dumb bumpkin. Perhaps you can calculate, how it is possible according to your information that more than twenty percent of the national territory is protected forest area, when more than eighty percent of the forest area, which covered only sixty-four percent of the total land area, has already been razed to the ground. While you figure it out, I can calmly tell you a sad story about my family and how I came to be what and where I am today."

Anabelle's jaw drops in astonishment about this well-crafted statement that was perfectly in tune with the sarcasm she had just dished out. Perhaps this uncouth native is not as clueless as she first thought him to be. To be on the safe side, she writes down the numbers he mentioned and listens to the sad family saga Monty begins to relate.

"The country had been settled from the south in the 17th century by people from the Spanish provinces of Galicia and

Catalonia. The mountains of gold promised by the early 'conquerors' were not found, but fertile land and a relatively mild climate in the central valley, which wasn't densely forested. At that time, by decree of the king of Spain, the lands belonging to the governorship of Guatemala were generously distributed to the families who promised to cultivate the land and pay taxes to the king from their proceeds. Since no natural resources classified as 'important' were found, neither gold, nor diamonds, ores or minerals, the settlers practiced agriculture and animal husbandry. And because there were no problems with unruly savages, who had been wiped out with cross and sword, typhus and tuberculosis, or decimated to the point where they no longer dared to rebel, one lived in relative poverty but relative contentment for many years.

"That all changed in one fell swoop in the mid-19th century after the country had gained independence, when a German immigrant was the first to grow coffee commercially, export it and make a huge amount of money with it. Every high valley dweller wanted to emulate this gringo's success. In order to obtain the necessary land for coffee plantations, forests were cleared on a large scale for the first time. The wood, when it was not used for building houses, was burned and the ash used as fertiliser. The country achieved economic prosperity very quickly with considerable coffee exports from the highlands.

"Other settlers in the hot, humid lowlands of the Atlantic coastal region followed suit with the cultivation of bananas and thus created a second lucrative export business. Whether in the pleasant climate of the high valley or in the hot lowlands, the population lived in relative prosperity and relative contentment for two centuries.

"The great turning point came with the end of the Second World War and the economic upswing of the victorious power USA. Satisfaction was no more. Greed took over! The tremendous demand for coffee, bananas, and beef drove prices to such heights that even the smallest landowner believed he could get rich overnight if, yes, if only he had arable land for plantations and pastures. Logging began on a massive scale to remove the useless trees many Costa Ricans call *mala hierbas*, 'bad weeds' to this day and turned the worthless rainforest into what they thought was valuable agricultural land. But most landowners, instead of getting rich overnight, lost everything and became impoverished. They hadn't realised that the soil of the rainforest, with a humus layer of less than twenty centimetres, was not suitable for agriculture and animal husbandry. The tropical rains washed away the fertile soil and the erosion turned their land into karst areas. Within twenty-five years, almost 21,000 square kilometres, or forty percent, of the country had been turned into barren lands without trees where the only sign of life is the occasional dust whirl during dry periods.

"Since this insanity of uncontrolled clearing had taken a hold of tropical countries in the Americas, Africa and Asia, an economic branch which had been regarded as insignificant developed into full bloom - the business with tropical timber. Of course, tropical woods such as mahogany, teak, bitter cedar, pochote and ceiba had also been felled for export in earlier years. But the heavy workload in inhospitable lands with the constant dangers of malaria, yellow fever, snake bites and attacks from other animals, as well as the relatively small profit to be made with timber exports, had made the effort of this business not worthwhile. When the first signs of a shortage of these woods began to appear, the prices shot up. The more expensive the wood became, the more it became a status symbol in the economically strong countries of North America, Europe, and Asia. More and more people who 'had made it' wanted, indeed had to decorate their homes with it so as not to appear to their friends and acquaintances as have-nots. Realising the profits to be made, the madness of forest destruction in the timber-exporting countries took on method. In most Latin American countries, the owners of forest areas, unless they belonged to the oligarchies, were expropriated by government decree, chased away with the help of the military or, as was usually the case with indigenous people, shot and killed when they did not want to give up voluntarily and insisted on standing in the way of 'progress'.

"In Costa Rica, where they had foolishly abolished the military, they had to come up with something else. Since it is a democratic country where violence is 'detested', they had the idea of declaring the still standing rain and cloud forests to be part of the national heritage of natural beauty, which, according to Article 89 of the constitution, has to be protected. It became public property under the care of the government, and thus came under the control of the oligarchy. Within eight years, from 1976 to 1984, the majority of forest owners had been persuaded to give the rain and cloud forests over to 'conservation' with a settlement of initially $1 per hectare that rose slowly to $100 per hectare, and lofty notions of

48

patriotism, protection of god's creatures, and the eternal respect and thanks of the people and government. This 'nature protection program' was quickly trumpeted to the whole world and the applause that could be heard from everywhere even drowned out the noise of screeching chainsaws and roaring bulldozers, with the help of which the deforestation of up to hundred square kilometres per year continued and the forests were used 'economically'.

"That's how my father was pulled over the hot embers. He was notorious as an eccentric who refused to 'cultivate' his land. He believed that nature had to be preserved and respected, and categorically refused to have the forest of his land cut down. There was enough arable and grazing land near the river for growing vegetables and animal husbandry. One year, after the neighbours had their entire properties turned into wasteland, a government official, who identified himself as the 'Personal Adviser to the President of the Republic in Matters of Nature Conservation', came to visit him. He announced that my father's entire 19,938 hectares of forest had been designated for conservation and produced a certified cashier's cheque for exactly $19,938 or $1 per hectare. The money that was offered and the glowing words of the adviser, not only persuaded my father to sign a transfer agreement, but also to write a letter of thanks to the President for his foresight, love of and respect for nature and the fatherland. He then handed over the ownership documents and all the historical papers in exchange for the cheque and a copy of the contract.

"The very next day, a photo in the national press showed the President in the company of the Minister of Forestry, his Personal Advisor in Matters of Nature Conservation, and the representative of an international environmental organisation. The report underneath the photo proclaimed in bombastic terms that the President was indebted to the noble donor for his generous contribution to the nature conservation of the beloved fatherland. Symbolically, he had handed him the ownership documents for 19,938 hectares of jungle in the Río Negro area. In turn he received a cheque for $897,210 and the deed of donation of the environmental organisation. Also, the original documents were returned to the president. Now the rainforest belonged to the people.

"When my father read this, he realised that this so-called environmental protection representative had actually paid $45 per hectare for the area of jungle that he had owned until the day before. That corresponded to a price increase of 4,500 percent in a few hours. He grumbled that the presidential bandit had cheated him out of several hundred thousand dollars and the people out of almost 20,000 hectares of rainforest. He suffered a heart attack, collapsed, and was hospitalised for six weeks. When he was back home, he watched from his sick bed every day how heavy machinery that was brought in cut down his beloved rainforest almost in front of his house. He suffered a second heart attack and died.

"My family was told the brazen lie that the land was cleared for landless settlers. But after the trees were felled and the valuable timber was hauled away and sold, all that was left was an inhospitable, ruined landscape. All life was destroyed. Birds, snakes, and lizards had been scared away or had died and jaguars, tapirs, coatis and monkeys were shot and killed. What had been a joyful habitat of life, unbridled in its power and grown over thousands of years, was all gone in a few weeks thanks to German chainsaws, American guns and bulldozers, Canadian forest technology and Japanese innovative business acumen.

"Some years before I was born a certain Mr. North, who was called 'Ollie' by everybody, had come to our neighbour's former property that had been destroyed like my father's. Ollie's American comrades, who were called pioneers, were supposed to build a road and bridges and drill wells. However, they built an airstrip large enough for a fully loaded Galaxy transport plane to land and take off. Everything was subject to the strictest secrecy, and no one was allowed to enter the cordoned off area. Our government called it 'absolute nature protection'. One day my aunt got too close to the end of the airstrip while looking for wild guavas on the edge of the site. One of the 'pioneers' shot her like a rabid dog without warning. Two country constables carried her home on a stretcher. She was still alive and told my family about bald men with faces painted black and a motorway leading straight to our house. She meant the so-called pioneers and the airstrip. An ambulance had been called, but it was over three hours late. An American in the uniform of our rural police had stopped it claiming communist terrorist gangs had been seen in the region. Meanwhile, my aunt had bled to death. The next day, the newspapers and television reports, as well as the president, ranted about the outrageous attacks on the sovereign territory of Costa Rica by communist commando groups from neighbouring Nicaragua. It was just an excuse to get my family out of our house and home that was declared to be too close to the 'danger zone'. They had to prevent the two curious brats snooping around and finding out the true state of affairs and possibly blab about it in public. My father put up a big fight in court, won his case, our family stayed, had four more children that included me, and for the years until my father's death we were left in peace. When my mother died from cancer a year later, my sisters, brothers and I ended up in care homes. I ran away some years later, drifted around for a while before I settled in this area. That's my story."

Monty takes a sip of beer, sees the dejected faces of his audience, and says dryly, "Hey, what's the matter? You look like your hereditary aunt died and left you nothing but debts. For everyone's amusement, I can whistle our national anthem on my hollow tooth. It's a real treat for all lovers of bad music."

Rico chuckles restrained and Martha wipes her eyes. Anabelle shakes her head in disbelief. Then she puts a hand on Monty's arm and says: "It's astounding what you've been through and survived. You're a real badass. Now if you would please tell me who knows where that film diva has a mansion here in Bahía Potrero. That is extremely important for me and my employer."

Monty is amazed at this woman's persistence. Did everything he said pass her by? Hasn't she understood anything?

He takes a deep breath and says, "Listen, Anabelle. You should drive back to San José first thing in the morning, go to the central land registry office, and submit your questions. You'll find out in no time that there is no American film diva living in this country or owning a mansion here. The only famous people who settled here, at least for some years, were criminals, like the multi-million-dollar fraudster Roberto Vesco, who bought the Cabo Velas peninsula, built a palatial mansion, a bunker, and a private airport where he could fly in and out unmolested by migration officials. A few old mafiosi also settled right here, and got involved in smuggling drugs, but most of them were lured back to the USA where they spend their last days in the klink."

Anabelle looks at him warily. "That's a big disappointment for me. Within half an hour, everything turned inside out and upside down. Nothing seems right anymore. I'm extremely disappointed and at the same time incredibly agitated. Why doesn't the rest of the world hear anything about what you told us? Whenever you read or see a report in the mainstream media about Costa Rica, it's only good news besides the rare natural disaster. Well, while I'm in the process of clearing up some misinformation, answer me this question. Is it true that crime is as good as unknown in this country with the exception of a few burglaries?"

The burst of laughter sloshing around her is answer enough and she has to wonder if she has just told a wonderful joke.

Rico calms down a little. "Where did you hear or read that? Did you get it from the tourism institute? They are the biggest liars under the sun, rivalling any politician for dishing up unbelievable stories and twisting the truth. I have to disappoint you in this respect, too. At the moment the situation is so bad that we even let some offenders go because we cannot keep up with building more prisons. The jails we have are overflowing with murderers, hired killers, rapists, drug pushers and dealers, fraudsters, burglars, and pickpockets. In this respect at least we have the good news that the criminal investigation organisation solves many crimes that lead to the arrest of the perpetrators."

"Well, it's reassuring that there are at least a few burglars among the captured offenders," remarks Anabelle with mild mockery. "Is that first-hand information, Rico? Can one feel safe in Costa Rica?"

"Yes, it is first-hand information. Whether you can feel safe here, apart from the fact that the feeling of safety is a very personal and subjective matter, I would like to answer your question cautiously in the affirmative. We are not a nation of criminals, although we have problems that have been exacerbated in recent years by the widening social gap. Above all, we don't have enough good role models in our society. It suggests that our problems will be getting much bigger. In this respect, Costa Rica is already no longer a developing country."

Quite sad Anabelle looks into her glass. "Now it feels like I never left home."

Martha notices her sadness and wants to cheer her up a little. "Not everything is bad in this country, Anabelle. There really are some incredibly beautiful sites. Despite the destruction of the environment, we still have over 1,000 species of trees and plants unique in the world. More than 1,200 species of orchids, over 850 species of birds and 200 species of mammals such as jaguar, margay, tapir, tepezcuintle, anteater, coati, agouti, and monkeys can be found wherever there are still intact forests, and don't forget all the amphibians. Do you know of any other country that has so much to offer in such a small area? You can enjoy beautiful beaches, some of which are actually clean. And then there are our wonderful mountains, where everything is green and thriving at an elevation up to 4,000 metres. Costa Rica is a little paradise if you look only on the bright side. That's why the progressive destruction of our environment is far worse than can be expressed in numbers.

"With every square kilometre of destroyed environment at least one plant that is unique in the world and had a very specific purpose growing on our planet is gone forever. Humanity has not yet understood that we rob ourselves with all that destruction of the possibility of ever finding out its potential healing power.

"If you have no longer a reason to write a report on stately homes, Anabelle, why don't you write a report about the monstrous destruction of the environment? Such a report might help us put a stop to it. Then your journey wouldn't have been a waste. What do you think of that?"

Anabelle smiles vaguely and nods. She digs a cell phone out of her handbag, switches it on, and notices there is no signal.

Monty watches her lifting it up and holding it in every direction. "You can put that thing away. It's of no use around here. Landline phones also work only occasionally. Jungle drums are the only reliable form of communication."

"I'll ask Flaco if I can use his phone for an overseas call."

"He doesn't have a phone. He can't afford to pay the vast amount of money demanded for installing a landline."

"Goodness, if he doesn't have a phone, I have to go back to the hotel. I must call my editor. This has become a very urgent matter."

Chavez hears their exchange and says from behind the bar, "Let's see if the pulpería, the little grocery store is still open. You can use the public phone that's installed there."

Martha gets up and looks in the direction of the village houses. "I think you're in luck. The lights are still on, and some kids are hanging out in front of the store. You should go and ask if the phone is working to save you having to go back to the hotel."

Anabelle gets up ready to leave. Martha joins her to stretch her legs a bit. The two women walk away and disappear in the dark.

Left alone, the two men don't say anything until Rico asks Monty, "Have you ever thought of taking the fraud of your family to court or to find at least the president's advisor that ripped off your father?"

"Yes, of course, I have thought of it. But I haven't got the funds to afford a lawyer and I don't have any documents to prove my case. I travelled to San José to find copies of the documents in various government departments. But those guys dealing with the preservation of nature or its destruction informed me that either the statute of limitation of my case had expired or I would have to provide the exact coordinates of the property to get any information at all. And as far as the guy is concerned that ripped off my father in the name of the president, I don't want to see him ever again. He is essentially guilty of my father's death, and I would become a murderer if I ran into him. The cruel joke is that a friend of mine, whom I showed the picture printed in the newspaper, told me this guy had been here various times, you know, over on Playa Flamingo, to talk to Don Federico."

"Don Federico? What's his family name?"

"I don't know exactly. Paletti or something. Flaco told me it's an Italian name."

"Is his name perhaps Poscietti?"

"Yes, that's possible! Once I saw it written down and couldn't pronounce it. Funny, isn't it, that a Don with an Italian name was an American gringo of the best sort."

"What do mean 'was'? I came here to visit him tomorrow."

"You're too late, *caballero*. The rural police detachment of Santa Cruz had set a trap for him, one of the worst kind to lure him to the United States so they could continue with the drug smuggling on their own.

"The guy who betrayed my father, he is said to have thought of the trap. As far as I know, he came here with the news that the Don's daughter was on her deathbed and had only a few days to live. Naturally, the Don wanted to see her and moved heaven and earth to organise a clandestine flight. That was almost impossible because he was wanted in the States as a capo of the mafia. But the local betrayers of his trust got a plane with the help of the FBI to take him to Miami, uh, Chicago, oh no, I remember now, to Philadelphia. The Don had no idea that his trusted collaborator in the States had been taken into custody, turned on him, and could walk free if he could get the Don to come home. The Don arrived in Philadelphia and went to his daughter's house where he was arrested. The last I heard of him was that he's in jail awaiting his trial. I guess, we will never see him again. That's very sad because he was a fantastic man."

Rico shrugs and says, "Even the best man who has become a criminal must face justice according to law."

Monty squints at him suspiciously. "Hang on a second, hombre, I know the difference between law and justice. As far as I'm concerned, the law was upheld, but Don Federico's trap and arrest had nothing to do with justice."

Rico gives Monty a curious look. Somehow, he had expected this answer from him. How could a young man who has not received what he considers justice think differently. Monty saw only the person of the Don and didn't know anything else about the activities of the mafia, nor did he care because he was not affected by it. Rico is tempted to make a long statement. He drops the idea because he had not come here to lecture a local resident about law and justice. Instead, he asks, "Was Don Federico a respected man in this community?"

Bright eyes and a happy smile underscore Monty's answer. "Oh yes, he was. Don Federico was a big-hearted man. Everyone here in the village was hoping to do him a favour so that he would turn to him and say: I owe you one. Those were the magic words and when he had said it, something good always happened afterwards. This village only became a real community after the Don built his house on Playa Flamingo and actively helped all the people to solve their small problems. He got Carlos a new boat with a motor so that he and his men could go fishing again. He had the school painted, new furniture brought in and paid for a qualified teacher out of his own pocket. The football field was levelled, and goals with real nets were installed. He donated money for a kindergarten. He found permanent jobs for many men and women in the nearby hotels, on construction sites, on yachts anchored here, and on the haciendas. But the best thing happened to my friend Angelito who hails from San Antonio. He was given a new bus as a gift after he had provided the Don with crucial information to help him get rid of the American mercenaries who had threatened him. We were glad when they disappeared from our village."

Rico interjects, "Angelito is your friend's name? Is that his first name?"

Not noticing how Rico tenses, Monty continues to relate what he wants to say in the tone of happy memories. "No, that's his nickname. He told me of his aunt Maruja Villafuerte in Sardinal who regarded him as an angel of good luck while the people of San Antonio see him as the Dark Angel. That's why he had wings painted on his bus. His real name is Felipe Suárez. He is a bus driver who gets around a lot, often all over the country. You may have crossed paths with him by chance."

Rico relaxes notably. What a stroke of luck! "Yes, indeed, I met him once. He made a somewhat headless impression on me."

Monty laughs. "Yes, yes, that's Angelito all right. Always a bit in panic when things aren't as perfect as he wants them to be. But he has a heart of gold. And he is honest, a virtue I value very highly. Only last weekend during his visit, I told him that his honesty would be his undoing one day. But he said, Monty, when you've turned all limp from your constant mountaineering, my honesty will not have broken my neck. He lives according to the ten commandments although he never goes to church on account of a quarrel with the priest who called him a devil's disciple because of his origin and the luck he has apparently all the time."

Before he digresses any further, Rico brings him back on course with the question, "What's the story with the bus the Don gave him as a gift? Felipe must have performed a real miracle to deserve such a huge present."

"You can say that again," says Monty and lowers his voice to a conspiratorial whisper. "Angelito provided Don Federico an enormous service. It's a while back when the mercenaries were still here and behaved like John Wayne in one of his shitty wild west romances. Down here in the beach hotel a whole unit of these wacko guys had moved in and behaved as if they owned it. Behind every bush they saw a terrorist, interrogated people who wouldn't show them signs of respect, and shot and killed sea turtles that came up the beach to spawn. Okay, those leatherback turtles can be up to two metres long and over one metre high. So, these morons probably mistook them for amphibious assault vehicles. Just imagine, Rico, these clowns pretended to be tourists.

"Angelito comes regularly to Potrero with a busload of revellers who want to enjoy the sea and a bit of fresh air. On those occasions he visits his aunt in Sardinal. Anyway, one day he burst into the mercenaries' circus with his busload. He was observed until he was alone and then forced at gunpoint to take them to Cabo Velas. Angelito had to oblige and listened to these turkeys during the drive. Suddenly their leader became suspicious that the driver understood every word, which was true to an extent. Angelito speaks a bit of English. That idiot of a leader jumped up, pointed his gun and screamed, 'This is a hijack! Take us to Cuba! A hijack, you understand?' Angelito understood very well but couldn't admit that, waved a hand and said, 'Hi... Jack.' While the other guys fell off their seats with laughter, their mocked leader didn't think it was funny and fired his gun right behind Angelito's neck out through the side window. Angelito got such a scare, he let go of the steering wheel, and the bus lurched into the ditch. The trip had come to an end, and the mercenaries ran off into the bushes. Fortunately, a truck passed by, and the driver helped Angelito pull 'Lucia', he had named his bus after his mother, back onto the dirt road. The bus wasn't too badly damaged and could be driven. He thought to have heard the mercenaries talk about a Fred Paletti they wanted to kill, steal his money and big yacht, and burn down his house. He asked around about a Fred and he was told that there were four, one village resident and three gringos that lived nearby. None of them owned a yacht or was very rich. Nobody thought of the Don since everybody only knew him as Federico. It was Flaco who connected the dots when he heard the name Paletti and said where the Don lived. Federico must have been surprised when this clapped-out crate of a bus drove up to his mansion. Angelito told him what he had heard and asked if he could help him in any way, but the Don only thanked him and said if everything turned out to true, then he owed him one. The magic words.

"Now here's a twist. The leader of the mercenaries and a couple of his flunkeys actually worked temporarily for the Don on his yacht. They had helped to overhaul the big engine and finished the job that day. So, it was ready to go out to sea and plausible that it could be stolen later in the night. Don Federico realised how close he was not only to lose his yacht but also his life. It meant Angelito's information had become invaluable and crucial for the Don's survival. He had to think of a ruse. The completion of the job on the yacht was the perfect excuse to invite the leader of the mercenaries and his sidekick to a party in one of the beach houses. Have a look, over there where a light is blinking. The Don was waiting for them with his bodyguards. A wild dance started with a lot of bangs and lead in the air. Then the two severely injured men were taken to the motor yacht, the 'Aquarius' that's still anchored in the bay, and taken out to sea. They have never been seen again. There are a lot of sharks near the Catalina islets.

"The following day the mercenaries received notice about their leader's disappearance and they fled like a flock of chickens never to return. Six months later, Angelito received a letter from a car dealer in San José informing him that his new bus was ready to be picked up. He was invited to drive to an address where a buyer of his old bus was waiting. He had no idea if this was some kind of prank or for real, so, he drove to that address. It was a scrapyard where Don Federico was waiting with the documents for the new bus. He gave Felipe a hug, thanked him, and gave him the ownership papers. He slapped him on the shoulder, said 'Good luck, son!' and drove away in a limousine with tinted windows. Since that day everybody in San Antonio claims that Angelito, my friend Felipe, is a mafioso in addition to being the Dark Angel."

Rico listened to Monty's long-winded story about Felipe Suárez without interruption despite the parts that raised some doubts in his mind. Whatever Federico Poscietti had done, if he had engaged in all that humanitarian work and had killed the two mercenaries or not, is of no interest to him. He wants to know more about Felipe. "Are you sure, Monty, that Felipe's contact to the Don was limited to this event? He didn't provide any other service for him as a courier or messenger?"

"What are you thinking?" is Monty's indignant response. "You are on the wrong track to think that Angelito was doing other work for the Don who ran a tight ship. He was very well organised with his men and didn't need any amateurs. I know the Don was shipping drugs, but he could only do that so successfully with the help of the Santa Cruz rural police that provided crucial information and security. Perhaps he carried some of the Don's mail that was given to him at the beach hotel but without knowing the sender. That's it. What are you getting at? Are you a cop?"

Rico ignores the questions and states, "I received the accusation of Felipe Suárez having cooperated with the drug mafia and being in a close relationship with a mafiosi. I came here to refute those allegations."

"Oh, I see. You're a lawyer," responds Monty with raised eyebrows. "I had that suspicion. But you can believe me, Felipe had no business with the mafia. You know how I can prove it to you? The accusation was raised by his colleagues in San Antonio. They are envious of his fantastic new bus and his generous sponsor. That's correct, isn't it? One or more of his colleagues are trying to get dirt on him, right? Yes, yes, I know you can't answer my questions and confirm what I just said. But I am right, right?"

Rico smiles in response to Monty's fidgety questioning. Based on his statement, he cannot see Jorge Alfaro's claim about Felipe's contact and cooperation with the drug mafia as entirely invalidated, but he's pretty sure that this trail is cold. The drug mafia has nothing to do with Felipe's murder. Somehow he is quite happy about this turn in his enquiry. Now he can relax with Martha for a few more hours and continue his search for clues in Sardinal in the morning.

He has one more question for Monty. "How did you and Felipe actually become friends. Did you live in San Antonio?"

"No, I could never live in that cool mountain climate. It was during one of his early trips bringing people here for a day on the beach that we started talking right here. In the course of our talk, I asked him if he knew where the land registry office was in San José. He told me and offered to take me along on his return trip. I had very little money, couldn't afford to stay at a hotel, and he invited me to his place. The next day he gave me a ride to the registry. I was very grateful for his help. So, the next time he came here, I invited him for a meal at this cantina and our friendship flourished."

"That's a nice way to make friends. Did you ever go back to San Antonio to visit Felipe?"

"No, I had no reason to go again to San José after my experience at the land registry."

"I understand," says Rico and the conversation comes to a stop.

Martha still stands in front of the pulpería together with Anabelle who looks a little clueless. She had had a highly unsatisfactory telephone conversation with her editor in Switzerland. Firstly, he had been very annoyed to have been rung out of bed in the middle of the night. Then he simply did not want to accept that the 'dream houses', as credibly described by his friend, the economic attaché of the Costa Rican embassy, do not exist. He also did not want to know anything about environmental destruction. It contradicted the reports of his friends from Switzerland, Austria, Italy, and Germany who had settled there and constantly described the country as a glorious paradise. Only a friend from France had complained about the deforestation. But that was to be expected. "The French, hah, they always complain," he said. How could he justify publishing a report that contradicts the exultant reports of the 'newly found vacation destination' in Central America, where clean mountain streams murmur merrily, the jaguar roams in the wild of pristine nature, and thousands of colourful birds sing their happy songs?

Anabelle responded to his naïve remarks and objections to a report about rainforest destruction with 'Tweedledee, tweedledum, only dead fish swim with the stream'. Outraged he ordered her to return to Switzerland forthwith and ended the call abruptly.

At least he had not fired her on the spot because he knew what an outstanding journalist he had in her. She dismissed his angrily banging down the phone with a shrug. She knows him well enough to know he can be persuaded to publish a damning environmental report if she provides the documented evidence to back it up. And that's the big hurdle she faces. How can she get hold of the necessary evidence in only four days?

She asks Martha this question as they walk on the rocky and dimly moonlight lit path back to the cantina. Martha suggests that she should go on a tour with a local who knows the country really well. He could show her the full extent of the devastation and she could collect more than enough photographic evidence backed up with accurate geographic information that would convince the readers of her report and even most sceptics. She should just ask this guy Monty if he is willing and has the time to go on a four-day tour with her. He knows the country and what is going on very well.

Anabelle expresses her doubts as to whether it is a good idea to drive with this braggart around in the country. Although she considers his personal story to be credible, but what he had to say about the fraud with nature conservation was surely laid on very thick and can only be based on half-truths and rumours. Martha counters with the question what her information from 'very reliable sources' about the film diva house, the crime rate, and the state of Costa Rica's nature is based on. She goes on to say that she finds everything he told quite believable and can confirm that much is amiss in the country where corruption and fraud are the order of the day in government circles. Her lucid statements make Anabelle think again about her hasty judgement of Monty's stories.

They stop while Martha recounts in very measured tones some facts that illustrate the country's contradictions. "Costa Rica has relative to its size the largest conservation program of any country in the world, at least on paper. At the same time, the country has the highest rate of environmental destruction and pollution per capita of any country in the world. The country boasts of having the most endemic plants in the world and, according to botanists

60

and ecologists, destroys many of these unique plants every day. The government boasts of providing free health care, while more people die each year from stomach cancer than in Japan and from pneumoconiosis than in England or the USA. The pneumoconiosis is not caused by intensive mining, but the dust storms on wasteland after the massive clearing of the rainforests. These storms also cause severe eye infections and hideous skin eczema, especially in children. Over 90 percent of the population gets water piped into their homes. But what good is that if you can't drink the water or use it to prepare food? More than half of all households receive tap water contaminated with heavy metals and highly toxic chemicals, according to the Ministry of Health's test results. The run-off of the uncontrolled application of pesticides, the dumping of chemical industrial waste and faeces in rivers and streams, and the use of any land area as a garbage dump poisons groundwater to an alarming extent and is worse than in any industrialised nation."

Anabelle mutters, "I have to take notes of all the data you've mentioned. This is devastating information."

Martha waves it off. "You don't have to take notes. You can read all of it in reports written by some of our courageous ecologists, biologists, botanists, and protectors of wildlife. They write and publish these reports despite the danger of getting fired from their jobs and never being allowed to work again in our country in their field of expertise. If we stay in touch, I can give you some of these reports. I keep them at home."

"That would be wonderful, Martha. I'm grateful for the chat and would like to stay in touch with you anyway."

"Then let me finish what I have only started to tell you about the state of our nation. Everything I have mentioned so far is possible due to the vast number of corrupt civil servants. They turn a blind eye to the worst crimes, especially those committed by big multinational corporations for downright ridiculous bribes. As long as the civil servants do not abide by the country's constitution and consider the well-being of the people but follow only the directives issued by the government, which is led by corrupt politicians, nothing will change. The fight against corruption also has no support from the economically strong nations. They know that an end to corruption in Latin America would result in its economic resurgence and would withdraw it from the industrialised nations' economic sphere of influence. Then we could set the prices of our products. Despite all protestations to the contrary, the industrialised nations are very satisfied with the status quo. They get tropical fruits, coffee, textiles and much more at the low prices they dictate. Why would they want to change such an advantageous situation? As we say here: It's very beneficial for your own wellbeing to let other people slide on their bare arse over burning coals."

Martha pauses, somewhat exhausted. The two women smile at each other. Anabelle listened very thoughtfully. They walk down to the beach, enjoy the mild sea breeze, and admire the stars in the firmament that seem close enough to touch. Anabelle would like to continue the conversation but has nothing to add at that moment. She is very happy about this acquaintance. Rarely has she met a person like this woman with whom she had such a strong spiritual link after a brief conversation.

Chavez is serving another round of drinks and mentions that the fish will be ready in a *momentico*. He leaves and returns with a large plate of salad. The long-awaited fish finally arrives as well. Linda gasps under the weight of the serving tray she places in the middle of the table. She smiles contentedly and wishes everyone with "*Que aproveche!*" a good appetite.

The red snapper, fried in its full size, looks scrumptious. The crispy brown skin has been decoratively scored for thorough cooking of the meat. It is garnished with lemon and lime wedges, mango, pineapple, and guava slices. Linda outdid herself this time, says Monty. He breaks off the tail fin, the locally prized delicacy. He hands it to Anabelle and gestures to bite off the crispy edge. Hesitantly, she follows his request, chews on the crumbling pieces and raises her eyebrows in appreciation. Now the small feast begins for the others too, during which not much is said.

A certain restlessness sets in after the meal. Monty wants to get a little closer to his goal of bedding Anabelle and wonders how he could achieve it.

Anabelle wants to know if, when, and where she could meet the oft-mentioned contractor, a broker involved in logging protected forests, or a conservationist with insider information. Martha is tired and wants to go back to the hotel and sleep. And Rico turns to Monty with the words: "Didn't you say that a friend recognised the President's personal advisor in an old photo of a newspaper? Was that your friend Felipe?"

"Yes, yes, that was Angelito, my friend Felipe. He recognised him. Wait a sec..." Monty pulls a plastic pouch out of a back pocket, takes out a yellowed newspaper clipping, carefully unfolds it with pointed fingers, and places it on the table. "The one in the photo on the right is the guy. Angelito said he met him a few times in San José when he was picking up letters or packages as a courier. He is sure he saw him here visiting the Don, but Felipe doesn't know his name."

Rico looks intently at the dots of the pixelated photo, holds it at a distance and then looks at it up close again. "I think I know the guy. The picture is old, but I'm sure it's Octavio Muñoz. He was Special Advisor to the President until six years ago."

"Son of a bitch! So, he was promoted to Special Advisor after he had ripped off my father. What's he doing now?"

"Monty, I don't know. But guys like him never lose. He is likely involved in some other dirty business as he proved with his visits of Federico Poscietti."

Martha yawns and blinks sleepily. "Excuse me, it was a long day. Can we go soon? I'm really tired."

Rico nods in agreement. "Yes, we'll do that, my dear." He turns to Monty. "It was truly interesting to listen to you. My wife and I would like to meet you again. Come and visit us when you are in San José. We live in Montes de Oca. Here, I'll give you my telephone number. Give us a call before you take the trip and I'll pick you up at the bus station."

Then he addresses Anabelle, "It was a privilege to make your acquaintance. I wish you all the luck in your endeavours. Hold on to Monty. You can get material from him for an interesting report about our country. You're staying at the little beach hotel, aren't you? Will we see you for breakfast? It would be a real pleasure."

He and Martha go to the bar, and he settles the entire bill. They link arms and after a friendly farewell of "*Hasta muy pronto!*" they walk along the beach in the darkness towards the lights of the hotel.

"What a marvellous couple," says Monty. "Did you know he's a lawyer?"

Anabelle shrugs and scrutinises Monty. She wonders if she should ask him to accompany her on a trip around the country to see all the devastation as well as some of the beautiful sites and intact rain forests. Wouldn't he misunderstand such a request as an invitation to more than she wants to pursue at the moment?

Cautiously she formulates her question. "I was wondering if you could help me with my research for a report of the destruction you described so vividly, Monty. Would you like to do that?"

"I'd love to help you, Anabelle. When do we start?"

"Why don't you accompany me to the hotel? I'll invite for a drink and we can discuss all the details of the trip I'd like to take."

"With the greatest of pleasure, Anabelle."

Monty follows Anabelle out of the cantina with a big grin. Chavez chuckles, shakes his head, switches off the lights and shuts shop.

Maruja's Hunch

The waiter serving breakfast to Martha and Rico mentions with a wink that Anabelle left early at 06:00 o'clock in the morning with 'Monty in her luggage' swaying her rear like a cayman swings its tail. Rico thinks it is a funny comparison while Martha considers it a bit rude.

Anabelle left a note for them stating that she persuaded Monty to accompany her on a round trip to show her the thrilling sites of the country. She has only three days to take the photos she needs and gather all the data before she has to return home. Before her departure on Thursday, she would like to see them once more and will give them a call on Wednesday.

Reading the note Martha chortles and wonders out loud what exactly Anabelle meant by 'thrilling sites'.

Rico looks out over the waves of the ocean and says, "From what she knows about Costa Rica, I'm sure she means palm trees and tasting some coconuts. However, if I assess Monty correctly, he'd like her to have another taste of his nuts."

Martha almost chokes on a piece of papaya and slaps Rico's arm. "That's outrageous! How can you say that?"

"Why do you think she was swaying her behind like a cayman's tail? In expectation of sitting in a car without air conditioning for the next few hours, in anticipation of seeing chopped lumber, or happy memories of a night well spent?"

Martha shakes her head. "Men are all the same. Thinking only of one thing every seven seconds."

"Actually... I'm thinking about only one thing all the time without interruption. Wanna know what that is?"

"Enlighten me already, you old sexpot."

"All right, here goes... Our trip to Potrero has turned out to be redundant. The hot trail I followed transpired to be ice cold. The man I wanted to interview is no longer in the country, moved to a permanent residence in an American prison. So, let's relax for an hour or so and wiggle our toes in the ocean before we go home via Sardinal. I want to talk to Maruja Villafuerte, an aunt of the murder victim in San Antonio. It's only a matter of learning a bit more about the victim's background. I don't expect it to take very long. There is no information to be gained in this region that could help solve the case. Okay? Are you with me?"

Of course, she is with him. They go to the beach, collect shells and sand stars, and then relax in the shade of a gnarled *acajou* tree that produces cashew nuts and refresh themselves eating its delicious pear-shaped juicy fruits called *marañón*. Their tranquil rest comes to a sudden stop when Martha wades in the shallow water by the beach. Her high-pitched scream of disgust after an encounter with turds and condoms floating on the calm waves wakes up Rico dosing under the tree. A closer look by him confirms the sea is full of faeces as far as the eye can see.

They talk to the hotel manager Pablo, an old gringo with a grizzled goatee, and complain about the filth. He says that they must be dreaming and shows them the document of the tourism institute certifying a clean and safe beach, sea, and resort.

Pablo refuses to have a look himself. He does not care one iota about the state of the sea, is already too drunk to tell the difference between shit and chocolate and would probably eat either when served decoratively on a platter.

Rico and Martha leave this pretentious place located on the edge of an open sewer earlier than planned and have the firm intention never to return. They drive along a dusty road in the north-eastern direction past desolate pastures where emaciated zebu cattle is chewing the cud. The landscape looks mostly burned. The dark brown of the vegetation scorched by the sun is only occasionally interspersed by the green of a field of sorghum or a papaya plantation. Rarely do they see a guanacaste tree with its enormously widespread crown providing shade for the cattle.

A billowing plume of dust trails behind their vehicle. After a steep incline that demands everything of the car's engine, they reach a wooded area where the temperatures are more bearable.

The dirt road turns into a rugged, rocky path that leads through low streams and dense undergrowth. A horde of howler monkeys loudly announces its presence in the treetops. A coati crosses their path and disappears quickly in the bushes. Colourful shimmering butterflies flutter by, and the cicadas' haunting concert accompanies the cawing of the montezuma oropendola orioles.

Behind a turn in the road shortly before reaching Sardinal, they are stopped by a rural policeman wearing camouflage. After a brief greeting, he declares the road is closed and orders them to turn around and go back. After a harsh exchange of words, he says the community of Sardinal is blocked off and nobody is allowed to enter or leave. Direct questions he refuses to answer on orders from above. Not even Rico's identification as an OIJ detective inspector impresses him enough to let him pass.

Rico brings the standoff to a rapid end. Without uttering another word, he steps on the accelerator and drives off at the highest speed his car can deliver. In the rear-view mirror, he sees the policeman drawing a pistol, aim, and then tuck it back into its holster as if ordered to do so. In response to Martha's worried question, if it was the right move to disobey the policeman's order, Rico tells her not to worry. He knows how to handle these unpredictable cops that were bootblacks yesterday and behave insolently in police uniform today to see people around them tremble in fear.

They enter Sardinal on the road between the football pitch and the church where they are stopped by heavily armed policemen. The captain demands to know in a harsh tone how they got into the village. Rico shows him his identification. The captain is surprised and wants to know what the detective inspector wants. The OIJ has not been called and is not needed because his men have the case under control and can handle it without outside interference.

A bit baffled Rico asks the captain for clarification of what case is under control.

The captain asks. "Don't you know?" He points to a neat little house on the other side of the pitch and explains, "The teacher who hanged herself. Early this morning we responded to an anonymous phone call informing us about her suicide. We went to her house and found her dangling in the living room."

Rico nods and asks, "So, what's with all the armed policemen?"

The captain lowers his voice. "We found a kilogramme of cocaine hidden in her bedroom. It confirmed my suspicion that she ran a drug transhipment and distribution point. She was known to frequent a known drug dealers' den over there in that dilapidated house near the corner of the football pitch. We raided it immediately and arrested the inhabitants to interrogate them. Now the village is in turmoil. A few people don't want to accept the teacher was a drug dealer. Some villagers even claim Maruja was murdered and cocaine was purposely hidden in her house. We have arrested some of these loudmouths as well and are interrogating them. They will change their opinions quickly. I suspect we will find more drugs in the course of our raid of every known drug dealer's house."

Rico feels a little dizzy listening to the captain's prattle. He asks, "What did you say was the name of the teacher who hanged herself."

"Maruja Ortíz Cordéro? Why do you ask? You know her?"

"No, I don't know her. I need to talk to someone else."

"Who's that? Can I help you find that person?"

Rico looks at the captain's face almost bursting with curiosity and staring at him like a gluttonous mutt who has just been shown a juicy steak. "No, thank you, Capitán. Just tell me where I can find the Villafuerte family."

"I thought so," shouts the captain. "What has this nasty riffraff done now? Should I have all of them arrested? What do you want us to do with them? Interrogate them? We can do that. We have proven methods to get at the truth!"

"I know, Capitán. I'm familiar with those methods. Just tell me where they live."

"They live dispersed all over the village. Ask the old man over there who is shaking his walking stick and threatening us. He is one of them."

"Thanks, Capitán."

Rico leaves the disappointed looking captain behind, drives around the football pitch and stops in front of the house made of hewn planks and nods to the old man as he gets out of his car. He provides the image of the village's Methuselah with his grey week-old stubbles on his chin, baggy jacket and pants, a stained, greasy hat, and the gnarled walking stick reaching up to his shoulders.

He greets Rico with a barrage of foul-mouthed assumptions about his sexual preferences and his mother's assumed night-time activity. A friendly smile and arms spread wide calms the old guy and astonished he holds onto his crutch with both hands.

Rico addresses him in a low voice because a policeman stands nearby. The old guy gives him a critical look and sputters, "You have to speak up! I don't understand a single word!"

On the dusty wooden steps behind the old man sits a young boy chewing on a piece of sugar cane. He removes the hard rind in strips with his teeth and bites into the juicy marrow. Judging by the strips of bark lying around and the lumps of sugar cane pulp he spat out, the boy has been sitting there since the early hours of the morning watching the activities of the heavily armed police force.

Rico points at the old guy and asks, "Is this your gramps?"

The boy shakes his head and keeps on chewing.

"Where can I find a Villafuerte in this village?"

The boy points at the old man. Rico sighs and asks, "And where does he and the other Villafuertes live?"

The boy points with an outstretched arm into the wide circle of the village and, with a happy grin, thumbs at the house on whose steps he is sitting. The old man laughs baring his toothless gums.

Rico would like to enter the house and points up the steps to the door. The old man puts on a devilish smile, rips the greasy hat off his almost bald head with a gesture bordering on grandezza, bends even lower than he already stands, and invites Rico with a gesture to go up the steps.

He knocks on the door. It is slightly ajar. Nobody responds. He pushes the door open and faces a family sitting around a large table having breakfast in a gloomy room.

"Oh, I am sorry. Excuse me bursting in like that. Good morning. My name is Rico Ramírez. Are you the Villafuerte family?"

A giant of a man sitting at the end of the table rises amidst the menacing looks of the men and women. "Yes, we are part of the bigger Villafuerte family. Who are you? What do you want? Are you a pig? Then get out! This house has already been searched!"

Rico watches the man coming around the table with heavy steps and hastens to say, "If you mean the rural police outside, I can assure you I have nothing to do with them."

The giant snorts scornfully. "So, what do you want? I can smell you are a cop. Was one myself not that long ago."

Rico holds up his identity card for him to read. "Here's my identification. Who are you, please?"

"I'm Benigno Villafuerte."

"Okay, Benigno, you seem to have a fine nose. You should be working for us. Or can you only sniff out pigs?"

The man studies the OIJ card briefly. "We have nothing to do with the murder of the Ortíz women, Señor Ramírez."

"Call me Rico, please."

"Okay, Rico. Call me Ben."

"You said murder? The captain said she committed suicide."

"He would, wouldn't he? He's a liar like all his corrupt party friends who installed him as police captain."

"Yes, I understand but that's not why I'm here. I have a message for Maruja Villafuerte and would like to talk to her."

Ben gives Rico a probing look. "Is that in connection with the Felipe Suarez' murder? We know all about it. If you have a message, you can give it to me."

Rico is taken aback. "How would you know of Felipe's murder? The case hasn't been publicised yet, has it?"

Ben sneers, "Jungle drums..."

Rico is annoyed. Could Ben not have told him, just for a change, how the news spreads in this country like a dry grassland wildfire in the absence of modern communication devices? Nobody is willing to say how the rural population gets detailed information of a crime often before the police has been notified.

He sighs and says firmly, "I have to talk to Maruja. Where can I find her?"

"She's not here. She left."

"Is that so? How did she leave the village that has been blocked since the early hours and the police won't let anyone in or out?"

"Listen, Maria isn't available to talk to anyone."

"Maria? No, I want to talk to Maruja."

"Rico, Maria and Maruja is one and the same person. Maruja is her nickname in the family circle. Keep that to yourself. Not a word about it to any of the pigs outside, is that clear? Otherwise, she will also get killed tonight."

"I don't understand. Why would she get killed?"

"We are absolutely certain Maruja Ortíz was hanged, and the cocaine was placed in her house by the captain. Whoever killed her, only mistook her for Maria. I knew that the moment I heard about Felipe's heinous execution style murder."

"That makes no sense. Maria is supposed to get killed because Felipe was killed? You have to explain that to me. Besides, it's not absolutely certain that Maruja Ortíz didn't commit suicide."

"Unplug your ears, Rico," says Ben with budding anger. "Until fourteen months ago I was the police captain in Sardinal. I know who deals with drugs in this village. Maruja Ortíz did not. She was a young woman with a lust for life, had a fiancé in Liberia, wanted to move there and get married as soon as her transfer request had been granted. She was the only teacher who had stayed in Sardinal for more than two years. This bright woman never touched drugs. She was hanged. That's a cert!"

"And how is her case connected to Felipe Suárez' murder?" asks Rico. "Do you have any idea who might have killed the Ortíz woman and why?"

70

"Who killed her? Felipe's murderer, of course! Listen carefully to what I will tell you. Maria was Felipe's confidante. He told her of his courier job and the corruption and dirty deals he discovered. What he knew, she knows as well. You can be certain that the motive for Felipe's murder was his accumulated knowledge. His murderer must have found out that Maria knows just as much. But he knew only what he assumed was her first name and the village where she lives but not her family name. Therefore, he hanged the wrong woman, the only one here with the proper first name Maruja. Our Maria is the next target within the next twenty-four hours if her nickname becomes public knowledge and the present police captain transmits it to the powers that made him captain."

Rico ponders what he heard and thinks of the witness statements in San Antonio.

Jorge Alfaro had mentioned Felipe's aunt Maruja in Sardinal who could provide information of all his courier activities. Jorge had entered it in his statement.

Edwin, the police captain probably read the statement and called his contacts to let them know of his discovery. The file containing all the information should not have been left in the care of the captain for pickup by an OIJ courier. Rico damns himself for his oversight of this small detail and not taking care of the file. An innocent woman had to die because of it. He feels guilty and lambasts himself for having ignored for a brief moment the criminalist's wisdom of tiny details that solve a case. Now he has to prevent further mayhem and bloodshed.

Anxiously he says, "Maruja, uh, Maria probably has information that is crucial to solve Felipe's murder and locate the murderer. She could be the key witness in any trial of the accused. If she is in immediate danger of getting killed, I can take her to safe place."

"How do you think you can do that with this mob of plods?"

"I can claim taking her to an identification parade in a prison."

"Forget it. In which prison would Maria be safe? You ignore how far the immense tentacles of our governing gangsters reach. It's easy to persuade a lifer to kill her in return for an early release."

"I'm not suggesting putting her in a prison. I could take her to San José to be safe with friends or relatives."

Ben turns to the family and sits down with them to discuss the option of taking Maruja to safety. After a while of intense whispered discussion, he returns to Rico.

"We have no friends or relatives in San José. You could take her to San Jerónimo where my uncle lives. Only, how long would she be safe until a murderer finds out about her whereabouts?"

"As long as nobody knows her real name. They would always be looking for a disappeared Maruja."

"How did you actually hear of her nickname?"

"It was Jorge Alfaro, Felipe's colleague in San Antonio, who wrote her name in his witness statement. He cited an Aunt Maruja in Sardinal who could possibly help us with the enquiry."

"Jorge Alfaro? I know that guy. He's a straight shooter and was correct. Who has his witness statement now?"

"If the courier of the OIJ hasn't picked it up, it's still in the hands of the rural police captain of San Antonio."

"*Cojones!*" belts out Ben and continues in a whisper, "That explains everything! The captain probably passed the information on or transmitted it directly to the assassin. If you can find out to whom Jorge's statement was transmitted, you will know who Felipe's and Maruja Ortíz' murderer is. How come you know Maria's family name?"

"That happened by chance during a conversation with José Antonio Castro in Bahía Potrero last night. He mentioned your family name when he said his friend Felipe has an aunt in Sardinal."

"We are not Felipe's family, I mean, blood relatives, but Monty doesn't know that. He is a nice guy but often not well informed." Ben looks to his family sitting around the table and shrugs. Most of the men and women nod in support of him and he continues, "I don't know why I should trust you, Rico, but I do. Let's visit Maria."

They leave the house and see Martha having a chat with the sugar cane chewing boy. Rico speaks loud and clear for the nearby cops to hear when he suggests going by car to Maria's house, but Ben prefers to take a walk. He says that the fat woman should follow them in the car. Rico enlightens him about Martha.

Upon hearing that Martha, the 'fat woman' is Rico's pregnant wife, Ben gives him a disgusted look and whispers, "Taking your pregnant wife on an investigative tour is irresponsible and should get you suspended from duty. How could you? The corruption of morals in San José is getting worse by the day."

Rico chews his lower lip and trudges after Ben harried by yet more feelings of guilt.

72

At the edge of the village, they stop at a neat house of weathered planks. Windows are shuttered and the door is closed. A few chickens are picking seeds in a small front garden. A brown mutt gives them a friendly greeting, wagging his tail, and sniffing their trouser legs. Ben knocks on a window shutter but nobody answers.

"Maria, it's me, your cousin Benigno. Open up."

Nothing stirs in response. The only sound is the clacking of the hard leaves of an almond tree in a light breeze. Ben murmurs, "Is she hiding in the corn field? That wouldn't be a wise move and could turn out to be fatal."

Both men go to the back of the house and notice some movement in a chicken coop underscored by clucking chickens. Rico casts a wary look back at the street where Martha drives up followed by two policemen armed with automatic rifles. He stands in front of the shed and says calmly, "Maria, is that you in there? I've come to help you. Please, come out."

Ben adds, "Hurry up, Maria. You can trust this man. He's from the OIJ."

A groan can be heard and then Maria passes with her slender body through the narrow door. She carries a little straw lined basket with eggs that she hands to Ben. He puts it aside on a crate in anticipation of having to be ready for any irrational move by the two policemen watching them.

When one of the plods approaches with his rifle at the ready, Rico stops him by showing his OIJ badge and says firmly, "You're disturbing my investigation! Get out! Get lost!"

With the cop back on the street, he turns to Maria and says, "You're under arrest! Follow me!"

Maria turns pale and faints. Ben catches her and hisses, "You didn't say anything about arresting her. How can I be sure that you're not a hired killer, huh?"

"You have my name and my number," whispers Rico. "Do you think, I would take my pregnant wife along, if I had the intention of liquidating someone? We have to play-act to prevent the fuzz becoming suspicious and asking questions. You have to trust me. Fetch some water. We must get Maria back on her feet."

A vat filled with rainwater stands next to the shed. Ben takes off the lid, dips an old plastic bucket into it, and pours the water over Maria's head. She splutters under the brief torrent, sits up, and clings to her cousin's leg.

"I have done nothing wrong, Benigno!" she howls.

He pats her wet hair and whispers, "Come on, Maria, this is just for show. You must play along. The inspector only wants to help you. He has a few questions and will take you to a safe place."

Rico bends down and says, "We'll go into your house. I want you to pack enough clothes for a few days. Then we put on a big act for the cops, and I'll take you to a safe place. I implore you to participate."

Maria gets up with some difficulty and wipes water and tears off her face. She goes to the backdoor of her house, unlocks it, enters the bedroom, and changes out of her housecoat into a dark green, unadorned dress.

Rico looks into the kitchen almost identical to those he has seen in the houses of the impoverished rural population and remembers well from his parental home. The water faucet on a plastic pipe sticking out of the wall above a cast concrete sink, the shower niche behind a curtain in a corner, dented aluminium pots and bowls on rough wooden shelves, a small table next to the fogón, the open wood fire stove, a colourful collection of plates, cups and bowls, the sock in its wooden rack for filtering coffee, and spoons, forks, knives, and a ladle in a flat box. Everything very simple and clean.

In the light of a bare lightbulb Maria rummages in the wardrobe for underwear and packs it into a small travel bag. She is crying and completely unsettled, looks at Ben standing in the doorway and shakes her head. He nods with an encouraging smile and locks the backdoor.

Rico enters the living room and opens the front door. The policemen stand there and want to rush into the house.

"Stay out!" barks Rico. "Guard the house until I am finished with my investigation!"

He leaves the house, pulls the door shut behind him and goes to his car. He winks at Martha, gets handcuffs out of the glove compartment and his gun out of a holster under the driver's seat. He sticks the gun into his waistband and takes a roll of OIJ crime scene tape from the backseat. Martially equipped he goes back to the house. Five more plods have arrived on the scene. They do not want to miss a single move of the OIJ inspector and all seven crane their necks until the door is slammed shut.

Rico asks Maria if she has packed everything she needs. She nods and holds up her travel bag. He tells her and Ben to come outside with him.

Maria locks the door and looks at Rico with a vague smile until he proclaims loudly, "Maria Villafuerte, you are under arrest!"

He handcuffs her and whispers, "You should cry now."

That was one comment he could have spared. Horrified by the sight of her sparkling bracelets, she howls with all her might. He leads her to the car, opens the backdoor, sits her down and puts her bag next to her before asking quietly, "Are you comfortable?"

Confused, she raises her shackled hands and shakes her head. Martha gets into the car to sit beside her and calm her down.

Rico goes back to the house, asks Ben to put down the basket with eggs and help him apply the tape to the door and all shuttered windows. They repeat the action at the back and Rico murmurs, "That should keep the vultures at bay."

He sees one of the cops step up to the car and attempt to flirt with Martha through the open window, Rico scolds him, "Piss off, you lunkhead! That's my boss!"

He is just about ready to have a final word with Ben and get into the car, when the captain comes panting along the street, waving a hand, and shouting, "Hold it! Wait! I have a few questions to ask you!" Sweating profusely, he asks, "Why did you arrest Maria Villafuerte? You can't take her away! We have to search her house. She is part of the inner circle of suspects in the Ortíz case."

Rico looks at him with a stone-faced expression. "Inner circle of suspects in the Ortíz case? You insisted that the teacher committed suicide. Are you telling me now, she was killed and Maria Villafuerte hanged her?"

"Yes, uh, no! Of course not!" The captain is confused and gestures to his men to surround the car. "This Villafuerte woman is a major suspect of smuggling cocaine."

Rico smiles sardonically. "May I assume that you have sufficient evidence to support your accusation, Capitán?"

The uniformed 'guardian of the law' is shaken to his foundations when Rico continues, "Your accusation of Maria smuggling cocaine has turned this case into a national matter. It is no longer a local affair. In my function as representative of the national crime investigation organisation, I demand that you present to me all the evidence to support your claim. If you can't produce any evidence, I'll have to arrest you, take you to San José for further investigation, and support Maria Villafuerte in her lawsuit against you for slander. So, where is the evidence?"

The captain suddenly looks very sick and ready to toss his half-digested breakfast all over the car. Frantically he thinks how he can get out of the hole he dug for himself and stammers, "The evidence is, uh, in her house. I received information that she stores the cocaine there. We have to search the house. I demand that you break your seals and open the house."

"Capitán, I have searched the house from top to bottom in the course of my investigation and didn't find a trace of cocaine or other illicit drugs. You know very well that one of your men will have to hide drugs in her house for others to find it. Should you insist on searching the house, I will appoint Benigno Villafuerte as my OIJ deputy with the authority to subject every person, including you, to a thorough corporal search using latex gloves, a suitable lubricant and a large spoon. Any person carrying drugs will be arrested immediately. You should be familiar with the consequences you and your division could face. If you insist on going ahead with the search, let's get to work, Capitán. Alternatively, you may officially withdraw your allegations."

The captain chews on his lower lip for a moment. He knows that one thoughtless statement would expose him as a ninny and waves a hand indicating his withdrawal of the allegations. Rico points at the cops surrounding his car and says, "Should you have any notion of preventing me from leaving this town, I will start disciplinary proceedings against you for hindering an OIJ officer in the execution of his duties. Have I made myself clear, Capitán?"

There is a tense calm after these words. Suddenly the captain smiles triumphantly, waves his men aside, and marches away with them without uttering another word.

Rico shouts a farewell to Ben, gets into the car, and drives with his two passengers away leaving a cloud of dust behind. Without incident they reach Liberia and the Pan-American highway to San José. Rico speeds up.

"Can you stop soon at a restaurant?" asks Martha with a pained expression. "The excitement has affected my bladder."

Rico stops looking in the rear-view mirror. "Yes, of course, but I'd like to find out if that car behind is trailing us. Since we left the city limits of Liberia, it's following at the same distance."

Martha and Maria look out the rear window and see a yellow car without a license plate on the front bumper at a distance of about ten car lengths behind. It could be someone who uses Rico as a shield against speed traps because he drives about forty kilometres per hour over the indicated limit. But Rico thinks of the captain's triumphant smile and fears that a commando of the Rapid Reaction Force was sent after him. Should the Felipe Suárez and Maruja Ortíz cases even be remotely connected, and the rural police is once again deployed to help in the cover up of a murder case, then this dreaded special unit, which does not shy away from committing any crime, is also part of the set-up and Rico has become a hunted hunter.

His suspicion is reinforced when he does not overtake a bus despite the oncoming lane being free of traffic, and he reduces his speed. The yellow car stays behind at the same distance. Warning signs announce the very hilly and snaking stretch of road near the town of Pozo Azul. Overtaking is not only forbidden but also very dangerous. One can hardly see more than thirty meters ahead on the narrow road. Already driving in the no-passing zone, Rico takes his chance to dash past the bus with flashing headlights and honking the shrill horn. He teases all the performance out of the engine of his car, pulls away at top speed, and 'lays rubber on the road'.

Some distance later before a descent, a billboard with a Toucan painted on it announces a restaurant one kilometre ahead on the left behind a bridge. The bus and the yellow car are out of sight in the rear-view mirror. While still on the bridge, Rico touches the brakes, steers at great risk through oncoming traffic into the entrance to the left and shoots down into a hollow where the restaurant is located on the banks of an almost dried up river.

Rico parks under the spreading branches of a guanacaste tree, jumps out of the car and runs back to the side of the road. Cowering behind a bush, he observes the traffic. The bus comes along the road towards the bridge when the yellow car overtakes it with squealing tires and roaring exhaust. It is an American car built in Argentina, the Rapid Reaction Force's favoured vehicle. The absence of any identifying sticker or license plate confirms it. He only sees a blur of the two occupants in checked shirts, part of the trivialising standard clothing of the special police unit members. Wishing them a speedy trip, he returns to the shade of the tree.

Martha has been trying to free Maria of her shackles for a while but cannot get them off. She stands cross legged and whines that her molars are floating because she has not been able to relieve herself. She did not want to drag Maria into the restaurant with the handcuffs on display. Guests inside might mistake her for an escaped convict. Rico removes the manacles quickly and sends the women on their way. He himself waters the tree.

In the restaurant, the women want to fill their growling stomachs with 'arroz con pollo', a deliciously smelling mix of rice, chicken and chopped vegetables. But Rico urges them to hurry up. In no more than twenty minutes will the yellow car drive back in search of them and the two guys might detect their car in the hollow. He orders six toasted cheese sandwiches and three cans of soda pop. A few minutes later they get their order and are again on their way.

A few kilometres south, he turns off the highway onto a gravel road that leads east into the mountains. Wedged between two dump trucks on their way to a quarry their car rides along in a thick cloud of dust that creeps into the car despite tightly shut windows and switched off ventilation. Covered in a light layer of grey they chew rubbery cheese on burnt bread rather reluctantly and wash it down with carbonated, lukewarm imitation orange drink. After the trucks have turned off the road, Rico can speed up and go as fast as the rocky path permits. He switches to four-wheel drive when they hit a muddy stretch and slowly get closer to their destination of San Jerónimo from the south-east.

Maria calms down once Martha explains to her why Rico had performed this charade with her. The only problem she has had were the handcuffs preventing her from crossing herself whenever they passed a church or graveyard. Since she has been freed of her shackles, she catches up on that activity eagerly before every steep ascent and descent, and when seeing a church or cemetery. She has an animated conversation but interrupts the dialogue ever so often with cries of joy when she spots a particularly enchanting vista of the far-off ocean, a mountain, or valleys. She comments on the variety of birds and blossoms she has never seen before. With the exception of short trips to Santa Cruz and Liberia in Guanacaste she never left Sardinal and knows hardly anything about the nature and sights of Costa Rica. She is happy just living in her own little world.

Passing through small settlements along the way, they close the dirty windows to block the view of curious people. If at all possible they want to reach San Jerónimio without being seen clearly or recognised by anyone. Their trip has to remain largely undetected.

They reach a farmstead on the right side of the road before they drive into San Jerónimo. A young man seems to await them, opens a gate, and points in the direction of an open barn. Rico asks Maria, if it is the home of her uncle.

"Yes, it must be! That boy is Immanuel, my cousin. We have arrived!" jubilates Maria and crosses herself one last time.

In the barn they get out of the car and are greeted by a younger and cleanly shaven version of the old man in Sardinal who comes across the yard. He embraces Maria and welcomes her with kisses on both cheeks. He introduces himself to her escorts. His name is Ignacio Villafuerte and he guides his visitors into his house.

Rico asks if he could use his telephone to call in San José. Ignacio looks at him with his joyful eyes and says, "Such a thing I don't have in my house. I don't think much of these newfangled devices. If you have to tell your colleague something important, then he will know it already."

Rico looks at him baffled. What did he mean by newfangled device? Did he not understand his request? He asked only for a telephone. It had been invented over a hundred years ago. Should the people of Jerónimo be so far behind the times? And how did Ignacio know that he wanted to call his colleague? He starts to feel uneasy fearing that Maria's hiding place may already be known.

"My sons will wash and polish your car," says Ignacio. "Nobody will know that you drove along dusty roads and visited the coast."

"Did you know of our arrival?" asks Maria.

Ignacio puts on his inscrutable smile, points out the window into the garden at a large head chiselled out of pumice and says, "The Súkia told me in my dream when I held my siesta."

Rico's mind is now fully in a spin. The news is sloshing ahead of him like a bow wave. For once he would like to know how this transmission of news functions in the absence of any technology. Jungle drums! Talking pumice rocks! What else will these people invent to guard their secret? Morse code pecking woodpeckers?

Ignacio invites his guests to have a seat. A young woman with a friendly round face almost identical to Maria's serves coffee. She notices Martha's extended abdomen and asks if she would prefer a glass of fresh milk, which is gladly accepted.

Rico thinks that he can at last focus on the reason for spiriting Maria away and ask her a few pertinent questions. But before he gets started, Maria surprises him with a hunch that turns the theories about his investigation topsy-turvy. What she has to say would have to make him look not only for one culprit of Felipe's murder but require and demand investigations into the highest levels of government, including the President of the Republic.

She says haltingly, "Felipe was killed on order of a high-ranking government official. People who know too much about corruption and dirty business deals are not allowed to roam free. They have to be eliminated. That's why I'm afraid to be the next targeted victim.

"I was Felipe's confidante. He told me all about his activities as a courier to get it off his chest. I know as much as he did. Getting rid of me has already been decided in government circles."

Her words nearly knock Rico off his chair. "What are you saying? A member of the government ordered the murder and had it carried out because Felipe knew too much, and your murder is already a done deal to be carried out in the next few days? Are you aware of the implications of such a claim? Do you have any facts to back up what you said and convince me, an OIJ inspector?"

Maria nods earnestly and reaches far back into Felipe's origin and history to tell his story and put it in the proper perspective.

"Yes, just some of the papers Felipe was ordered to copy have to be found to provide the facts you need. All the original letters and documents were secret or confidential government correspondence. But let me tell you first about Felipe's background and origin.

"Lucía Suárez, his mother, had to leave her home in a village in Spain during the time when Franco was still 'El Caudillo', the dictator of the Spanish people. She escaped her captors by going across the border to France and embarked on an odyssey of Latin America that came to its end in Costa Rica. Since Franco's hated secret police was also active in San José, Lucía settled in San Antonio and worked in the capital in an inconspicuous position as a typist for a lawyer. With the money she had brought from Spain, she bought a cheap piece of land on the slope above the village and had a simple wooden house built.

"Everything would have been fine if Lucía, as an attractive and stately young woman with long reddish-brown hair, a fine face with a narrow, prominent nose, a slim, well-proportioned figure and cool demeanour, had not fitted into San Antonio like an elegant doe into a herd of swine.

"She had hardly any contact with the villagers and wouldn't let the village boys under her skirt. The people knew nothing about her origins, apart from her being Spanish due to her accent. Soon the wildest rumours about her began to circulate. She was expelled from Spain for witchcraft, it was claimed, and had come to San Antonio to continue her evil work. She was accused of practicing black magic when the lights in her small house were seen burning late into the night. She just smiled about these silly assumptions, didn't do anything about it, and people felt encouraged to try other outrages to lure her out of her shell.

"The former owner of her piece of land claimed he had been bewitched by her to sell his property cheaply. He went to court and challenged her rightful ownership of the land. The devil had guided his hand when he signed the deed of sale. The judge even believed him, since the man's signature, distorted by his lechery, did not correspond to his usual handwriting. However, since witch hunts were no longer common in the 1970s even in Costa Rica, the trial dragged on for years. Then the young village priest, Padre Alfonso, denied her access to the church one Sunday morning. Lucía waited outside the door until the hypocritical congregation came out of the church, and she cursed the entire village with a short, fiery speech.

"After that, strange things happened. The bus carrying the village football team, on the way to a game, fell into a ravine and all the village boys who were after Lucía died in the accident. The previous owner of her land was eerily killed one night. As he staggered past the cemetery in a drunken stupor on his way home, the ground shook very briefly and the stone cross on the entrance's archway fell on him, crushing his skull. At the same time, the entire vegetable harvest, the village's main source of income, suffered a plague and was destroyed. Dairy cows and pigs died of a mysterious illness soon after. The village was in uproar and all the accidents and mishaps were blamed on Lucía. Night vigils with burning crosses stood in front of her house, she was accosted and physically assaulted. They wanted to drive her out of the village for allegedly practicing witchcraft. Only the mayor stood by her, knew how to appease the rabid mob, and one day turned up with the official cadastral documents of her property. Nine months later she gave birth to a strapping boy, her son Felipe.

"Lucía gave her son the name of a fellow political comrade-in-arms in Spain, a certain Felipe Gonzáles from Andalusia, who was once a big shot in Spanish politics. Since she wasn't married and kept quiet about the boy's paternity, Felipe's surname was simply doubled on the birth certificate so he wouldn't suffer the reputation of a bastard born out of wedlock. Thus, his full name was Felipe

Miguel Suárez Suárez. But only his mother called him by his first name. The villagers called him Diablito, the little devil, and their superstitions were soon confirmed.

"Lucía's liaison with the mayor, who was the brother of the village priest, continued, as did all his relationships with nine other women in the village. Since his brother had no interest in women and preferred buggering the church's choirboys, the mayor probably assumed that he had to act on his brother's behalf as well. With wise political decisions he kept most of the men in the village happy and while they were discussing his wisdom in the tavern, he delighted their women and satisfied them with his bursting masculinity. San Antonio was dubbed the 'Village of Smiles' throughout his tenure, until tragedy struck him down. The rumour persisted that the wife of a finance administrator, a certain Rosa Cisnero de Miranda, was the originator of the accident. She was better known as 'The Prodigious' since she had encouraged the entire football team, including the substitute goalkeeper, to have an orgy of a gang rape with her one night. Although she freely and evenly extended her favours to anyone who wanted to have sex with her, she was also known to be extremely jealous. That crucial night the mayor was having his jollies with Lucía instead of attending to her prodigious needs. It was alleged that Rosa, driven by jealousy, set fire to Lucía's house.

"That day the mayor had come to visit Lucía earlier than usual in the late afternoon before she had put her son to bed. The little boy had been spotted playing in the garden until nightfall. Then he went into the house where, probably cold and hungry, he lit a candle and snuggled up under the kitchen table in his mother's leather jacket. When he ran out of the burning house, it naturally suited the villagers to accuse the five-year-old boy of starting the fire, although Rosa had also been observed near the house. Lucía and the mayor died in the flames. Felipe was called *Ángel Negro* from that day on. It was alleged he burned his mother for spending time with the mayor instead of him.

"Nobody in the village wanted to have anything to do with this spawn of the devil. So, a lawyer, Lucía's former employer, who had looked after the boy's well-being, had no choice but to bring Felipe into the care of his friends, the Villafuerte family in Sardinal, for a few days. A few days turned into a few months until a place in an orphanage was found for the boy. When the attorney picked him up in Sardinal, he said that Felipe also had to appear in court in support of the defence in a case of the mayor's widow laying claim to his property in San Antonio. The little boy said goodbye to us with a straight face and the words, *"Adiós, hasta pronto"*, thus promising to be back soon.

"Felipe kept that promise in a way. The lawyer brought him back three days later and explained rather excitedly the orphanage burned down to the foundations a few hours after Felipe had arrived. And the next day, the mayor's widow with her three children in the car on her way to the court had a head-on collision with a huge truck. She and her kids died in that accident and the documents supporting her claim burned in the wreckage.

"We thought these coincidences to be really amusing only Felipe didn't laugh. He assured us that he had meant it when he said, *"Adiós, hasta pronto."* With this statement, he sent pleasantly creepy shivers down the spines of many family members. Perhaps there was some truth to the rumours involving him. We understood why the villagers of San Antonio felt their superstitions had been reaffirmed and didn't want to have anything to do with this boy. Yet, we welcomed him into the circle of our extensive family and I was happy to have him as my little brother.

"Nothing exciting happened during all his years in Sardinal. Only once did we receive a long letter from the lawyer concerning the priest Alfonso. He had made a claim in the name of the Catholic Church for Felipe's property and his brother's assets. The claim concerning the property was instantly thrown out. But he had made the mistake of publicly launching his claims and was joined immediately by nine women who dragged their offspring fathered by the mayor into the courtroom. Instead of bagging the land and financial assets in full, he had to settle for a tenth of his brother's money. Because he was unable to entrust all his deceased brother's worldly goods to the care of the Church, it was rumoured that he had been permanently relegated to the post of village priest and had no chance of ever being promoted to bishop.

"Felipe grew up in my care. I am four years older and was infatuated with my living doll. I slept with him, bathed him, dressed him, and guarded him like the apple of my eye for the next six years. Being a young girl who should have known better, I had the crazy idea when he injured his hand on a rusty wire one day to try and heal the wound with mud and mashed herbs. I had seen that in a movie. But instead of healing him, I gave him blood poisoning and he spent a long time in hospital. My mother was furious, called me a little witch, and since that day I was known in the family as *Maruja la bruja*, Maruja the witch.

"I felt very guilty of having almost killed him. When he came home, I embraced him warmly and squeezed him to my bosom. He had reached puberty and tore himself out of my arms shouting that I was still trying to kill him. Pointing to the tent in his trousers, he whined that my embrace was causing rigor mortis. It took a while to convince him otherwise and we had had our first affair. He liked this encounter so much that we had it off every day after that, often several times a night.

"This happy time came to an end for us some years later when he finished school at the age of sixteen. He said farewell with his usual "*Adiós, hasta pronto*" before he departed for San José looking for work. I had hoped to see him again three days later but it took more than twenty months, three weeks, and two days before I read about his fate in a newspaper.

"He worked as the gofer for the lawyer who had also employed his mother. One day he was sent to the bank and was taken as a hostage by a bank robber who got shot in the arm. He forced Felipe to drive the getaway car. Since Felipe's experience of handling a vehicle was limited to pushing carts in Sardinal, he crashed the car into a tree. The robber was arrested and Felipe celebrated as a hero. This incident became a key experience for him because now he wanted to learn how to drive a car properly. He obtained his license, scraped all his savings together, bought a used car, and came to visit me regularly.

"He got a taxi license and made a career in this business. Often he was asked to function as a courier delivering letters and parcels all over the central valley. He was noted for his discretion and gained the reputation of being a trustworthy messenger. Ministries and private persons entrusted him their secret and sealed documents for delivery and he got to know the odd behaviour of some very strange people. He witnessed their confidential conversations and unscrupulousness of conducting business. During conversations with him, I learned that 'those up there' have nothing in common with us simple rural people who work our fields and want to make a living selling our produce. Also, the majority of elected officials don't care about their electorate, only try to attract rich foreigners and listen to their wishes to flog the country and its working people to the highest bidders. At that time Felipe said often to be happy not to know too much about all that dirty business or he might get dragged into it and perish in this quagmire of corruption.

"He wanted to get out of the taxi business and get out of San José. With a loan he managed to have a house built on the site of his burned down birth place to the dismay of the villagers. The people who had trusted him as a taxi courier did not forget him and continued to call on him. His activity increased when the gaffer Rafael of the pub Linda Vista took phone calls on his behalf. When he had lunch at this place he received the messages and was on his way to pick up and deliver whatever was entrusted to him. It was so simple and also profitable and could have continued like that had it not been for a strange phone call one evening.

"The caller refused to give his name and just asked him if he was interested in expanding his courier activity and make lots and lots of money. Since he had to pay off the loan for his house he was very interested and the man told him to pick up a package at an address in San Pedro. Felipe figured it was worth a try and agreed to meet the man. But when he got to the place, there was only a dirty urchin waiting who handed him a grubby package with a phone number and the message to call right away. He called from a public phone and a different man answered and explained that the content of the package was a black box that facilitated opening and sealing envelopes without a trace. The man added that in future it would be Felipe's task to open all ministerial and business mail and make photocopies of documents and letters marked as confidential and secret, note sender and receiver of the mail, put photocopies and notes in an envelope, deliver it to a shop in San José, and call the number he had dialled to announce his delivery.

"Felipe listened with increasing anxiety and told the man he couldn't be of service. The man suggested to return to San Antonio, have dinner at the Linda Vista, and think about it. When he got to the pub, Rafael had an envelope for him a courier had delivered. It contained another envelope and the message 'Too Late'. He called the number of the man who had given him the instruction to ask what that message meant but his call was not answered. After dinner at home he used that black box by following the instructions on the back of it to open the second envelope. It contained five hundred American dollars, an enormous sum for him. But he sealed the envelope again and couldn't see a trace of it having been opened and sealed. That was very impressive, yet he hesitated to accept the activity because it was an abuse of his clients' trust in him, no matter how much he disliked most of them.

"The next morning he called that man and told him he was neither interested nor willing to get involved in this activity. The man explained that he could no longer back down. It was 'too late' for that. He knew already too much, and the only way out was in a coffin. Full of fear, Felipe complied. He carried out the work conscientiously like all other work that had been assigned to him. It turned out to be easier than he had feared. He delivered the envelopes with the photocopies to the assigned shop, where he immediately received his payment in American dollars. His income was actually a mighty lot more than he had anticipated. Sometimes he would make over 2,500 dollars in a week and in just one year he had amassed enough money to fulfil his long-cherished dream of owning a brand-new car.

"But as if his 'telephone ghost' had guessed what he wanted, the next time Felipe called, he was instructed to buy a used bus instead of a car and become self-employed. He was given precise instructions where to buy the bus and with whom he had to talk about financing. Under no circumstances was he to pay the total amount for the bus in cash, although he could afford it. Felipe was supposed to purchase it on an instalment plan to prevent attracting curious snoops and envious neighbours. He followed the instructions to the letter and everything went smoothly. He joined the public transport cooperative as the proud owner of a used bus and was his own boss with an assigned route. It was as if the wind carried him on invisible wings.

"One evening, when he visited me, we watched the news. Suddenly he sat up startled. During the broadcast of the trial of a minister accused of corruption and nepotism, he was sure to have recognised his telephone ghost's voice and manner of expression. The plaintiff, a former ambassador who had been removed from her post for failing to follow government directives, won the case. Naturally, the minister's trial and sentence was the number one issue of the news reruns and panel discussions. But the trial scenes and witness statements were never shown again, and Felipe was no longer sure if he had recognised his mysterious contact by his voice.

The next day he called the television station and asked about the witness who had been featured on the original newscast. He was tersely told that the six o'clock news had not shown any witness testimony. Although he still didn't know who that witness was, he was sure it had to be a very influential, powerful bigwig who could manipulate the news broadcasts.

"After that experience, Felipe's anxiety increased day by day. Not only the doubts about the legality of his work as a courier gnawed at his nerves. It was also his immense knowledge of the crimes committed by members of the government, which he had gained through opening, reading and copying confidential documents and letters. He needed to ease his conscience a little and confessed to me everything he knew. And I took everything in like the kind friend I was to him and calmed him down.

"The revenue of drug deals, the profits of arms trafficking to any warring party regardless of supplying cursed communists, tolerated fascists, or respected bloodthirsty dictators, development aid funds, economic aid grants, donations for nature conservation, and the money received for the sale of national park forests, everything serves the personal enrichment of some government hotshots. And the money thus embezzled all goes to their private accounts in foreign tax havens. The Rapid Reaction Force, a 1,500-strong paramilitary group formed under pressure from the US government 'to protect the country's borders', as it was cynically stated in response to a question in parliament, is nothing more than the bodyguard regiment of our corrupt politicians. The special unit carries out its orders in the name of 'public security' with unbelievable efficiency and brutality by letting undesirable persons disappear who are aware of illegal deals and even gets rid of their families. It disguises these murders as a tragic accident or suicide in every case. Felipe suspected that often he was the bearer of decisions to have one or another 'undesirable' eliminated who knew about corruption and embezzlement.

"He once made the mistake of implying to a government official that he already knew about a case and would deliver the letter to the recipient in Alajuela without having received his name or address. Although the officer only nodded politely, Felipe bit his tongue and expected to be killed any day because he had admitted being knowledgeable of the following fantastic scam. An $8 million conservation debt write-off had been negotiated with Sweden, and the Department of the Environment was given $6 million to establish a new 125-square-kilometer rainforest national park. The conservation area in question had the mysterious ability to move about with just the slightest modification of its geographical coordinates and was therefore never recognised as one and the same for every further upcoming deal. When the deal with Sweden had been signed, sealed, and delivered, the rainforest in question was sold to a Korean businessman for $25 million and licensed for commercial use, that is, to be cut down. Meanwhile, economic aid to the tune of $15 million was given by Germany and Italy to build power lines through this very site, and the coup was augmented and rounded out by another $9 million from Canada to reforest the area of rainforest that had not yet been logged.

"The total income, along with the debt relief, resulted in gross proceeds of $63 million for the property, which a government official had bought from a certain family Villalobos for $1.25 million. The roughly $55 million net profit was divided among those involved in the scam. Felipe knew all of them by name. The money flowed into their private accounts in foreign countries. Felipe also learned that the money released by the debt relief was distributed by the then governing party among its party faithful during its re-election campaign.

"Apparently, Felipe's slip of the tongue wasn't a big deal for the government bigwigs, because Felipe wasn't harassed or bothered any further. However, his verbal slip had been noted and some comments were made. But on his next visit, the government official received him as kindly as usual and handed over the letters to be delivered with confidence.

"Even so, the alarm bells in Felipe's head just kept ringing. He knew if his client, the secretive man on the phone, made just one mistake and caused all the letters and documents copied by Felipe to fall into the wrong hands in one fell swoop, all activities could be traced back to him, since he had been the only outsider through whose hands the copies had once passed."

Maria has finished telling her story. She can no longer control her inner turmoil and lets her tears flow freely. Martha and Ignacio stare at her spellbound, but Rico looks sullen. His expression reveals that he is not satisfied with Maria's story. What she said was interesting but she didn't provide specific references to persons and events that would get him further in his investigation. He lets her cry for a moment and then encourages her to reveal more details of what she knows, such as names and dates.

She gathers her thoughts to talk about incidents she can remember. But they turn out to be just further examples of corruption and misappropriation of public funds.

Maria's account reaches as far back as the disappearance of funds for the construction of the highway from the capital to the Caribbean coast, the embezzlement of the national emergency fund to the most recent scandal surrounding the new 'superhighway' from the capital to the Pacific coast and, of course, the continued sale and clear cutting of thousands of hectares protected rainforest every year.

Rico adds up the amounts mentioned by Maria and is overwhelmed by the total of billions of dollars transferred to private tax haven accounts of the beneficiaries. She describes a monstrous morass of corruption and fraud. He wonders what the consequences would be if she could back up her account with solid, documented evidence that would stand up in court. Along the same line of thought he had hoped to get some solid clues to help him in his investigation of Felipe's murder or at least point to a perpetrator, the actual murderer or the people pulling the strings. None of that has emerged from her statements. It's only when she incriminates herself for the underlying reason of the murder does he get the one clue he has been waiting to hear.

Maria looks at Rico with her reddened eyes in an expression of deep despair. "I suspect I could be blamed for the murder of Felipe. It was not an act of jealousy or revenge on my part, just innocently talking to a stranger. You see, Felipe and I had a very close bond based on love, trust and respect for each other and we had on occasion discussed getting married and have a family. But there were the two insurmountable and undeniable obstacles namely, I was older than him and he didn't want to live in Sardinal while I didn't want live anywhere else. So, we drifted apart a little in so far that our relationship became platonic. Oh, he still came to visit me regularly and people were asking when I would start handing out cookies in the tradition of letting everybody know we were engaged.

"But then he met Olga and they fell madly in love. Within a year they announced their engagement and the planned wedding. I wished them lots of happiness and a healthy family. He mentioned to me his plans for their honeymoon and escape to Spain where he had still some distant relatives. It was an act of desperation to get away from the clandestine activity of copying confidential and secret documents. He was scared of this mysterious man he had never met and who had threatened him with death should he ever quit his activity. In preparation for his honeymoon trip overseas, he withdrew all his savings from the numerous American dollar bank accounts he had opened years before.

"Four days ago, last Thursday, a man driving one of these very expensive luxury cars visited me and claimed he and Felipe were old friends who had lost contact with each other. He was very courteous and friendly and enquired about Felipe's well-being. I said he was happy and doing very well especially as his marriage to Olga was imminent. He was surprised to hear that and asked where the couple had planned to spend their honeymoon. I didn't think anything bad. His friendly manner had lulled me into feeling free to gossip a little. So, I told him they were going to Spain. He raised his eyebrows, muttered such a trip would be very expensive and asked if Felipe could afford it. I laughed, said he should remember his frugality, and added he had saved enough to stay in Spain for a year or move there permanently on account of his mother's nationality. I saw in the man's eyes that he wasn't at all happy to hear that but he remained very friendly. He said farewell and requested to give Felipe his best regards when he came to visit. Only then it occurred to me that the man had never introduced himself by name. I wanted to ask him, but he went quickly to his car and drove away. That's why I noted the car's license plate. It is the number 01.334, hence a car of the government fleet.

"Inspector, I am absolutely certain this man pulled the strings and probably gave the order for the murder. He spoke in exactly the same elaborate Cervantesian form like the people of our so-called upper class as well as the mysterious man Felipe had described as the one who gave him his orders."

Rico looks at her critically. "It's possible. But then I would have to assume that Maruja Ortíz' murder is not connected to Felipe's or that she did commit suicide. If this friendly stranger knew you and your house why should Maruja Ortíz have been mistaken for you?"

"No, no, Inspector," Maria replies excitedly. "The man addressed me only as Maruja. I'm sure he didn't know my real name. When he asked me what I'm doing all day long, I told him that beside my work in the field I work also in the school. Of course, I didn't tell him that I'm only the charwoman who cleans up after the kids. And then look at my house. Is it not almost identical to house where Maruja Ortíz lived? It's a wooden house of weathered planks without a paint cover. When one describes my house, it could be the teacher's as well. No, Inspector, Maruja has become an innocent victim because of a mix-up with me and I, yes, I will be the next victim. Felipe was murdered because he knew too much about the scams and especially how this country will become a wasteland unless the environmental destruction and pollution is stopped. He would have been a credible witness at any court hearing because of his vast knowledge of details of the confidential documents and the people who received them. And I know everything he knew. You took notes of it, didn't you? This volume of knowledge is simply too dangerous for me to be permitted to live in this country. My days are numbered."

Maria begins to cry again. Rico touches her arm attempting to calm her. "Maria, here you are safe for now, aren't you?"

Her uncle Ignacio had been listening slack jawed and in disbelief the whole time. He takes a sip of his cold coffee to wet his parched throat. Outrage flares up in his eyes as he shouts, "That's monstrous! I'll have to clean my old shotgun! I'll go to the village and shake up my old comrades from 1948! I'd call on Don Pepe, our liberator from back then, to guide us once more, if he was still alive. We will march on San José like we did then and get rid of this ragtag bunch! Yes, we will!"

They are words of indignation Ignacio utters. They are an old man's memories of better times when one still thought to have a future. But the future is no longer what it used to be, thanks to the abuse of the privileges and entitlements fathers had created for their sons and daughters. Rico lets Ignacio thunder on and finish. With a vague smile he asks him, "And how are you going to prove your allegations when your horde of old men and women stand shouting in front of a government building?"

With the gnarled index finger of his calloused hand, Ignacio points at Maria. "She just said it! She listed every shabby detail of the dirty dealings! She can testify! She's our witness!"

"And how is Maria going to prove what she just told us?" counters Rico.

"Young man, I ask you! We know Maria doesn't lie! She has never lied! She is honesty incarnate!" insists Ignacio.

Rico reassures him, "You may be right about that. Gathering enough information to file charges against more than 100 people in industry and government circles, as you know, could be a very simple matter in our country. But when it comes to a trial, one has to present relevant documents to prove the charges beyond any doubt. With logic, a comprehensible course of events and witness statements that are dismissed as implausible without documents, you won't even win a flower pot as a consolation prize. Not one judge in the practice of judicial decision-making would accept that there has been a murder without a corpse. To see this in the context of our country and in relation to the probable motive for the murder of Felipe Suárez let me put it this way: If there is only one tree left in our country, the defenders of the existing system will present it as a rainforest, and it will be the duty of the prosecutors to prove with documented evidence that it is not the case, that our knowledge is not only knowledge, but based on legally irreproachable and documented proof.

"To summarise, we know that government officials are cheating the nation by hawking the country's most valuable natural resources to the highest bidder. We know that many of the people's representatives, elected in free, democratic and secret elections, have no scruples to personally enrich themselves with the millions of dollars obtained through illegally sold people's property, the protected national parks. We know that unpleasant accomplices in these dirty deals often disappear without a trace. We know that the Rapid Reaction Force is largely responsible for the cases of people who disappear without a trace as well as countless murders disguised as accidents or suicides. We know that under the protection of the police, many representatives of the people are engaged in arms and drug trafficking on a large scale. We know Maria does not lie. But can we prove it?"

Don Oduber's Tirade

Monty looks sceptical and hooks his thumbs into the belt of his jeans. He stands in his boots ankle deep in thick mud and slowly sinks deeper into it. He shakes his head and says to Anabelle, "You can't get out of here with that cart. Why did you rent this useless subcompact? On these roads you need a big car with a powerful engine and four-wheel drive or you're lost. Did I tell you how a couple of tourists disappeared without a trace driving such a tin bubble on wheels? They sank into a mud hole like this one and were found a few years later when the Rincón de la Vieja volcano spat them out. They were..."

"Shut up, Monty!" screams Anabelle in a shrill voice. Her nerves are at breaking point. She could howl in anger. How could this have happened to her? She clutches the steering wheel. The car's engine roars with a cheap tinny sound when she steps on the accelerator. The rear wheels spin and the car sinks a bit further into the mudhole. Utterly frustrated she screams, "I've had enough of your stupid stories! Try to get us out of here! You guided me into this mess! Now do something to get me out!"

In response to her verbal barrage, he gets a comb out of a back pocket, combs his thick black wavy hair straight back, shoves a hand into it at the front, pulls the mane over the forehead and adjusts the odd curl on either side. After all, one wants to look good when one goes to work, or at least pretends to get cracking.

Anabelle watches him and feels a screaming fit coming on. What a jumping jack flash, what a fine specimen of totally useless Latin-American macho dickhead that guy is. Okay, she has to admit that last night he lived up to what she expected of him on the sofa, the coffee table, under the shower, and in bed. But that was it except his telling of funny jokes, his ease of handing out compliments, his natural charm, and his undiminishing prowess of making her feel like a queen for a couple of hours. She expects more from a man than the ability to keep 'It' up for an hour and have 'It' rise to the occasion the moment she touches him and wants some more.

She wants a man of decisive action who knows what has to be done in every and any situation, a lifesaver, a creative thinker who is also good in bed, on the sofa, or on top of the fridge when her urges demand it. But does such a man exist?

Monty doesn't fit that category, that's for sure. She curses his inactivity. They have only a couple of hours until the sun goes down and darkness will envelop them. They can't go back. The rocky path is in far too bad a shape and dangerous to navigate in the dark. And who knows what lies ahead? It is incomprehensible why this damaged road is marked on her map in red as paved. Even Monty's taunt of those brazen foreign governments simply not shelling out enough money for this poor, poor country's road maintenance and refuse to pay more than is needed to cover the corruption didn't help to contain her anger. Yet the condition of this road fits right into the picture of the various forest destruction sites Monty showed her in Guanacaste Province. She photographed them from every possible angle. So, this day of her limited time will not have been a complete waste even if nothing else of note should crop up.

She was shocked to see barren land and massive soil erosion wherever they went in those northern parts of the country that were marked as completely forested on her tourist map. But when Monty told her that most of the area had been clear cut bit by bit over the past fifty years, she knew that all of it would be nothing more than a marginal note in anything she could write and deliver. A report about general environmental destruction, poisoned groundwater, and villages swept away by mudslides does not impress readers anymore nowadays. They are tired of learning that developing countries repeat the mistakes of developed countries as if on cue and complain about the destructive problems of climate change caused by industrialised and large emerging nations' excessive use of fossil fuels, a habit they find very difficult to relinquish.

She wants to see forests in the process of being razed, collapsing rainforest giants, lumberjacks active with enormous chainsaws, bulldozers crushing everything, animals dying in agony, evidence of the wantonness of destruction of life, the disaster in the making in all its staggering proportions. She knows the editors of illustrated magazines and daily and weekly newspapers well enough to know that she has to come up with one 'mighty hammer' of a photo report if it is to get any attention in the publishing world saturated with daily sensationalism of mayhem, murder and war reports.

"Holy frustration!" she shouts at Monty. "Can you move faster?"

Smacking sounds are heard when he pulls one booted foot after another out of the mud. Finally he moves! By the side of the road he rips out clumps of grass and picks up rocks. He stuffs everything into the mud behind the rear wheels and stomps on it to create a firmer base.

Wading to the front of the car, he grabs the bumper, and pushes against the bonnet with all his might. With the engine roaring and the rear wheels spinning, the vehicle moves slowly at first and then with a sudden jerk backwards out of the mud hole. Monty falls face first into the gunk. Slowly he gets up looking like a monster from the lagoon. He guides Anabelle with hand signals onto the firmer part of the path and she drives forward stopping next to him.

She opens the passenger door and tells him to get in. But first he wants to clean himself up a bit and asks for a rag or a towel. It doesn't matter if he gets the car dirty, she says. They will stay overnight in the next hotel where she can clean him and the car with a powerful jet of water.

"Stay in a hotel? No way, rosebud!" says Monty. "We are on the way to visit Don Oduber Madrigal, an old friend and neighbour of my family, and stay there overnight. I must introduce him to you because he will confirm every one of my stories, yes, every word you doubted. You'll see!"

"So, I'll have to prepare for a very long night," she sighs. "Can we even show up in this condition and unannounced at your friend's house?"

"But of course! He's a friend!" he responds emphasising the word 'friend' as if she wouldn't know the true meaning of it. "He and his family adhere to the age-old rules of hospitality. You can rely on that."

Anabelle is very sceptical. "Really? And how far is it to your friend's abode?"

"Uh... fifteen kilometres... *más o menos*," says Monty cocksure to have provided a fairly accurate estimate of the distance between the Earth and its Moon.

"More or less?" asks Anabelle. Hearing him using the phrase *más o menos* reminds her of the many times she heard it already in response to questions concerning time, distance and amounts. It's nothing more but a wild guess. She has learned to half or quadruple the numbers and is relieved he did not say 150 kilometres.

Monty ignores her question and happily chats away. "Don Oduber is well informed about everything in the northwest of Alajuela Province. He can tell us where a forest is being cut down. We'll take a look at it, you to take your dramatic pictures and then we drive on to the Caño Negro refuge on the northern border where we'll see some fresh clearcuts. At noon we continue to Sarapiquí, where you can meet some of your compatriots who turn the finest tropical wood into cheap charcoal and supply the civilised world with the enormous quantities produced. They cut down more than twenty hectares of rainforest year after year and have done that for the past twenty-five years. I understand you like grilled meat, don't you? Good! Next time before you bite into a juicy piece of grilled meat, check the bag of charcoal first. The inscription may tell you that the superb smoky flavour you cherish so much is a greeting from our clear-cut rainforests. Hopefully the bite of meat will stick in your throat in memory of Sarapiquí.

"In the evening we visit another friend of mine in Guápiles. He can show you some environmental disasters that should really satisfy you. So that you Europeans as well as Americans, Canadians and Japanese only get the finest bananas, the extremely sensitive 'Cavendish A' banana, the American fruit companies have received permission to divert entire rivers to control the irrigation of their plantations for the paltry bribe of ten thousand dollars. Huge nature reserves in Tortuguero Province were transformed into arid landscapes in just one year. It's amazing what you can still get for ten thousand dollars these days, isn't it?

"The day after tomorrow we drive to a smuggler's nest on the southern border. You'll meet some interesting guys who are willing to do anything for a little bit of money. The forest companies get lumberjacks there because they can count on their confidentiality or can have them eliminated without anyone complaining or questioning their fate. You'll have to shell out a few bucks to loosen their tongues, though.

"At noon we drive to San José, where you can probe the bureaucratic Moloch that pulls the strings of orchestrating the dirty deals. You're going to have a lot of fun with corrupt government employees who will lie the blue out of the sky for you and claim the moon is made of cheese. With a few tricks and the pretence of being an international consultant, you could even find out how

96

much of a bribe you have to pay to be allowed to cut down a large rainforest.

"On Thursday or is it on Friday I will take you to the airport and say goodbye to you with the heartfelt wish that you will visit me and our beautiful country, this paradise of untouched nature again really soon. Hmm, what do you think of that?"

"Hold your breath, Monty," says Anabelle. "You aren't planning my roundtrip. I decide where I will go and what I want to see."

"Aw, don't you like my plan?" he asks in an ironic tone.

"Well... uh, yes, I do."

"So?" Monty raises his hands to shoulder height and grins triumphantly.

She gives him a brief, angry look and would like to strangle him. His ironic talk, his sarcasm that she had to suffer the whole day is the main reason for the frustration she feels. Evidently, he is very knowledgeable about his country, the corruption, fraud and theft. She does not understand why he does not do something about it, help organisations with his knowledge. Surely he is not alone or the only citizen of this country with such wealth of information. What is he waiting for? Do foreign environmental organisations have to become active? Doesn't he understand that far-reaching societal change only happens from within? Obviously not! She will have to talk to him about it.

Monty points to a large homestead on the left. "We've arrived."

They drive through the open gate and are critically viewed by a stout man standing on the porch of his house in a blue shirt, white trousers and a white sombrero.

Monty jumps out of the car in front of the building. The stout man smiles and shouts, "*Chorlito*! I haven't seen you in ages. You look like a pig. Have you taken to wallowing in the mud?"

Monty laughs. "Yes, but it was an accident, Don Oduber. I had to push the car out of a mudhole and..."

Anabelle gets out of the car and the man stops him in his tracks. "Shut up, *Chorlito*. Who is this pretty cayman you brought along? She is far too good for you."

Oduber whistles appreciatively, comes down the two steps from the porch, and approaches Anabelle with arms wide open. He taps Monty on the shoulder. "Won't you introduce me, you lout?"

Monty apologises and introduces them to each other. Oduber doffs his hat, turns to her, shakes her hand, and says, "Anabelle!

What a beautiful name. How long will you please me with your presence? Welcome to my humble home, Señorita."

He kisses her on both cheeks and tries to embrace her. But she isn't comfortable with this exuberant friendly greeting. She feels overwhelmed in her normal distance from strangers, stripped naked by his gaze, and groped in the embrace. Can so much displayed warmth be real?

In the cooler atmosphere of her home, subtle signals of their femininity are hardly noticed, at least not seen as a signal to get fresh with her. An accidentally undone button on her blouse might draw the looks of a young man with a hormone disorder. Here she would feel exposed because of a missing button. It hasn't yet dawned on her that in the rural regions of these latitudes, sex is not an abstraction, but a reality that exists in the nether regions. So, she tries to keep her distance and balance.

"*Chorlito*, your cayman is very reserved," says Oduber with a chuckle, takes them both by the hand and leads them onto the porch of marble tiles and thick pillars. He turns around, whistles shrilly across the yard and roars, "*Chorlito*!! Go to the grocer and get a bottle of heating oil! But the finest! We have guests! Don't come back with *guaro*!"

In the white-washed reception hall decorated with relics of native craft he booms at the same volume to the left, "*Chorlito*!! Cook something tasty! Don't forget the beans! Rice! Salad! Bread! Cheese! Chilis!" He claps his hands. "Hurry up! Our guests are starving!"

Then he yells to the right, "*Chorlito*! Bring shirt and pants! Our friend needs to wash and change!"

He gives Monty a shove and points towards the bathroom door. "Go wash yourself, *Chorlito*. I'll have a little chat with your cayman."

With these words he leads Anabelle into the living room. As dusk falls, she looks out through the panoramic windows and sees orchids in wire baskets hanging in the trees of the garden outside. He invites her to sit down. But since she is not quite comfortable with the strange greeting, she remains standing. She wants to get away from this rude man and asks a little irritated, "You seem to call everybody *chorlito*. That's not very nice to call anyone a person who does things without thinking and is not judicious. Who are these *chorlitos*? And why do you keep calling me a cayman? I'm not an alligator."

Oduber laughs a little embarrassed and explains, "I call any man on my farm *chorlito* so I won't confuse them. They are my six sons, labourers, and visitors." He sighs and looks at her with a serious expression. "I'm sorry you don't like to be called a cayman. You're not familiar with the expression, are you? It's actually a compliment based on the lyrics of a song that said every woman, even if she wiggles her behind like an alligator, should be treated with caution and respect. You never know if she's going to snap and hurt you or regard you as a friendly source of comfort and food. Okay?"

Anabelle is not convinced that calling a woman a cayman is actually meant as a compliment. She would like to leave this house as soon as Monty has cleaned himself. But for the moment she needs to sit down and flops into an easy chair. The backrest gives way and the chair turns into a lounger.

Oduber sees her lying there and struggling to get up. He laughs heartily. "Now that's very forward of you, Anabelle. Is that supposed to be an invitation?"

He helps her get up, puts the backrest in the upright, and locks it in that position. He asks, "What is your full name?"

"Oh, does that interest you?" asks Anabelle in an uppity tone. "You just said that all women are alligators. Why don't you keep calling me cayman? Then our fleeting acquaintance will remain as anonymous as it should be."

Oduber sits down on the sofa, tries to put on a sad face but snickers when he proclaims, "In our circles nothing remains anonymous, my dear. You are another victim of civilisation who never gets in touch with untamed nature. Surely you live in a big city in Europe and enjoy prestige and status. And like your fellow citizens, you're concerned about having your aura touched. You must keep up the pretence of your image. No one shall discover that beneath your exterior is a human being that laughs and cries, feels happiness as well as grief, and may suffer depression. How unfortunate, really very unfortunate. But now will you tell me what your family name is, or shall I guess?"

Anabelle is overcome by a feeling of rising anger. Who does this rude bloke think he is? Calling her a victim of civilisation who never gets in touch with nature? That sounds like an insult! She is in touch with nature practically all the time. She has potted plants she cares for and cherishes, a dog she takes for walks regularly, and when she has time, she goes on long hikes across the pastures of the mountains near her home. She knows what it means to be in touch with nature.

He is a klutz who knows nothing about good manners, an uncivilised hunk who disregards the normal restraint of fellow human beings, imposes himself on them and takes them by surprise. With a scowl, she asks him, "What do you know about civilisation? Without it humanity wouldn't be where we are today. We would still be living on trees."

Amused by her anger, he looks at her and nods. "You are so right. And thanks to that civilisation we have not enough trees left for humanity to live on, clean air to breathe, or untainted water to drink. On the other hand, though, it has given us such great achievements as little flowers printed on toilet paper and a society whose members rush past each other, have barely any time for each other and are becoming increasingly distant from each other thanks to the virtual reality of social networks. Oh, how glad I am to know so little about this civilisation and to be hardly touched by it, Señorita Anabelle Bouchard."

Shocked she sits up and asks, "How do you know...?"

"Well, I won't reveal that to you. However, you should always be prepared for surprises among uncivilised people. Your craving for image reveals to us, who look, hear, smell, feel with sharp senses, everything that you would like to keep secret. Come on, let's have a look to see if dinner's on the table."

He gets up, takes her like a father his little daughter by the hand and pulls her along into the dining room. Monty stands by a table large enough for sixteen people. He looks funny in a shirt and jeans he could wrap twice around himself, yet Anabelle does not laugh. She is quite content to see his familiar face and gives him a light nudge. In turn he introduces her to five of Oduber's sons and their wives while the sixth son is still rushing around putting bowls and large plates full of food he prepared on the table.

After the extensive meal Oduber slouches in his high-back hardwood chair at the end of the large rectangular table made of one broad plank cut from a rainforest giant. He burps and apologises in the direction of Anabelle. His family and guests have been well fed, that is to say fattened. Roasts, steaks, chops, goulash, grilled chicken, rice with carrots and peppers, cabbage salad, tossed salad, tomato salad, marinated chili peppers, caramel pudding, white bread, hard cheese, homemade soft cheese, beer and freshly squeezed fruit juice had been served to eat and drink and all is gone down the gullet of twelve portly men and women as well as two slim guests.

Anabelle is stuffed. She had to taste a bit of everything, and she was given portions that would normally last her a whole day. She still wonders how she was able to eat all the food she was served. Luckily she will be in the country only for three more days. She can imagine that after a longer stay she would totter through the streets like a barrel on stilts and look more and more like many of the local women.

She understands, judging by the portions she saw Oduber and his six sons and five daughters-in-law eat, why stomach cancer and obesity are the most common health problems in Costa Rica. Monty, the wiry lad, was an exception as she could see at the table. Father, sons and wives gasped through lard-covered tracheae and, because of their paunches, could only see and shovel the food in from afar.

As if he could read Anabelle's mind, Oduber says, "One eats and celebrates in the same manner one works." He clicks his tongue and continues, "When the stomach is full, the heart is content. Come on, let's get comfortable in the TV room."

When he passes his youngest son, he puts a hand on his shoulder. "That was good, Chorlito, very, very good. Even if you don't have a bride yet, you prepare meals like a real man. Will you make some coffee for our guests?"

His son almost bursts with pride upon hearing these appreciative words in the presence of the visitors. He confirms the coffee order with an eager nod of his round head and storms off to the kitchen.

Don Oduber and his guests enter the room stuffed with American style upholstered furniture, Venetian figurines of multi-coloured glass and, and a gigantic, Korean TV set. The walls are decorated with floral wallpaper, retouched colour photos of family members and two monumental hams of a snow-covered Alpine landscape and a bellowing deer. The contrast to the dining room, with its fine wood furniture and wood panelled walls, is stunning. Symbolically, they step from an underdeveloped country into a civilisation of plastic, worthless imitations and high technology, from the warmth of being into the cold of pretence.

"You're a journalist?" asks Oduber and lolls in his armchair. Astonished, Anabelle stops digging in her handbag for cigarettes. She rarely smokes but after that meal she has the urge to light up and assist her digestion. Before she can answer, he continues, "Do you like our country? What do you like about it? The peace, democracy, unspoiled nature, or perhaps all the nice people?"

Anabelle lights up, takes a drag, coughs slightly, and looks at her inquisitor who lies in his chair like a three-hundred-pound cabbage roll and blinks at her from underneath languid eyelids. She asks herself why he presents his questions and statements in the same tone as Monty.

Is it a characteristic of the people who live in the north-western region of Costa Rica? Do they use irony and sarcasm as a defence to maintain their sanity in view of the countryside's devastation she got to see today? She leaves these questions aside to answer his question.

"Señor Madrigal, I came only three days ago to your country and will not provide the blanket assessments your questions demand of me to deliver. I've heard a lot of good things about your country but found very little confirmed so far. I have met a few people who impressed me with their warmth and open-mindedness while I haven't seen anything yet of the famed nature. Democracy? Peace? These are relative terms, misused by most politicians around the world on a daily basis. The oligarchies of the so-called upper classes throughout Latin America are showing day in, day out and before the eyes of the world their outrageous misuse of these political terms. In this country, too."

Oduber sits up and grins. "What? In this country, too? What gives you that idea?"

She does not respond to his challenge but says instead, "I don't want to be pretentious or rude, but what I've heard so far about the local society's upper class hasn't impressed me. Yet, I would have to find out much more about the high and mighty before I will pass any judgement. As I stated already, I arrived in the country only three days ago and don't want to offend or hurt anyone's feelings. I have to learn a lot more about this country and the rural life in the tropics. Why don't you tell me about the struggle of yourself and your family?"

Oduber tilts his head back and squints at her. "You are cunning, very, very cunning and clever."

He turns to Monty, sitting like a sack of laundry an arm's length from him. "Chorlito, you ugly scarecrow, I told you before, this cayman is far too good for you. She floats about three miles above you. But if you're a good boy, she'll let you kiss her feet tonight."

102

He smacks Monty on the knee, causing his foot to slip. He reaches for his wrist to show he is only joking. "What you haven't grasped in your twenty-five years, she figured out in three days, namely how one has to behave in this country to strike back one day with all the might you can muster. If only you had stayed here with your siblings when I offered it to you. I would have made a real man out of you, a fighter and not a cuentista who wastes his powder with the continuous repetition of tall stories. Do you still have it in you? Can you still fight like you did ten years ago? Or are you just a rooster who refuses to put on weight?"

Monty looks embarrassed. The oversized clothes he wears make him appear like a little boy who does not dare to fight for his property after his football was taken away by the neighbourhood bully. He seems to sink into the sofa. Anabelle can see how he is struggling with himself. She feels sorry for him because she knows he still has the tinder to start a fire but doubts he will ever fight for his rights. He is not the type who realises he has nothing to lose but the pitiful remnants of his manly pride.

"Doña Anabelle." Oduber lets her honorary title and name glide over his tongue like a sip of good wine. "What a pretty name for an attractive woman. If you were a queen, our people would crouch at your feet, myself included."

Anabelle is glad the youngest son brings in the coffee and stops the Minnesinger. She doesn't like compliments like that. They are embarrassing to her. She wants to be noticed and respected for her intellect. She can do without platitudes about her feminine attributes. Nevertheless, she also wants to be seen as a woman and Oduber's unabashed courtship, although she rejects it, goes down like warm honey. She much prefers it to the jaded, cool ramblings or pathetic come-ons she hears in the trendy pubs and bars of Europe and North America.

Only she and Monty are served coffee and she asks Oduber who is pouring cognac if he does not drink the beverage that made Costa Rica famous.

"No, never!" is his very firm response. "I won't touch that stuff. Others may want to poison themselves with it, I don't. Coffee, or gaghwa as the Arabs call it, is an invasive plant from Africa and doesn't belong here. It was at the root of the massive destruction of our land. And what have we gained? Some alleged economic benefit that has put us at the mercy of international traders in London. They dictate the purchase and sale prices. We get about fifty cents for a kilogramme of harvested coffee beans that are sold at more than forty times the price in the consumer countries. It's a fraud."

"But there are medicinal properties to coffee that have been proven to prevent Alzheimer's disease for instance."

"Fine, then let the Africans grow it and we import whatever medicinal properties we require. That would be beneficial for the economy of many African countries and us. They could make a fortune with the export of coffee beans and we would have relatively little expense for the import of these beans to satisfy the people who want to drink the beverage and any medication we may need. Then we would have vast expanses of intact rainforest whose plants could be intensively studied and explored for all their secrets of medicinal properties they can provide. With every part of our rainforests razed to the ground to grow coffee we destroy habitat for a myriad of creatures and thousands of unexplored substances of plants that might help to prevent or cure diseases."

Depressed silence follows this eloquent rebuttal of the benefit of growing coffee outside of Africa until Oduber resumes, "Doña Anabelle, let's consider your desire of learning about rural life in the tropics. Would you like me to confirm the many good things you read and heard about our 'Land of Peace'? I'd be happy to do that. When I talk about the wonders of our little paradise, I sometimes even believe it myself. It gives me inner peace and I can sleep well until I am ripped out my dreams by howling chainsaws. Or would you rather hear a tirade of my honest opinion about life in this tropical paradise? Then you should call a doctor, because I usually get a heart attack after half an hour of talking about it."

"Can you keep it to half an hour of expressing your opinion without a heart attack?" Anabelle responds in his ironic tone.

"I'd do anything for you, Doña Anabelle. For you I'd ride a porcupine bareback."

He sips the cognac and winks at her with an amused twinkle in his eyes before he proceeds.

"The economy of Latin American countries is largely based on agriculture. Even in oil-producing nations such as Venezuela and Ecuador or industrialised Argentina and Brazil, the majority of the population works in agriculture. It means that most people's income as well as the national economies depend on the sale and export of agricultural goods. However, since the importing

104

countries have no interest in the huge variety of tropical fruits and only demand cheap mass-produced goods, the farmers of the producing countries are forced to set up huge monocultures. These crops, be they banana, coffee, cocoa, mango, papaya, avocado, palm oil, or flower plantations, are highly sensitive to all kinds of diseases and pest infestations. They are kept alive with highly toxic imported pesticides whose prices bear no relation to the depressed prices of tropical products. The low prices of tropical mass-produced goods dictated by the commodity exchanges abroad mean that most *haciendados* and *finqueros*, the large and small farmers, earn barely enough to pay their debts, let alone make a decent living and save something for their retirement in old age.

"Let's take the mango for example. Consumers in Europe, North America and Asia pay more than three dollars for a mango weighing 300 grammes. The farmer who produces it receives for a box of thirty-six top quality fruits in the best case about six dollars, more or less fifteen cents for each mango. That's a twenty-fold price increase from producer to consumer. The coffee business is even more brutal.

"The overseas consumers pay without complaint sixteen dollars for one kilogramme of low-grade blended Arabica coffee of half *Suave* highland and half *Robusta* lowland beans, while the *Cafetaleros*, the coffee producers get less than forty-five cents for the same quantity. The consumers pay on average thirty-four dollars for one kilogramme of finest select *Suave* coffee beans while a trader or wholesaler paid a maximum of about seventy-five cents per kilogramme! Not even the world-wide operating 'Fair Trade' organisations that demand for their coffee over forty-five dollars per kilogramme with the excuse of paying the growers a 'fair' price, pay the *Cafetaleros* no more than one dollar for a kilogramme of coffee beans. Those are price increases between thirty-three thousand and forty-five thousand percent.

"These enormous differences between purchase and sale prices cannot be justified with the often-cited transport costs either. Shipping five thousand tons of our products to Europe costs sixty-five thousand dollars, less than two cents per kilogramme. Import and sales tax add about fifteen percent to a retail price. It is the extreme profit maximisation, the avarice of brokers, wholesalers, and retailers, that drives up consumer prices and denies the producers a fair income. Therefore, a satisfactory livelihood cannot be achieved with agriculture alone in the tropics.

"Country life in the tropics lacks any romance. It's tedious and hard. So, it's no wonder that every landowner and farmer, especially those who possess forest areas, have an open ear for any opportunity of additional income in the hope of making a quick buck, be it with an airstrip for the drug traffickers, the cultivation of coca, poppies or marijuana, the razing of an entire forest and the sale of tropical timber. Thousands of abandoned homesteads are testament to the failed attempts of millions of farmers across Latin America to make a quick buck by taking the great risk of betting everything they owned on one or another nefarious scheme, lost it all and left a destroyed landscape behind."

Oduber pauses as he appears to be out of breath. It's the opportunity for Monty to add his bit of mustard.

"If I may, Oduber, I can confirm what you said about people trying to get a bit of extra income by any means imaginable. In my circle of family and acquaintances scattered all over the country, there isn't a person who won't try to earn a bit of extra money on the side by crooked means.

"The entire population, it seems, is degenerating into bootleggers, smugglers, drug traffickers, and people willing to peddle anything, including themselves, for a few bucks. In our country schooling is compulsory up to the age of 14 by law, but you see children who contribute to the livelihood of their families with their work as newspaper vendors, shoeshine boys, harvesters on the coffee and sugar cane plantations or in child prostitution. The father as a craftsman or the mother as an office worker simply do not earn enough to at least buy a Canasta Basica, a basket of staple foods and still have enough money in their pockets to pay rent, utilities, buy clothes and maybe afford a little pleasure like a cheap bus trip to the beach or a visit to the cinema.

"Everyone wants to make money as quickly as possible, also in a criminal way, stash it away and do not pay taxes because the corrupt government just wastes the revenue anyway. The country's social problems are enormous and get bigger every day. What really upsets me are loud-mouthed foreigners, be they representatives of the World Bank, businesspeople, or tourists who come here and believe that with a few shithouse slogans like 'discipline, law and order, hard work, and tighten your belt' they are conveying the panacea to end the people's misery. And when a bum like that opens his mouth, I get so angry that I would like to smash my fist into his or her face."

"Why don't you?" asks Oduber. "That's what a fighter would do and suffer the consequences. When you end up in court and state publicly your reason for assaulting the loudmouth, you can count on huge support from the people. Everybody is tired of hearing these slogans and even more so of governments regurgitating this garbage and continuously tightening the belt of those who have least. I could sing a song about it.

"Almost all of my neighbours were tempted to make a quick buck. The few who fell for the lies they were told, like your father, Monty, they were cheated out of their possessions by corrupt civil servants. With a lot of luck and a bit of cunning, I kept my head above water. When my father had divided his property in three equal parts to be inherited by my two brothers and me, I took out a huge mortgage to pay my brothers and keep the property intact. The sale of 650 hectares of land with hot volcanic springs to a foreigner who wanted to build a health resort there, which he never did, as well as my wife's dowry, and the sale of all my cattle brought in enough cash to pay most of the mortgage. Some smart refinancing of the remaining debt, switching from cattle farming to growing vegetables on the fifteen hectares near the river, and my brothers selling my vegetables in the central valley, helped me and my growing family to get through difficult times. Thus, I didn't succumb to the temptation of using my 4,850 hectares rainforest 'economically', as many profiteers and experts had suggested.

"The rapidly advancing destruction of forests in my neighbourhood raised interest in my property. A broker specialised in tropical timber dropped in and calculated how many cubic metres of timber in board metres my forest contained. He appeared to be well informed about my financial situation and offered me one million dollars cash for the sale of the forest and my hacienda. A quick calculation showed that he offered me twenty dollars per cubic meter of timber. I showed him a report about the price in the USA of almost $2,000 per cubic meter in the shape of boards. I demanded one hundred million for my forest and a further twenty million for my hacienda. The man cursed and left to make room for the next lot of 'experts'. Every one of them had some fraudulent intention and I chased them away. I gained the reputation of being a blockhead from Aragón who'd break his neck one day when my entire property could be had for an apple and a song. Consequently, I was left alone for a while.

"The clear cutting of forests in the north of the country from the Pacific to the Caribbean coasts continued and left the landscape devasted. It had a dramatic effect on the climate. Year after year I noticed the rise in temperatures and less and less rainfall. When El Niño struck, I was sure the bell of my final hour had tolled. If you are not familiar with the phenomenon of El Niño, it is the reversal of the normal weather pattern caused by a turbulence of the Pacific Gulf Streams off the coast of Peru. For its duration it brings only gentle breezes and hardly any rain to Central America. The absolute drought we experienced dried up my river almost completely. In my distress I thought for the first time of using all my savings as a bribe to get a clearing licence for my forest. But my wife persuaded me to tighten my belt, live off our savings, and ride out El Niño. When there was still no rain worth mentioning after fourteen months, we were in despair. My good wife and mother of my sons decided to go to San José and work in her sister's bakery to support our family. Two days after her arrival, she was found dead with her throat cut behind the bakery's stall in the Mercado Central. She had become the victim of a robbery. It was the absolute low point of our family history.

"Her life insurance allowed me and my sons to survive financially for another six months until the first harvest of our vegetables after the dry spell and we recovered slowly. The family tragedy and my financial difficulties had been noticed by many people. Especially the adventurers on the hunt for a piece of forest contacted me again. It was inevitable that one day the government officer, who had already done the dirty on Monty's father, approached me with an offer of having the entire forest declared a protected area, and laid a meagre certified cheque for two hundred and fifty thousand dollars on the table. When I asked him innocently which green organisation or country had just offered fifteen million bucks for nature conservation, he stuttered and asked how I could possibly be informed about it. He noticed his verbal slip-up and hurriedly left my house without saying another word.

"The mental distress suffered due to our family tragedy seems relatively minor compared to the running battle which began after that visit. The very next day we received visits from police officers in plain clothes who questioned me and my sons for seemingly endless days. They pumped us about contacts with government agencies, radical organisations and revolutionary cells, which we couldn't answer because we didn't know what they meant. They searched the house and yard, even went into the forest, accused us of seditious intentions, and tried to incite neighbours and my brothers against me. Eventually they left and were replaced by the tax investigation auditors who claimed to have received tip-offs of tax fraud. They went with a fine toothcomb through all my income and expense books. Luckily, my wife had drilled it into me to keep every receipt neat and tidy, and to have my annual tax returns signed off by a state auditor. After four weeks of fruitless efforts, they certified that I was probably the only citizen in the country who paid his taxes correctly and on time, and they left very disappointed.

"But worse was yet to come. In the name of 'Nature Conservation' my license for selectively cutting down a tree and collecting firewood was withdrawn. That meant I couldn't even cut posts for my fences. To enforce this order, the rural police hung around every day and controlled our every movement. Once a week a police patrol came to our property and searched the house and barns for freshly felled wood. My remaining cattle were stolen without one of these useless cops ever seeing or noticing any of it. I did file a complaint against person unknown and about police inaction, but I never filed a lawsuit. I was smart enough to know that a court action would have ruined me financially. Then the fight continued with even harder bandages. One night my truck, already loaded with over 2,000 cases of vegetables, caught fire that burned down my barn as well. The last major action was an alleged terrorist hunt across my farm and into the forest that ended with a monstrous shooting of invisible or non-existent opponents. My youngest son was shot when he ran out of the house to see what was going on. Luckily he was only grazed and not seriously injured.

"It was all part of the endless campaign to soften me up and sell or give up my forest for 'conservation'. It's been a bad time and will get worse. The more forests are cut down, the more valuable the trees on my piece of preserved nature become. Nevertheless, I am confident that I will survive with the help of my sons. I have one great advantage thanks to an entomologist from Italy who studies spiders and a herpetologist from Japan who studies frogs and other amphibians. These two researchers initiated the support of their universities and a few months ago my rainforest was registered with the United Nations as a national heritage site. The 'frogman' from Japan is here right now, and I'm expecting a group of researchers and students to stay here for a few months to explore my forest. This will of course be exploited in a big way by the government to provide the world further proof of our nature conservation. I don't give a damn as long as it keeps the philistines away who want to harvest, as they call it, my forest."

Oduber looks exhausted. He gives everybody a refill of cognac, raises his glass, and says, "Cheers to the future."

Anabelle had listened intently and took copious notes. His refusal to sell his land for a price that would make him an instant millionaire has raised her suspicion. She has heard only of natives in the Americas refusing to sell their land at whatever price was offered. Immigrants and their descendants appear only too ready to flog their real estate in exchange for a life of leisure, acquire money for investments, or simply to survive in the vast majority of cases. Thus, she assumes purely economic interests motivate Señor Madrigal, who is doing quite well, apparently, to hold on to his property. She asks herself how she can get at the truth. But at the moment another question surges to the fore: If the government buys up areas of land for conservation with international financial support and the law declares these areas to be protected public property, how can parts of it be sold again for clear cutting without anybody noticing and protesting against it?

She asks him this question and notices that he hesitates to answer as he scrutinises her. Instead of giving her a prompt answer, he requires her to treat anything he has to say in this matter and the source of the information with the utmost confidentiality.

She assures him to keep it secret.

Oduber takes a deep breath and oils his vocal cords with one more sip of cognac before he speaks.

"In a geographic coordinate system, measurements are expressed in degrees, minutes, and seconds. A degree is 1/360th of a circle. Each degree is divided into 60 minutes, and each minute divided into 60 seconds. The sale of forests in protected areas and national parks is very simple and is referred to as the 'phenomenon of migrating protected areas' by those in the know. Each piece of land, whether privately owned or by the state, is registered in the central land registry office by its geographic coordinates that are based on survey data. At its simplest, it looks like this: a property in the range of 10°25'30" and 10°24'47" north latitude and 83°50'25" and 83°49'52" west longitude has a total area of about

110

135 hectares. Making half of it available for sale without causing a stir, the coordinates are changed to 10°25'51" and 10°25'08" north latitude and 83°50'58" and 83°50'25" west longitude, for example. Thus, about 67 hectares of woodland were moved out of the originally protected area and can be sold as unprotected land by 'migrating' the original area 21" north and 33" west.

"The 67 hectares of previously unprotected land that has by some bureaucratic miracle become part of the protected area can be used as before because the owner, in case it is held privately, is not informed about the shift. Should the area be state owned, it makes no difference since the central land registry office is under government control. At the international level, protected areas are only indicated with markings such as rivers, mountains, coasts or roads and coordinate corrections are the order of the day. So, the corrections aren't unusual and don't stand out as long as the total area stays the same. The prerequisite for a successful manipulation and migration of the area is therefore, as in this example, an adjacent area to the east and south of the protected area that is appropriated and corresponds in its extent to the forest area to be sold.

"Karst areas are preferred as replacement land for the sold forest areas. Firstly, they're cheap if they have to be bought, and secondly, they can be used very profitably for the reforestation programme of the internationally funded 'Debt Relief for Conservation'. In connection with the term 'nature conservation', it sounds like sheer mockery, but corresponds to practice.

"To a layman, a tropical rainforest is nothing more than a dangerous, monstrous thicket. The government officials of the industrialised nations who fund conservation are laymen as far as tropical nature is concerned. They take the position that such a thicket should first be cleared and swept with a broom for them to count the trees for which money should be paid. Only concrete figures count in this business as in any other business where billions of dollars are at stake.

"However, since it is practically impossible to come up with specific figures for a rainforest other than its dimensions, relatively little money is made available for the protection of existing nature. If, on the other hand, the wish is expressed to reforest a devastated area, a wasteland without bushes or trees that can be surveyed and measured, then the bureaucrats of the donor countries sit up and take notice. They understand and know it from home and immediately ask how many seedlings are to be planted. The debt relief, the support for 'reforestation' depends on the exact number of seedlings to be planted.

"First, an exact calculation determines the size of the land that is slated for reforestation. Then a price is agreed for each seedling and the cost of labour to plant it, which is multiplied by the number of seedlings per square meter and the number of square meters to be reforested. The result is a verifiable sum that can be used in the calculation of debt forgiveness or as a donation. Although such reforestation programs have little to do with nature conservation, they are used very effectively in the political arena.

"For instance, a politician who says that fifty square kilometres of rainforest have been preserved thanks to his personal intervention is quickly discredited for advocating to do nothing. But a politician who boasts that thanks to his efforts fifty square kilometres of karst have been transformed back into a flourishing landscape with the planting of 200 million little trees is applauded. His assertion isn't remotely true, since a monoculture susceptible to disease was created, not a flourishing landscape with healthy nature. But who cares when impressive numbers are bandied about, especially when it comes to billions of dollars spent on conservation. The industrialised donor nations carelessly promote the progressive destruction of nature in developing countries by supporting politicians who quickly realised that by preserving nature their debts are cancelled once in a best-case scenario and quickly forgotten, while deforestation and reforestation sets in motion an endless flow of money they can use to enrich themselves.

"In Costa Rica, conservative politicians recognised more than five decades ago that the sale of forest areas to foreign timber companies, export taxation of tropical timber, donations for nature conservation, and the foreign financing of reforestation, created four constantly flowing sources of money. This financial instrument is now played with such uncanny virtuosity that the country could show a surplus of billions of dollars each year instead of a deficit if most of the money raised was registered with the auditor general rather than transferred to foreign accounts of politicians and top bureaucrats.

"The money they bag is derived from forest sales, export taxes, conservation donations, and reforestation funding, as well as percentages of donations for research, road and port improvements, communications systems, and public housing construction."

Oduber is exhausted. "Now you know how the sale of protected forests functions, Anabelle, and more importantly why."

Somewhat irritated she looks up from her notes. "There is one thing I don't understand at all. Your portrayal and Monty's stories show that you and many others in this country are very well aware of the fraud, corruption and destruction. I suspect you have enough evidence in your hands to bring charges against those in power. Why don't you? Why aren't you doing anything against the system of which you are so critical?"

Oduber looks at her with eyebrows raised. "I'm surprised you ask me such questions. Being from Europe you must know that the judicial system is part of the total system. Ask yourself what would have happened to you during the Nazi regime, if you had accused the government of concentration camp mass murder before a German court."

"Hang on a second," objects Anabelle and slides to the front edge of her chair. "That's an outrageous comparison. In Costa Rica it is not a fascist terror regime in power, but a freely and democratically elected government. According to the constitutional law, you have the separation of judiciary and government, which makes the judicial system independent, and you don't even have military in this country."

"Anabelle, you'd be an excellent ambassador of our country. Like an ignoramus you regurgitate everything the government states to represent itself and the country in the most favourable light."

He scratches his balding pate and looks at a loss for words, before sweeping her arguments away like a hurricane. "A while ago, you mentioned the Latin American oligarchies trampling the concept of democracy, peace and freedom and abusing it on a daily basis. In this country too, you added. Do you actually know about it or are you just pretending? Do you have any insight at all, or at least a perspective? Do you know that the presidents of our country's modern history come from only six extended families and are all related? In some other countries there are even fewer families who regard the country as their private property. They control the press, radio and television, industrial licensing, import and export business, tourism and agriculture with an iron fist. They have the country and the people in their back pocket, so to speak.

"Do you actually know what democracy means in Latin America and especially in the much-cited model case, our beloved Costa Rica? The people are called to go to the polls every four years and elect a president from among four or five members of the oligarchy. In order to camouflage the family ties and keep up the appearance of democratic elections, the candidates stand for allegedly differently aligned political parties. Yet it is irrelevant who wins the election. All the candidates have the common interest of carrying on as before to ensure they can enrich themselves while in office.

"Freedom in Latin America means, with very few exceptions, that the oligarchs move about their respective countries like buffoons in their house. The people must keep peace, be calm and not disturb the taking of liberties. The military, where it exists, and the police, both of whom are nothing more than the guards of the upper families, will ensure peace - graveyard peace, that is.

"You came to our country only three days ago and have heard many good things about it. Democracy, peace, freedom, friendship, and no military. That's very impressive. But you also said, it's all relative. That applies to our absent military as well. It's true that we don't fire cannons and tanks don't roll through our streets. However, under pressure and with funding from the United States, our country has for the past fifty years one of the most powerful paramilitary commandos in the world. Its members are trained by officers of similar US, Israeli and Argentine military special forces at a camp in Santa Rosa National Park. They don't wear uniforms, appear in civilian clothes, are as far as possible only active at night, and use silenced weapons exclusively. Here this unit is called a 'Special Police Unit' that doesn't officially exist. In other Latin American countries such a troop is called a death squad. Here, as elsewhere, it is the long arm of the oligarchy that no one can escape. Every year more than a thousand people disappear without a trace in our land of peace - men, women and children. Once you have observed how the Rapid Reaction Force operates, you may not have any proof but no more doubt who is responsible for most of the disappearances.

"I hope this gives you some insight into the true nature of our freely and democratically elected government. Maybe now you see why I or Monty couldn't, indeed, can't do anything about it. Only suicidal maniacs open their cakehole about fraud and corruption, or let it be known publicly that they know something. I can say all

114

I want to say here in my house and in a private conversation with a foreign journalist but never in public. If I did that, I'd have just under three hours to live. If someone opens his big trap and then disappears without a trace, we say he was bitten by the bigmouth snake, whose venom works within two hours and lets the victim vanish into thin air. My knowledge alone is enough to be eliminated. So, I asked you to keep everything you hear from me confidential."

Oduber is breathing heavily and puts a hand on his chest. Saliva forms little bubbles in the corners of his mouth. He wipes them away and takes a long swig of cognac. Anabelle stares at him mesmerised. Monty looks at her with a satisfied smile and is silent when she clutches at one last straw. "What about the media? There are big newspapers, TV stations and radio stations in this country. There has to be someone who can really unravel this whole dirty business and get a public reaction!"

Tormented, Oduber laughs at the top of his lungs. "You want to see me break down tonight, huh? You're an adamant and tough woman, Anabelle."

He groans, leans forward with elbows on his knees, and mutters scornfully, "The media, I told you already, is also controlled by the government. We have the *Instituto Nacional del Periodismo*, the National Journalism Institute for that function. Officially it's the guardian of the quality of journalism. But really it should be called the 'Institute for the Testing of Paper Pushers Toeing the Line'. Any person who wants to work in the media in this country, yes, even just a disc jockey announcing songs for a radio station, is subjected to a thorough examination. It has to be determined whether the candidate has had the required brain amputation and can recite by heart the 365 variants of 'Runaway Cat in Tree was Rescued by Fire Department'. Anyone with an ability to think or a critical attitude is denied a license to practice his or her chosen profession. So much for the media. Any other question?"

"I'm too depressed to ask any more questions," says Anabelle, looks at her notes, takes a sip of her drink and says quite innocently, "I suppose I may quote you in my report, Don Oduber?"

"Have you gone completely insane?!" he yells and flops back in his chair. "What have I done to you to want to kill me? Or are you deaf? I answered your questions openly and honestly to open your eyes and for you, a foreign journalist, to know how everything works here. Now you can deepen your research and collect your own evidence. That's what your reports has to be based on not the tirade of an old fart like me. I gave you the pointers so that you can sideswipe effectively and strike where it hurts. Reports abroad that denounce and document the quagmire in this country are our only chance for something to improve."

Royally pissed about his harsh tone, she replies, "If the system is indeed as sophisticated as you make it out to be, a report abroad might stir up some dust, but it won't bring about any changes in Costa Rica. That has to come from within. As Albert Einstein said, the world is a dangerous place to live, not because of the people who commit evil deeds, but because of the people who don't do anything about these evil deeds. He meant to say that improvements have to be brought about by people like you and Monty. I have little time left to do much research and gather evidence for a hard-hitting report. In the two full days I have left I want to take some dramatic photos and will hardly be able to turn the country on its ear."

"But you could if you really wanted to," insists Oduber. "I didn't suggest putting the country on its ear. Select a case scenario to follow through and get the documented evidence for your report."

"How am I supposed to do that? I have no information other than what you and Monty told me and no contacts in the country. I don't even know what case scenario would yield the results I need."

"Then I'll have to think of something," says Oduber in a tone that suggests his mind is elsewhere. He yawns and rubs his hand over his face, sees Anabelle looking again through her notes, and asks Monty if she has ever seen a rainforest.

He looks at him astonished. "No idea, but I don't think so. Since I told her what had happened to my family and our property, she has shown interest only in destroyed forest areas. Why do you ask? Were you thinking of taking her on a guided tour of your jungle?"

Oduber grins. "Yes, that's the idea. Tomorrow morning before sunrise we'll go and take our shotguns along. With a bit of luck, we might kill a Guatuso or even a jaguar."

Anabelle looks up startled. "What did you say? You want to kill a jaguar? You're not allowed to do that, are you?"

Oduber laughs so hard that his paunch wiggles. "That reaction I expected to see from you. Such a comment would derail your

116

train of thought. But what gives you the idea that I can't kill a jaguar in my forest? Do you want to stop me from going through with it?"

Stunned, she struggles for words to wipe this man's laugh off his face. What kind of person is this who claims to be fighting to save his rainforest and is then willing to shoot and kill one of the world's rarest life forms for his pleasure? Oduber's continued amusement completely confuses her. "Surely you must know that hunting and killing endangered animals in the wild is banned around the world and an offense carries most severe penalties. If you kill a jaguar, the government and police really have every reason to make life miserable for you and confiscate your forest."

"Oh, all right, but shooting and killing a Guatuso is okay?"

"I don't know what a Guatuso is."

"I see... So, the tourist map you were given doesn't show the village San Rafael de Guatuso just a few kilometres away from my place? Very smart."

"What do you mean? There's a village of animals?"

"Well, some of our officials would like to put it that way to justify the killing of our natives, which they consider equal to animals."

Anabelle starts to stutter. "Wha... wha... what? Guatusos are natives and you're allowed to shoot and kill them?"

"No, I'm not allowed to shoot and kill any of them, but if I did and left the corpse in my forest, there wouldn't be an investigation. The Guatuso are one of our tribes of natives, like the Chorotega in Guanacaste Monty may have mentioned. Most of our natives were only recognised a few years ago as citizens of Costa Rica and many in the southern region on the border with Panama are still not recognised as such, are a divided people with one half living here and the other half in Panama where they are recognised citizens."

"That's incredible! How can they not be recognised in this country? They lived here long before any of the settlers."

"Indeed! But Costa Rica is no exception to the rest of the world. Racism is alive and well in our lovely country, too."

Anabelle looks forlorn and with her eyes downcast she pauses for a moment to digest what she heard. She takes a deep breath and says, "Oduber, Monty, both of you have told me so many depressing stories about what's going on in your country. Wouldn't you like to live somewhere else?"

The two men respond in unison, "No! Oh, no..."

"Why not?"

Monty is quick off the mark with his comment, "This is my country, my home. I want the pretence, the lies, the hypocrisy that everything is fine to stop. I want it to be a better place where any worker is paid a fair wage and have enough money to feed and clothe a family, can afford to rent or buy a proper home, and..."

Oduber butts in, "Fair wages would reduce the rate of petty crime immediately, but the drastic increase in wages it requires won't happen. Living in some other country? Where? Do you know of any country that is not run by oligarchs? The word oligarchy has been mentioned often in our discourse said so far. You know what that word means, don't you? It refers to the few that rule, meaning the very rich business leaders who are only interested in amassing more money, dictate the politics and don't give a flying fig about societal norms and needs. I can't see how that will ever change."

"But what about you?" enquires Anabelle. "Aren't you part of the oligarchy? You are a big land owner and very wealthy."

"Wealthy? No! I'm well off but not wealthy. I was very lucky to have inherited the remnants of land that was bequeathed upon my ancestors by the Spanish king many centuries ago. I could be wealthy if I sold my land but I will never do that. Tomorrow morning I will show you why. It's late and we have to get up very early. Let's call it quits for tonight, okay?"

Sudden Death

During the drive home in the dark from San Jerónimo to Montes de Oca, Rico doesn't say a word. Only occasionally does he move his lips in silent soliloquy or raises a hand and lets it slap back onto the steering wheel.

Martha looks at him and is ready to help if he opens up and asks. She knows what's going on in his mind. It is a colossal process of sorting, structuring and mental digestion of his investigation's findings so far and the interim conclusions he gained. The gathered information is in a clinch with his search for the one starting point that, like a loose thread, would allow him to unravel the entanglements of the Felipe Suárez case like an old woollen sock. Whole card indexes of thoughts he shuffles back and forth in his head while keeping a keen eye out for the potholes on the roads and cruising along with the bravado of a sleep walker.

Martha leans her head against his shoulder. Patiently she waits for the liberating "Aha!", "Yesss!" or "Got it!" that would indicate the end of his mental digging for a clue. But she waits in vain. Not a word can be heard from him even when he carries their luggage and his gun into the house, locks the car, and then tigers up and down in the living room like a caged animal.

When she calls him to the table for their late dinner, he waves her off at first but then joins her and eats a few bites of a delicious roast chicken while he looks at her apologetically. He knows very well that he should be sitting with his wife having a chat about their trip or watching some programme on TV instead of being a pain in the rump.

Suddenly he gets up. "Martha, my dear, I must go to the office. Tossing these thoughts around in my head is driving me crazy. I have to get all the evidence, factors and aspect into a clear structure, draw a big diagram on a board to tie it all together, and write it all down. It will take some time and I don't know when I'll be back. Please forgive me for running out on you like this."

"Don't worry, Rico. I knew what I was getting into when I married a crime investigation detective. I wish I could be of help.

Don't you want to talk to me about it? I might see something that escapes you."

"I know that, my dear. But this case continues to draw wider circles and I may need Gus's help to get some secret file information. You stay here and be safe. Don't forget to lock the doors. I have a strange premonition that there could be trouble brewing."

She looks up frightened and asks, "What are you getting at?"

"You remember Maria saying that she is in mortal danger because some people know that she has all the information Felipe had acquired. Now you and I know about it and could be targets as well." He takes a deep breath and continues, "I wish I hadn't taken you on the trip because then I could rest assured that you are safe."

Abruptly, he goes to the guestroom, gets the gun out of its cabinet, and checks the magazine is loaded. He rushes back and puts the gun on the table.

"I want you to take this to defend yourself. You know how to handle and fire it, don't you?"

"Rico, you want me to shoot someone?"

"Yes, of course, when it's a matter of saving your own life! If I had to find out that you and our baby were murdered, I wouldn't want to live anymore."

"What are you talking about? I think you are getting carried away with your thoughts and theories. We should sit down and talk about your premonition."

"I know, but... I haven't got time for a long discussion. Let me give you a brief summary. It's all about the motive for the murder of Felipe. He worked for someone who paid him a lot of money for making copies of confidential contracts and letters. I have no idea what these documents were but I presume it has to do with corruption, bribes, fraud, drug money laundering and other dodgy business. If any of this becomes public knowledge, there will be a shitstorm of indignation and a lot of people may end up in prison. It's my theory that two competing groups of very rich and influential people are fighting for dominance of this dirty business that may allow whoever wins to dictate the political course of our country. Now... the people who used Felipe made a bad, a really bad mistake by having him killed. When they found out his plan of getting married and leaving the country, they should have invited him for a chat, paid him a vast amount of stolen money like half a million dollars and send him and his wife off to Spain. Then

120

they could have started a huge hue and cry about a courier having escaped with stolen money and discredit him that way without demanding his deportation. Had he ever opened his mouth about what he knew then nobody would have believed him and the whole case would have fizzled out. Instead, they decided to kill him and want to eliminate anyone they assume to know about the dirty business and their fight of wanting to take over and dominate it. This fight is like a sudden death game that's decided in overtime by a point or goal. Don't be surprised if high-ranking officials and possibly our president, a former president, or a future candidate will be in court on charges of embezzlement and corruption. If it is known by now that I'm investigating the murder and took you on the trip to follow some trails, it makes you and me potential targets."

Martha listened and nods. "I see your point but it's only a remote possibility that someone will want to burst in here and kill me."

"Remote or not, it's still a possibility. Please, be on your guard and ready for the worst."

"Yes, I'll lock the doors. Also, we have grilles in front of all windows. Our house is like a prison. Who could get in here?"

"Anyone determined enough to do so, will do so. Let me get the USB stick and I'll be off."

She watches him rushing around, gives him a hug and pulls the wrought iron door grille shut when he gets into his car and drives away. She locks the grille and the door and clears the dinner table.
***
After a hectic drive, Rico enters the OIJ headquarters. In his office, he switches the desktop computer on, sticks the USB stick into its slot and reads what he had written about the initial investigation in San Antonio. He discards previous conclusions and assumptions but jots down the facts about Felipe and Olga, the pathologist's findings, the police officers in San Antonio and Sardinal, as well as the presumed murder of the teacher in Sardinal. Then he steps up to the large whiteboard and referring to all his notes, he draws a diagram of the facts in San Antonio and the encounter with Maria Villafuerte in Sardinal and San Jerónimo. Based on what he can see now in all its clarity, he starts to write a new report.

It is well past midnight when he finishes a first draft, reads it, compares it to his notes and makes a number of corrections. He goes to the kitchen, makes himself a cup of coffee and ponders his findings. It strikes him that he began to follow a line of investigation focusing on the motive and background and deviates from finding the murderer of Felipe. He will have to make some corrections and find the San Antonio case file that was hopefully delivered to Gus. He hopes that it will have been expanded by the reports of the pathologist and forensic laboratory. Back in the office, he opens Goicoechea's filing cabinet and looks for the case file.

He looks under 'S' for Suárez and San Antonio, 'F' for Felipe, and under 'Open Cases'. He can't find the file and curses under his breath, "Where the hell did he put it?"

A familiar voice behind him asks, "Where did I put what?"

Startled, Rico swings around and faces Gus. "Shit! You scared me there for a sec, but I'm glad to see you."

"Why? It's past midnight, man. You should be home, have a snooze and not rummage through my files. Whatcha lookin' for?"

"The Felipe Suárez murder case."

"Ha! You think I'd keep it in an unlockable cabinet? No way! I know a lot of people are keen to get their hands on it and destroy it. Let me tell you, it's not just a murder case but reaches into the highest echelons of big business and government. It opened a huge barrel of effluent with some really big turds floating around in it."

"Very picturesque description of big business and government. You're not planning a Basque uprising, are you? So, where is this file? Where do you keep it?"

"You're standing on it, well, almost."

Rico looks down and takes a step aside. "What? Where?"

Gus whispers, "See the patch of carpet that's under the legs of the cabinet for no reason? I put the file there so nobody searching the cabinet would get the idea to look under his or her feet."

Rico bends down, lifts a corner of the carpet and pulls out a file. He looks at it. "This isn't it. Where's the Suárez case file?"

"A bit to the left or the right. Can't remember. But it's there."

Rico pulls out five more files and puts them on the desk. "What's all this? Why do you do that? These are all current cases."

"I know and every one of them has some links to officials and powerful business types. Why do you think I hide them?"

"You are a rebel, aren't you? Can't deny your heritage."

"No! I'm not rebellious. I only safeguard the files."

"Sure. Including this one about the mother who killed her child? What's that got to do with big business and government?"

122

"A lot, let me assure you. Saw that woman a while ago. It's one of those cases that wants you to quit criminal investigation and look for a job selling toilet brushes door to door. Once the woman's head had cleared up, I interviewed her. She doesn't remember a thing, is inconsolable about the loss of her child. She's an addict all right. Was high on china white, cocaine and meth when she killed her child. She confessed to be involved in the trade and spilled the beans about the big shots that pull the strings. I really don't want to talk about it. It's too depressing. What about your case?"

"Let's grab a coffee and I'll tell you about it."

Rico and Gus settle in their office chairs nursing their mugs of fresh brew and Rico tells him everything he found out.

In turn Gus enlightens him with some details about Felipe's murderer. "On the assumption the victim stood upright, the degree of the cut to a vertical line tells us that the murderer is about the same height as the victim of one metre sixty-eight. He must be incredibly strong to slash through the neck in one blow even with the very sharp machete. Either the murderer is a skilled assassin or was incredibly lucky to have placed the cut between two vertebrae. Had he struck a spinal bone in the neck, he wouldn't have succeeded decapitating the victim with one blow. It would've turned into a holy mess. On the machete they found blood particles that matched the victim's blood. There were also partial finger and palm prints unique in the entire house and assumed to belong to the murderer. The prints didn't match any on the finger and palm print data bases. So, it's a local boy in the employ of people who hired an assassin. One last thing, I was talking about a man as the suspect because lab tests established the power required to cut right through the neck with one blow of the machete. It's highly unlikely that a woman, even a specially trained athlete, would have the upper body strength to do that. We don't have such trained female athletes in this country or hermaphrodites with a criminal record in this line of business. We can leave women and hermaphrodites aside and look for a monster of a man."

"Hmm, that narrows the field of potential suspects, excluding children and most old guys down to about 1.2 million adult men. A task of about ten years or so."

"Yes, if you're kept on that long. Yesterday afternoon I got a call from the big cheese expressing outrage about you taking your pregnant wife on an investigative trip."

"I don't believe it! How could anyone in the OIJ have found out about it? That was a decision taken on the spur of the moment. Nobody was told."

"Whatever. The big cheese found out and he wants to talk to you today before ten o'clock possibly in connection with an anonymous call from some ministry. Omar told me about it. You're supposed to be taken off this case immediately or there would be dire consequences for you and your wife."

"My wife? You sure that she was mentioned specifically?"

"Yes, I thought it to be strange and asked Omar twice. He confirmed it and was just as puzzled as I was."

"Shit! I must call her and go home."

***

Martha had finished cleaning up, settled on the sofa and watched a French crime film on the university TV channel, a so-called European cultural contribution for the third world. When the film's highly predictable tale of two constantly brawling detectives who used a trouser button found at a crime scene as evidence to convict a Minister of State of the murder of a prostitute and some associated corruption finally came to its long-overdue end, Martha went to bed just before midnight. But she couldn't sleep - not on account of the film but Rico's warning to be on her guard and ready for the worst. She had put the gun and an extra magazine on the bedside table, looked in its direction in the dark and was prepared for the worst.

After some tossing and turning, she hears the sound of a car stopping nearby and a car door being shut gently. She begins to doze again when the faint metallic sound of someone trying to unlock the grate in front of the door can be heard. But there is no snap of the lock indicating a successful opening. Her first happy thought of Rico having come home is gone and she thinks of his warning. Yet, she can't imagine someone wanting to break in and kill her. The metallic sound ceases. Martha relaxes and dozes off again.

She is wide awake when she hears a thud followed by the scraping sound of metal on mortar. In haste she gets up, grabs the gun, and peers into the living room. In the darkness she can't see a thing. Where is the flashlight? In the kitchen in one of the drawers. Silently she rushes on her bare feet past the table, stubs her little toe on a leg of one of the chairs, hops on one foot to the sideboard and rips open the drawer. She finds the flashlight and hurries to the front door. She can hear someone trying to force the grate open. She holds the gun behind her back, touches the door lock, switches the flashlight on, unlocks the door and rips it open the moment the lock of the grate gives way with a sharp bang. The grate swings back and she stands almost face to face with a man who has the facial features of a gorilla.

Without hesitation she raises the gun, unlocks the safety and fires three shots into his chest. The man drops the crowbar he held in his hand, collapses and falls down the four low steps into the narrow strip of grass bordered by a low hedge that passes for a front garden.

In shock and like an automaton, Martha reaches out, pulls the grate closed, steps back and shuts and locks the front door. She staggers to the sofa and sits down. Carefully she locks the gun and puts it next to her. The flashlight casts an eerie looking circle on the front door. She switches it off and leans back when she feels the baby kicking. She holds her belly and mumbles, "We are safe, little one, yes, we are safe for now. Mommy takes care of you."

Tears begin to stream down her face as the initial shock subsides. She slaps her hands on her face and cries bitterly giving her emotions free reign.

The telephone rings. Martha gets up, staggers in the dark to the side table, and picks up the receiver. "Yes?"

"Martha!" yells Rico. "Is that you? It's me, your husband! Say something! Are you all right?"

"No," she whimpers. "I'm not all right. I just shot and killed a gorilla in a black T-shirt and blue jeans."

"What? A gorilla in a black T-shirt?" asks Rico dumbfounded. "What's going on? Are you safe? Say something!"

"I'll be safe until the police gets here," she says quietly. "He's lying in front of our house. I'm sure he's dead."

"Who? Who is dead? Tell me already!"

"I don't know who it is. I've never seen him before. He tried to break in and broke the lock of the grate. That's when I shot him."

"You mean you opened the door for him? Never mind, never mind. It's okay, Martha, as long as you are safe. I'll come home now and be there in twenty minutes or less. Don't open the door for anyone, your hear? Don't open the door for the police and definitely not another burglar! Okay?"

She hangs up and goes to the front window to look outside from behind the gauze curtain. The squealing of brakes can be heard. It is a police truck with an extended cabin. Four men in grey uniforms get out, stand around and look at the front door of her house. One of them steps onto the narrow strip of grass where the corpse lies. Martha can't see what he is doing but then she hears him say, "He's dead, the useless fuck."

A sedan pulls up next to the truck and somebody with the insignia of an urban police officer on his uniform gets out. He talks quietly to the men.

Martha goes to the sofa, grabs the gun and the flashlight, rushes to the door, unlocks and opens it, and says firmly, "What is going on here? Who are you? What are you doing in front of my house?"

The officer looks at Martha, as far as he is concerned a pregnant woman in a nightgown, and barks, "Get back inside and shut the door! This is none of your business!"

Martha shines the flashlight at the man she shot and says loud and clear, "None of my business? There's somebody lying in my front garden! Is he drunk or something? Get him out of here!"

"Madam!" shouts the officer. "This is my last warning! If you don't get back inside and shut your mouth and the door, I'll have to put cuffs on you and arrest you for interference in police business! You got that?"

Martha steps back and shuts the door. Standing by the window, she watches the limp body being picked up and dumped in the back of the truck. It seems to hold a cell phone in one hand. One man picks up the crowbar, gets into a car parked nearby and drives away.

The officer waits in his car for the remaining men to climb into the truck. They leave and everything is gone like a haunted apparition.

In the kitchen, Martha makes herself a camomile tea to calm her nerves. She waits for Rico to have a word or two with him about his premonition of the incident that came to pass.

A car is pulling up at the front of the house, a door slams shut, the front door is unlocked, and Rico storms into the house. Where he expected to see a mess, he sees his serenely smiling wife leaning against the kitchen cupboard sipping a cup of tea.

He whispers, "Put that cup down. I have to give you a hug."

And they hug for a while before sitting down on the sofa. She tells him every detail of what had happened.

Rico picks up the phone and calls Goicoechea who answers the call with a tired sounding voice. Rico gives him a brief summary of Martha's encounter with the burglar, the removal of the corpse and asks, "How can I find out who that failed assassin was?"

"Go to the city morgue and check out the corpses that were delivered during the night."

"What would that tell me? He is probably stored in the freezer under unidentified victims of a crime. I want to know who he is."

"Listen, Rico, I was packing it in for the night and go home. I pass by the morgue and can have a look. If he's there without a name tag, I can take his fingerprints on the pretence that I'm looking for a victim of a shootout."

"That would be great, Gus, if you could do that for me. But I have one more question. Would you have a contact in a ministry I could call to find who drove a black limousine with the licence plate 01.334 for a trip to Sardinal last Thursday?"

"Call? Forget it, man. You should know that you would be bombarded with all sorts of question why you want to know that. Hang on a minute. I have to check if I can access the data for the government fleet of vehicles. Then you'll know at least to which department it is assigned."

The clicking sound of Gus typing on the keyboard of his computer can be heard. After a few minutes he asks, "Did you say a black limousine? Are you sure you got the correct licence plate?"

"Yes, I'm sure it's the correct number."

"No, Rico, can't be right. That licence plate belongs to one of those Korean pickups for general use by any department. It's been in the repair shop for the past two weeks."

"Damn! That means somebody borrowed those licence plates for the trip. Well, at least I know that it must be somebody from a government department."

"Not necessarily so. The repair shop is public. Anyone can walk in and borrow licence plates for a bit of cash."

"Oh, great! I guess, I can mark that as another dead end."

"That's the luck of the draw. But don't go to sleep, yet. I'll give you a call as soon as I leave the morgue. Okay?"

They end the call and Rico starts to pace to and fro again. Martha gets up, holds his hand, and looks him in the eyes. He appears to be far away in thought and she knows she'll have to go to sleep alone. Rico makes himself a cup of tea and sits next to the telephone.

Half an hour later, the telephone rings. Rico picks up the receiver, "Yes? Is that you, Gus?"

"Indeed, it is I, the Gus for all seasons. Guess what I found out."

"At this late hour? You better tell me what you found."

"Did Martha tell you that the guy had the face of a gorilla, wore a black T-shirt and blue jeans?"

"Yes, that's how she described him."

"Well, hold on to your hat. I found him under unidentified victims. You won't believe it but that son of a bitch wore a mask, you know one of these theatrical mask made of rubber or something. I peeled it off and who did I see? Our former colleague Benito Bonilla. You remember him? Was fired for manipulating evidence. Joined the Rapid Reaction Force, at least for a while. I don't know what he was doing lately but it appears he was associated with the urban San José police."

"Did you tell the guys in the morgue his name?"

"Are you kidding? They would pass on the information of a detective inspector of the OIJ identifying him and I'd get dragged into this barrel of effluent. We'll have to wait and see if he gets a police burial or is cremated. Then we'll know what his function was. Police burial would be evidence of him being a member of the force. Cremation is reserved for hired assassins. Tomorrow we can compare his finger prints on the OIJ files against the partials that were found on the machete."

"Thanks, Gus. You're a great help. I'm sure that Benito was not the killer of Felipe Suárez. I'm back at square one with my investigation. I'll have to keep digging."

"Certainly. But leave that until tomorrow. You and I have to get some sleep now. Good night."

"Good night, Gus. See you in the morning."

More than a Walk in the Park

In the very dim first light of the day, before the sun breaks over the horizon and awakens nature in all its glory, Oduber, two of his sons, Anabelle and Monty, hike in rubber boots along a muddy trail across pastureland towards the rainforest.

She has her two cameras at the ready. One is a single lens reflex camera loaded with high-resolution film and the other a digital camera, both of them fitted with large zoom lenses. From the belt of her trousers dangles an extendable monopod she can stick in the ground to support a camera. Every few steps she stops to take atmospheric shots of the mist hovering over the grass and hiding the trees in the distance. And there are many more scenes to observe as she walks along.

Fascinated she watches a fat bishop spider consuming a cicada entangled in a large web decorated with finest dew pearls. On the spider's back she can clearly see the outline of a smiling face under a mitre, a bishop's hat, and takes close-ups of it until she has to put a new film in the camera.

A curious opossum watches Anabelle taking pictures, sits up on its haunches and holds still until it is photographed.

At the edge of the rain forest, on a thick branch of a pochote tree, a sleepy iguana waits for the first warming rays of the sun.

Coral hibiscus blossoms attract bees to their bright yellow stamens, the pollen-containing filaments, while the blossoms of the queen of the night close for the day.

The two-kilometre hike is quickly covered. The men wait for Anabelle to catch up with them before they enter the forest.

They stand between hanging lianas, prickly palm trees and tall ferns next to a gigantic bitter cedar overgrown with araceaes, bromeliads, passion flowers and other parasitic plants. The parasites derive all their nutrients and water they need from the host plant and will slowly kill it. Once the tree collapses, the parasites go down with it and together they will fertilise the ground and provide fodder for insects as well as nutrients for new trees and other plants to grow.

A finger put to his lips, Oduber urges everybody to be silent. Aside from the soft crackling sound of hundreds of busy leafcutter ants, there is still early morning silence. An eagle soars high above the trees. In the distance a couple of chicken vultures are hopping awkwardly on the grassland. The world is at peace.

The sun rises, the first rays split the layers of fog horizontally and present a subtle spectacle of colour. Due to the reflections, two fireballs appear to glow above each other on the horizon for a moment. Anabelle is overwhelmed by this rare natural phenomenon and takes photos of it. The four men next to her hardly seem to notice, as if it were an everyday spectacle.

The denizens of the forest make themselves heard with a loud concert of squawking, croaking, whistling bird calls and the screeching of capuchin monkeys in the treetops.

Parrots of various shades flutter in pairs from the canopy of the jungle to disappear in the direction of individual fruit trees. Toucans fly into a nearby tree that stands a little off the edge of the forest. They shoot through the still cool morning air like arrows. They reinforce the impression of projectiles with their rapidly flapping wings and powerful beaks stretched straight forward.

Anabelle sneaks under the Toucan gathering. It's amazing that almost a hundred, or so it seems, of these colourful birds have gathered in one tree. They don't let the clicks of the camera interrupt their morning palaver. Anabelle photographs until a black, white and brown blob causes opacity of the lens.

"You little shit! You only had to voice your objection to having your picture taken," she murmurs as she strides back to her companions and cleans the lens.

The small group enters the forest. Immediately everyone sinks up to the ankles into the dark mud. The forest canopy is closed and only a little light shines horizontally into the wooded area. It looks gloomy and yet the trees, bushes, tendrils and leaves are clearly recognisable in the splendour of shades of green, brown and yellow.

An assembly of fiery red frogs catches Anabelle's attention. Enthusiastically, she picks one up and lets it sit on the palm of her hand. She admires the tiny creature's orange eyes, red torso and black 'pants'. One of Oduber's sons whispers to her that it is one of the notorious poison dart frogs. Terrified, she puts the amphibian back on the forest floor and rubs her hand on the seat of her pants. The companions grin at her reaction.

A peculiar roar is heard that sends a mighty shiver down Anabelle's spine. She looks at her arms. The fine hairs stand on end.

Excited, Oduber just murmurs, "Jaguar!" He follows a barely recognisable path. Every few steps he points at green frogs, bright blue palm-sized morpho butterflies, gigantic dragonflies, and wonderfully patterned snakes slithering away.

A grey anteater trundles past unfazed by the human intruders, and an ai climbs up a tree at the rapid pace for a three-toed sloth of almost half a meter per minute. It even finds the time to wink at them with its typical broad grin.

When the sound of an animal fleeing through the undergrowth is heard, Oduber stops. He is certain to have recognised the clomping steps of a tapir and that the jaguar is probably hunting it. No animal will be seen now at the watering hole.

As Oduber speaks, Anabelle feels a sensation in the back of her neck, as if someone is watching her. She turns anxiously, makes eye contact with a small margay, takes a photo, and gone is the spotted cat as it disappears silently into the bushes.

The troupe laboriously struggles on through the deep mud, slides over rotting trunks of fallen trees and everyone hardly looks up anymore. Anabelle has to be admonished several times to remain quiet. For her, being a 'civilised person', the slightest disturbance of her balance is reason enough to announce it loudly, as if she slipped up in a massive pile dog poo back home. Apparently, she hasn't noticed that each of her companions speaks only when absolutely necessary and then in a whisper. Her cackling and whooping really grates on the men's nerves. Monty finally reprimands her harshly and a bit offended she finally shuts up. With the silence that now prevails, she notices at last the difference between a botanical garden and the rainforest.

The temperature has risen noticeably in the almost two hours since they entered the rain forest. Droplets of water are coming down and Anabelle says that they should have taken some rain gear along.

Oduber shakes his head and points to the canopy that is closed like a manmade roof. He explains to her, "It is called a rainforest not because it rains on it constantly. The rising temperature causes the water on the ground to evaporate. The vapours rise to the canopy, cool down, condense and drop down again in droplets. It is a closed cycle."

They walk on until they reach a small clearing where two big trees had recently collapsed. About ten meters above ground on one of the upright forest giants presents itself the lush bouquet of a guardia morada, the almost extinct national flower of Costa Rica, a violet orchid whose vivid colour seems out of place. Anabelle looks up impressed but is mesmerised by another event. A short distance from her, a single ray of sunlight hits a closed blossom on the protruding branch of a bush. The beautiful burgundy blossom with subtle dark blue markings, a crown of white stamens and a delicate black pistil opens slowly in response to the intensity of this singular ray of light. She is fascinated by the spectacle and makes a slow-motion recording of it with her digital camera. No one says a word as long as she keeps an eye on the interlude of flora in motion.

It is time to turn around. On the way back Anabelle is deep in thought and very quiet. Neither does she notice the horde of monkeys high up in the trees accompanying them on the way out of the forest nor does she complain about liquid mud in her boots or the very high humidity. She is captivated by the vitality and beauty of this eternal life cycle of flora and fauna, which seems magical to her.

All living things strive towards the scarcely available light. Each plant feeds on other living or dead vegetation and struggles to survive in this self-contained area of life, where each plant, animal and insect has a specific task. When something dies or is killed, it serves the sustenance of flora and fauna in the immediate vicinity and thus becomes a source of life. Life and death are not separate abstract concepts but part of the reality of a perpetual cycle.

Standing on the grassland, Oduber points a thumb back at his forest and asks Anabelle, "What do you think?"

She gushes, "I have never seen nature like this before. I have taken over five hundred photos and would probably take five thousand more if I stayed a couple more days."

"Have you seen the one thing or should I say creature that was totally out of place and didn't belong into the forest?"

Anabelle ponders the question for a while, shakes her head and says, "No, I can't say I noticed anything out of place."

"You would have seen it if there was a mirror installed. It is us, humanity that has no place or function in there to add or contribute to life. We can and might want to take some of the fruits or other life sustaining substances like heart of palm out of it as long as it doesn't kill the source of it. But otherwise, we have no business in there. We only interfere and destroy the existing lifecycles."

He pauses and asks after a while, "You asked me last night and I ask you now if you would sell these almost 5,000 hectares forest for a million or even a billion dollars if you were the owner?"

She is emotionally overcome by that question and tears well up in her eyes as she says, "No! Oh, no! I could never sell it. Compared to the little snippet of life I saw on our walk, money means nothing. It is just numbers printed on paper or plastic or embossed on round pieces of metal that lose value all the time. This forest will never lose its value when kept in its present condition and I'm sure you will see to it."

"I'll do that," says Oduber and adds, "And here's the reason: A wise person, a man or a woman, I don't remember, said some years ago, nature can live and thrive without humanity, but humanity cannot survive without nature. Have you heard that before?"

"Oh yes! You hear it all the time when environmentalists and climate change activists get together to demonstrate."

"So, you're familiar with that phrase. Let me add my own little bit of wisdom to it. When humanity carries on destroying nature as it has done at an ever-increasing rate over the past four hundred years, then the question of environmentalists and climate change activists if humanity can survive will become entirely irrelevant. It will be replaced by the question of 'who dies last'."

Stunned, Anabelle looks at him with fear in her eyes. It takes her a moment to let his words sink in and imagine a world with the human race dying out and flora and fauna destroyed. Timidly she asks, "Don't you think humanity will come to its senses and stop the destruction?"

His response is prompt and harsh. "No! That's because the majority of human beings are a bunch of nutters who believe in some apparition in the sky they call god, who they claim sits up there with a goose quill and a huge book looking after every activity of every one of almost eight billion people. Supposedly, he created this world and trillions of planets and stars and commands all human beings to subject nature to their will. And most of them follow this command because they are subconsciously aware of their insignificance, have no trust in themselves and their ability to see reason. Therefore, they put their trust in some non-existent, imaginary being and claim to obey his command. So, their destruction of everything they need most to live and survive is not their fault. It's all god's plan. Isn't that a wonderful pile of bullshit?"

Anabelle swallows hard thinking of her own upbringing and years in a convent school. She can see the reason for his outburst but doesn't want to get involved in a lengthy debate about religion. It seems so out of place after her walk through this majestic piece of intact nature. She nods towards Oduber's house, turns and slowly walks towards it in her squelching boots.

After a shower and a hearty meal, it is time for Anabelle and Monty to get ready and be on their way. She has a lot to think about and to digest. For starters she doesn't see Oduber any longer as a boorish country bumpkin with a big mouth and bad manners. He is a smart human being fighting for his and his sons survival and goes about it in a very dedicated manner. From the perspective of his remote vantage point, he has gained insights that remain hidden to most other people stuck in the hustle and bustle of social processes, because they are too busy with their superficial self-expression in a civilised world lacking profound values.

She cannot say whether his explanations of the morass of the country's upper classes, which he presented in the course of yesterday's conversation, are based on his personal experiences or were logical conclusions he draws from the facts and data he collected. But now she trusts his assessments and believes him. He was right when he said that his statements were only pointers to the path she must follow now to collect the evidence on which her report must be based if it is to be accepted as credible.

Leaning against her rental car, he summarises the course of action he had proposed. "First call the Society for Investments and Economic Development and make an appointment with one of their consultants for tomorrow morning. Don't let them turn you away. You must take and keep the initiative. These guys only respond to pressure and tempting offers. With my cheques of an American bank, I gave you, the offers will look enticing enough. As soon as you have an appointment with a consultant from the investment company, call the forestry and economic ministries and make appointments subject to the confirmation by the consultant. Insist on a meeting at state secretary level, or even better with deputy ministers. Once you had the meeting at the Investment Society, you can play one of the interlocutors out against the other and have all the documents you need for your report in one day.

"Don't forget to have business cards printed under an assumed name. These cards are very important in Costa Rica and are worth more than a passport. An impressive title added to your name, the business card will open all doors for you.

"One last point: as a precaution, I suggest that you leave Costa Rica the same day tomorrow evening. You have to get out of here as quickly as possible before the authorities get wind of your activities and find out they've been had. Fly to Panama or Miami, anywhere you can get a connecting flight to Europe. And don't worry about me. I'm going to make a big fuss about my 'stolen' cheques in San Jose the day after tomorrow and report it to my bank in Florida. Since you will pull off the caper under a false name, there shouldn't be any repercussions for you back home.

"That's what I had to say to you. Good luck, Anabelle. Visit me again when you are in the country. I hope to see you soon. And watch out for your companion. He's also known as Brother Lightfoot, aren't you, *Calavera*?"

Monty laughs and gives Oduber a light jab in his paunch. Anabelle embraces her host with the warmth and cordiality he had tried to show her when he greeted her the day before. Oduber beams a happy smile and hugs her like an old girlfriend.

As they drive away, he stands on the porch and waves a bit wistfully until his guests have disappeared beyond the horizon.

Feeling the Iron Fist

Martha enters the spare room very quietly where Rico sits at a small table and stares at the screen of his laptop computer. He is editing the update of his interim report entering a few minor corrections.

Speaking softly she asks, "Would you like to eat something? You had only a slice of toast for breakfast and no lunch. Aren't you hungry?"

He looks up and shakes his head. "No, I'm not hungry. I want to finish my report. Writing the request for your police protection or better protection from the police took me a long time. I'll be done in a minute and go to the office where I'll eat something."

"You should call in and say you're sick. Weren't you supposed to meet your boss at ten o'clock this morning? It's almost two."

"Yes, I know. To hell with that meeting. He's a pompous old windbag with nothing to say, a government appointee who was never involved in crime investigation but tries to tell us how to do our job. It's a waste of time talking to him."

"But you have to talk to him. He has to approve your request for police protection and he could fire you for taking me on your investigative tour."

"He wouldn't dare. And if he did, I'd apply for a job with one of the international police organisations. I'm not worried. Let me finish my report."

She leaves and hears a few minutes later the printer spitting out Rico's report and what she thinks are some photos. He comes into the living room with a file under his arm.

"Okay, dear, I'm done. I'll be off then and see you later."

Martha takes him by the hand, pulls him to the kitchen table and says, "Sit down. I won't let you go without having eaten something. Here, I made you a nice egg sandwich."

Unwillingly he takes a seat and wolfes down his snack.

"May I go now?"

"By all means. Don't you feel better now?"

"No! Now I'm really hungry."

Before she can respond, he gives her a hug, rushes to the door, and asks, "When is the locksmith coming to fix the grate?"

"He should be here at three."

"Good. Make sure he replaces the frame and anchors it well. Otherwise a new lock will be useless. Take care."

Twenty minutes later he enters the office he shares with Gus who greets him with the words, "Heh, you blind chicken! Have you finished picking your report? I was going to send a search party on behalf of the furious boss. Called twice to find out where you are."

Rico drops his file on Gus' desk and frowns. "Yes, that's all the old windbag does. Demand that we stand to attention at his beck and call. I may see him later. I have to eat something. I'll be in the canteen while you read my report. I'd like to know what you think of my investigation results so far and what you think of my chances to close the case."

"Okay, I'll read your romance novel. May I suggest not to eat the smelly tacos. They gave me gas. Want a sampling?" asks Gus.

In the knowledge that Gus isn't shy about spreading his evil smell, Rico leaves the office in a rush.

Gus picks up the file, thumbs through the pages and mutters, "Six pages! Does this case need such extravagant literary efforts?"

He reads every page studiously and puts the file aside waiting for Rico to return. In the meantime, he takes another call from his boss, states that Rico is in the house and has to listen to a whole litany of complaints. He puts the receiver on his desk, lets the boss prattle and works on one of his cases. When he hears the question, "Are you still there, Goicoechea? I just asked you a question," he picks up the receiver and says, "Of course, Señor Carrazo, I listen most attentively. I have nothing to add and agree wholeheartedly."

The call comes to an end with the boss stating that he is glad to know Goicoechea being on his side. Gus wonders what the hell the boss' question was and leans back in his chair.

When Rico returns half an hour later, he asks him, "What took you so long? Man, the boss called again with his complaints and demanded you to see him right away."

"Of course, but first I'd like to know what you think of my report. Any good?"

"That's strong tobacco you stuffed in that pipe. Who do you think is going to read it without a coughing fit? As far as I can see, the details are extensive and correct. But your assumption about

138

two clans of oligarchs fighting over the spoils of this country and that one of them ordered a contract killing of Suárez, although I agree with it, you should have kept to yourself until you can prove it with solid evidence. But you signed it and it's only an interim report... so, fly with it. I hope you won't have a crash landing."

"You touch a sore spot there. I struggled with putting my assumption into the report but it was the only way of showing that my conclusions make any real sense."

"Yes, I understand that but still... by the way, your request for a police escort for your wife... You won't get it!"

"We'll see. The three photos of the broken lock and frame should be sufficient evidence of a break-in to harm or kill my wife."

Gus waves the comment off. "Carrazo is going to ignore the photos. Even if Benito Bonilla was still alive and you dragged him in with a signed confession, he'd deny police protection. And as far as your report is concerned, he will blow his top when he reads it and let it disappear. Wouldn't surprise me if he tries to get you fired or at least suspended and condemned to blowing dust of the files in the archive. You know how vindictive Carrazo is when a report clearly aims to denounce the corruption of his benefactors."

"Sure, but he won't fire or demote me. You wanna bet?"

"Of course! That's easy money. How much?"

"A red rag?"

"Wow, a thousand colones! That's a buck fifty! With that win I can afford to buy a small loaf of bread tonight. By the way, I took the liberty of making a photocopy of your report and request."

Rico takes his file and mutters, "Why? You intend take over and do your own investigation?"

"No, it's just a safety measure. Once the old geezer has read your scribblings, the file will disappear."

Rico gathers report, request and photos and puts them in a folder. He sighs, salutes Gus and leaves.

At the door to the boss' office, Rico reads the sign stating name and position of the occupant, *Ángel Gerardo Carrazo de Gallego - Comisario de OIJ*. Rico thinks that the first name Ángel of the commissioner must be a misnomer because Lucifer would be much more appropriate.

He enters the antechamber occupied by the secretary, a plump woman with an elaborate hairdo and lots of makeup. He greets her and says that the boss wants to see him.

She picks up the phone and asks, "What's your name?"

"Rico Ramírez."

"De Gallego?"

"No, madam, I'm not that pretentious to claim that my ancestors came from Galicia."

Judging by her reaction, he might as well have poked her in the eye with a blunt stick. "Señor Comisario, a Rico Ramírez is here."

The response is an angry, "Send him in!"

Rico opens the office door and Carrazo, a rotund man with a combover dyed black, gets up behind his desk and shouts, "Where have you been? Your insubordination is out of order! What have you got to say for yourself?"

"Good afternoon," says Rico with a smile and holds out his file.

Carrazo rips it away and keeps on shouting, "Taking your pregnant wife on a dangerous mission to the coast is outrageous! I should suspend you for such a breach of protocol!"

Rico looks at him with contempt. "You don't have to shout, Señor, I'm not deaf. And I didn't take my wife on a dangerous mission. It was a pleasant Sunday drive to the coast where I followed up a few leads. All quite harmless and all in my report."

Carrazo opens the folder, puts on reading glasses, and points at the page. "Request for a police escort for your wife and protection of your domicile? Are you insane? Who do you think you are?"

"I don't think who I am, Señor. I know who I am. Read the reason for my request and you may understand."

Carrazo skims the request, puts it aside and says, "That's a load of nonsense. There was no police activity in front of your house and no corpse was removed."

"Indeed? How would you know? Have you spoken to the urban police about it? If you did, what was your reason to do that?"

Ignoring Rico's questions, he leans back and fleetingly reads Rico's report. He puts it aside and says, "Short on facts and evidence but long on conspiracy theories. How dare you accuse the leaders of this country and the... the captains of industry and commerce, the cream of our society of having ordered this heinous crime?"

"I did not accuse anyone, Señor. I suspect some influential people in positions of power ordered the killing of Felipe Suárez because he knew too much about their dirty business. That is a suspicion demanding enquiries to establish facts to prove it. And I will dig up those facts."

"You are despicable, Ramírez!"

"I know, Señor, I am as despicable as all detectives and investigators who uncover the dirty business of the people that parachuted you into your position."

"Son of a bitch! You're fired, Ramírez! You hear? Fired!"

"Good, Señor, very good. Please put in writing and have the notice of my dismissal delivered to my desk before I go home today."

"No! No, no, I will suspend you. Yes, you are suspended and will do archive duty."

"That's not a good idea. If you banish me to the archives, I'll still be in the building, have access to computers, and can study all the old case files. Imagine how much dirt I can dig up. I could start a revolution! No, firing me is much safer."

"Why are you so keen on getting fired?"

"It's the only way to get rid of you."

"What?!?"

"You see, Señor, I'm not a government appointee like you. I am a state employee chosen on merit. If you fire me, there will be a public enquiry into your reasons. That will give me the opportunity to present my case and have you removed from your position. Please, go ahead and fire me."

Carrazo turns pale and says, "I won't do you that favour. You're suspended from duty! Get out of my office."

Rico gives him a sarcastic salute, "Yes, Señor! By the way, all my colleagues know of my case file having been delivered to your usual care. Should it disappear, it'll be on your record."

"Get out!!"

Rico smiles at him, turns, and leaves.

Back in his office, he drops the promised 'red rag' on Gus' desk.

"What's that?" asks Gus.

"A red rag."

"I can see that. But why?"

Rico points a thumb to the office door, puts a finger to his lips and whispers, "I have company. You were right. My request was denied by that pompous bastard. He turned pale when he read my report and condemned my suspicion about a contract killing by people in power. I had to mention Maria Villafuerte in my report. I'd appreciate it, if you could keep an eye on her in San Jerónimo and make sure she won't have a fatal accident."

"Why me?" hisses Gus.

"Why do you think I dropped the red rag on you?"

"Oh, holy trinity! Are you saying that I can visit you in the archives starting tomorrow morning?"

"Perhaps, suspension is the price one has to pay for suspecting oligarchs of dirty business and put it in a report. Remember when our president announced after his inauguration that he would rule with an iron fist? What exactly he implied becomes clear only now."

"Right... Who will take on your case? Any idea?"

"Carrazo didn't say. I'll keep an eye on it in my own time and appreciate you letting me know of any developments."

"I'll do that, Rico. For sure."

The Sting

The trip from west of San Rafael de Guatuso to San José was a horror for Anabelle. A few times she thought the car would break apart or at least break down when hitting the potholes along the country roads. Twice she was stopped by police. They wanted to know if she had been drinking because she wasn't driving around the potholes. Her reply that she would have to be drunk to do that didn't help but they let her go as soon as they saw that she was a foreign tourist.

Monty's comment that they would reach a motorway soon with hardly any potholes as far as he could remember did not put her in a better mood. She was angrily aping him when he suggested not to take her anger out on the car. Her driving style made him wonder if all Europeans turn into wild road hogs as soon as they feel an accelerator pedal under their right foot. He did not understand her haste and complaints about running behind schedule. It was a completely alien concept that meant nothing to him. It took a mighty speed bump in the road jolting the car and causing Anabelle to hit her head against the roof to finally slow down and adapt her driving to the road conditions.

All along the way she thought reaching San José would improve the situation but realised that she jumped essentially from the frying pan into the fire. Crawling into the downtown area along the main artery Paseo Colón stuck between busses and trucks burping swaths of black diesel fumes took her breath away. Motorbikes and mopeds screeching past gave her one fright after another. Howling sirens and flashing red and blue lights of ambulances and police cars forced her into the gutter.

Following Monty's directions, she drove suddenly into a madhouse of narrow one-way streets, construction sites, roadblocks and loudly screaming street vendors. Oil drums used as rubbish bins on the roadside emitted a stench that made her want to vomit. At each stop, dirty children approached the car and thrust newspapers, scissors, watches, fruit, chewing gum, cigarettes, fried plantains or homemade pies at her. Some of these poor urchins simply stood there with open hands in the hope of a charitable gift. A strong gust of wind whirled bits of paper, plastic bags and grey-brown dust through the traffic-clogged streets.

This is not how she remembered San José from her early Sunday morning drive out of town and wished she could turn around and drive back to the coast.

The sleazy hotel suggested by Monty, located between a brothel and a beer hall near the Central Market, gave her the creeps and she rejected it out of hand. The dirt, stench, and clutter of the congested streets was too much for her to bear. All she wanted was to get away from this noise and commotion, find a quiet place and clean air to breathe. Slowly she fought her way through the sluggish traffic of the city core, found a luxurious apartment hotel near the Sabana city park and booked a room.

She revives after a brief refreshment, puts on an elegant dress and contemplates Don Oduber's plan. Monty sits uncomfortably on a footstool, makes himself very small, squints from the large dining room glass table with the heavy, white-lacquered cast-iron chairs to the low coffee table surrounded by leather armchairs, the pompously framed paintings of abstract art on the walls and the huge bed in the next room. He feels extremely uncomfortable in this environment that is foreign to him, contemplates escaping over the balcony, down the drainpipe and flee - away from here, far away and back to the little hotel next to the brothel where he would be treated with respect and be more than just 'somebody'.

He can hear Anabelle calling but doesn't respond. She comes out of the bedroom admonishing him, "Come on, Monty, get moving! We don't have much time left. My goodness, we have so much to do and you're sitting there like the personified heap of misery. What's the matter with you? Did you at least call the printer and order our business cards?"

Monty shakes his head, lights a crumpled cigarette, takes a puff, looks at her bleakly, and says very quietly, "This won't end well. I have a really sick feeling. I won't come out of this alive if I go along with it. I think it's better I go home now."

"What do you mean? What won't end well? We haven't even started yet. You are supposed to be my personal advisor and need to get you some business attire for the occasion. You can't walk into a meeting looking like someone driving cattle. I'll call the printer and order our business cards. Then I'll set up an appointment with a consultant of this economic development corporation. We'll leave in half an hour to find a gentleman's outfitter. And please take off that ridiculous amulet."

"No, I can't do that. It's my lucky charm."

"You can put it on when you go home. Then you may need all the luck it can muster."

Monty gets up and stands on the balcony while Anabelle sits down at the coffee table, picks up the phone and calls the printer Oduber had recommended. She asks for José-Louis and provides him with all the data for their business cards. Then she checks the phone directory, calls a couple of gent's outfitters and asks for suits, accessories and shoes of European brands. Having done that, she takes a deep breath and calls the Society for Investments and Economic Development as well as the ministries. She demands appointments for the next day with the coolest arrogance she can muster. She ignores all the excuses of the secretaries and assistants and cajoles, harasses and threatens the respective women and men until she has reached her goal. Relieved, she hangs up the phone.

She calls Monty to come in from the balcony, "Are you ready to leave? Then let's go. First is the printer and then we have to get you a proper outfit. And you can do with a good haircut."

"Haircut? For me? Forget it!" he protests.

"Oh, yes. You will get a haircut. It has to look neat and trim just like a bureaucrat. Remember you have to look the part of an advisor to a multi-million-dollar investor. When you look the part, I want to have a really scrumptious dinner in your company. Okay?"

"Sorry, can't do that. I don't have any money."

She picks up her handbag, takes out a one-hundred-dollar bill and stuffs it into his jeans pocket. "That should be enough for a decent dinner for two or we'll go Dutch and I pay half. Let's go."

They stop at a nearby barber shop and the old hairdresser with a pencil moustache gets busy right away. He clips Monty's hair according to what he understood to be Anabelle's request. Ten minutes later he says, "There you are."

Anabelle gives it a critical look. "No, no, no... you have to cut the loose fringes. I don't want to see any unruly curls. Give him a cut you would give the president."

"The president? I wouldn't sell that corrupt toerag a used comb and be sorely tempted to cut his throat."

"Okay, but I want to see a razor-sharp cut with some class. Imagine your favourite film star sitting in your chair."

"You want me to shave his head? My favourite film star is as bald as a coot."

"Of course not. Just get on with your job. You know what I want. And don't forget to trim his moustache to a fine line."

"Out of the question!" protests Monty. "Then I'll look like the Minister of National Affairs."

"Okay, just trim his moustache. Don't use any greasy hair cream and give him a parting on the left."

"Parting on the left? Are you crazy? I'm not queer! Only poofters have a parting on the left. Real men comb their hair straight back."

The old figaro confirms that assertion with a hefty nod that cause his remaining tufts of hair to droop over his ears.

Anabelle gives up. She cannot compete with this onslaught of male vanity and ridiculous prejudices.

She becomes aware how little the people of all parts of the world differ in their basic features. In the so-called developed world almost every car owner is ready to start a war over a dent in the mudguard or a scratch on his shiny shitbox on wheels and don't give a damn about the pollution the six-litre engine of their pathetic pickup 'truck' causes. In Costa Rica this madness expresses itself only in a different form. A parting on the left, right or none at all concern the people more than the destruction of their country's environment. Personal vanities are the focus of human attention the further the destruction of the environment progresses. A comparison of the way of life in the concrete jungles of the big cities with the areas where nature is still intact highlights this difference perfectly. When thinking about living in harmony with nature is no longer required, humanity faces up to the challenges of fabricated symbolism, ritual gestures and facial expressions required to conform to the masses and confirm the assumed self-importance that belies individual insignificance.

Fifteen minutes later they are on the way to the printer in a taxi. They pick their business cards and Monty reads,

José Antonio Castillo Montalban de Gallego

Forestry Advisor - Asesor Forestal

Zürich y Río Negro

He pulls a funny face and asks Anabelle quietly, "Who is this? And why is there a 'de Gallego' attached to the name?"

"Have a look in a mirror and you see Señor Castillo Montalban. The 'de Gallego' is attached in allusion to the conceit of many

Costa Ricans who claim to be descendants of early migrants from the Spanish province of Galicia although they may have come from Murcia or nor at all from Spain. Oduber told me about it. It'll impress anyone getting your card and demand their respect."

Monty sighs and says in an emotional tone, "My father would have been proud had his full name been printed on this card."

"You can have cards with your real name printed when we're finished with our sting operation. For now we have to use our fake names." She pokes him in the ribs with an elbow and adds, "If your father could see you in a short while, he wouldn't be just proud of you, he would burst into tears of joy although he'd have difficulties recognising you."

She hails a taxi that takes them to the gent's outfitter.

Inside the shop, Monty is attracted to the special offers of suits in screaming colours that would be perfect for a clown at a child's birthday party.

Horrified she pulls him away, takes an elegant navy-blue pinstripe suit off the rack and asks the salesman for one in Monty's size and a pair of black shoes in soft leather. The assistant takes all the measurements, hands over the requested items and Monty disappears in a fitting room. She chases the salesman around with more orders for underwear, black socks, white shirts and neckties. He shows her a selection of yellow ties made of polyester, latest fashion from the USA and she asks him if he is colourblind. A yellow tie with a navy-blue pinstripe suit would look as if he had peed on his shirt. She wants a light blue silk tie that contrasts yet matches the style of the suit.

She hands shirt, tie and shoes into the fitting room and a moment later Monty steps out not quite sure of himself. She pulls him in front of a tall mirror where he sees her smiling over the shoulder of a young businessman to whom he would obediently doff his hat. He sees himself as a stranger. Anabelle turns him around and slings his necktie into a Windsor knot.

"Are you going to the theatre?" asks the shop assistant.

"No, we are going to act out our play tomorrow," she responds.

"Oh, I see."

Anabelle takes a step back to look at the 'new' Monty in his elegant suit, white shirt, tie and shiny black shoes. It is strange that she is usually suspicious of guys in this finery, mostly bores from the financial district or computer consultants. But not Monty. He is perfect in this masquerade and looks quite appealing to her.

Dressed to a T they enter a restaurant of her choice. After she has chosen their meals, the appetiser is served. Monty wants to return it. That's fraud, he complains. There are at most two full spoonfuls' soup in the cup and then nothing is in it, not a bean, just a clear, red-brown broth that looks like tea. Mrs. Sherry, who according to the menu has prepared it, doesn't seem to know much about proper cooking. When Anabelle remarks that a fine sherry beef broth is about quality, not quantity, he replies that a decent quantity of the quality she lauds would be even finer. The waiter pours him a sip of wine into his glass for a taste. He looks up questioningly and demands a full glass. After all, he will have to pay for the whole bottle. In the presence of the expectant-looking waiter, Monty downs the wine like a beer in one long draft. His sour expression is thoroughly misunderstood until he opines that the grapes must have been mashed with unwashed feet because the juice has gone off.

Anabelle is amused by his boastfulness. He tries to portray how he thinks a man of the world behaves and is proving with every word and gesture and without any further thought to be a cocky, commanding, clumsy, and brazen individual who knows nothing and is nothing. That is not far from the reality that she, as a journalist questioning socialites, had to deal with often every day. This behaviour is accepted in many 'civilised' countries as normal. Monty performing unintentionally and subconsciously a parody is the subtle difference that raises the otherwise embarrassing situation to the level of an excellent comedy.

After dinner, the two discuss the plan for the next day. She mentions the appointment at the Society for Investment and Economic Development at 08:30 o'clock. It is not yet certain which advisor they will meet, but that is not all that important. It is most salient to have a foot in the door. A follow-up meeting with the Secretary of State for Forestry is scheduled for 11:00 o'clock. Anabelle suggests inviting this gentleman to lunch in order to get more information out of him. Finally, they still have the appointment with the deputy economics minister at 15:00 o'clock.

In addition to the cheques for the 'purchase' of the rainforest area, the logging license fee and a 'donation' for reforestation, she will also give each of the interlocutors an individual bonus cheque as a reward for the 'efforts' to bring the negotiation to a successful conclusion. That will sweeten the deal even more. At the end of every single consultation, Anabelle would like Monty to take

148

photos of her and the respective representative shaking hands to properly document her visit and provide conclusive evidence.

Monty advises against photography most vehemently. That's too risky. If one of the guys got wind of it, or if she made even the slightest mistake, she wouldn't get out of the country alive but disappear somewhere without a trace. His life wouldn't be worth a centimo either. She should remember Don Oduber's warning about the Rapid Reaction Force - death squad he called it.

Anabelle whispers excitedly then the whole action can be called off. She insists that she must provide photos of these guys they will take for a ride and preferably showing them in her company. It is the only way to convince her magazine editor of her report's authenticity and get it published. After all, that is the purpose of the entire campaign.

Monty replies laconically it would be a better idea to commit suicide right here at the table if she insists on her plan.

The tension of the muted argument is underscored by clenched fists resting on both sides of the table. In the mellow candlelight and against the background of constantly droning music, the other guests in the well-attended restaurant hardly notice anything about the clash of persistently defended points of view.

The waiters, on the other hand, have their ears wide open like radar antennas to catch a word, a phrase here and there. They whisper near the kitchen door. Can this foreign woman and her rude companion not pay the bill for their expensive dinner? Are they having a dramatic love affair? Wasn't suicide mentioned just now? Shouldn't this couple be asked to leave before a fight breaks out and blood is spilled? One should inform the manager!

Over coffee and liqueur, Anabelle and Monty agree to drop the idea of taking photos at the end of the talks. Instead and if at all possible, she will take secret snapshots of the guys or search international press photo archives for their mugshots. Even without any of these photos, Anabelle hopes she will have enough evidence in her hands to prove the credibility of her report.

Exhausted after a long day, the two fighting cocks go back to the apartment hotel for a good night's rest.
***

"Señora Berndorf, Señor Castillo, I extend a warm welcome to you at the Society for Investment and Economic Development."

Roberto Zuñiga, a young man with freshly oiled black hair and wearing a silk suit of an indefinable shade of grey-green, greets

Anabelle and Monty with a handshake and the usual exchange of business cards.

"I have been assigned to you as your investment advisor. I speak some German. We could have our conversation in your language."

"German is not my first language, as you assume," retorts Anabelle in perfect Castilian Spanish. "Señor Castillo and I are both Spanish speakers and prefer to conduct the negotiation in your mother tongue. My advisor is a compatriot of yours."

"Oh, really?" mutters Zuñiga and has a look at Monty's card. "But you, uh, live in Switzerland and I believe in, uh, Brazil?"

"No, I live in Río Negro," says Monty.

Zuñiga smiles helplessly. "Yes, that is in Brazil, isn't it?"

Monty snorts contemptuously. "No, Río Negro is located in the north-eastern San Carlos region about 120 kilometres from here."

Zuñiga stares at the card. "Well, well, I didn't even know we had one, too. I assumed you as forestry consultant and rainforest expert..." He leaves his assumption unfinished, looks up and continues, "Let us go to my office. We can talk privately there."

Zuñiga leads his visitors in single file out of the reception hall that is lined with mirrors and polished steel. Carpets swallow every sound of their footsteps. At the end of a corridor with locked office doors is an open space where Zuñiga tells a secretary not to put through any phone calls. He opens the door to a luxuriously furnished office and motions Anabelle and Monty to enter.

They sit down under a plastic palm tree on leather upholstered tubular steel chairs grouped around a low coffee table with a heavy lead crystal tabletop. An oversized desk with a ten-centimetre-thick top made of fine, light-coloured ceiba wood looks overwhelming even in this large office. Three telephones and a desktop computer are strategically placed on it. But despite the other typical office accessories and a large relief map of Costa Rica on the wall behind the desk, this office doesn't give the impression of a work environment and Zuñiga seems somehow out of place.

Zuñiga seizes the moment to speak. "Señora Berndorf, it is my pleasure to receive you and your advisor this morning to discuss the Madrigal Group's planned investments in Costa Rica despite the difficult circumstances and the tense situation we are facing in this sector at present."

Anabelle purses her lips mockingly, glares coldly at the man who tries very hard to put on an impressive style of speech, puts her briefcase on her knees, opens it, and pulls out an envelope just far enough to expose the corner with the name of an obscure Bank in USA. She unlocks the pause button on her digital voice recorder and lays the case, slightly ajar, on the floor between her and Zuñiga's chairs. His eyes are fixed on the corner of the envelope as he relaxes and licks his lips lightly. He is familiar with the ritual of being presented with cash or a cheque right at the start of the conversation and anticipated it.

"Tense situation in this sector?" asks Anabelle. "What do you mean by that?"

With an erratic hand movement, he tries to forewarn of the importance of his upcoming remarks and explains, "Every day we receive investment enquiries from all over the world. Costa Rica's reputation as the engine of the Latin American economy is well known in the global business community. Investments flow in constantly and to an increasing extent. But usually, our company's foreign offices receive advance notice from investors and their intentions, and we have enough time to prepare for talks with them. Since I know absolutely nothing about the Madrigal Group of Companies and their investment intentions, I would of course like to find out who this Madrigal Group is and why their intentions are presented by a consultant in this unconventional way."

Anabelle pauses briefly and explains, "The worldwide rainforest situation is a delicate matter. Therefore, Madrigal prefers to remain in the background. This procedure is the same everywhere and we haven't had any difficulties in Brazil, Thailand, Ghana, Sri Lanka, and Indonesia. Consequently, we do not expect to be confronted with any problems in Costa Rica either. I gather information on site with the help of my local advisors and should a specific area turn out to be of interest to us, I submit our offer to the decision-makers without lengthy correspondence and a potentially embarrassing paper trail. You see, we keep our actual activities as secret as your company keeps its actual activity secret as well."

Zuñiga doesn't seem to have heard her explanation and insists, "I have to gather information about potential investors to avoid conflict of interest situations. We have to be extremely careful with this type of investment. We have a great interest in securing investments, but we are also forced to turn away funds from ambiguous sources. Otherwise we would open the door to the drug cartels and help to legalise its capital generated by criminal means.

In order to rule out this possibility, I contacted your office in Zurich, Switzerland after your request for an interview. Unfortunately, I have not received an answer regarding the solvency of the Madrigal organisation. Can you explain that, Señora Berndorf?"

Anabelle can hardly resist a sardonic grin. "I can and I will," she says with a somewhat menacing undertone, since his superfluous talk is already grating on her nerves. "Firstly, there is no organisation behind the name Madrigal, but a group of Spanish private interests that are represented, verified and classified as absolutely honourable and trustworthy by our financial consulting company. Secondly, our client works only with local subcontractors who are recommended and assured to be reliable by appropriate bodies of trust in, which takes care of your concern about conflict situations. We trust you to advise us on this point and are in your hands. Thirdly..."

She pauses again, then fires a full broadside. "We are not the only ones who know that your company works unreliably, even sloppily. You are known to reply to legitimate enquiries by fax with photocopies of newspaper clippings and out of date data tables not relevant to the enquiry. Therefore, I assume your unreliability, which is lamented in the international business world, is not being handled better by your representative offices overseas. It would have been a miracle had Madrigal received scant and incorrect information within six weeks of enquiry."

That blow hit the target. A painful smile covers Zuñiga's face. He leans back evidently offended and glares at Anabelle.

His reaction encourages her to continue in her arrogant voice and a sharp tone. "Publicity is poison for our business, as you well know, Señor Zuñiga. As investors of millions of dollars, we have a legitimate interest in an unbureaucratic and speedy settlement of this deal. And don't tell me any stories about your relationship with the drug cartels. We are extremely well informed about that little sideline of your business. And now I come to my conclusion."

Zuñiga is reeling and his face takes on a slightly green tint. Is there anything this woman is not informed about? What is her information source? How can he get rid of her, he wonders and tries to pump himself up for an act of insulted dignitary while he watches her put the briefcase back on her lap.

Anabelle takes four envelopes out, opens one and holds up a cheque for him to see. "I have been commissioned to present your government with a cheque of an amount equal to twenty percent of our forest area investment for a reforestation program upon the successful completion of our business. Use of this donation is at your discretion and Madrigal would appreciate you announcing the source as anonymous."

Zuñiga's facial complexion returns to normal as soon as money is mentioned and he relaxes. He leans forward in a conspiratorial attitude, reads the amount entered on the cheque and in no time at all calculates the amount for the purchase of a forest area. "That is a very satisfactory proposal, Señora Berndorf. I believe we will be able to reach an agreement quickly. However, it is very unusual to work with crossed cheques. Generally, we only accept irrevocable letters of credit and forms of direct cash transfer."

Anabelle realises she cannot give this financial philanderer an inch of space and is grateful for Oduber's detailed preparation for this meeting, particularly his accurate characterisation of the advisors. She responds to Zuñiga's remark in a slightly ironic tone. "Irrevocable letters of credit, as you should know, are only issued for the delivery of contracted goods and entail a jumble of documents. You don't provide shiploads of harvested tropical timber, but only property documents and licenses that give us for a limited time and our own risk the rights for economic exploitation of an area of rainforest. Thus, you can't expect us to work with this type of capital transfer. And direct cash transfer, I have to assume, was just a bad joke. Correct? Since I'm not representing a drug cartel, surely you didn't expect me to come waltzing in here with a suitcase full of plain brown envelopes stuffed full of cash."

Zuñiga looks embarrassed and gropes for an acceptable reply. "Direct cash transfers are quite common in Latin America, even for transactions of the targeted size. Surely you will have had this experience in Brazil. However, we will be able to live with your payment method. So don't worry. What do you want to know of me now? How do you wish to proceed?"

Anabelle is relieved to have taken the first hurdle and proceeds to the next, which concerns the selection of the forest area. "We, by that I mean my advisor, Señor Castillo, will point out our envisaged forest areas. With your help, we would like to reduce the rather long list to two and preferably only one specific location. I expect you to convince me that the modalities of the finally selected area do not pose any problems for Madrigal. I also count on your support for the negotiations scheduled for today with the Ministry of Natural Resources and the Deputy Minister of Economy. A phone call from you should suffice to confirm the meetings and to assert that today is the only day available for negotiations. Time is money and limited when it comes to handing out a lot of money. As soon as our discussions have been satisfactorily concluded, I will notify my client to arrange the release of the submitted cheques for payment according to the following procedure. The Madrigal Group's bank in the USA will clear the cheques upon my assurance to have received all ownership transfer documents of the area. The amounts are instantly at the recipient's disposal."

She holds up another cheque. "It applies to your personal bonus as well, Señor Zuñiga."

He ignores the cheque and scowls at Anabelle. She is shocked and cannot interpret his reaction. Did she make a mistake? Is the amount of the cheque insufficient? Zuñiga, noticing her sudden tension, lets her hang out to dry for a moment. The lady has become too bold. He has to make up ground he lost to her.

"All financial matters concerning me personally I discuss only in absolute confidence and in private," cuts his voice through the noticeably cooled atmosphere.

Before he can continue, Anabelle agrees hastily and asks 'Señor Castillo' to leave the room for a moment. Monty gets up and is brought to the door by Zuñiga who orders the secretary to make coffee for two. He closes the door gently and without fuss gets to the point where the shoe pinches him. "The cheque you just showed me isn't worth the paper it's written on. It's a crossed cheque that's not certified and neither is the recipient entered. I can only accept a cashier's cheque in my name that I can cash today."

Anabelle takes a deep breath, sits up straight in her chair, and glares at him. In a clear voice, she says, "I think we should end our conversation here and now. If you think for one moment that you can impose conditions, you are sorely mistaken."

She grabs the envelopes and his cheque, deposits them in her briefcase, and stands up. "I will notify my client of your outrageous demands. He will initiate further steps and will note with dismay that his planned investment of sixty million dollars fell through due to the objection of a junior consultant. The consequences for Costa Rica, your so-called consulting company and as far as your person is concerned... you can do the math yourself, Señor Zuñiga!"

His eyes seem to pop out of his head for a moment when Anabelle walks towards the door. He hastens to beg her, "Señora Berndorf, that is a misunderstanding. Please, excuse my hasty comment. Of course, with an investment of this magnitude, we should be able to accommodate you. Can we discuss the cheque issue once more?"

With one hand on the door handle, she says, "There's nothing more to discuss! We have to abide by your land acquisition customs and you have to accept our terms and conditions! Basta!"

Zuñiga, who has been standing, needs to sit down. Instead of gaining ground, he kicked loose a landslide and is now a lost sentinel in the wilderness of his own making. He has never met a negotiator as tough as this woman. Business people from North America, Europe and Asia usually come in, put plenty of cash on the table with an arrogant smile, await and receive their desired contacts and appointments and are on their way again. But this woman strikes a whole new pitch. He looks at Anabelle with the eyes of a wounded dog and begs, "Señora Berndorf, please sit down again. I approve of everything you have said, but you have to understand that we need reassurances."

Anabelle is outraged about this lying little bastard. She would like to give up the charade and confront him like a proper journalist with all the questions she has and tie him up in his network of lies and pretence. But what would that achieve? She overcomes her anger and returns in a second to her lead role. "What are you actually allowing yourself? Do you think that I, an internationally respected financial adviser, would waste a minute of my time with a farce? Then I expect you to say so bluntly to my face."

Zuñiga writhes in agony. *Caca! Mierda!* Wherever he turns and twists, he always steps into his own cowpat mines. Luckily at that moment the secretary comes in with the coffee. After setting down the tray and leaving, Anabelle follows his gesture encouraging her to sit down again, also because she really needs a cup of coffee right now, if not something stronger, to get her nerves back on track.

Zuñiga tries to appear even-tempered, but the frenzied stirring of his coffee and his cracked voice betray his inner turmoil. "Señora Berndorf, I wonder if you are aware of the actual function of our company. It is my job to sound out the investment offers that have been presented to us. Once I have checked whether the strict requirements of our country are met, I give the go-ahead for the talks with the ministries. So, it is my job to ensure that the conditions are in place for a mutually agreeable conclusion."

"Is that so?" Sarcasm swings in Anabelle's voice. "And one of the prerequisites is pushing cash over the table or that the cheques are confirmed by the bank and are to be paid out to 'bearer'."

"No, you misunderstand the customs of our country." Zuñiga ignores Anabelle's sarcasm and tries to keep things calm. "You mentioned that publicity is poison to our business. I agree. But just as your client insists on anonymity, neither do we want to appear in the public eye, at least not beyond a level we can control. You know, I'm sure, the press distorts the truth and presents a completely false picture. It destroys careers and is very detrimental to a project. We have a lot of experience with tropical timber ventures and so far have been able to get everything successfully aligned with our world-renowned nature conservation program. The selection, processing and delivery of ownership documents requires a lot of work and considerable pre-financing. Our state has very detailed legislation and we can't simply ignore the bureaucracy that often gets in the way. I hope, you understand my situation and also why I can speak to you only in a most confidential setting and why direct cash transactions would be very beneficial to your project."

"Yes, of course I understand you, probably better than you would suspect." Anabelle speaks now in unctuous tones. "But surely you will understand that I have to meet my obligations as well. Direct cash transfer, that is to say payment in plain brown envelopes stuffed with cash pushed over your table, will not take place under any circumstances. Our experience with cash payments is very negative. Instead of our contractually agreed demands being met, unabashed demands for more cash were sent to us. Even you can't give me a guarantee that an amount received today will grease all squeaky wheels tomorrow. The pre-financing you mentioned will have to come out of your pocket. We anticipated these requirements and will follow the Brazilian model of paying a premium over the market rate for rainforest land. Our premium payment should remove all your concerns. Are we getting closer to a compromise?"

Zuñiga listens to her words with growing enthusiasm. The clarity with which this woman expresses her position suggests that she would be an excellent advisor for the Society for Investments and Economic Development. Figures amounting to many millions

156

of dollars for the purchase of land and the licence to clear cut the forest rumble in his head.

A warm shiver runs through him and his heart skips a little. He takes a sip of coffee to wash down his excitement. "Yes, a compromise is in sight. How big an investment did you have in mind? Is the bonus cheque you showed me a clue?"

"Yes, it is two and a half percent of the total investment." Anabelle is keeping a keen eye on him now. She has to register every one of his motions, tempt him to make more thoughtless statements, and be careful not to expose her farce in the process.

"Oh, just two and a half percent? Normally I'm entitled to at least five percent."

He sees Anabelle smiling contentedly and wishes he could take back his words. Did he step into a cowpat mine again?

But Anabelle doesn't raise her voice or express the anger seething in her and explains matter-of-factly, "Normally, you're not at all entitled to a personal bonus, Señor Zuñiga. I've been informed about that as well. Your company gets the usual five percent of the total investment and you get a share of that amount. Because of the fifteen percent premium we are willing to pay over the market price for rainforest, the amount you can expect to receive will be considerably higher than usual."

He stares into his empty cup. "You are indeed well informed. May I ask who your informant is and why you need our services?"

Instead of answering his question directly, she serves up the noncommittal reply he should have expected. "One can never have enough friends in our business. I'm a lot more comfortable knowing you to be on our side than having you against us."

After a brief pause, she continues, "Let's get back to the business of actual concern. We considered the purchase of a 5,000-hectare primary rainforest area. We're offering around sixty million dollars plus the twenty percent reforestation donation plus the personal bonuses. There should be enough small change left to grease the bureaucratic wheels, don't you think?"

Zuñiga smiles for the first time since greeting Anabelle and Monty. "Yes, considering the sums you mentioned, I agree with you. We can probably say we have found a compromise. Shall we call Señor Castillo?"

"One moment," says Anabelle and raises a hand. "We always work on the basis of mutual trust. That means we trust you to deliver the required documents quickly and correctly and we can go about our work undisturbed. In return, you receive more money from us than you can expect from other investors. We don't question your work and you trust us with our cheques. Should you or one of the other interlocutors come up with the idea of contacting our bank in the USA, we have an arrangement with the bank to cancel the entire project immediately. We had to take this precaution because my client does not like snoopers in his finances. Discretion is the word on which our good name is based."

Zuñiga takes a deep breath to respond, thinks better of it, goes to the door, and invites 'Señor Castillo' to come in.

Monty explains swiftly which areas he selected. He points at areas on the large relief map undaunted by the fact that most of them are located in the middle of national parks and wildlife reserves. Zuñiga only knows the whole country in the form of a blue-white-red grid, blue for the zones that are 'productive', white for zones that are deforested or native reserves that cannot be acquired, and red for available forest zones. He corrects Monty a few times, but a deal is quickly struck.

An area in the country's north, in the western section of the Barra del Colorado National Wildlife Refuge near a proposed road, is acceptable to both parties. The selected area suits Zuñiga fine, because deforestation is already going on there and a few more timber transports on the country roads will hardly be noticed or raise eyebrows. Furthermore, subcontractors working there can be hired without him having to spend enormous bribes to keep them silent.

He calls the Secretary of State for the 'Economic Utilisation of Fallow Forest Areas' in the Ministry of Natural Resources and gives him the coordinates of the forest area. After a short time he gets the data as well as the appointment for Señora Berndorf and Señor Castillo confirmed. He receives his personal bonus cheque and with greatest relief escorts his visitors back to the reception hall where he bids them farewell.
***

A young man receives Anabelle and Monty in the Ministry of Natural Resources and walks ahead of them upstairs to the department where the meeting with the Secretary of State, Manuel Cardenas will take place. Monty can hardly contain himself about the guide's awkward mincing and tries to imitate him by putting one foot in front of the other like a fashion model. Anabelle admonishes him with hand gestures to stop it but has to suppress her amusement when they meet more young men who lure each other with spurious calls and conspicuous hip movements. On this floor of the office complex is only one woman in sight, a lonely typist in an anteroom.

They have to wait a moment to be announced and called into the Secretary of State's office. Zuñiga had informed Cardenas with a second call about his meeting. He warned him to treat that tough negotiating woman with greatest caution and utmost respect. It was a necessary warning because it is known that Cardenas loathes negotiating with women. In his opinion, women are barely useful for filing papers and only indispensable for making coffee and tea. Negotiate with them? The very thought is repugnant to him.

Anabelle and Monty notice Cardenas' cool, dismissive tone when he greets them. Their amused faces and poor attempts to suppress their snickering does not improve the greeting they receive. They take their seats across from him on the other side of his desk and he begins a monologue with his eyes fixed on Monty's belt buckle. Fortunately there isn't much to talk about, Cardenas says, since the selection of the forest clearing area is final, the financial matters have been settled, albeit in an unconventional way, and only the exact land survey data have to be brought into line with the land registry. A letter corresponding to this effect, as well as a short declaration of the purchase of land by the Madrigal Group of Companies, represented by its financial consultant, a certain Señora Elisabeth Berndorf, are in the process of being typed. Now all they have to do is wait for the letters to be handed in for his signature, the state secretary explains.

When he is finally finished with his discourse, Anabelle enquires if he has visited the Barra del Colorado Wildlife Refuge. Instead of answering her question he starts to regurgitate texts of tourism brochures without letting Anabelle get a word in edgeways. Evidently he endeavours to prevent her asking any more questions and raves about the country's beauty, the eternal spring, and the immensely diverse flora and fauna. Impatiently he calls on his phone a couple of times enquiring very abrasively what the holdup with the letters is.

A proper conversation with him is not possible. He cuts them off a couple of times when Anabelle wants to query how he squares the beauty of the country with the pollution and ongoing destruction and when Monty points out that a national park he claims to be in the north is actually in the south bordering Panama.

They conclude that he has scant knowledge of his country and is a pretentious, self-important, arrogant, and abusive loudmouth.

The two letters are at last delivered in triplicate. He signs them, gives one copy to his assistant for mailing to the registry office, stuffs one into the drawer of his desk, and hands the original to Anabelle. He receives the two cheques for the land purchase and his personal bonus and declines her invitation to join them for lunch stating to have important appointments. Once he has tucked the cheques rather carelessly into a pocket, he gets up hastily, guides his visitors to the door and waves them out with a short greeting.

After a more or less one-sided talk of just over half an hour, Anabelle and Monty are back on the street looking perplexed. Contrary to their intention, they didn't get any additional information about the sale of protected nature reserves out of him but are now in the possession of documents declaring the Madrigal Group to be the new owners of just about 5,000 hectares of rainforest allocated to be cut down.

They enter a restaurant with an open terrasse in the vicinity of government buildings, order lunch, and eat their meals in silence.

After the meal, Anabelle begins to show signs of a burgeoning depression. Monty wants to cheer her up a little. But she doesn't want to hear any of his stories. She fears that they will not only come true but will be overtaken by reality in the most brutal way, like almost everything she has heard from him so far.

On the wide pavement in front of the restaurant, she sees only happy people who could be posing for photos in brightly coloured brochures. A group of smiling men and women on the way back to work, a mother with a full shopping bag holding her child by the hand, young lovers cuddling and kissing in the shade of a tree in the park across the street, three old men on one of the benches probably exchanging memories and chatting about days gone by, friendly traders passing by the terrace offering assortments of clay pipes, hammocks or American newspapers, and even an old beggar woman with snow-white hair stretching her gnarled hand out of a niche to the passers-by - everyone smiles, everyone seems to have only kind words for their fellow human beings - everything is so *tranquilo* as they say here, so calm, so peaceful, so normal, so bloody awfully normal! Doesn't anyone of them know what is going on around them? Do they all take a double dose of tranquilisers for breakfast? Haven't they noticed how they are being cheated out of their own and their children's future? Or does it simply not concern them that their forests are being destroyed, the rivers and lakes poisoned, and the coasts polluted?

Anabelle has to severely restrain herself from shouting out these questions and stopping the people's daily activities to admonish them. It is war, Folks! A slow, cruel, horrible and almost silent war is waged against you by the greedy people you elected and many of those who administer your bureaucracy!

Tears well up in her eyes and Monty feels utterly helpless in the face of her barely suppressed grief.

"All lies!" murmurs Anabelle. The tourism brochures boasting about untouched nature, clean rivers, cheerfully babbling mountain streams, the cleanest beaches in the world - All Lies! And nowhere is a trace of organised protests against it! Why not? Don't the people know or don't they give a damn? The whole system seems to be so well set up that people cannot or will not do anything about it. Or are they just scared? And why is hardly anything known about it in North America and Europe and nothing at all in Asia?

The environmental organisations are always railing against the cursed tropical timber dealers, the unscrupulous transnational companies and the stupidity of the consumers who still demand and buy teak and mahogany furniture. But are they really the culprits? Aren't the main culprits the greedy bigwigs who initiate the disastrous process with the lament that their poor country needs every dollar it can get and organise and promote the environmental destruction with the indirect and direct support of creditor countries, international banks, and financial organisations?

Would the destruction of forests and environment stop if all timber traders, companies, and consumers in North America, Europe and Asia suddenly refused to buy tropical timber and products made from it? Highly unlikely! Mankind's stupidity is infinite and profiteers like Zuñiga and Cardenas and their comrades-in-arms would quickly find other ways to make a disproportionate profit for their personal enrichment with the sale and destruction of the natural resources humanity needs most to survive.

"I need a drink," says Anabelle abruptly. She orders a large single malt Scotch whisky and a glass of still water with an ice cube on the side. Monty orders a jug of beer. They clink glasses before she takes out a notepad and starts writing her report to use the time they have until the next meeting productively.

***

Anabelle and Monty visit the Deputy Minister of Economy, Roberto Chaverry just before 15:00 o'clock. He is a jovial, funny fellow who hardly gives his two visitors a chance to speak. He tells anecdotes about his trips to America and Europe and how much he liked it there. Cleanliness, order, progress, efficiency, punctuality and economic strength - his enthusiasm degenerates into rapture. He mentions the construction of industrial parks, huge tourist centres on the 1,800 kilometres of undeveloped coast, large international airports and seaports - those are the goals for his country.

Eventually he becomes aware of the presence of his guests and the reason for their visit. But Chaverry steers the conversation straight back to his favourite topic, the massive industrialisation of his country. He wants to know whether the investor represented by Señora Berndorf is only interested in nature conservation. Or would he also be interested in progress? Oh, really, the investor intends to invest in the furniture industry? Wonderful! Then the issue of the license to clear cut the forest would be a mere formality.

Chaverry does not notice his contradiction of enquiring about nature conservation and granting a licence to clear cut a forest in the same breath. Anabelle makes a note of it and wonders if he understands nature conservation to be an asphalt covered parking lot with plastic palm trees and small strips of grass like those in Florida he waxed so enthusiastically about.

Unencumbered by and probably unawares of his misstep, he continues to plough his furrow of industrialisation. He asks if the investor has the intention of starting a furniture manufacturing company. No? Oh, contact has already been established with suitable companies to discuss partnerships? Excellent! But he could still recommend the company his brother founded last year. Would that be of interest to them? Yes? Fabulous! Then they should please take his business card and call him at the next opportunity. I beg your pardon? Shouldn't they talk about the actual reason for their visit? No, that would not be necessary. He will get the license issued shortly and everything else has been taken care of, as Señor Zuniga and Señor Cardenas had confirmed by telephone. The Madrigal Group can start harvesting the tropical wood in a few days of less than a week. Yes, not everything works only mañana here.

162

Chaverry gets a brief phone call and beams a broad smile at Señora Berndorf. The licence application received the minister's approval and the licence is in the process of being formalised. It should be ready shortly and will be handed over by his secretary.

Anabelle hands over the three cheques for the licence, the reforestation programme and Chaverry's personal bonus. The deputy minister is overjoyed looking at the amounts entered and asks if she would like to suggest a specific area for reforestation, an area that might be particularly close to her heart. No? He is free to choose how the donation is to be used and the noble donor wants to remain anonymous? Well, that's fabulous! The money will be put to good use, yes, yes, definitely.

Chaverry stuffs the cheques totalling thirteen and a half million dollars into his jacket pocket with a hearty laugh and shakes hands with his visitors before he compliments them out of his office. In the anteroom his secretary hands over the licence and accompanies the visitors on their way out.

It is 15:45 o'clock when Anabelle and Monty stand on the street in the choking fumes of the rush hour traffic onset.

Monty smiles at her. "We've done it. You got everything you need. Now listen... don't you think you should follow Oduber's advice and leave Costa Rica tonight before these jokers wake up to the fact they've been had? I'll take you to the airport and be on my way as well. I guess I'll be missed back home."

She looks at him angrily. "I'm supposed to run away now? Do you even understand what happened today? I just bought a huge forest and got the licence to put the axe to its nearest tree. If more people had done the same thing today, there wouldn't be a tree left standing in this country in four weeks. Don't you realise that?"

Monty is amused. "You look really pretty when you're angry."

The grin is wiped off his face when she hits him in the head with her briefcase.

"Ouch! Stop... that! Stop... hitting me! Yes, yes, yes... I know what happened here. It is exactly what Oduber and I told you. If you'd believed us, you wouldn't be angry now but happy to have the evidence for your report in your hands. Do you want to stand here, scream and protest? That wouldn't do any good. You can't change the system. So, what's it gonna be? Let's pick up our luggage from the hotel and I'll take you to the airport. All right?"

She shakes her head. "No, my flight is tomorrow. I want to do what is evidently the tradition in this land of graveyard peace in recognition of the advanced destruction of all life! Noble shall the world perish! I want to get totally shitfaced to forget the horrors I experienced and do a funny little dance to *La Canción del Final del Mundo* by Rúben Bládes. His fiery song about the end of the world should be your national anthem with just a minimal change of the lyrics! But first I need to do something urgently. Let's go!"

She hails a taxi and they are dropped off in no time at the hotel. She drags Monty to the elevator who is puzzled about the sudden rush. In the room, she changes into trousers and T-shirt. Then she rips open her backpack, takes out all the exposed films, removes the memory chip from the digital camera, rips the pages of her almost finished report off the notepad, folds them together with the documents she received, and puts everything into her handbag. She stows her briefcase back in her backpack, urges Monty who is getting out of his suit to hurry up and put on his regular clothes. A little while later they hail another taxi in front of the hotel and she asks the driver to take them to an international courier company.

The guy asks if her goods are supposed to be delivered the next day. She confirms it and he states only airlines at their airport counters accept courier goods for next day delivery until two hours before departure of their respective flights. The courier companies have a cut off time for next day delivery of goods at 16:00 o'clock.

At the airport, she goes straight to the counter of an airline with direct flights to Europe and asks for courier service. The attendant wants to know what she wants to send. Anabelle puts all her goods on the counter and requests them to be sent on the night flight. A heavy-duty upholstered envelope and a customs declaration form for the description of the items is handed to her. Sixteen rolls of exposed film and the digital disk receive the identical entry 'Nature Photography' and the papers are described as 'Report about the natural wonders of Costa Rica'. She puts the items in the envelope and seals it, addresses it to her home in Zurich, attaches the custom form, and hands the package over.

The attendant reads the declaration. "Did you take nice photos?"

Anabelle points at Monty and responds excitedly, "I took unbelievably gorgeous photos on a walk through the unspoiled nature up north thanks to my guide who took me there. My photo reportage will be published in a nature magazine that is also on sale here at the airport. Everything going well, it should be in next month's edition."

"I look forward to reading it and seeing the photos. What is the value of this package? It must be worth thousands of dollars."

"Well, that's difficult to say. But what does it take for the package to pass through customs speedily without a hindrance?"

"Anything less than one hundred dollars."

"Good. Then write $99.50 on it. That should do the trick."

And with that entry, the package is tossed into the bag of an international courier company. Anabelle pays the enormous delivery fee, gets a receipt and leaves with Monty in tow.

Back in the downtown area they enter a bar that is almost empty at the still early hour, sit down on the barstools and order drinks. Anabelle checks her purse to count the cash she has left. Two hundred thousand colones and three hundred dollars is less than she thought. She takes three fifty thousand colones banknotes, folds them, and tucks them in Monty's shirt pocket. He takes the money out, counts it and mumbles his thanks. Their drinks are served. She gulps down her vodka martini and orders another one.

He sips his beer and adds up how much money he has now. With the one hundred dollars she gave him the night before, he has almost three hundred fifty dollars and feels quite rich.

Her second drink goes down her gullet just as quickly and she looks listlessly at her third. The drinks don't have the desired effect. She begins to brood and realises that all she really wants to do is get away from here. She would like to escape this cruel emptiness of the civilised world. She thinks of Bahía Potrero. Her world was still in order back there. How long ago was it? About seventy-two hours.

Monty takes another small sip out of the bottle while he thinks of his wife and four children. A feeling of guilt is pushed aside by the fact of the money in his pocket. His wife is used to his absence and knows about his dalliances. The kids love him even more when he turns up again after a few days. He will buy all of them a present. His wife would be happy about a new blouse or a necklace. He has enough money to buy both or a nice pair of shoes. Yes, shoes, he will buy her shoes. And each of his kids shall have a present as well. A toy truck for Daniel, a doll for Marcela, a diving mask for Manuel, and an ocarina for the youngest addition to the family, little Carlos.

Ocarina? Oca? He turns to Anabelle. "Hey, *conchita*, didn't you want to call this guy Rico and his wife in Montes de Oca before you take off?"

"Hombre!" she shouts and grabs his arm. "Why didn't you think of that earlier? I'll call them right away. You'll join me to visit them, won't you, if they are home?"

Instantaneously her depression disappears. The memory of Martha comes to the fore and how comfortable she felt in the company of this calm and thoughtful woman. She will describe the experiences of the past three days and ask her opinion. Whatever she has to say could become the fulcrum of her report.

After a lengthy phone call they leave the bar, take a taxi back to the hotel, get into her rental car and follow the route to Montes de Oca Martha had described. They stop at a supermarket and buy two bottles of wine, a dozen ready-made tamales, several tins of smoked mussels, a pound of Turrialba cheese, freshly baked baguettes, and a big jar of palm hearts.

In Montes de Oca they drive along until they see Martha standing in front of a plain townhouse with barred windows and a trampled low hedge. Martha, Rico and Anabelle embrace like old friends in an exuberant greeting and Monty is given a hearty welcome. They take a seat in the sparsely furnished living room and Anabelle unpacks the goodies she has brought along.

After her initial appreciation of the bottles of wine, Martha looks a little helpless. She has no *chuncho* she says while twisting her hand. Now Anabelle looks puzzled and asks why Martha would need an oddball. They all laugh when she points to Rico and says Martha has one and a really splendid one at that. She is told that in Costa Rica *chuncho* is the term used for any utensil when one does not know its proper name. Holding a corked bottle in one hand and twisting the other indicates that one needs a corkscrew. Aha, she needs a *sacacorcho* says Anabelle. Martha replies dryly that in Spain it may be called corkscrew but in Costa Rica it will always be a *chuncho* even when the country drowns in wine. She goes to the kitchen, returns with a screwdriver, hands it and the bottle to Rico and declares him to be the official *sacacorcho* for the evening.

In this relaxed atmosphere, Anabelle quickly drops her pent-up bitterness. With a touch of humour she describes her experiences of the past two days since they met in Bahía Potrero. Even the events of the day that had so upset her come easily over her lips. The turbulence in her head clears up, she recognises the structures of the system, and begins to understand the connections and components. She mentions the historical aspect of the 'Old World'

166

with its colonialisation having initiated the current situation. It is maintained and promoted by industrialised nations with their avarice for the tropical world's natural resources, their protection of economic spheres of influence, and their support of corrupt governments of the so-called 'Third World'. She concludes that her report will fall like a sledgehammer on society's corns.

While she speaks it dawns on her that she will have to improve her report to take on a more acrid form.

It instils a little fear in her. It is after all her first report in the critical sector of investigative journalism and totally different from her reports so far about the lavish lifestyles of the rich and famous. Is she after all a 'disguised revolutionary', as some colleagues call her when she is harping on about the lack of attention paid to gender equality and women's rights and demanding a radical change of society?

The ambiguousness in her mind about her report is not mitigated when Rico expresses his doubts with a wry smile that such a report would be published in Costa Rica. It would be swept under the carpet, the journalist could have his or her accreditation revoked and, in the worst case, will never be heard of again.

Martha does not agree. "That's not quite true, Rico. I can prove it to you. Hang on a minute."

She goes to the guest room where well-thumbed magazines and newspapers and books are stacked on a shelf. Rummaging through the publications, she pulls out an edition of the magazine *Rumbo* and two of the daily *La Nación* and one little book. Triumphantly she holds them aloft when she returns to the living room.

The magazine has the bold headline *Costa Rica - El Paraíso Muere* on its cover, suggesting 'Costa Rice - The Paradise Dies' above a close-up photo of an *Ara Macao*, a scarlet macaw. Martha opens it up to page 14 with an article under the headline *Paraíso Casi Perdido* meaning 'Paradise Almost Lost'. It shows contrasting photos of a jaguar in the wild and a deforested area with only a few stalks of dead trees. The book has the title *Crisis ecológica de América Central* - 'Ecological Crisis of Central America'.

She hands the magazine and the book to Anabelle with the words, "Read this article and the book. Then you won't be afraid to have your hard-hitting photo report published."

She holds the *La Nación* reports out to Rico and says, "Here is an article about drug smuggling cops being sentenced to ten years in prison and another about the trial of our former president Calderón for corruption. It should reassure you of fair, open and free reporting in our country."

Rico waves off her comment. "Look, Martha, these articles and the book were published years ago."

"I know but due to limited distribution, at least of the *Rumbo* magazine and the book, hardly anyone got the information to find out what's going on in our country. That's why nothing has changed and the people still elect these useless candidates who carry on business as usual."

Anabelle looks up from reading the report and says, "That's a good point about the electorate. One government after another is ineffective, the people know it, and yet they vote for the same candidates to form another excremental administration. Costa Rica is not alone with this problem that is usually a result of a biased media and rich donors who support and finance the campaigns of these useless candidates."

"That's true," says Rico, "but it goes deeper than the media and rich donors. It starts with the education system that churns out mostly semi-literate graduates at best. They can read an article but don't get the message because they haven't been taught critical thinking. So, they read the headlines and think they have all the information they need. That's a problem not unique to Costa Rica."

"But look at this report," challenges Anabelle. "What's not to understand. It presents facts everybody knows."

"True," says Martha, "but consider the small distribution of the magazine. The majority of readers who are aware of the facts don't want to bother with more bad news. The few who read the article found confirmed what they know and can't do anything about."

"I have to remind you also of the time the report was written," argues Rico. "It was a time when there was some rebelliousness among the journalists against the censure of the National Journalism Institute and the public had an open ear for any news that went against the grain of reporting everything in conditionals and not stating blunt facts. What do we have today? A bunch of yahoos posing as journalists who describe everything as beautiful and progressive to promote Costa Rica as the top Latin American destination for investment and tourism."

"I doubt that," says Martha. "Costa Rica was rated as number five right after four Scandinavian countries as having an unencumbered free press."

"Sure, and the list you quote was published on an Internet site that also publishes lists of the healthiest and cleanest countries. And guess what? Just a few days ago, it claimed that the United Kingdom of Great Britain and Northern Ireland is number five of cleanest countries in the world because of its clean and safe water supply despite the fact that for years the water companies are dumping raw, untreated sewage into rivers, lakes, canals and onto the seashores. How does that add up? It is based on national journalists' opinion about their country. The rating of freedom of the press by Reporters Without Borders shows Costa Rica only rated in eighteenth place."

"My goodness," clamours Anabelle for attention. "The situation is really bad. I thought forest depletion was the biggest problem but this report mentions the annual loss of 680 million metric tons of fertile soil due to erosion caused by the forest massacre and the use of 11,500 metric tons of pesticides each year on the infertile ground to get anything to grow. And then all that pollution. Incredible! This writer's knowledge could be crucial for my report and put it beyond any doubt. Where can I contact him?"

"I'm not sure," says Martha. "I think he lives in France. There was a book published by Carlos Cortés. You'd have to contact the book writer to find out if he wrote this article."

"And about 30,000 more gentlemen by that name in more than 50 countries," pipes Monty in and chuckles.

"Why do you say that?" asks Anabelle.

"Because around the world live at least that many men by that name," says Monty. "As far as writers by that name go... Martha, have you read any more articles by Carlos Cortés?"

"I don't think so. Also, the magazine folded some years after his article was published and I don't know if any other publication would have accepted his critical writing."

"There you are," says Monty to Anabelle. "As Rico said earlier, it's likely these critical writers had their accreditation revoked and were never heard of again. Martha only knows of one who published a book in France. You'd have to start looking in all Latin American countries and several more. He could be living anywhere."

"All right, but what about here in this country?" asks Anabelle. "Couldn't I find out if he still lives here?"

"Possibly," says Rico, "but you need good contacts to other writers who know him and finding those is just as difficult."

"What about the writer of this book, Alexander Bonilla Durán? Is he still in the country?"

"I don't know," says Martha. "I haven't heard of him lately. If he lives here, I wouldn't know where to find him. Anabelle, I think it is best to quote the article and book. That should be sufficient."

It concludes that discussion and after a brief moment of silence, Monty says, "Now that I'm in the central valley, I should visit my friend Felipe in San Antonio before I go home tomorrow. I'm sure he'll be happy to see me."

Rico gazes at Monty out of the corner of his eye, sees the smiling face of this still young, carefree man, and looks down embarrassed at the red-brown tiles of the floor. He says, "Monty, that won't be possible. I'm a detective inspector of the OIJ and the purpose of my visit to Bahía Potrero was to investigate a trail of the case involving your friend. He was murdered. I'm sorry to have to tell you this here and in this way."

Shocked, Monty looks at Rico in disbelief. "Felipe? Murdered? Who killed him? Which bastard did that?"

"I don't know. We don't know. The investigation is ongoing, but my colleagues hold out little hope to ever find the killer. We have been able to establish so far that Felipe's murder is closely linked to what you and Anabelle experienced today."

"What? He was involved in selling protected nature reserves?"

"No, not as an active party. I shouldn't say any more for two reasons. Firstly, the investigation is ongoing, and, secondly, when I presented my interim findings and conclusion to our department boss yesterday, I was officially suspended from duty without an explanation for four weeks."

"Has it something to do with your findings? Is that possible?"

"Possible, Monty? Sure, it's possible. The last entries in my report concerned the findings of the laboratory tests. Accordingly, Felipe was beheaded with his own well-sharpened machete. Tiny particles of the victim's skin and blood were found on the blade of the weapon. It was undoubtedly an execution. Everything else is pure speculation. We don't have any evidence, but we know Felipe was working as a courier for a mysterious group of people who had good reason to eliminate him. His accumulated knowledge of their fraudulent business meant he had become too dangerous for them. My speculation about the motive and the people who may have ordered his murder was possibly cutting too close to the bone of those in power and they would like to cover up this case."

170

Anabelle listened intently and questions are piling up in her mind. Any answer could shed light on another dark side of the illegal rainforest sales and she asks, "Is this fraudulent business linked to the rainforest deal I pulled off today? Does it mean that knowing too much is sufficient in this country to be executed? That would put a whole new twist on what's going on in Brazil where you get killed for just wanting to find out what's going on."

Rico notices her leaning forward, awaiting an answer. But he declines. "Sorry, Anabelle, but I can't say. I've already said too much. But tell me when you are going to leave and return home."

"Tomorrow on a flight to Madrid and on to Zurich."

"I'm glad to hear that," mutters Rico and takes a deep breath, "but it would have been safer if you had left today. If these guys you hoodwinked find out that their cheques are not worth the paper they are printed on, they'll move heaven and earth to get a hold of you. And what happens if they succeed is anybody's guess."

"Monty suggested it, but I couldn't face a long flight. I've sent the incriminating evidence and my exposed films back home by courier. It should be on its way by now."

"Good," says Rico and turns to Monty. "Here's a bit of strange news. You mentioned that Felipe was known in San Antonio as the Dark Angel. Consequently, nobody is willing to bury his remains."

"What? Are these villagers stupid? They can't leave a corpse lying around in the open."

"No, it won't lie around in the open. Once the autopsy has been done, the bodily remains are put in a plain coffin. It has been sent back to San Antonio today or will be sent tomorrow morning."

"In that case I will go tomorrow morning to San Antonio and pay my last respects to my friend and bury him. Could I count on your help? A coffin with a corpse inside is heavy and I may not manage to move it all by myself."

"Yes, of course, I will come along and give you a hand. Perhaps the grave digger can be persuaded to assist us."

After a short deliberation, it is decided that Anabelle and Monty will meet Rico and Martha at the gate of the San Antonio Cemetery at 09:00 o'clock the next morning.

El Cholo

The light in the *Club Torre Blanco* bar is dampened by dense tobacco smoke. The pounding staccato rhythms of rock music boom out of loudspeakers installed in the low ceiling. Any attempt at normal-pitch conversation is lost in the cacophony. The nightclub manager turned the volume prudently up to the level that has been scientifically researched and proven to encourage drinking. The louder the guests have to talk, the quicker their throats get dry. The clients play along and drink until they succumb to their alcohol binge, run out of money, or find a partner with whom they can retreat to one of the club's quiet cubicles or the sauna.

At first glance it is not obvious that the club is a gay bar. The gentlemen who are present wear suits of the finest thread and the ladies are men dressed in expensive designer clothes. The few foreign tourists who stumble in by chance are directed to stand near the door to the contact toilet. The manager gave his employees the strict instruction of one bottle of beer as 'max' for these unsuitable guests, not to serve them cocktails or long drinks, and collect cash payment immediately. After consuming the beer or protesting against the club's strict rules, they are complimented, if not to say thrown out to prevent them disturbing the harmony of the business. This is a high-class nightclub for the entertainment of gentlemen who expect to spend some time of untroubled fun and relaxation.

In front of the club, in a yard to the side of the entrance and in the shade of some bushes, stand two stately men in dark suits who are known in the club by their pseudonyms Rodrigo and Bruno. They smoke cigarettes and talk in whispers.

Bruno, with his full black hair, even features and prominent chin could pass for a schmaltzy lover of the silent movie era. Carefully he peers towards the front door, making sure that no one is within earshot. Looking up at his counterpart, he whispers, "I was relieved to learn that our little problem was solved so quickly. I mean, I applaud the speed of execution, but not the method. It must have been a huge mess that played out. Couldn't our friend have been garrotted, you know, in the best of Spanish traditions? That would have left him just as speechless."

Rodrigo, the slightly taller man with somewhat aristocratic features, murmurs, "All of us would have preferred a fake suicide of hanging the guy, but there was simply no other way. I was assured the situation demanded quick action. You yourself had warned me that our friend had the strength of a bear because you once saw him repairing his bus and handling the transmission like an empty briefcase. Believe me, just a little delay would have resulted in disastrous consequences and, well, you know, our man Cholo for these jobs kicking the bucket instead."

"Yes, I know, I know," is the surly reply. "But did it have to look like a ritual killing, yet with a machete? That should be reserved for labourers in the sugar cane fields to solve their conflicts when they are drunk as skunks."

Rodrigo pushes his receding chin forward and shrugs. "Unfortunate, yes, of course, but I was assured there was no other way. Now it can't be changed anymore. Water under the bridge. Let's forget about it."

After a moment's reflection, he continues, "By the way, I've had all of our friend's connections traced. It's proof of how much we needed his permanent silence." He takes a folded piece of paper from his jacket pocket and hands it to Bruno. "Here is the list of our required clean-up operation. Take good care of it and see to it that all the people are dispatched as quickly as possible. The one at the bottom of the list poses the biggest problem."

Bruno skims the list of names lets the paper disappear in his jacket pocket. "Yes, I agree. Ramírez, the nation's super snooper does pose a big problem. He gets a lot of protection from his colleagues. But I thought he had been put on ice."

Rodrigo drags on his cigarette and flicks the butt out into the parking lot. "You're quite right. He's been put on ice for four weeks, but that doesn't mean he won't continue sniffing around. At least we have sufficient time to prepare his demise. Two variants were suggested. First, his jalopy could be manipulated, you know, the steering or brakes, causing him to have a fatal accident. The other variant would kill two birds in quick succession. It concerns his wife. As an innocent bystander of a gun fight she could have her head blown off on the street where she goes shopping. Then we could fake her hubby's suicide over the loss of his wife."

Nervously, Bruno lets his gaze wander around and whispers angrily, "Wait a minute! Eliminating Ramírez and his wife would bring the entire OIJ onto the scene. You know how these gumshoes react when one of their own suffers a fatality."

"I thought of that," says Rodrigo and waves the objections aside. "We're not so stupid to get the OIJ to investigate an accidentally fatal shooting followed by a suicide of one of their popular colleagues and his pregnant wife. That's why Charro and I came up with another variant that's very solid. Ramírez confiscated a drug courier's attaché case at the airport a few weeks ago. We had it spirited out of the evidence room of the OIJ with the help of Ramos. It contains over two million bucks. The case has to be placed in Ramírez's house where it will be found by his own colleagues after a tip-off. He'll be out of his job and it's certain he'll be going to the slammer for at least ten years. Consequently, we are rid of the problem of his unconventional investigative methods and when he gets out of jail, we bump him off. Could you take on the task of having the attaché case placed in his house? I make sure it will be of considerable financial benefit to you."

Bruno pulls the corners of his mouth down appraisingly and nods. "Yes, I can have that done for you. But I'm not interested in financial benefits. I'd much rather see some movement in my career. Our project is progressing smoothly as if by magic and I would like to go back to work in the public sector again. Since you mentioned the attaché case, I understand that an attaché for Colombia is still being sought. Could you arrange something for me in your position of Secretary of State?"

Rodrigo glares at his counterpart. "You're not supposed to use my title in public, you idiot! If anyone hears that, the shit hits the fan and we'd end up with more than just freckles on our faces! And my name is off limits too, is that clear? In this environment everybody appears incognito and my name is Rodrigo. Got it?"

Embarrassed about his slipup, Bruno pokes a toe of his shoe into the turf. "Sorry, uh, Rodrigo."

Rodrigo breathes heavily while keeping his anger in check and says without a second thought, "If you really want to go to Colombia, that's no problem. I can arrange it tomorrow and in ten days you'll be in Bogotá. But do you even have a clean slate?"

"But of course! You know me, don't you? I've always paid everything on time, right up to the last parking ticket. I'm clean."

Rodrigo gives Bruno a strange look and thinks about the people he had eliminated and the fraudulent deals he executed in the past five years of their joint activity. He was always reliable when entrusted with these activities but letting him loose in Colombia is a different matter. He knows why Bruno wants to be transferred to Bogotá. Great changes have taken place in that South American country since the transformation of the cocaine cartels into a global business empire, and the effects have already been felt financially by most people involved in the shipping of illegal drugs. The use of Costa Rica as a land bridge for transferring cocaine and heroin destined for the US West Coast from the Caribbean to the Pacific coast has declined dramatically, and many government officials have written off this revenue stream entirely. It is certain that Bruno wants to revive the old drug routes, which would be a welcome development from the standpoint of the substantial revenues involved. But going it alone outside of Costa Rica and in Colombia of all places entails the danger of him acquiring too much knowledge of the secret dealings with the new cartel of the second and third generation of drug lords and thus gaining enormous power, which is not at all desirable.

Rodrigo had a suspicion for some time that Bruno was collecting information on members of the government and business tycoons and as his nervous collaborators fear had already acquired enough knowledge to bend the state apparatus to his will, manipulate political networks, and pervert election outcomes. That's why he commissioned one of his underlings to investigate whether Bruno, the Thrice Resurrected, as he is disparagingly called because of his turbulent past, doesn't have greater political ambitions after all. Bruno must be kept on a short leash and under control until this suspicion is confirmed or clearly disproved. The position of attaché in Bogotá and thus direct contact with the drug lords would remove him from such control. In case of the worst outcome, it would increase his knowledge and his power could get out of hand. Rodrigo is also mindful of the president's admonition of Bruno potentially possessing the suspected information and already having enough power to place a politician into a ministerial or even the presidential chair and remove him or her again from office at will upon presentation of dirty laundry to the media and public.

After this brief exercise of mental acrobatics, Rodrigo turns to Bruno, "Wouldn't a more prominent position than that of an

176

attaché appeal to you even more if you really want to work in the public sector? I'm thinking of the position of Special Envoy for Nature Conservation, which I suggested and has been approved by the President. We are looking for a high-profile personality, a seasoned businessman and diplomat. The job will include all Latin American countries getting attuned to our model of nature conservation. Embarrassments such as the sale of the Yasuni National Park in Ecuador to an oil company and the public slaughter of the Yanomami natives in Brazil must never be repeated and progressive, humane approaches like ours in Costa Rica must be put in its place. This task requires a great deal of finesse, as you have demonstrated to have aplenty. The activity is also very profitable. You can assume a ten percent share of all forest sale revenues after the introduction of our model. Does that appeal to you?"

Bruno thinks about it for a while. "So, this is a completely new position and includes travelling to all Latin American countries? Yes, that sounds good. I can do that."

Rodrigo hears the acceptance of his suggestion with some relief. "Good, then I'll cram your approbation process through the committees as quickly as possible. I don't expect any objections since you were a state employee a few years ago. But now let me come back to a small problem that we have to solve. You have to take care of that. It concerns our suddenly speechless friend. Can you imagine that nobody wants to bury his corpse? The people in that mountain village are nuts. They claim he is the Dark Angel and none of the villagers want to touch his coffin out of fear of his revenge."

Bruno can barely contain himself. "The Dark Angel? Hard to believe unless these villagers still live in the Middle Ages."

Rodrigo does not look amused. "I'm afraid that's not funny. The case needs to be closed as soon as possible. Ramos will have the OIJ case file corrected with the usual reference to farm equipment accident as the cause of death, but to close the case we still have to bury our friend, preferably in an unmarked grave. Once grass grows over it..."

Bruno roars with laughter. Rodrigo looks ready to strangle him. "What are you laughing at like a moron? I'm not telling jokes! Control yourself!"

Bruno wipes laughter tears from the corner of his eyes. "Sorry... It was grave and grass growing over it. You understand?"

Disgusted, Rodrigo looks into the distance and curses quietly, "You are such a simpleton! Pathetic! Can you have Cholo take care of the burial or do I have to look for someone else?"

Bruno nods his agreement.

Rodrigo continues, "Remember that Cholo also has to dig the burial pit and act like a friend to create the impression of 'what one wouldn't do for an old friend'. I've already got a funeral wreath. It's in my car. You should take it and have the grave decorated to make it look real and believable. So, if you're ready, let's go to my car for the wreath."

Bruno lights up another cigarette and squints at Rodrigo. "Just tell me why our friend wasn't cremated. That would have solved the problem of nobody wanting to bury his remains by simply letting the wind take care of a bucket full of ash."

"We had thought of that from the beginning when you were told to instruct our man for the job to make it look like a suicide. But as you know, it didn't work out that way. The crime scene investigation team found a death insurance policy when the house was searched for items of evidence. It wouldn't have been paid out in case of a suicide. Since it was a case of murder, the beneficiary, our friend's fuckbuddy, she is due to receive some money."

"Isn't our friend's, uh... girl on the list?"

"Yes, right at the top."

"Then we should let her disappear."

"I see what you are getting at. But it can't be done for a few more days. She's still in hospital under observation. Letting her disappear is impossible until she is released. And forget about bumping her off. That would cause even more intense investigations. Let's go ahead with a proper burial for our friend to avoid an investigation about the whereabouts of the corpse."

"But can't we let the insurance policy paper simply disappear?"

"No, it's already in the hands of San Antonio's mayor who is aware of the coffin having been delivered to the graveyard. It's sitting on a cart but apparently not even the gravedigger wants to go near it as far as I know. We are stuck with finishing the job to stop the bureaucrats from posing all sorts of stupid questions."

Together they go to the parking lot next to the club building, Bruno moves his car next to Rodrigo's limousine, they open the trunks and swiftly transfer the wreath.

Rodrigo points to the quite large attaché case. "You might as well take care of the case now."

178

Bruno grabs it by the handle and is surprised about the weight of the case. "What the hell is in that case? Lead bricks?"

"No, paper bricks."

"Paper bricks? What do you mean?"

"Money, you moron. Bundled one-hundred-dollar bills to the tune of two point three million bucks."

"Oh, shit." Bruno lifts the case and stows it in the trunk of his car. "If this is found in Ramírez's house, it'll be..."

Rodrigo shushes him with a sharp gesture. They shut the trunks and Rodrigo is ready to leave.

Bruno feels it necessary to reassure him once more. "I'll have everything arranged tonight. I'll assign Cholo to do the job. He'll follow my instruction to be at the graveyard tomorrow morning around six o'clock for the burial and put the case in Ramírez's house when it's safe to do so. Okay? Will you join me for a drink now? I really need one and Armando is waiting for me as well."

"No, I have to go home. My wife has a do arranged with her friends for her birthday to celebrate at midnight. But tell me, this Armando, is he clean?"

With enthusiasm in his voice, Bruno replies, "Oh yes! He is absolutely clean and pleasing and flexible like a hooker in a Turkish whorehouse. Only the other day, he..."

Rodrigo cuts him off, "That's quite enough. But perhaps you could turn Armando over to me once you're on the road as a special envoy. I'm tired of Raúl. He always wants money, he's always travelling. Oh, and his boasting! He's a hideous hot air merchant. Besides, I have the suspicion that he's having it off with these wimpy fellows in his travel agency. He always has new staff. He should have a revolving door installed in his personnel office. I'm really tired of him and some fresh meat would do me good."

Bruno listens to him quietly and thinks Rodrigo is complaining like a cat in heat. Armando would be the perfect fit for him. They would make a couple that hadn't searched for but found each other anyway. He watches Rodrigo get into his car and drive away. He turns and goes slowly back the entrance of the club.

"That turned out better than I dared to hope," he murmurs pulling the folded paper out of his jacket pocket. He reads the list of names and chuckles. He has deftly guided the government into a dead-end road and stalled its rampant investigation into the leaks of classified information with the sacrifice of a dogsbody that can be blamed on Rodrigo. Also, his aim of getting the post of Special

Envoy for Nature Conservation has gone as he wished. His confidant in the Presidential Ministry had been right when he said that there was no way he was going to get the post in Bogotá but had to ask for it to be considered for the only other vacancy at the moment, the post of Special Envoy. Thus, one of his biggest hurdles, the lack of public exposure, will be cleared out of his ambitious path to the highest office in the country. If he handles it smartly and pays sufficient election funds into the coffers of the right party, he could be considered a serious contender for the presidency in as little as three months and be the prime candidate by the time of the next election.

His load of secret information is safely stowed away in his safe at home. It enables him to drag any opponent into the dirt, including his sideline collaborator Rodrigo, that arrogant prick, who thinks he is in charge. It has been worth the years of suffering the humiliation of being considered nothing more than a better errand boy of the government and having swallowed the insults of being a gay swine and the president's doormat. Due to his well-known submissive demeanour, the suspicion had never been raised that he would ever be anything more than a highly intelligent misfit who, while able to amass vast amounts of money in a short time, lacked the stable odour to be automatically qualified for higher office in the eyes of the oligarchs. Now his time has come to prove them wrong. He vents his inner excitement with a brief, vigorous rub of his hands.

Before walking into the nightclub, he gets out his cell phone and dials a number very familiar to him. "Cholo? It's me Bruno. Could you come to the Club Torre Blanco in about half an hour? I have several very profitable jobs for you. Okay?"

In a dark corner of the club he greets his lover, a rather diminutive and somewhat fragile looking transvestite. "Hello, Armando, have you made yourself look pretty for me?"

"Oh, hel-lo, Chief! I thought you had stood me up tonight. I put so much effort into my make-up just to please you. It's not too much for your taste, is it?" Armando lisps carelessly.

"No, it's exactly how I'm used to see and smell you," says Bruno and nods his confirmation. "If you gave up your damn stupid lisp or at least talk like a Spaniard, I would let you blow me right here at the table."

"That is not nice to call me damn stupid because of my speech impediment," protests Armando.

180

"I didn't call you stupid but your damn lisping," Bruno flares up. "You remind more and more of my mother. She lisps just like you when she wants something and claims to have a speech impediment. When she doesn't get what she wants, she stops lisping and argues like a birdbrain just like you. Moreover, when I heard you recently speak on the phone, you didn't lisp once. So, give it up for my sake."

"You listened to me on the phone? Are you spying on me? Don't you trust me anymore? You don't love me any longer. I can feel it," squawks Armando without lisping.

"Rubbish! I asked you only to stop lisping," hisses Bruno.

"But you used a tone suitable for military barracks, Chief."

"Shut your cakehole already. And don't keep calling me Chief. It makes me want to vomit."

"What am I supposed to call you?" rebels Armando. "Chief makes you want to vomit. I'm not allowed to call you by your first name and your pseudonym Bruno is pathetic."

Bruno groans, drains his glass of whisky and fills it again from the bottle on the table. He leans over and whispers in Armando's ear, "Listen, would you like a career move? A good friend of mine, he's a Secretary of State, has just expressed an interest in you. He thinks you're gorgeous and wants to meet you."

Pretending to be close to tears, Armando sniffles, "You want to get rid of me, don't you? I knew it! You can be so cruel."

"Nonsense, he's a good friend of mine and very influential. That's what I meant by career move," Bruno soothes him. "He has a crush on you. You should visit him. His connection would be of great benefit to you and help me a little bit as well."

"Is he a pervert? You know I wouldn't go along with SM. What's he got, uh, how is he built, that Secretary of State?"

"No, he's not a pervert. He is a nice guy. He's inclined both ways, well, you know what I mean. He runs on AC and DC," says Bruno proudly.

"AC and DC? Wow! One could have a threesome with him in the middle," exclaims Armando. "And how is he built?"

"Very athletic and about thirty centimetres," lies Bruno. "You could suggest your trio idea to him. Knowing him, he wouldn't be averse to participating. Who knows, maybe you'd show up here with a third guy and dance as a threesome on the bar counter."

Armando starts whinnying and shakes with laughter. "Just imagine! Three guys do a number standing up on the bar counter while they tap dance! The whole place would be swimming in cream of leek soup in no time with most of the patrons wanking to the rhythm of the music. No, the idea is just insane. *Dios mío!* You said the guy has 30 centimetres? Man, he's fit to cover a mare! What's his phone number?"

"You want to be unfaithful already?" Bruno asks amused and looks at his watch. "I'll arrange a meeting for you next weekend. You can meet him here or at your place. I'll be very busy the next few days starting tomorrow. Have to get up at five in the morning. It'll be a long day. I better go home now and get some sleep. Will you bring me to the door?"

They get up and head to the exit. Armando slings one arm around Bruno's waist and slips his hand into the jacket pocket in his usual quest for some money. But instead of banknotes, he touches a folded paper, pulls it out, and unfolds it in a flash. He sees the list of names with the name of Felipe Suárez on the right side marked with a cross. Immediately, he asks in a shrill voice and without a lisp, "Who is Felipe Suárez? You're going to see him now, aren't you? That's why you want to offload me onto this secretary of state! I knew it! I knew it!"

But before he starts howling and can tear up the paper, Bruno snaps it out of his hands, stuffs it back into his pocket, and snorts derisively, "You know nothing! Felipe Suárez is dead! Now shut your trap!"

Armando whimpers, "Dead? He is dead? Was he one of us? Who killed him? You? You killed him, didn't you? Yes, it was you! Tell me, just tell me!"

"I told you to shut up!" barks Bruno and tears his arm out of Armando's clutches. "You assume something that amounts to a load of rubbish! He's dead! It's over and done with! Water under the bridge. He wasn't one of us, as you put it. He was a filthy little cockroach who had stolen important information that affected my business most severely. He was the head of a ring of snitches and spies and had to be silenced. That's the way things go. You stick your nose into affairs that are none of your business, and - zap! - it is cut off! It's as simple as that and you better remember it."

Armando whines like a puppy, "Oh, my darling, I'm so worried about you. Don't play with fire!"

"Don't start to imitate my mother!" Bruno snaps louder than the pounding music. "I hate your parodies. By the way, your dress looks awful, your perfume stinks, and one of your fake tits has slipped out of your bra and hangs below your navel. And your whorish gold plastic shoes with high stiletto heels have been out of style for over twenty years. Let's get out of here!"

"You uncultured lout!" Armando bawls while fishing for the fake tit. "Insulting a fine lady like that!"

Outside Bruno tells Armando to wait, waves to the driver of a black sports car, and rushes over to him. The driver, a bulky, very muscular man gets out of his car, they shake hands and have a brief chat. Quickly they come to an agreement and the driver is given the list of names before he carries the heavy attaché case like a featherweight and puts it into the trunk of his car without any problems. Bruno hands him the wreath, has another brief chat with him, points over his shoulder with his thumb to Armando, and the driver nods.

Bruno returns to Armando "You better go home as well. My friend has agreed to give you a ride. Okay? I have to rush. I'll probably see you tomorrow. Wait for my call. Good night."

Abruptly he turns away, gets into his car and leaves the parking lot at high speed. Armando totters over to the black sports car.

"Hi, Cholo, how are you today?" he asks after settling in the passenger seat. The driver's hands clutch the steering wheel while he steers the car out of the parking lot.

"Hi, you old poof. How're you doing? What did you find out?" asks Cholo in a surprisingly soft and supple tone.

Armando shifts in his seat to feign excitement. He knows he doesn't have much to tell and fears Cholo's enormous strength and fits of rage. "What I have to tell you will launch you into orbit and cost you a pretty penny."

"Then get your tongue wagging already," answers Cholo calmly.

"Can I see some moola first?" teases Armando.

"No! You know our agreement. First the goods then the moola for what the goods are worth. So, what are the exciting news?" asks Cholo with a menacing overtone in his voice.

Armando knows what this slight change of tone means and bursts out, "Bruno wants to put me in touch with a state secretary, his friend and closest confidant in his business. He didn't mention the name of the state secretary, but for the coming weekend he will arrange a rendezvous for me. Then something really big should go down with this stallion, and I will bring you a lot more information. But the sensation is something completely different. Imagine,

Bruno told me that this Sánchez, no, wait a minute, Suárez, yes, that was his name, that he exposed this Suárez as the head of a conspiracy ring spying on his business and he killed him. I'm sure he must have drowned him because he said something about water under the bridge, but he didn't tell me which river that was."

Cholo is quiet for a moment before he gives Armando a quick, disdainful look. "Is that so? What else?"

Armando looks astonished. "That's it. It's enough, isn't it?"

On a bridge crossing a railway line near the Centro del Pueblo, Cholo slams hard on the brakes, stops the car, and says in a low menacing voice, "Listen, you stupid faggot. We've put you onto Bruno's tail to squeeze his balls for information not to suck them dry! You're just giving us information we already have, that are false or worth a donkey's fart! Get out! Piss off, *maricón!*"

Armando protests, "I can't get out right here in the middle of nowhere. You're supposed to drive me home."

Cholo repeats, "Get out and piss off!"

Armando whimpers, "No, I won't."

Cholo gets out, walks around the car, looks left and right to make sure there is nobody nearby and no cars are coming, rips open the passenger door, lifts Armando by his right arm out the car, grabs his behind, and tosses him like a full bag of garbage over the bridge railing.

Armando screams as he sails down head first. He crashes onto the rails twelve meters below the bridge and lies very still with his skull split open and a broken neck.

Cholo closes the passenger door calmly, gets back into the driver's seat and drives away without any haste.

Sweet Revenge

Monty sits in the passenger seat and directs Anabelle along the curvy roads of the central valley's southern mountainous terrain towards San Antonio. Their luggage stands on the backseat in preparation for Anabelle's flight home and Monty's return to Bahía Potrero.

Heavy rain is pouring down. The windshield wipers provide only brief moments of a hazy view of the road ahead through the splattering water masses. They pass low adobe houses, old style little groceries, modern mansions imbedded in carefully styled gardens and protected by mighty cast-iron picket fences, and a couple of shopping centres that don't fit into this landscape like the neon lit hamburger and pizza joints at every intersection.

At a fork in the road the traffic splits with most vehicles taking the road to the left. Anabelle follows the one to the right and can finally speed up a bit. She dashes into the next village almost missing the turn to San Antonio but takes it in the last second thanks to Monty pointing it out. The narrow, asphalted road leads uphill and they overcome a climb of over four hundred metres for the next ten kilometres until they reach their destination.

Anabelle spots Rico's car parked under a tree at the police station and comes to a stop behind it. She and Monty rush into the low building past the young auxiliary policeman Eduardo who stands by the door in his khaki-brown uniform, shiny boots, and peaked cap pulled down to his eyebrows. He plays with his new rubber truncheon and pays no attention to them.

They enter the guardroom the moment they can hear the captain of the rural police say to Rico, "I'm sure you're too late, Señor Comisario. A good friend of the deceased came here before six o'clock this morning and asked the guy on night duty about the location of the graveyard. He came to pay last respects to his friend, he said and to bury the coffin. He has done the job by now, I'm certain of that."

"Good morning, Anabelle, Monty. How are you?" greets Rico his friends. "Did you hear what the Capitán just said? An old friend of Felipe started the burial over three hours ago and probably has finished the job."

Monty nods. "I'm pleased to hear that Felipe had more friends than me alone. We bought a bouquet of flowers and would like to pay our last respects by decorating his grave. I also want to say a prayer and ask for his salvation. Only after my farewell will I be able to live in peace with the thought that he is no longer with us. Will you accompany us to the graveyard, Rico?"

"But of course," says Rico. "Unfortunately, Martha couldn't join me this morning. She feels a bit under the weather."

"I hope it wasn't the food and drink last night," expresses Anabelle her concern.

"Oh, no, not at all," he reassures her. "It's the stress of the past few days and realising that very little has changed in the past thirty years after reading some of the old reports. It must be very disheartening for an expectant woman to wonder what the future holds for her kids."

"I understand," agrees Anabelle. "It's the reason for millions of young people gathering every Friday protesting and demanding that much more has to be done to assure them of a future."

Rico goes to a window and looks outside. "We have to wait a little longer for the rain to let up before we can go to the cemetery."

He turns to the captain. "Although I'm not here in my official function of detective inspector but only as a mourner, could you tell me of any new insights in the Suárez case?"

"Oh, you aren't here in your official function?" gloats the captain. "Are you not in charge of the Suárez case any longer? I'm so sorry to hear that."

Rico knows the captain is lying but plays along instead of asking who informed him about his suspension. "Yes, Capitán, also in the private life of a detective inspector exist certain priorities. I've handed the Suárez case to a most capable colleague and taken four weeks' vacation to be with my wife and stand by her during the most difficult time of her pregnancy. It is our first child, you know?"

Suddenly the captain looks almost human when he beams a big smile and pumps Rico's hand. "My most sincere congratulations to your wife and you! I hope everything goes well and you will soon welcome a healthy strapping boy, your son into the family. I can remember my wife's first childbirth. Oh, how I suffered in those days. I think I suffered more than my wife. But after a while

I got used to it. After the birth of my sixth child I stopped the business in my butcher shop only for five minutes to share a beer with my employees. Yes, that's how it is. The human is an animal of habit."

"I can only agree with that sentiment," says Rico. "It is also a human habit to steer clear of unpleasant questions and if that isn't possible to avoid giving an answer. Therefore, I ask you once more if any new insights have emerged in the Suárez case that may result in the arrest of the killer."

The captain bloats his chest like a balloon. "Well, uh, Señor Ramírez, uh, of course, I cannot give you as a private person any information about the ongoing investigations conducted by the police and, uh, the OIJ. You are well aware of that, aren't you? But let me put it this way, we are following every lead and tip-off and the arrest of the perpetrator is imminent."

His voice dripping with sarcasm, Rico replies, "Thank you, Capitán. You've learned the Senior Policeman's Handbook by rote and memorised it very well."

All those present spend the next little while in silence and occasionally look out of the window. When the rain finally stops, Rico, Anabelle and Monty drive to the graveyard. The captain had pointed out that Felipe's intended burial site is on the slope near the eastern boundary, separate from the crypts and graves of 'honourably' deceased villagers.

Although the cemetery gate is wide open to drive through, they park their cars by the side of the road in a little bay set up for this purpose near the entrance.

Monty carries a huge bouquet of white lilies and together they walk uphill over the crunching gravel of the wide main path past old, whitewashed family tombs decorated with angels and simple graves with tombstones or cast-iron crosses.

Facing the open area without any graves, they have to turn left onto a narrow path where a luxurious black European sports car is parked between tall juniper bushes. A men's suit is hanging inside the car by the rear side window.

Along the way, a large flatbed cart blocks their passage. A sign on the side identifies it as belonging to the cemetery. Rico pushes the branches of a few bushes out of the way and they walk past.

Felipe's grave has to be somewhere around here. They look up and down the slope but can't see a fresh burial mound with bouquets of flowers or a freshly dug grave. About ten metres ahead of them, somewhat obscured by dense vegetation, the thin end of a simple spruce box protrudes from a mud hole.

"Is that a coffin?" asks Monty, puts his bouquet down on a patch of gras and walks slowly over the softened ground towards the box.

"That is a coffin!" he exclaims when he get closer. "If that is the way they bury people in this village, I'd rather fall overboard on the high seas and get eaten by sharks."

"Where is Felipe's friend and the gravedigger?" asks Rico

"In this heavy rain of the past few hours, they probably went to the pub and didn't give a damn about the coffin," presumes Monty.

When the three mourners stand at the end of the coffin that sticks out of the ground, Rico looks dumbfounded. "I don't understand. If this is the coffin with Felipe's remains, I wonder why it isn't in the ground yet. The captain assured me that digging the burial pit had been finished yesterday. I can only imagine that the heavy rain caused a mudslide and closed the pit partially. Perhaps the friend wanted to fix the pit this morning and got surprised by the cloudburst. In any case, now the grave site is filled with mud."

Anabelle remarks, "It's strange the pit was dug lengthwise along the slope and not at a ninety-degree angle to it. Makes no sense unless it was the intention of the coffin slowly sliding downhill and never to be found again." She looks at the end of the box and tries to read something written with a black marker. "Come here. There is something I can't decipher. It seems to be upside down."

The two men bend down and read, "..árez – San Anto.."

Rico whispers, "It is Felipe's coffin."

"That must be a very peculiar friend who came to bury him," voices Monty his outrage. "Takes off to the pub and lets Felipe's corpse do somersaults into a pool of mud."

"Oh, how awful!" exclaims Anabelle and points to the long side of the coffin facing some bushes. A hand sticks out of the soil seemingly waving farewell.

Rico has a look and warns, "It's possible the coffin broke open and the corpse is sliding out! Don't touch anything! I will call the captain and the gravedigger to help clear up this mess. It is best for you to stay away from the burial site."

He rushes down the path to the cemetery gate. Anabelle and Monty take several steps back. She says, "Come on, let's go to the car parked amongst the bushes and check it out. Perhaps we can find something out about Felipe's friend."

She opens the unlocked driver side door, sits down and checks the glove compartment. It contains a gold ballpoint pen, mint candies, and a road map but no clue about the car's owner. In the pockets of the suit hanging by the rear side window are a handkerchief and a folded piece of paper. It is the list of names including that of Felipe Suárez. She gets up and shows the list to Monty who opened the trunk and fiddles with the locks of an attaché case. He can't make any sense of the list but points to the little cross and the note 'elim.' next to Felipe's name and turns his attention once more to the case.

Anabelle returns the paper to the suit pocket. She will give Rico a tip to have the car forensically searched. She shuts the car door and returns to see how Monty is getting on with the case.

"Any luck yet?" she asks him.

"No, the left lock won't open."

She takes the case by the handle and puts it in an upright position. "Bloody hell, that case is heavy," she mutters.

Only the right lock snaps open when she presses the release lever. The left one remains firmly shut and won't budge however hard she presses and fiddles. The solid metal frame of the case's lid with only one lock open won't allow bending it to have a look inside. Monty wants to smash the stubborn lock with a rock but Anabelle stops him.

She says, "This is a German car and there is always a small toolkit somewhere for changing a flat tire."

"Why would you want a tool for changing a tire?" asks Monty.

"To open the case. I want to see what's in it."

"Aw, don't bother. It's just full of worthless papers to judge by the weight."

"Exactly, and I want to see some of these papers."

She pushes the case to one side and pulls up the cover for the spare wheel. Neatly in its proper slot and wrapped in a piece of cloth is what she has been looking for. She takes it out, unwraps the tools and picks the wrench for the wheel bolts. It has a flat end like a big screwdriver that might be perfect for breaking the lock. She hands the wrench to Monty and shows him how to apply it as she pulls the case closer. Monty pokes the wrench under the lock's lever and applies force. With a bang the lock snaps open. Anabelle lays the case down flat and lifts the lid. Both are speechless for a moment when they see the neatly bundled one-hundred-dollar bills, seven across and three deep.

"Worthless papers, what?" says Anabelle.

"That must be thousands," whispers Monty.

Anabelle sticks the fingers of one hand between the bundles, probes the layers and says, "No, it's much more than a few thousand! I wonder whose pile of money it is. Let's shut the case, put it and the tools back into their place and shut the trunk. If the owner of the car turns up, we could be in a lot of trouble."

Monty shoves her aside. "Are you crazy? That amount of money in the trunk of a car means in this country only one thing! It is illegal! Finders! Keepers! Should the owner turn up, I'll kill him with this wrench!" He grabs a couple of bank note bundles, laughs insanely, and shouts, "I'm rich! I'm rich!"

Anabelle recognises the typical reaction of a man or a woman for that matter who has never held a real amount of money is his or her hand. Monty's sudden change of behaviour is frightening. She experienced it once before when a good friend had had a big lottery win. He was a pleasant guy without any great ambitions in life who turned within a few hours into a monstrous pain in the butt, an extremely repulsive, repugnant piece of human garbage. He 'acquired' new friends giving lavish parties because all of his old friends had turned their backs on him in disgust. After a short time, he had no money left but a mountain of debt. He turned to criminal activities, was caught, found guilty of fraud, and ended up in prison. When he got out and was penniless, he remembered his old friends and begged them for help. Only a few stepped up to the plate and helped him, but they came and helped. Who would be there to help Monty? She could see him following an identical path as her former friend and also that there would be nobody to help him. There was only one way to cure him. He had to be brought back into reality, if necessary with brute force. She tears the two bundles of dollar bills out of his hand, tosses them back into the case, snaps it shut and quickly closes the one functioning lock.

"Now you'd like to get pissed and brag to the whole world that you're rich, huh?" Her sharp voice slashes through his dreams. "You have to stay calm! Especially now! The police will be here any minute. You want to boast in front of them as well?"

Monty wants to tear 'his' case away from her but she has an iron grip on the handle. He howls, "*Hija de puta!* You filthy whore! Give me my money!!"

He pushes Anabelle. She keeps her balance holding on to the heavy case and pushes back. In the ensuing scramble, Monty gets too close to the open trunk lid, slips up, and bangs his left eye into the trunk lid's corner. His howling changes from one instigated by greed to one caused by pain. He clutches his face with both hands and sinks to his knees.

"I'm sorry, Monty, but greed has its own reward. So there."

She takes off her jacket, drapes it over the case that she heaves out of the trunk. She had not expected the case to weigh over twenty kilogrammes, almost drops it and is ready to abandon her idea. But she continues, slams the trunk shut, slings her arms around the unwieldy but very valuable piece of luggage and takes the first step on the way to her car.

"Wait here!" she shouts at Monty and rushes as fast as her legs carry her and the heavy load to the cemetery gate. A couple of times she almost buckles under the weight but makes it. She unlocks the car and stows the case under the passenger seat just in time to see Rico return with the captain.

"Anabelle! Are you leaving us already?" asks Rico as he gets out of the car. "I guess it's almost time for you to think of your flight."

"No, I was thinking of driving onto the cemetery," she replies. "Monty is not in good shape. He has gone to pieces over the death of his friend and this awful failure of burying the remains."

"I understand. Don't let me stop you taking care of Monty."

She pauses, locks the car and says, "No, I've changed my mind. Now that you are here, I'll walk with you up there."

Monty still sits in his elegant suit on the soft sod at the back of the sports car. He is crying in anger, pain and disappointment. He mumbles to himself, "I'll show that bitch that you can't cheat a Castro that easily. Not even sharing the booty with me is unforgivable. Foreigners, fucking foreigners! You can't trust any of them! I'll go to the police, talk to the captain and have her arrested. I will tell the press and in court all about her fraudulent purchase of the rainforest with forged cheques and testify for the government people. This *puta madre* of a devious slag will rot in prison, yes, she will! There is still justice in our country!"

His confused mind games are interrupted by the crunching of gravel as Anabelle, Rico and the captain approach. He blinks at them with his bloodshot eye, gets up and wants to throw himself at this woman, this witch, this creature from hell, this foreigner, in order to at least strangle her. But in his blind zeal he trips over a rock and slams face first onto the gravel path at Rico's feet.

Rico helps the pitiful Monty to his feet. "Santa Maria! Has your friend's death affected you that much?"

"She has..." he starts to bleat with his voice drowned in tears but is cut short by Anabelle before he gets really started.

"Quiet, my dear, stay calm," she says, hugs him, and pats his head, "Come, let's sit in this car where you can cry on my shoulder."

She moves Monty and sits him down on the passenger seat. Watching the drama, even the captain is moved close to tears.

Monty gets himself under control and bleats, "Rico, I have to tell you something awful!"

Rico looks at his bloodshot eye and sees small scratch marks on the bridge of his nose. He gives Anabelle a critical look who smiles trustfully back at him.

"Yes, it's all right, Monty," he says and pats his shoulder. "Later you can tell me all about it. Cry your heart out now. Let out all your grief and you'll feel better soon. But the Capitán and I have to take care of your friend Felipe."

He knows Monty has not been overcome by grief for his dead friend. Something dramatic and very serious must have happened during his short absence. But later they will have time to discuss it in peace and quiet. He gives Anabelle another critical look in the hope to get more than a trusting smile and he does when she whispers, "You have to check the pockets of the suit in this car."

He gives her a brief nod and turns to the captain who blows his nose into a red hanky and says poignantly, "You know, I've seen many grieving people in my life but this young man takes the cake. I never knew that Felipe Suárez had such good friends."

"Yes, wonders never cease," agrees Rico. "Come, Capitán, let us go to the burial site. One of your subordinates called the gravedigger who should be here any moment. Then we'll have to see how we can clean up the mess."

He points to the narrow path and goes ahead of the captain.

Anabelle thinks it is not a good idea to stay within earshot of Rico and the captain, drags Monty out of the sports car, and says, "Let's go to my car. There's a bit of a surprise waiting for you."

When he resists, she grabs him forcefully by the arm and pushes him ahead of her down the gravel path. Once seated in her rental car, he howls, "Give me my money!!"

"Aw, shut up, you fool!" she says coldly. "You're sitting on it. You can have the whole bloody lot. I don't want a single dollar."

"Where? Where is it?" he screams and lifts himself out of the seat to look for it.

She wonders if this poor devil can still be helped and gives him a resigned look. "The case is under your seat."

Monty grabs below the seat, feels the valuable object, wants to pull it out, rummage through 'his' money, throw the bills into the air, and scream 'Rich, rich, rich at last!'

Anabelle watches his convulsive efforts mad with greed for money. "Don't bother! You can't get the case out that way. Now shut up and listen to me! Or do you need a broken nose to shake you out of your insanity?"

Monty squints at her, sees the edge of her hand inches away aimed at his nose, flinches and bangs his head against the door post.

Anabelle can't contain herself any longer and barks, "You rabid dog! Will you finally listen to what I have to tell you?"

Petrified, he looks at her with his face contorted in fear. "You don't want any of the money?"

An uncontrollable anger boils up in Anabelle. She would like to hit him square in the face. What an imbecile! How can he assume that she wants any of the money? "No, I don't want any of that filthy lucre! I don't want or need it! How could I get it out of the country and then declare it to customs back home? It is all yours and your family's! Be happy with it, you fool!"

Realising the exact state of affairs, he relaxes and begins to cry in shame and stutters, "I... I'm so sorry about everything."

He wants to lean over to her and put his head on her shoulder but still sickened by his behaviour she pushes him away. "Are you ready to listen?" He nods and wipes snot from his nose adding a couple of cross stripes to the pinstripes on the sleeve of his elegant suit.

Looking disgusted she continues, "We have to get cartons for you to get away with the loot. We'll buy shirts, underwear, socks and that kind of stuff to fill the cartons, split the money in equal parts and hide it among those goods. You have to add a note addressed to your family members explaining not to spend the money right away. We wrap the cartons in sturdy packaging paper and send these parcels by courier to whoever you choose to receive one."

Anabelle looks at him almost pleadingly in the hope that he listened and understood everything she said because he is staring out the window in disbelief as if in a dream.

And he is dreaming of what he can do with all the money that is all his although he has no idea how much it is. He will be able to dress his wife and children properly, build a solid house on his parcel of land near the beach, buy machinery and tools and become a proper hacendado, a big land owner. "How much money do you think is in that case?" he asks.

Anabelle shrugs. "I don't know. I have never seen so much money in one heap. Judging by the weight of the case, it's probably more than a million dollars."

Monty turns pale and looks ready to faint. "That much? I thought it was perhaps a hundred thousand."

"That would have been a few thick bundles of bills. You have to learn how to take care of that amount. Split it amongst your family members, brothers and sisters. Then it won't raise suspicion."

"I was going to give them some of it anyway but now... how much should I give each one of them? What do you think?"

"That's up to you. You can decide whatever you think is best when we pack the parcels. I suggest we go to the graveside to see what's going on and if that shabbily dressed man who walked into the cemetery a minute ago is the gravedigger."

They get out of the car. Although Anabelle locks it and checks the four door handles and the hatchback, Monty is not happy about leaving his value object unguarded.

He walks around the car nervously looking for a way to prevent it from getting stolen. He thinks of taking off the steering wheel but that would take too long, and he would need tools he does not have. He heard about disabling a car by removing the distributor arm, but with this Japanese car, he would not know its location. Letting the air out of one tyre would stop anyone from driving away with the car but it would not stop a thief from breaking in and stealing his riches.

Anabelle snaps at him, "Come on already! You're wasting time. That old guy passing the car is almost at the grave."

Mentioning the grave gives him an idea. "Listen, can you drive the car into the cemetery to a spot where I can keep an eye on it?"

"Whatever next?" she asks but gets into the car and speeds up the gravel path until she can see Rico and the captain.

194

Monty has to run along the path. Out of breath he reaches Anabelle just in time for both of them to see Rico get into a tussle with the captain who looks panic stricken and wants to get away.

Anabelle and Monty rush along the narrow path to the burial site to find out what is going on. As they get closer, they hear Rico shout, "Nonsense! There is no witchcraft and no Dark Angel. In this broken coffin are the remains of a brutally murdered man. We have to move it carefully and I expect you to lend a hand."

"No!" bleats the captain. "I'm not going to touch a broken coffin with diseases lurking inside that could kill all of us."

The situation is exacerbated when they are approached from behind by the shabbily dressed old man who snickers about their kerfuffle. They spin around and the captain looks ready to soil his pants. Now the old guy laughs out loud. Rico turns to him. "Who in the devil's name are you and what are you laughing about?"

"I'm Humberto, the gravedigger" says the man, takes out a cigarette, lights up, takes a puff, and blows the smoke in the captain's face. "I'm laughing about you two nitwits. There is no disease lurking in the coffin and it isn't broken."

"But a hand sticks out," says Rico. "Have a look. The coffin broke open."

Humberto looks at the coffin's side. "Are you guys blind? The coffin isn't broken. That hand sticks out of the mud. It's probably the hand of the arrogant bastard that came to bury his friend. Chased me out of the cemetery, my place of work. Can you believe that?"

"What?" ask Rico and the captain in unison and Rico continues, "Why are you so sure the coffin didn't break open?"

"Have a proper look at it. These coffins are sturdy and don't break from sliding into a pool of mud," says Humberto, takes a puff and flicks the cigarette away. "I can pull it out with a tool I have for such a job on my cart. Stand aside. I don't need your help."

He goes past Anabelle and Monty, acknowledges them with a nod, picks up a tool consisting of a long steel bar, a winch with a steel rope, and a large clamp. He returns to the burial site. The mourners and the captain stand aside and watch him put the clamp around the narrow end of the coffin sticking out of the ground. He attaches the rope to it that passes through the mechanical winch, pushes the steel bar into the ground a few metres away from the pit, and starts to move the winch lever to and fro. Slowly the rope tightens and starts to pull the coffin bit by bit out and up the slope. Before the coffin is removed to its full length and secured, the mourners look at what the pit reveals.

Horrified they pull back at the sight of a man's face with its open mouth filled with mud. The sharp bottom edge of the coffin dislocated the nose and scraped skin off the forehead. The corpse holds a shovel in his right hand while his left sticks out of the mud.

Humberto secures the coffin, takes one look into the pit and grumbles, "Told you so. I advised him to put the coffin on the slope below the pit. He didn't listen and put the coffin up here in the hope of it sliding in by itself. The cloudburst this morning did it for him while he was in the pit trying to clear out some of the mud that washed in during the night. That's what you get for not listening."

"Do you know this man?" asks Rico.

"No," says Humberto, "but I've seen him a couple of times. About a week ago he seemed to inspect Felipe's house and a day later he had a meal in the Linda Vista pub."

Rico gets excited. "Hang on everybody. I'll be right back."

He rushes down the path to his car parked at the gate and returns clutching his cell phone in one hand and a plastic bag in the other. He climbs into the pit. Carefully he removes dirt off the fingers and palm of the dead man's hand, takes some foils out the bag and takes the prints. Humberto gives him a hand to get out of the pit. Rico calls his colleague Gus on the phone.

"Hello, Gus, it's Rico. How are you? Uh-huh. Listen, I'm in San Antonio. What? No, no, I'm here for the funeral. It went sideways. No, the coffin wasn't buried but it slid into the pit and looks as if it killed the guy who tried to bury it. I took this guy's finger and palm prints. Can you send someone up here on the double. What? No, I have a suspicion. I want you to match the prints with the partials found in the lab. Yes, indeed. Could be. The corpse has the figure to have been involved. Okay? Great! I'll wait for you."

He ends the call and the captain gets all curious. "What was that all about? Why did you take the prints? I thought..."

Rico cuts him off, "I can't tell you anything, Capitán. I'm not here in any official function. You have to wait for my colleague who may tell you something in his OIJ function if he feels that it's safe to do so. The case is now in the hands of the OIJ. Okay?"

The captain gets grumpy. "But surely you..."

"No, Capitán, I can't tell you anything for a number of reasons. I'm here as a private citizen helping the OIJ in its enquiry. That's it. You should return to the station. Duty calls, but I can't give you a ride. I have to stay and wait for the OIJ officer."

The captain turns to Anabelle but before he can ask her to give him a ride, she waves him off. Sloughed off like that by a tourist and a private citizen, he wants to say something, thinks better of it, and slowly walks away.

Rico whispers to Anabelle, "You said earlier that I should check the suit in that black sports car. Did you find papers that identify the dead guy in the pit?"

"No, nothing to identify the owner of the car. But there's a paper in a suit pocket that could help you with your enquiries."

"Thanks, I'll have a look." Rico turns to Humberto. "What are you going to do about burying the coffin?"

"Well, that's a good question. Lots of stuff has to be done."

"Like what?"

"First the corpse has to be got out of the pit. I guess the OIJ wants it and should come to help me. I can't do that alone."

"Sure, I'll let the OIJ know to send the forensic team. Don't change anything. Leave the coffin where it is now."

"Okay, but can't I shore up the pit? It should be safe for the team to get into it."

"No, leave it as it is. The forensic guys know what to do. They'll be done by early afternoon and then you can finish your job."

"Then I'll look for a better burial ground that isn't on a slope and dig a new pit."

Monty butts in, "What about our bouquet? And over there in the high grass I saw a wreath. It was probably supposed to be put on the grave. Would you do that?"

"Leave it to me. I'll take care of it. Back at my house I have some wooden crosses. I'll put one on his grave. It'll look nice."

Monty goes to the coffin, puts a hand on it and kneels to say his prayer. Rico calls the OIJ general number on his phone to inform them of having found an unidentified corpse in San Antonio and the need for a forensic team to investigate it. When the woman asks who is calling, he gives a fake name and ends the call. Then he goes with Anabelle to the black sports car. Meticulously he searches the vehicle for any identification like a driver's licence or car registration but finds nothing. He takes the suit and digs through the pockets. He finds nothing besides a hanky and the folded paper, tosses the suit onto the backseat of the car, and unfolds the sheet.

He reads the list of names and says to Anabelle with a low voice, "This is a hit list. My name is right at the bottom. The names of Felipe's fiancée and his aunt are on there as well. But your and Monty's names are not. That means nobody has become aware of your rainforest sting. But I think I should accompany you to the airport for your safety. I still have my badge and could pretend to deport you. That would result in a re-entry ban but you'd get out of the country and home alive."

"Aw, come on, Rico," expresses Anabelle her doubts. "It can't be that bad. This is not a fascist dictatorship."

"True, and it doesn't need to be," says Rico. "As a result of more than sixty years of conditioning the general public has gone fast asleep and believes that Costa Rica is the land of peace. They are oblivious to what is going on in our country.

"So, the criminal elements in our government and its administration can satisfy their greed with impunity. That doesn't mean that every government official is a criminal. Far from it. There are a lot of good, honest people who'd go public with any attempt of bribing them. But if you told them about their criminal colleagues, they'd deny it. They'd even deny that one of our former presidents, Carazo, made millions supplying arms to the contras during the Nicaragua conflict or that another one, Monge rifled the national emergency fund and put the millions of dollars in his pocket. Also, our Nobel prize winner Arías is still under investigation for ceding control of a large national park to some Canadian gold diggers in return for a hefty baksheesh. The only one that was ever prosecuted for corruption was the latest one, Calderón. He pocketed over half a million dollars in bribes from a Finnish medical supply company. But what did he get for his crime? Three years of house arrest and he wasn't even banned from running again for the presidency.

"As far as your deal is concerned, just think that over eighty-five percent of our rainforests have been destroyed. Many of the small clumps of rainforest left are owned by rich gringos who live cloistered in their forest enclaves and pretend that the entire country is full of beautiful flora and wildlife to attract tourists who pay top-dollar to see a monkey and a parrot. That's it. As you said, our government is not a fascist dictatorship but you have to beware of the criminals in business, government and administration. None of them will shy away from having anyone standing in their way bumped off, including foreign visitors."

Rico has hardly finished his monologue when they can hear a car pulling up at the cemetery gate. Moments later Gus Goicoechea comes trotting up the gravel path. Rico does the introductions. He shows Gus the clear plastic bag with the finger and palm prints he took and Gus takes a small plastic envelope from his shirt pocket with the partial prints. Carefully he takes the foils out of both envelopes. He puts them on top of each other and holds them up to the light. With bated breath he shifts them to match the lines of the partials with the complete ones.

He says, "Yes, Rico! They match perfectly. The guy who was killed by a coffin was the killer of Felipe Suárez."

Monty pipes in, "Did I hear that right? The dead guy is the killer of Felipe? Then the villagers were right when they called my friend the Dark Angel. He got his sweet revenge!"

Rico waves him off. "Don't promote superstition, Monty. It was an accident. The guy didn't heed the gravedigger's advice."

Gus asks, "Can I see that son of bitch? I'm familiar with many of these underworld types and may know him."

"Of course," says Rico and holds out the list of names. "But first have a look at this hitlist. It includes a minister, a lawyer, three top bureaucrats, two case witnesses and me as well. All of them, including myself, seem to be somehow linked to Felipe Suárez."

Gus skims the list of names quickly. "I think I'm going to shit a brick. This case draws much wider circles and is bigger than anyone could have imagined. If the people on the list are killed, we'd have to investigate a bloodbath of immense proportions. But we can use this list to nail the bastards that want to have them killed. I suggest you take out a private investigator license and interview each one of the people on the list in that new capacity. You'll have the four weeks of your enforced vacation to solve the case. I can help you. My son hacked the Public Security Ministry's computer system and found a list of all the passwords. We'll have no more exclusions from accessing all the information we need. Okay?"

"Hmm, yes," says Rico in a very pensive mood, "now let's look at the corpse."

Gus rolls up the plastic envelopes containing the fingerprints and sticks them into his shirt pocket. He walks around the burial pit to have a good look at the corpse's face. He goes down into the pit, scrapes some of the mud off the dead man's chest, sticks his fingers into the shirt pocket and pulls out a small plastic pouch. He flips it open and gives a driver's licence the size of a credit card, the car registration and insurance in the name of the Ministry of Natural Resources a brief look. Then he proceeds to check the trouser pockets, finds a car key and a thin wallet. He reaches up to hand all items to Rico and is helped to get out of the pit. Standing next to Rico, he looks over his shoulder to see what is in the wallet. There are two more driver's licenses and the card identifying him as a Costa Rican citizen. All four cards bear different names but the same photo.

"We got a proper oddball here. Do any of the names mean anything to you, Gus? Did you recognise him?"

"No, although he looks oddly familiar. It's difficult to say with his smashed nose. I seem to remember his face with a full beard a few years back. The different identity cards are real as far as I can see. They are proof that he must have had direct contact with very influential bureaucrats and the ministry listed on the car registration. He's a hired killer, I'm sure."

"Might he be a member of the Rapid Reaction Force?"

"Definitely not. If he was, he wouldn't have carried these licences and identification cards but only an RRF badge. I should take care of these cards. If the forensic team finds them, they'll only hand them to our boss who'll let them disappear."

Rico hands the citizen card, driver licenses and wallet to Gus. "So, what're you going to do now?"

"Since I'm out of the office, I might as well go to the site of a smashed corpse on the railway line near the Centro del Pueblo. A train passed over it and mangled it. It's a transvestite, some skinny young man in a woman's dress. May have committed suicide jumping off the bridge or was flung over the railing. Then I'll go back to the office, upload the fingerprints and check every database I can access now."

"Be careful, Gus. Every unauthorised access is reported."

"Not to worry. I installed a virtual private network and my unauthorised access can't be traced back to me. It could have come from anywhere."

"Good luck. I'll think about your idea of getting a private investigator's licence. Keep me up to date, will ya?"

"Of course! Don't forget you are on the hitlist. Take extra care and grow some eyes in the back of your head. I'll be in touch."

Gus leaves and Rico turns to Anabelle holding out the car key for the black sports car as well as the registration and insurance. "Would you like to drive an expensive imported car with government license plates? No cop would ever dare to give you a ticket even if you park in a no-stopping zone."

"That's very tempting, Rico. But what about the rental?"

"Leave it here. Let the air out of one tyre and call the rental company to pick it up. Problem solved."

"Are you sure?"

"Yes, as long as they are informed that you didn't steal the car."

"What are you going to do now?"

"I'll wait for the forensic team to clue them in and then I want to interview the first person on the hitlist."

"Who's that?"

"It's the murder victim's fiancée. She's still in hospital."

Anabelle takes the car key and Rico goes to the cemetery gate.

As they approach the sports car, Monty voices his concern. "It's not a good idea to drive that car. If the guy who drove it was a hired killer, then the guys who hired him may recognise it. When they see you driving it, they'll send somebody to bump both of us off."

"That's a fair point," answers Anabelle, thinks it over for a moment and then rejects his concern. "Don't worry. All we'll do is go to a supermarket to get cartons, the clothes for your family and relatives, pack the cartons, take them to a courier company and leave for the airport. Then you can take a taxi home and I have to wait for my flight to take off. That's all."

Reluctantly he agrees with her and moves their luggage and his value object, the attaché case into the trunk of the sports car. He presses a key on the pin of the right front tyre's valve and lets the air out. While he is busy, she takes six bundles of dollar bills out of the case and tells him to wait a moment. She goes down the gravel path to see Rico who sits in his car reading the hitlist.

Seeing her, he lowers the window and asks, "What's the matter? Is something wrong with the car?"

"No, the car seems to be in good shape," says Anabelle and holds the bundles of dollar bills out to him. "But look what I found in the trunk hidden beside the spare wheel. You should take it as evidence or to enhance your pension fund."

"I can't take that."

"Of course, you can. It belonged to the killer and now it's yours. Nobody will be any the wiser when you use it as you see fit."

He takes the bundles, stashes them in the glove compartment, and asks, "Is Monty aware of your find?"

"No, he is busy letting air out of a tyre. It's only you and me who know about it and I'll be gone later today."

Rico ponders the situation. "I can't use that booty for myself but I know someone who will be in dire need of it."

"Well, that settles it. You take good care of yourself and give my warmest regards to Martha. She really opened my eyes. I'll be going home a completely different person. I'm very grateful to her."

"Thanks, I'll give her your regards. Don't forget us. Drop us a line to let us know how your report was received."

"I will, Rico. Bye-bye."

She rushes back to the sports car, tells Monty to get in, sits in the driver's seat, adjusts it and the rear-view mirrors, starts the engine, and they leave the cemetery on a ride as smooth as silk.
***

Edwin, the police captain left the cemetery in a huff. There were two people with cars and neither one of them wanted to give him a ride back to the police station. He had recognised the dead man in the burial pit who is known to his confidants as Cholo. His contacts had to be informed about the tragic development. Having to walk the two kilometres to the station had caused an unnecessary delay and he got angrier with every step he had to take.

As soon as he gets to the station he chases his loitering underlings out of the guardroom to phone his contacts in relative peace and quiet. He makes eight calls to bureaucrats and friends in the government to inform them about Cholo's unfortunate demise and also that this suspended detective inspector Ramírez is against all orders mixing it up again together with a strange couple of a foreign woman and her lover boy of national origin. Action should be taken immediately to forestall any further developments that could blow the lid off his friends and associates' clandestine operation he heard about. Having done his duty, he relaxes noticeably and thinks of the reward he may receive.

His phone calls raise the level of panic in various government departments to new heights. It has already been discovered that the Investment Corporation, the Ministry of Natural Resources and the Economy Ministry had been duped by a fraudster who was probably a journalist. The woman had bought a large area of rainforest in the Barra del Colorado Wildlife Refuge the day before

202

with cheques that were stolen and not even covered, as the owner of the account, a certain Oduber Madrigal, had credibly assured. The woman had received property papers and a logging license for her fraudulent efforts.

These documents have to be recovered under all circumstances. This woman, who went by the alias Elisabeth Berndorf and her, judging by his accent, local advisor named José Antonio Castillo Montalban de Gallego, must be arrested and handed over to the Rapid Reaction Force for further handling of this delicate matter.

The major blame for this disaster is heaped on Roberto Zuñiga for not following proper due diligence procedures to ascertain the credibility of a potential investor in the country's natural resources. He could have phoned the Economic Attaché at the Swiss Embassy who would have assured him within five minutes that the financial brokerage company stated on the female scammer's business card does not exist, is purely fictitious.

The Minister for Public Security is called in this matter to determine who these fraudsters are. An intensive search of the migratory files determines according to all known criteria of gender, origin, nationality, profession, and language there is only one woman fitting that bill, a certain Anabelle Bouchard who is due to leave the country today.

So, there is an excellent chance to arrest her at the airport or any border crossing once all the relevant bodies have been informed. The case of José Antonio Castillo Montalban de Gallego required a search of all citizen registers until it is determined that such a person has never existed and does not exist. But not to worry, assures the Minister of Public Security, there are the closed-circuit videos with the exact date and time of the visits of the corresponding buildings and a good still shot of the faces of these swindlers can surely be found and then distributed nationwide.

Rodrigo is on high alert despite all these assurances. He worries about the whereabouts of the attaché case with over two million dollars in cash.

He calls Bruno and learns that he had given not only the wreath and the list but also the attaché case containing the drug money to Cholo with the order to finish the burial of Felipe Suárez and to place the case in Rico Ramírez's house. That casts a new light on the case and he orders a couple of his subordinates to drive to San Antonio to retrieve Cholo's black sports car and one other guy to search Cholo's apartment for the attaché case.

After a tense thirty minutes, he receives scary bad news. The sports car was not found near or on the cemetery of San Antonio but in its place stood a white vehicle with a flat tyre, which according to its licence plate was a rental of a company operating exclusively at San José's international airport.

The black sports car was used by a woman and her escort according to the gravedigger Humberto. Rodrigo gets to hear as well about Rico Ramírez who was not 'mixing it up', as the captain had claimed, but was at the cemetery only as a mourner of the Felipe Suárez funeral and cooperating with the OIJ's forensic team as a private citizen.

The next phone call causes him severe heart palpitations when he is informed that the attaché case was not found in Cholo's abode. Where is that damn case? It has to be found. With any luck the securely locked case is still in the sports car.

He sends out an alert to all police forces and the Rapid Reaction Force to find that car and arrest any and all occupants for their illegitimate use of a government registered vehicle.

Nervously he paces around in his office and curses these developments of the day. Not only will it be noticed that the case had gone missing out of the OIJ's evidence room, but also Ramírez cannot be accused of going against orders of his suspension or, for that matter, having stolen the case and storing it in his home.

What a disastrous day!

Farewell to Paradise

The black sports car handled really well on the curvy roads out of San Antonio and Anabelle turned into a bit of a race driver. At full speed she drove into the parking lot of the first shopping centre they reach, parked the car, got one bundle of dollar bills out of the case, locked the doors and double locked the trunk.

Inside the centre they found all the shops for their purchases. The cashiers were happy to accept dollars for payment of the goods of cartons, sticky tape, wrapping paper, underwear, socks, shirts, dresses, and shoes as well as some jewellery and watches. They pushed the overloaded shopping cart into the parking lot, dropped all the goods into the trunk, and Anabelle moved the car to a secluded spot where they filled eight cartons. Hastily they packed everything with Monty not paying attention to how much money he put in each carton as long as the biggest amount went into the one for his wife. But he did not write a short note advising the recipients not to spend any of the money for a couple of months until the anticipated search for it had cooled down.

For himself he kept fifteen of the dollar bills, wrapped the parcels properly and wrote the names and addresses of the recipients on it. All done with that task most parcels didn't fit into the trunk and they put them on the narrow back seats. Monty wanted to keep the empty attaché case but Anabelle insisted he discard it in one of the large rubbish bins. Then they were on their way to a courier company. It took them a while to find one in the San José downtown area near the central bus station and carried the parcels inside.

The clerk is suspicious and wants to know what all these parcels contain addressed to people in various villages and towns. Before Monty can give a longwinded explanation that would be exposed as a lie, Anabelle shows her passport and says, "It's clothing and shoes for my friend's extended family. One of his sisters is getting married and there will be a big get together. Since I have to fly home today and can't join in the festivity, I thought of getting nice clothes for everybody to look their best."

"Oh, they are so lucky. Did you buy all of it?"

"Yes, and I gave my friend some money to buy wine and beer. It's going to be a great fiesta."

The clerk is satisfied, asks no more questions and finishes the job of putting the parcels away for next day dispatch. He is not even surprised when Monty pays with a couple of large dollar bills. He just looks at Anabelle and wishes that this apparently rich woman would ladle out some money for him.

Anabelle and Monty have a quick bite to eat in a nearby restaurant and are on their way to the airport. She drives into the long-term parking lot. When she wants to pay the required deposit, the attendant just asks for her flight number and the government department's car registration. She shows him the papers, he jots Ministry of Natural Resources on a piece of paper, stamps it, tells her to put it on the dashboard and waves her through.

Inside the airport terminal building she goes to the counter of the car rental company, hands over her rental contract and explains that she had a flat tyre. The car is inside the cemetery confines of San Antonio and is otherwise in good shape. No accident to report. After a lot of questions she has to pay an extra fee for the flat tyre and for having the car picked up. She settles the bill and is finally ready to check into her flight.

She did not notice that a young female employees at the car rental counter checked a computer terminal and saw a slightly blurry but well recognisable video still shot of her taken by one of the security cameras in a ministry building. The woman calls the number of the Rapid Reaction Force underneath the photo.

Anabelle goes with Monty to the airline counter area. Looking at him, she wonders if she will ever see him again. She got to know him as a 'big boy' who trundled through life without a concrete plan, without a future. During the few days of their trip, she recognised him is a smart guy who in many ways would have the talent to bring about change in his country but she doubts he will ever break the matrix of his cultural and social environment.

She sees him now as a good friend who has a future, if he uses his money well. But how will all that money on its way to his family and relatives going to change him? Putting all these thoughts aside, she says to him, "This is the place to say good-bye, Monty. I have to check in and go through passport control. Let us part here and go our separate ways. I hate long emotional farewells. Okay?"

Monty drops the bag with his regular clothes and gives Anabelle a long, firm hug. "You're something else, Anabelle. I'll never forget you as long as I live. Have a good flight. *Vaya con dios!*"

She looks at him with tears in her eyes, abruptly turns away and goes to the airline counter where she presents her ticket and puts her backpack on the conveyor belt. It is dutifully tagged with its destination Zürich, Switzerland. She gets her boarding pass, an exit form to fill in, and her passport. While she puts the documents in her handbag, a guy with a crew cut, sunglasses, his checker shirt hanging over his jeans walks up beside her and asks if that is her luggage on the conveyor belt. She confirms it, he nods to another identically dressed guy who grabs the backpack and rips it open. Against her vehement protest he shows her briefly a plastic identity card and mutters something about airport security and a bomb threat. The airline employees watch respectfully and Anabelle helplessly how her personal belongings are thrown to the floor, searched and stuffed back into the backpack that is kicked onto the conveyor belt.

Monty almost faints knowing exactly that these thugs are members of the Rapid Reaction Force. He sees them grab Anabelle by her arms and drag her away down a stairway against her vociferous protest. He thinks he hears her cry, "Run, Monty, run!"

It takes him a moment to react, looks around for any other thugs in his vicinity, picks up his bag, and walks slowly to a staircase going upstairs. As soon as he reaches the first step, he scurries up like a cat in flight. He looks for the bar, sits down in the dark corner at the end of it and orders a beer. Before he takes the first sip, he notices two thugs coming out of the gents toilet. They shrug and give a signal to somebody he can't see. Instinctively he knows they are looking for him and he is still dressed the same as he was when he and Anabelle pulled off their caper. Monty thinks of Don Oduber's warning of the perfectly functioning and deadly system of detecting and silencing opponents of the oligarchs. With over two million dollars of their money in his possession he must surely be counted as one of the most obnoxious adversaries.

He realises how wise Anabelle's advice was to split the vast amount of money into manageable lots distributed over eight parcels. At best only one or two small lots of the money will be found by pure happenstance. On the other hand, it won't make any difference to the Rapid Reaction Force how much money they will find. They will beat all of it out of him with torture and let him disappear without a trace. The thought of how he will be killed and thrown to the sharks puts extra pressure on his bladder. He looks around for any of the thugs, sees his way clear, grabs his bag and sneaks off to the gent's toilet. In a cubicle, he gets out of his suit, shirt and tie and puts on his usual attire of loose shirt, jeans and cowboy boots that he carried in the plastic bag. By the sinks he finds a filthy sombrero, puts it on and pulls it deep over his forehead. He looks into the mirror and sees the Monty of old who has little if anything in common with Señor Castillo Montalban who took part in the rainforest sting. He digs into the bag and takes his amulet and the money out of the suit pockets.

The garbage container by the door is lined with a blue plastic bag. He pulls it out, stuffs suit, shirt, tie and shoes into it and slings a knot into the top of the bag. The cleaning staff will not inspect the full bag and simply toss it on the refuse cart. Relieved to be rid of the attire that made him easily recognisable as one of the wanted culprits, he steps out, sits down by the bar and drinks his beer.
***

Anabelle was taken down to one of the holding cells in the basement. Three guys subject her to a strip search, check brutally every orifice and slam her onto a chair. When she protests and demands to see the French ambassador, one guy takes a still shot photo from his shirt pocket that shows her face. He grins but doesn't say anything. Her cell phone is taken apart and the battery removed. Also her two cameras are taken apart. The film from the single lens reflex camera is removed. One guy looks for the memory chip in the digital camera. He asks where it and all her films are. When she says in Switzerland, he gives her backhander and drops the camera on the floor. In one of her trouser pockets he finds the small digital voice recorder. He can't get it to replay the recordings or erase what is recorded. He drops it on the floor, stomps on it and breaks it into little pieces. At last she is allowed to put her clothes on again. They check their watches. It is a couple of hours to go until her flight departure. They leave and slam the cell door shut.
***

Monty finished the first beer and wants to order another one. Listlessly he looks at the empty glass. He knows that he should keep a clear head if he wants to get away alive and go home. He wishes he knew how to drive a car. If he did, he could go to the parking lot, get into the sports car and drive away. But he does not know, has never driven a car in his life. The only way out of here is by taxi or perhaps by bus. He has no idea when or if busses to Guanacaste stop at the airport. He could go back to that dingy hotel in San José and hide there for a couple of days. He discards the idea he would have considered seriously without all that money in his pocket. So, he decides to go by taxi. Slowly he gets up and walks to the staircase. Cautiously he looks into the hall, cannot see any of the guys in checker shirt and jeans, goes downstairs, crosses the hall with his head held low, and exits to stand in line for a taxi.

The taxi marshal asks him where he wants to go. When he says Bahía Potrero in Guanacaste, he is told to go across the street to the long-distance taxi stand. But there is no taxi waiting. He sits down on one of the benches. The heat is getting to him and he takes off the sombrero to wipe the sweat off his forehead. At that moment the young woman from the car rental company steps outside to have a smoke, sees that lonely figure sitting on a bench waiting for a taxi and wiping his face. She recognises him as the other culprit shown as a wanted person on her computer screen, rushes inside, calls the RRF number, and provides details of the man's whereabouts.

A moment later a car stops in front of Monty. It is not marked as a taxi but the driver asks if he is waiting for a long-distance ride. Monty confirms it and asks him if his car is a taxi. The river confirms it and Monty wants to know how much it would cost to go to Bahía Potrero. He is told the fixed price is two hundred thousand colones. That is a steep price of over three hundred twenty-five dollars, but he agrees and asks if he can pay in dollars. Absolutely, he is told, pays the price and gets into the car.

The driver is quite a jovial guy and asks what Monty was doing at the airport. So, he tells him that a friend was returning home to Switzerland and that they had been in town for the funeral of another friend. The driver starts telling him some anecdotes while he drives along at the prescribed sedate speed of eighty kilometres an hour.

They follow the old Highway 1, not the new speedy Highway 27 to the Pacific coast that would be considerably faster. Since they are going at a steady speed and Monty is distracted by the driver's stories and anecdotes, he has not noticed the trailing yellow car.

When they pass a greasy spoon along the highway, the driver suggests taking a break to have a piss and then getting something to eat. Monty agrees and he and the driver stand above a cliff relieving themselves.

The yellow car rolls silently past them, stops, a burly guy gets out holding a cosh, sneaks up behind Monty and whacks him. Monty collapses and the driver goes through his pockets. He finds the money and Monty's identity card. He pockets the money and stuffs the card back into the pocket. The burly guy and the driver roll Monty's limp body with a few kicks to the edge of the cliff and drop it down. Their job done, they get into their cars. The guy in the yellow car drives back in the direction of San José and the fake taxi towards Alajuela.

***

The time has come for Anabelle's flight to take off. She is taken out of the cell. Her handbag relieved of any remaining money and the cameras are hung around her neck. Zip tie handcuffs are put on her wrists and duct tape is stuck over her mouth. She is dragged along a tunnel to an airfield exit, the waiting airplane and up the stairs that have been pushed to the airplane especially for her.

Inside, the flight crew, informed about the late arrival, doesn't question or protest the treatment of their passenger. They stand aside and a stewardess points to a seat in the last row of the business class. Anabelle has problems breathing, which is noticed by the crew but nobody dares to touch her and remove the duct tape.

A passenger on the other side of the aisle protests the treatment of this woman and is told by one of the goons that brought her onto the plane to shut up or he would get the same treatment.

The man rips out his diplomatic passport. He gets up and shouts at the three goons that this display of harsh and unwarranted treatment of an international airline passenger will have most serious repercussions for this land of alleged peace and friendship.

The purser of the crew intervenes and asks the diplomat to sit down and be quiet otherwise he will be ejected. The diplomat asks the purser calmly for his name and rank, tells him in no uncertain terms that he and the entire crew including the captain will be part of an official government enquiry in Spain into this unacceptable treatment of a female passenger. He demands to have the zip ties and duct tape removed since the airplane is Spanish territory.

The airplane captain comes out of the cockpit and explains laconically that the rule of Spanish territory applies only once the airplane has taken off. He wants the name and position of the diplomat and promises to have him arrested upon arrival in Madrid for an unnecessary delay of the flight.

And so the shouting match between several Spaniards continues until one of the goons tries to punch the diplomat. The other two goons hold him back and they leave the plane, which is finally ready for take-off.

The diplomat sits down next to Anabelle and against the protest of a stewardess peels off the duct tape and removes the zip tie cuffs. When the diplomat asks her, what the reason for such treatment was, she begins to tell him the entire story of the lies, hypocrisy and blatant pretence she experienced as well as the environmental destruction and the little pockets of indescribable beauty of nature that serve to support the lie of the entire country's environmental protection. He is shocked and wonders why the embassy and consular staff don't know anything about this state of affairs.
***

The fake taxi has arrived in Alajuela and stops in front of a mansion. The driver goes to the house, rings the bell and Bruno opens the door. They have a brief chat, the driver takes the bundle of banknotes out of his pocket, and hands it over. Judging by Bruno's expression, he is not impressed and asks if that is all. That is confirmed, Bruno peels two banknotes off the bundle, hands the money to the driver and shuts the door. A bit peeved about the small payout, the driver curses under his breath and swears to get Bruno a payback when the opportune moment for such action arrives.

Nothing Special to Report

Shortly after Anabelle and Monty had left San Antonio, Rico did the responsible citizen's duty of helping the OIJ forensic team and detective inspector Omar with a statement about detective inspector Gus Goicoechea's investigation. He assured Omar that he was not there in an official function but only as a mourner of the funeral of Felipe Suárez that had gone so horribly wrong.

His statement was dutifully taken down and he would have been free to go, had it not been for these two guys in tight trousers and colourful shirts who had been mincing up and down the gravel path and enquired what 'that guy' was doing there. Omar showed them the protocol confirming that a private citizen was helping with the enquiry but they demanded to see proof that 'the guy' was not there in an official function and wanted to see his identification. They were told by Omar to piss off unless they could provide proof of any authorisation to demand such identification of a private citizen. In turn, they started to ask what had happened to the black sports car. That was driven away by a woman and her escort. Everybody had assumed she was a representative of the Ministry of Natural Resources since she must have had the ignition keys in her possession. Disappointed they called their boss on a cell phone, were given a proper earful in response and left the scene.

Rico takes it easy on his way to the Hospital México where he wants to interview Olga Miranda Cisneros and give her the money foisted upon him by Anabelle. He is sure the money will come in handy since none of Felipe's savings withdrawn from his accounts in preparation for their honeymoon had been found and was probably stolen by the killer. He wants Olga to shed some light on the question of what the killer might have been searching for and if there had been documents of interest to the OIJ in his house.

When he gets to the station in the hospital the receptionist had told him upon presentation of his OIJ card, he is surprised not to see a policeman guarding Olga's room as had been requested. He asks the station's head nurse and is told that the policeman got a call yesterday evening to withdraw. The reason given was that protection of that patient was no longer necessary. A bit worried he hurries to the room and is relieved to see Olga alone in a room for two patients. She is sitting up in bed having a cup of tea.

"Hello, Olga," he greets her. "I'm detective inspector Ramírez. Do you remember me? I interviewed you in San Antonio and had you transferred to the hospital for observation."

Looking at him scared, she pushes the trolley with her cup of tea away and slides under the blanket as if it could provide some protection. She shakes her head in response to his question.

"Don't be scared. I'm from the OIJ and will assure you get the protection you need. You were in severe shock when I tried to interview you and probably don't remember much of what had happened that day. But tell me, are you treated well? Have you been told when you will be released?"

"No," she answers with her voice choking. "I don't even know why I am here and have to take all these medications that make me sick and sleepy all the time."

"I guess the doctors want to make sure you have a good rest. You need it. Do you remember what happened to Felipe?"

She shakes her head but says, "He is dead, isn't he?"

He nods. "I'm sorry to have to tell you that Felipe was brutally murdered. Let me assure you the OIJ is working to solve the crime. This morning we found Felipe's killer. He is dead. Had a dreadful accident. I can tell you about it later."

"How do you know the dead guy was his killer?"

"We found evidence linking him beyond a doubt to the murder. We are certain his motive was not personal or revenge but that he was the henchman of people in power. But it is early days, yet."

She is quiet for a moment and then motions him to close the door before she says, "Felipe and I suspected some people wanted to have him silenced. He knew too much about a lot of secret business deals and criminal activity. We wanted to get away for an extended period in the hope that they would forget about him."

Olga sheds tears at the thought of Felipe no longer by her side as her protector, her safe haven. Split from her family, she has nobody except a few girlfriends she would not consider her confidantes.

Rico is deeply touched by her emotions and knows that his wife Martha would react the same way if she was informed of him having been killed. He thinks of the hit list with his name at the bottom.

214

He asks, "Would you know if Felipe had any documents or letters in his house relating to these dirty deals?"

She shakes her head. "Oh, no, he would never have brought any of the documents and letters he copied for his mysterious contractor into his house or keep them anywhere else. He knew that he was doing this job for somebody who wants to get at those people who make millions right now with the sale of forest areas, drug deals, and blackmail. He told me about it but he never had any of those documents. Why do you ask?"

"When Felipe's house was searched by our crime scene unit, no papers were found except a life insurance policy. Normally one would find private mail, a letter, a postcard, but nothing was found. So, we presume that his house had been searched by his killer on the assumption that Felipe had stockpiled copied documents. That could have been the motive for killing him. On another point, we heard from another witness, his aunt Maruja, uh, Maria..."

"Oh, Maruja, you heard from her," interjects Olga. "How is she? Is she all right?"

"Yes, for now she is safe, but she is also in danger according to information I received. According to her, Felipe had withdrawn all his money in American dollar funds from his various accounts in preparation for the honeymoon. Do you have any idea where he kept that money?"

"Oh, yes. He had put it in a sealed envelope that was hidden in the lining of his mother's old leather jacket hanging behind the bedroom door. That jacket was the last memorabilia he had of his mother and he thought it was a good hiding place."

"Hmm, we found the jacket but there was nothing in it."

"Oh no! What am I going to do? That money was all we had. Now I have nothing."

"Not entirely," says Rico with a smile and takes the bundles of one-hundred-dollar bills out of his jacket pockets. "This money was found in what we have reason to believe was the killer's car. It may be Felipe's money he found in the house. It's all yours."

He hands her the bundles of cash but Olga seems strangely reluctant to accept it. She looks at the bank notes, sees they are all one hundreds and shakes her head.

"I can't take this money. It isn't Felipe's. It is much more than his savings and all in bills of one hundred. His savings were all different bank notes from fives to fifties with very few hundreds and they didn't have any band around it."

"Doesn't matter. Take it anyway and may I suggest you use it for a trip to Spain. Do you have any idea where Felipe's relatives live? Do they know that you are, uh, were his fiancée?"

"I have their address in a small town in Aragón south of Zaragoza. Felipe wrote to them about our upcoming wedding and planned honeymoon trip to Spain."

"Huh, Felipe was Aragonese? That explains a lot about him."

"What do you mean?"

"Well, in Spain the Aragonese are reputed to have heads of stone, to be tough, unyielding, and yet very smart. It was probably the reason why he was feared."

"Felipe wasn't really Aragonese. His mother was, but he was born and raised here. His father was unknown but very likely a Tico. But what am I going to do with all that money? I have no safe hiding place and can't put in a bank account."

"You could put it in a safe deposit box."

"I don't have one. Felipe did."

"He did? Why didn't he keep the money in there?"

"We were going to leave after our wedding in a few days."

"I see... Do you know where his safe deposit box is located?"

"Oh yes. I accompanied him when he put his last will and testament into it but I don't have the key for it."

"Well, as part of the OIJ investigation we could have it opened. That's no problem. But for now we should get the money out of sight. You have a handbag?"

"Yes, it's in the wardrobe with my dress."

Rico opens the wardrobe and wants to put the money into the handbag. He can feel a small rectangular object and takes it out. It is a tracking device emitting silent signals. He puts it in the back of the upper shelf, stows the money in the bag, takes all her clothing and the handbag out and puts the items on her bed.

"Please, get dressed, Olga. We have to get you out of this room. I'll talk to the head nurse and won't be a minute."

He goes to the station desk and tells the head nurse that Olga has to be moved to another room and nobody must be told about her move. The nurse rejects his request claiming not to have a free bed anywhere else because the other patient in Olga's room was moved this morning and took up the last available space. Hearing the nurse's argument, Rico is on high alert.

"Then I will have to take her out of the hospital. The patient is in grave danger of getting assassinated."

The head nurse appears amused. "Here? In the hospital? You're kidding, aren't you? This is a hospital..."

Rico cuts off her flow of speech and shows her his OIJ card. "Indeed! But it is not an impenetrable fortress. During visiting hours anyone can pass through. Is Olga in a condition to be moved?"

"I don't think so. I'd have to ask the doctor in charge."

"Then ask him. This is now a very urgent matter."

She picks up the phone while she looks down the hallway. "Ah, there he is," she says and shouts, "Doctor Madriz, can you come here for a minute? This gentleman has a question."

Reluctantly, the doctor approaches Rico. "Yes, what is it?"

"Olga Miranda Cisneros is your patient?"

"Yes, what about her?"

Rico shows him his OIJ card. "I am responsible for your patient's security. She will have to be moved. Is it safe for her to be moved?"

"Well, uh, yes, uh, no. No, she can't be moved."

"What now? Yes or no? I've talked to her, and she appears to be of sound mind. Why can't she be moved?"

"Uh, well, uh, I was given clear orders not to move her."

"Really, were you now? Who gave you those orders?"

"I can't tell you. The order was given in absolute confidence."

"Doctor, anything besides a patient-doctor relationship is not protected by confidentiality. You know that, don't you? Who gave you those orders?"

The doctor looks flustered, takes Rico to the side, and whispers, "I got a private phone call last night from a man claiming to speak on behalf of the OIJ who instructed me not to have this patient moved or released. He threatened severe repercussions if I went against his order."

"Okay. Who was this man?"

"He said his name was Bruno. That's all he revealed."

"Bruno?" asks Rico. "Sounds like a pseudonym. Leaving that aside for now, can Olga be moved or released?"

"Well, she's physically fit except a lot of bruises, but I would like to keep her here for a few more days of observation."

"That's out of the question, doctor. She will release herself and I will take her out of here. Her present room will be off limits to anyone. I will call my colleagues to guard it for the next few days."

"But why would you guard the room if nobody is in there?"

"It's a ruse, doctor. I tell you in strictest confidence not to let anyone know that Olga has walked out of here. Okay?"

"What am I supposed to say if anyone asks for her?"

"Nobody is going to ask you anything, not with one of my colleagues on guard at the door."

Rico rushes back into Olga's room where she is sitting on the bed in her soiled dress. "Are you ready? You have all your stuff? Don't forget your handbag."

"Where are we going? I can't go anywhere in this filthy dress."

"Yes, you can. First we'll go to your home. You'll pack all your belongings and then I'll take you to a safe place."

"But why?"

"Olga, you are in imminent danger to be silenced by the people who silenced Felipe. That's why I suggested you travel to Spain. Do you have a passport?"

"Yes. I got it in anticipation of my honeymoon trip."

"Good! That means you can be out of the country and on your way to Aragón in a couple of days. Let's go."

Seated in his car in the hospital's parking lot, Rico calls Gus to update him on Olga whose name is on the hitlist. He tells him she released herself from the hospital and is with him. He will take care of her and make sure she is safe until she leaves the country in a few days. When he asks to send an armed OIJ officer to guard the room Olga had occupied, Gus baulks at the request.

"I can't do that, Rico. Guard duty is for the urban police force. That's out of our jurisdiction."

"Okay, Gus, then send one of our juniors for observation duty. That is our jurisdiction, isn't it? Observation and investigation?"

"Yes, it is, but I'm still reluctant to grant you that request. And you want him armed as well. Why? You expect a gun battle?"

"It's possible although unlikely but whoever goes should be able to defend him or herself. Let me tell you why I expect trouble. I found a tracking device in Olga's handbag, meaning that her whereabouts are checked 24/7. I tossed it in the back of the top shelf inside the wardrobe. So, you can have it picked up for reverse tracking to find out who receives the signal."

"That's a good idea. It could have been one of the guys of this cloak and dagger operation whose initials I found in the wallet of the dead guy. Does M.C., R.Ch., or O.M. ring a bell?"

"Only the initials O.M. and they ring a thousand alarm bells if they stand for Octavio Muñoz. If that is the case, then the noose is tightening, Gus. I talked to the doctor to see if Olga was fit to leave the hospital and he told me of a call he received ordering him to keep Olga in her room. It was someone who gave only the name Bruno. Can you find out whose pseudonym that might be?"

"I'll give it a try but don't get your hopes up yet. Okay?"

"All right. If you can confirm Bruno is Muñoz's pseudonym, we are just a step away from solving this whole dirty business."

"Uh-huh," wheezes Gus into the phone. "But I doubt you can get at him. It was just announced on the news that Octavio Muñoz is going to be appointed Special Envoy for Nature Conservation with the task of attuning all Latin American countries to Costa Rica's model of nature conservation. Thus, that gentleman will have police protection 24 hours a day once his appointment is confirmed, and we won't get close enough to arrest him."

"That don't impress me much, as a Canadian country singer says in her bad English. I think I have a way of getting at this turkey to eliminate him and his associates. Then we can tell our boss, the case is closed and nothing special to report until these guys start to eliminate each other and we have to investigate their deaths."

"You're a sly son of a gun," responds Gus. "Go ahead, I wish you luck. But here's another bit of bad news concerning you. I was informed that the attaché case you confiscated a couple of weeks ago at the airport has disappeared out of our evidence room. We may have to let that drug money courier off the hook. Unless we can locate the case we won't have any evidence against him."

"How in the devil's name was it possible to remove the case from the evidence room. It's a secure area you can't enter without proper authorisation or a court order. Has the log been checked?"

"Yes. It showed an almost indecipherable signature with first name Ramos or something like that. Reason for removal was an alleged court procedure that couldn't be confirmed. I guess, it was done with the help of one of our higher ups."

"Well, Gus, if the case can't be located then let the courier go. He's just a cog on a tiny wheel of the drug business. He couldn't reveal anything about the drug pushers on our shores. Okay?"

"I guess you're right, Rico. Now go ahead and don't forget to take good care of Olga. All right?"

Rico ends the call. He starts the car, smiles at Olga and says, "My colleague told me to take good care of you. He also provided some interesting news that may resolve the entire riddle of Felipe's murder and more. That was all in all good news."

Wondering what the good news might be since she heard only his half of the telephone call, Olga is nevertheless content and calm. Instinctively she knows that good things are coming her way. They get to her place where she packs her few belongings, says good-bye to her friend who gave her shelter and pays her two hundred dollars for a month's rent. Everything stowed in his car, Rico takes course on his home in Montes de Oca.

Martha comes walking along the street with a bag full of stuff she bought for dinner, sees Rico and a woman in a dirty dress get out of the car, and wonders who he picked up this time.

"Hello there," she says. "You got a new friend, Rico?"

"I sure hope so," answers Rico. "May I introduce her? This is Olga Miranda Cisneros, the fiancée of Felipe Suárez. She will stay with us until her departure for Spain in a couple of days. Olga, this is my wife Martha, the best criminal psychologist this entire continent has ever seen."

"Don't listen to him, Olga. I'm just a housewife. But tell me, you're not going to Spain in that dirty dress, are you?" asks Martha. "Let's go inside to clean you up a bit and get your room ready. While you settle in, I prepare lunch. Rico, you can't leave on an empty stomach. Come on in and give me your update."

End Game

Gus Goicoechea is searching every fingerprint data base he can access since his phone call with Rico. It has become an obsession to find the name of the dead guy whose fingerprints identified him as the killer of Felipe Suárez. If he can prove his proper identity, he may find out other contacts he may have had nationally as well as internationally. But every data base of criminals or people suspected of involvement in criminal activity used by police organisations around the world shows no match of the fingerprints Rico took of the corpse.

Gus takes a breather and ponders who else takes fingerprints and keeps them on a data base. There are security organisations and companies who do it for exclusionary purposes but they are too numerous and their data files are offline and inaccessible by anyone from outside. He knows the military of most countries is taking finger and palm prints of all recruits and civilian personnel. They are under national security by most countries and accessible only by the authorities in charge. But what about soldiers that were dishonourably discharged and not prosecuted in a civilian court? He searches the regular Internet for such files without any luck, thinks of his son having used the dark net to hack the Public Security Ministry's system, gives it a shot and finds files of various countries. He hacks the biggest one of the United States and is overwhelmed by the thousands of records. A fingerprint matching facility is not provided. He downloads the massive file and converts it to one the OIJ's fingerprint system can plough through.

It takes a few minutes until Gus strikes paydirt. It shows the record of a John Walker Valenzuela, Costa Rican national. The legend says that his parents migrated to the States in the 1970s, where the couple had four children one of whom was John. He joined the U.S. Navy after graduating from college, absolved his training and was accepted as one of the Navy Seals. Despite an excellent combat rating, he was dishonourably discharged as a result of charges brought against him including violent assaults, drug use, and the theft of weapons and ordinance he sold on the black market. Six years ago he escaped from a military correctional facility and the United States for an unknown destination.

His destination might not be known to the US Forces but is well known to Gus. He checks the migration records and finds the entry of a J.W. Valenzuela by car dated six years ago. The contact address given was San Antonio. No further entries are found.

Gus puts on latex gloves and takes every card, paper and a couple of banknotes out of the wallet he found on the corpse. In a small pocket opposite the one that contained the list of initials he notices a thin hard object he had not noticed before. It is a key that could be for a safe deposit box. Probing the pocket once more, a small piece of paper emerges with the name Butch and a phone number on it.

Gus is baffled. He does not know anyone by that name. Since the phone number is national, he gives it a shot and calls.

A woman answers, "San Antonio butcher. Can I help you?"

"Possibly. Can I talk to Butch, please?"

"Butch? He isn't here."

"Where might I contact him?"

"In the police station. He is the captain of the police force."

"Very good. Then I will call him there. Thank you."

Gus ends the call and mutters, "Oh well, I have to take another trip to San Antonio."

After a quick drive to the police station, Gus rushes in, sees the cops sitting around watching the transmission of a national Primera División football league game and switches off the TV set. He turns to the captain and says in a stern voice, "I have to talk to you. In private! Get rid of your flunkies!"

The protest is loud and aimed at Gus personally. He takes out his OIJ badge and shouts, "Get out, you layabouts! I have good reason to arrest every one of you!"

The policemen clear out rapidly until only the captain is left. Gus slams the door shut, pulls up a chair and sits down opposite Edwin who has turned pale. His hands are trembling.

"Do you know or have an idea why I'm here, Butch?" asks Gus.

Hearing his pseudonym used to address him, Edwin is in panic. He knows that this nasty OIJ officer's visit has something to do with his old buddy Cholo's death.

"I'm Gustávo Goicoechea, detective inspector of the OIJ. And you are the Capitán of this police station. What's your name?"

"Edwin Rodríguez."

"Okay, Edwin or Butch, does the name John Walker Valenzuela ring a bell?"

Edwin blushes and stares at the tip of his boots. He clears his throat and murmurs, "Not really, uh, I remember him vaguely."

"In what capacity?"

"What do you mean by capacity?"

"Well, was he your friend, a colleague, a neighbour?"

"No, uh, he turned up one day and I gave him shelter."

"Do you do that often, giving shelter to someone who escaped military detention in the United States and needs a hiding place?"

"No."

"Look, Edwin, speak up and tell me what you know about Valenzuela. How did you meet him and had first contact?"

Edwin sits up straight and tries to calm down. "About six years ago, I got a call from a friend who has lots of contacts with Ticos who migrated to the United States. He asked me to provide shelter for a returnee who needed to go under cover for a while."

"Who was this friend?"

"Is that important? Do I have to tell you?"

"Yes, of course. If Valenzuela was your friend, he must have been an even better friend of him."

Edwin looks down and mumbles, "Bruno..."

"Bruno? Bruno who?"

"I don't know. You see, all the people who contacted me or I had to call used pseudonyms by which we address each other in case somebody listens to the phone calls. I have no idea who the real people are behind those aliases. All I know is Valenzuela was Cholo and I am Butch."

"You don't say."

Edwin hastens to add, "I think Bruno was only the front of a network of business and government executives."

"Uh-huh, and this network needed an executioner, a killer?"

"I wouldn't know anything about that. Why would they?"

"Why? Business and government executives don't get their hands dirty with a wet job. They hire someone who is trained for such activity."

"Yes, I suppose. But did Cholo have such training?"

"He used to be a member of a special operations force of the U.S. Navy that carries out the killing of high-level targets clandestinely. We have proof that he killed Felipe Suárez and know he was hired for such a clandestine job. He didn't know

Felipe and had no other reason to kill him except to do the job he was hired to do.”

Gus takes out his notepad and a pen. “You said all people of the network used pseudonyms. What are they?”

Edwin speaks slowly seeing that Gus writes them down. “There is Cholo... Bruno... Charro... Adan... Rodrigo... Chaco... Rich... Ramos... and, uh, Pedro whose number I was supposed to call only in case of a national security threat. That’s all I can recall on the spur of the moment, but there are many more. I can give you the phone number of each one. I have the complete list at home.”

“That would help.” Looking at the names, Gus snorts derisively and then continues, “Why was Valenzuela called Cholo? It would be a nickname for someone of European and Native parentage but as far as I could tell from his appearance, he has no Native ancestry.”

“I have no idea. I don’t know why this code name was given to him. In my case, being a butcher, it was an obvious choice.”

“Sure... So, for how long did you shelter Cholo at your home?”

“Uh... about three months, six months.”

“What now? Three months or six months? That’s quite a difference and you can’t remember?”

“No, but after three months of staying at my place every day he got calls for jobs, disappeared for a few days and then came back. Three months later he had enough money for his own place and left for good. Also, I got paid only for the first three months. The rent was paid on his behalf and delivered by courier.”

“Hmm... He stayed in your house for three months solid and on and off for another three months. Did you never talk to him? Come on, you give shelter to someone and don’t want to get to know him?”

“I tried to have a chat with him but he was very abrasive when I asked what he had done in the past and wanted to do. Generally, he was very reticent.”

“You mean to say, you never found out what jobs he did when he had disappeared for a few days?”

“No, he never talked about it. For a while I thought he worked as a butcher when he came back with his clothes splattered with blood. But he burned his shirts and trousers right away although my wife had offered to wash them.”

“Could he have joined our Rapid Reaction Force?”

“I don’t know. I wasn’t privy to such information.”

224

"Okay. When was the last time you saw him?"

"Since he left over five years ago, I never saw him again."

"Are you sure? You didn't see him on several occasions in the course of the past two weeks?"

Edwin blushes and stares again at the tips of his boots. "No, uh, no. I... I... I didn't see him... alive."

"Meaning what? That you saw him when he was dead and you recognised him then? Why didn't you inform Rico Ramírez who was with you at the burial site?"

"I couldn't do that for several reasons."

"Which were what?"

"For a start, Ramírez was there as a private person. Bruno had informed me about his suspension from duty. Then there was the gravedigger and this strange couple. Had I blurted out that I knew the dead guy, Ramírez would have interrogated me about Cholo's activities and I couldn't have told him anything. That would have looked like obstruction. It was better to say nothing. The day Cholo left my house to live in San José was the last time I saw him alive."

"I don't believe you. I put it to you that you didn't just see him but helped him locate Felipe's house and told him about Felipe's work schedule."

Edwin whimpers, "No, it wasn't like that at all! He came here to the station over a week ago dressed up with a fake beard, a floppy hat and dirty coat. I recognised him but he talked to my sergeant who gave him directions when he was told of a delivery for Felipe. The bus schedule hangs out at the bus stop and Felipe had marked his departure times with angel's wings."

Gus says coldly, "So, you did see him and you overheard him asking for Felipe's house. Didn't you know of Cholo's penchant for killing people and felt obliged to warn Felipe of the imminent danger of becoming one of his victims?"

"I didn't know Cholo was a killer and, uh, nobody in the village was talking to Felipe or had any contact with him."

"That's not true. Jorge Alfaro as well as Rafaelo, the landlord of the Linda Vista pub, stated they had a cordial relationship with Felipe when Rico initially investigated his murder. You, in your function of police captain, had the obligation to warn and even take steps to protect him. You didn't do that. Why not?"

"Well, there was his Dark Angel reputation."

Gus takes a deep breath and pauses for a moment before he asks, "Are you a good Christian, Edwin? Do you believe in the almighty lord and creator of all life, who's responsible for everything?"

"Yes, of course!"

"So, if you believe a god is responsible for everything on our planet, why do you put faith in this superstitious bullshit of a Dark Angel? Is that also god's work? If you believe it, then Felipe's bloody murder is also god's work and your god turns out to be a rather nasty piece of shit in whom I can't put any faith whatsoever."

Edwin stares at Gus in utter disbelief of what he just heard and stammers, "You... you don't believe... have no faith in, uh...?"

The response is immediate. "How can I have faith in some illusionary superior being with all the horrors I see every day? If it wasn't for people like some of my very few friends, I would have lost faith in all of humanity a long time ago."

Gus gets up. "Your game is up, Edwin. I charge you with being an accessory to the murder of Felipe Suárez. Let's go pick up the list of the goons' aliases and their phone numbers. Then I have to take you to OIJ headquarters for a complete interview."

He gets up, takes zip-tie handcuffs lying on the desk and puts them on Edwin's wrists who folds his hands and looks at Gus with tears streaming down his face, "I beg of you not to arrest me and suffer the humiliation of being dragged outside as a prisoner."

But Gus shows no mercy and puts the cuffs on. "You leave me no choice, Edwin. I wouldn't want you to become a fugitive. But there's a way out of this dilemma. Your interview will be recorded. If it is a full confession and includes the names of all people involved in the murder of Felipe Suárez, I'll have it transcribed. You can sign it, get yourself registered as a key witness and be home before midnight. Let's go."

***

Rico relaxes after a hearty meal in the company of Martha and Olga and listens to their conversation without adding his bit of mustard. He is preoccupied trying to figure out what he should do next.

His cell phone buzzes, he sees it is Gus calling, gets up, walks outside and sits down on the step at the front door.

"Hello, Gus. What's the good news?"

"Rico, do you remember when I said that the Suárez case has opened a huge barrel of effluent with some really big turds floating around in it?"

Rico chuckles. "Yes, vaguely. It stands out as one of your more picturesque descriptions of cases we investigate. I guess you've opened up the barrel and identified some of the turds."

"That's very perceptive of you. I checked every data base for matching fingerprints to find those of the dead guy in San Antonio. Found them on a file of the U.S. Forces. It is the dishonourably discharged John Walker Valenzuela, Costa Rican citizen. That led me to contact your old nemesis Edwin."

"Edwin? You mean the butcher of San Antonio?"

"That's him. Upon closer inspection of the wallet I took out of the corpse's pocket, I found a key to a safe deposit box and a shred of paper with the name Butch and a phone number on it. I called and a woman answered telling me that Butch is the police captain in San Antonio. I drove up there, interviewed him and he revealed that the entire network of turds works with aliases. He had a list of their phone numbers in his home that he surrendered to me. I checked the numbers and found a frightening network of business and government executives. One of the main players according to the initials O.M. on the other shred of paper in the wallet is Octavio Muñoz aka Bruno. Does that help you?"

"You can bet your bottom dollar on it, if you have one. That clears the path I want to take all the way to the horizon."

"Good but be careful. According to Bruno's telephone record, he is in contact with some bigwigs. The most prominent one is Rodrigo better known as Secretary of State Manuel Cardenas. They call each other several times a day. He's also calling Charro, the Minister of Public Security regularly. Then there is one more of interest to us. He is, uh, no... I'll keep you guessing."

"Could it be the one of whom I've been suspicious since the day of his appointment? If it is, I hope we find the evidence to catapult him out of his seat and on the garbage dump where he belongs."

"You're not much fun for guessing games, but yes, it is the one and we have all the evidence to have him catapulted. He signed the log of our evidence room with his pseudonym Ramos, meaning he picked up the attaché case in person. I found out by calling his number on Edwin's list from a public phone. When I heard Ángel's voice, I asked for Tomás and apologised for having dialled the wrong number. You're aware, of course, that he has unlimited access to information sufficient to break the neck of all the other turds and could solve the Suárez case in five minutes flat."

"Interesting. Let's keep digging for the evidence we need to clear out the barrel of effluent. I will get the ball rolling. I know which turd I need to take on first to get all the others up on the barricades. Once the resulting blame game is in full swing, they will reveal the details we need to charge and arrest the lot."

"Sounds like a good plan. I wish you luck. Take care."

"Thanks and I will take care. But I have one more question. You mentioned to have found a key to a safe deposit box. Do you think it belonged to the killer?"

"That's hard to say. We'd have to find the bank branch and open the box to see what's in it. Why do you ask?"

"Well, it could have belonged to the murder victim and be part of Olga's inheritance. The box could also contain documents related to his activity as a courier and help us solve the crime."

"Interesting but right now I don't have the time to find the bank branch and the safe deposit box."

"That's okay. I know a possible short cut. Give me the key and I'll ask Olga if she recognises it and can open the box."

"It's worth a try. Sure. I'll give you the key next time we meet."

"All right. See you soon."

Rico gets up and ponders the best route for public exposure of Muñoz aka Bruno, his first target, who was going to be appointed Special Envoy and has no immunity or presidential protection until the official swearing-in ceremony. Rico is trying to remember where Muñoz lives. It is likely that he will give a reception at his home to celebrate the announcement of his appointment. But where is his home? The only location he can think of is the town of Alajuela where Muñoz was once elected some years ago. Perhaps some of the people living there can direct him to his present residence. He steps into the house and bids farewell to Martha and Olga with the promise to be back in a little while, 'más o menos', so that they know he could be gone five minutes or five hours.

After driving into Alajuela, Rico stops at a bakery to buy some bread and a cake the two women at home would appreciate. A friendly elderly woman serves the customers. When it is his turn, he asks for a loaf of bread and then rubs his chin trying to decide which of the cakes on display he should purchase.

"Are you looking for a special cake, Señor?" asks the woman.

"Yes, which cake would you recommend to make two women happy? I would like to surprise my wife and her visiting friend."

"You're a real gentleman, Señor, thinking of making two women happy with a cake. This one with the chocolate glazing is a very nice sponge cake with layers of fruit and cream."

"Excellent choice, Señora. I'll take it."

The woman picks up the cake and puts it in a carton. At that moment a lanky baker of about the same age as the attendant comes from the workroom into the shop carrying a tray of bread rolls. It is the apt moment for Rico to ask, "Have you heard the exciting news?"

"What's that?" asks the baker and drops the rolls into a basket.

"It was just on the news. Your fellow denizen Octavio Muñoz is going to be appointed Special Envoy for Nature Conservation."

"Son of a bitch!" grunts the baker. "That scumbag always falls on his feet."

Rico does his best not to laugh. "Scumbag? I guess, you don't like him very much."

"How could I? When that turd was elected as an alternative rep for the two-year term he lasted, he acted like he owned this town, bought everything on credit and never paid his bills. I'm not the only one he screwed. He's a scoundrel, a scrounger, and a fraud."

"Really? I'm sorry to hear that. Actually, I would have thought that everybody wanted to congratulate him on his appointment."

The baker puts a chocolate cream pie on the counter top. "Why don't you do that on my behalf with this cream pie? When you see him, slam it in his face with my best regards. That would make me and many other merchants around town very happy."

"But I don't know where he lives."

"That's easy. Next intersection take a right. When you get to the first traffic light, take a left. Third mansion on the right is his."

The woman chortles while she puts the carton with the cake on the counter top. "You can't ask a total stranger to slam a cream pie into that bastard's face."

"Why not? You're not from Alajuela, are you, Señor? You look very respectable and are the perfect assailant. If you do it, Señor, I'll give you bread and cake free of charge for a whole year. You may even be appointed honorary member of the Alajuela Merchants Association. How does that grab you?"

"That's very tempting," says Rico with a smile, puts the cream pie on top of the carton and asks, "How much do I owe you?"

"The cream pie is on the house," says the baker. "For the cake and bread just give my wife whatever you think it's worth."

Rico hands over enough money to make the baker's wife happy and asks, "Next intersection to the right and then at the traffic light to the left? Correct?"

The baker and his wife nod and wave as Rico leaves the bakery.

Sitting in his car with the bread and cake on the backseat and the cream pie on the passenger seat, he asks himself, if it is right for him to cream-pie Muñoz. What will his colleagues and Martha say when it gets into the press? They will have a good laugh and celebrate him - for sure! He starts the car, opens the passenger side window, gives the baker and his wife a reaffirming thumbs up with a very determined look on his face, and gets applause in response!

It is a short drive to the side road. Turning left into it, Rico sees several cars and vans of TV stations, two police cars and a luxury limousine in front of his designated target. He takes the delicious looking cream pie and walks through the small crowd of news reporters and camera men towards the entrance of the mansion. A policeman stops him and asks where he is going with that projectile.

Rico looks at him indignantly. "How dare you call this delectable pie a projectile? It is a present from the Secretary of State Manuel Cardenas for Octavio to celebrate his appointment. Let me pass."

The cop steps obediently aside and lets him pass to the door where a few microphones are set up. It means the media is expecting Muñoz to come out and give a statement or short speech.

Rico wants to ring the bell when Muñoz walks out in front of an entourage of men and women, some of whom are familiar looking members of parliament.

"Hello, Bruno," says Rico. Hearing a stranger calling him by his pseudonym, Muñoz stares at Rico slack jawed who speaks loud and clear for the microphones to capture every words. "Look what Manuel Cardenas asked me to present to you on this great occasion. He is a bit pissed off with you for stealing the attaché case with two million dollars he had stolen from the OIJ's evidence room."

The smiling faces of the entourage suddenly express shock. Muñoz wants to say something when the pie hits him square in the face and some of the chocolate mousse splatters on the suits and dresses of the people behind him.

Chaos ensues as news reporters and policemen wrangle to get at the assailant first. One cop breaks through and manages to hold

Rico in an armlock. Familiar with that grip and being trained to get out of it, Rico takes steps in the limited room in front of the door to get his arm around the throat of the cop in an instant. The reporters are amazed and start to bombard Rico with questions about the words they captured just a second ago. The TV cameras swivel between his face for close-ups and that of Muñoz who scrapes chocolate mousse off his face and licks his fingers.

Rico releases the cop out of the hold and speaks into the microphones held out to him. "I have it on the good authority of the Alajuela Merchants Association that this man, Octavio Muñoz is a scoundrel, a scrounger and a fraud. Furthermore, although I cannot speak on behalf of the OIJ, I do know that an investigation is under way that will put an end to the careers of several high-ranking government officials for fraudulent deals of selling protected forests and wildlife habitats, ordering the murder of people who know too much about these dirty deals, as well as the theft of evidence of the ongoing enquiries into the trade of illicit drugs in our country. Muñoz is the leader of this pack of criminals. That is all I have to say. Please refer to the OIJ for more in-depth information."

The crowd is stunned. Nobody tries to stop him when he pushes through the small crowd of policemen and news reporters, enters his car and drives away. Rico is satisfied to have planted the seed for actions of revenge by Muñoz's collaborators against each other and many more of their supporting cast of characters as for example his boss who lets incriminating evidence conveniently disappear.

***

The mid-afternoon programs of all TV channels are interrupted with the breaking news of a heinous attack with a chocolate cream pie on the dignitary who is going to be appointed Special Envoy for Nature Conservation by the President of the Republic as it was announced in the morning news. The commentators do verbal somersaults to express their speculation about the beginning of lawlessness in the country of peace and friendship. The assailant's statement of Señor Muñoz being a scoundrel, a scrounger and a fraud and involved in fraudulent deals is shown only once. It is blended out for the victim declaring his innocence and that there is no premise for any of the ridiculous assertions. One of the channels can report the identity of the assailant and a brief interview with Ángel Carrazo de Gallego who declares that the assailant was none other than the recently suspended detective inspector Rico Ramírez. He will be fired to the great relief of all his colleagues and hunted down to receive the appropriate punishment for his unspeakable crime.

The breaking news interruption of the afternoon program is repeated several times. The work in the government offices comes almost to a complete standstill. The reactions are a mix of disbelief, laughter and congratulations for the assailant. Only Manuel Cardenas does not share this mix. He is outraged after hearing Rico stating boldly that Muñoz is in possession of the attaché case with two million dollars that was taken from the OIJ's evidence room. No OIJ officer, suspended or not, would say that in public without having concrete evidence. He calls an officer of the Rapid Reaction Force, explains his case, and requests immediate action to be taken to recover not only the attaché case with the money but also the incriminating forest purchase and clear-cutting licence documents. Furthermore, the silencing of everybody on the list has to be done and finished as quickly as possible. When the officer asks what list he is talking about, Cardenas remembers giving it to Muñoz who gave it to Cholo who is dead. He tells the officer to forget about the list and to focus on the retrieval of the two documents and the attaché case. Cardenas is ready to faint when he hears that the woman who had obtained the documents had sent them already by courier to Switzerland. Furthermore, she was deported. Muttering feebly, Cardenas pleads to get the case out of Muñoz's house under all circumstances and deliver it to him.

Cardenas has hardly finished his call when Chaverry is on the phone lambasting him for alleged cooperation with an OIJ officer who is known in government circles to have no respect for those in higher office. Cardenas rejects that allegation out of hand claiming that he never in his political career collaborated with the OIJ or the officer commonly called the 'Super Snooper'. Then how can he explain, retorts Chaverry, that the assailant mentioned Cardenas' name during the attack and very likely did not have enough time to mention his name as the plotter of the attaché case theft. Cardenas is stuck for an answer. He swears on his mother's grave, although she is still alive, to move heaven and earth to find the culprit who blew the whistle on this case. First steps had been taken to recover the attaché case and any other incriminating evidence. He will keep Chaverry informed and call him later in the course of the night.

***

Olga and Martha watched the breaking news and were perplexed why Rico would cream-pie a barely known man who is soon to be appointed a Special Envoy. What would be his connection to the killing of Felipe? When Rico steps into the house, he catches the final repeat of the breaking news and asks what they think of his deed. Their first shock gives way to smiles for seeing him hale and hearty carrying a loaf of bread and a cake in a carton. Upon his question if they liked Muñoz's face full of chocolate mousse their smiles turn to giggles until laughter echoes through the house. When they sit down to coffee and cake, he assures them that he has nothing to fear once concrete evidence to support his accusation can be presented. Martha wants to know what concrete evidence he is hoping to unearth. He mentions Gus who has been able to obtain crucial witness statements and proof of the involvement in the dirty business of several high-ranking government officials.

Martha says documented proof is better than unreliable witness statements and adds she knows someone who has documents that can provide irreproachable proof of fraudulent government business. Rico gives her a puzzled look. She reminds him of Anabelle's caper. He should give her a call. He looks at his wrist watch, does a quick calculation of the time zone difference, and says he will call her at about 02:00 o'clock at night when it will be seven hours later in Zurich.

***

Anabelle had a relatively pleasant flight after her ordeal at the San José airport. She and her companion, the Spanish embassy diplomat Marcos Gutiérrez, had a lively discussion until it was time to get some shut eye. After their very early morning arrival at Madrid airport, they exchanged addresses and phone numbers and promised each other to stay in touch. It was then that it dawned on her to have flown business class. She had booked economy and was wondering why none of the crew had asked her to change seats. She looked in her handbag for the boarding pass and the ticket for her onward flight to Zurich but found only her passport. She opened it and saw the bold stamp "Persona non grata" right across her personal data page. It was the confirmation of her being declared an undesirable alien prohibited from entering Costa Rica ever again. Despite the stamp, the Spanish migration officer gave her only a stern look, then smiled and waved her through. She thought she had to buy a ticket for her flight to Zurich but enquired with the airline if she was on the passenger list for the scheduled flight. It was confirmed and the young man was kind enough to issue her a boarding pass when she explained to have lost the ticket. Next she went to an electronics shop and acquired a new battery for her cell phone.

It was still early morning when she arrived in Switzerland. The passport control officer did not take kindly to the stamp across page two of her personal data and told her that the passport was invalid. He wanted to know why she had been declared an undesirable alien. She explained it was the price one has to pay for uncovering a multi-million-dollar fraud scheme involving business and government officials to which he replied, it should teach her not to snoop around it matters that are none of her business. Upon the presentation of her cards proving residence as well as her driver's licence, he advised her to get a new passport and let her pass.

Hardly arrived at her home apartment and before she unlocks the door, she can hear Zeus, her dog barking in her neighbour's abode who had taken care of the mutt. The woman opens the door, watches the joyous greetings of dog and owner, and hands her the envelope with films, report and caper documents that had arrived the day before. Anabelle thanks the woman profusely and says she would get a present for her in the course of the day. Her phone rings before they can continue what would have turned into a lengthy chat. She hurries into her apartment and answers the call. It is Rico who greets her with a jovial salutation on the assumption that she is all right and everything had gone smoothly. Her negative reply and the anxious question if Martha and he are all right and in good health is enough for him to realise that everything is not even close to being all right. She asks if she can call him back in an hour, explains to have just arrived at home and needs to sort out her stuff.

He agrees but before the call is ended, he asks, "Could you do me, I mean us, the OIJ the big favour of sending the purchase document and clear-cut licence to my colleague Gus Goicoechea at his home address by courier? It is a crucial piece of evidence we need to close the murder case and the swindle with the sale of protected forest areas."

"Of course, Rico, I will do anything to help you finish this death of paradise by a thousand cuts. I have to show these documents to my editor first. I have a meeting with him in the early afternoon. You can get some sleep until then. We will discuss all the details when I call back about 09:00 o'clock your time. Give my warmest regards to Martha. Talk to you soon."

That ends their call and it is time for Anabelle to take a shower and clear her head. Then she has a bite to eat, unpacks her luggage, tosses all the clothes into the washing machine, gets dressed, packs all her films into her handbag, and takes Zeus for his long-anticipated walk to the park in glorious sunshine. When she passes a photo shop that still develops films, she orders the film development and prints of every shot as quickly as possible. The shop assistant mentions something of a premium price for expedited processing. She agrees and is told the film and prints will be ready in an hour. At last she can relax and have fun with her pooch.

On her way home, she picks up the big package of prints and films and pays an enormous amount. She recalls Rico's request for the original documents of her forest purchase caper and wonders how he or his colleague could use them for the closure of a murder case. She decides to make colour copies of these papers that cannot be told apart from the originals upon closest examination. Her editor would get copies and she will keep some for herself.

At home Anabelle finishes and copyrights her report on the computer and prints the demanded three copies. Then she goes ahead with copying the documents, prints them with the colour matching scheme, and checks every detail with a magnifying glass. Happy with the results, she puts the papers into a folder and looks through the prints of her photos. She sorts out the best shots and then remembers the digital camera chip with her shots of the devastated landscapes. She puts the chip back into the camera, connects it to her computer and downloads the over four hundred shots. What she sees brings back horrible memories and gives her yet more reason to appreciate Don Oduber Madrigal's effort of protecting his patch of rain forest. She prints the most horrifying photos of seemingly endless destruction and makes sure that every shot has the date and time imprinted. Adding her selection of photos to the folder, she is ready to see her editor. Looking at her dog and seeing his sad eyes, she gives him a reassuring rub and says she will take him along. He smiles at her and his eyes seem to light up as if he had understood every word.

First she goes with her dog to a café just around the corner from her apartment building, orders a cup of coffee, some light fluffy pastry, and an ice cream for her canine companion. Refreshed, they go to the backyard of her home, get into her nippy little Peugeot and drive to the magazine's editorial offices.

The editor, Alfons Zuber, is happy to see her and welcomes her dog with the repeated question, "Who's a good boy?" Then he turns to Anabelle, "What's the good news? What have you got to report?"

She shows him her passport and the page with the big stamp. He is shocked and notices the absence of an exit stamp.

"Does that mean you were deported?"

"Mm-hmm. I was not only manhandled like a gangster but also declared a persona non grata and banned for life from re-entry. But I had a call with an officer of the crime investigation organisation this morning. He will have the people arrested who instigated my deportation."

"What? You have to pass that by me once more. The people who instigated your deportation will be arrested? For what?"

"You have to read my report to fully understand what my case is about and what's really going on in that little paradise."

"Huh, so, your report will not be suitable for publication in our social news magazine, I guess?"

"Definitely not! But some of the nicer pictures would make the cut. I could write a little diddy about one man's struggle to preserve his patch of rainforest. My main report should be published in our nature magazine with all the contrasting photos."

"Contrasting photos of what?"

"The absolutely breath-taking beauty of the tiny preserves of rainforest contrasting with the harrowing destruction of the land. Consider that eighty-five percent of Costa Rica's forested area has been clear-cut and turned into a dust bowl. What is left are mere clumps, little patches of forests that are offered to tourists as the greatest nature conservation in the world while at the same time Costa Rica has the highest rate of environmental destruction on a per capita basis of all countries in the world. Please, read my report."

"I will, Anabelle, I will. But let us call the major shareholder of our publishing house. He arrived from Germany this morning. He is a great fan of Costa Rica and should read your report as well."

Alfons picks up the phone and requests to speak with Herbert Glatzeck. "Hello, Herbert. Anabelle Bouchard has returned from Costa Rica with lots of photos and her final report. Yes, she arrived early this morning. Had a bit of a harrowing experience. What?

No, her report is not about celebrities' mansions. That was a canard bestowed on you by our friend at the Costa Rican embassy. Well, you know how they like to boast about their country. No... no, there are no celebrities living in big mansions in Costa Rica. Her report is about the state of nature. Wonderful. We'll see you in a minute."

A few minutes later, Herbert comes shuffling into the office. A gnarled old man with thinning hair, a wrinkled face, glasses resting askew on his nose, torso bent over, he looks cranky. He gives the dog an uneasy glance, ignores Anabelle, gives Alfons a nod, and sits down. "So, where is this report then? I expect to see it on the desk when I'm called to read it," he squawks.

It is the first time Anabelle sees the majority shareholder of her contractual employer, the Swiss publishing house of colourful magazines. He reminds her of the hobgoblins and bogeys that pick their noses and fart a lot as depicted in the Swedish children's books she loved to read as a little girl and remembers well. Glatzeck could have jumped right off one of the pages. She expects him to break wind and pick his nose to confirm the impression she has of him.

Anabelle opens her folder and presents one copy of her report to Herbert and one to Alfons. Herbert looks at the headline, 'Death of a Paradise'. He sniffles. Evidently he does not like it.

Alfons is a quick reader and his eyes appear to bulge as he turns to the second page. It gets worse when he gets to pages six and seven. He takes a handkerchief and wipes some sweat from his forehead while he casts a nervous look at Herbert who has barely started reading the third page and tosses the report on the desk.

Staring down Alfons, he rasps, "You're not going to publish this rubbish, are you? It is the biggest pile of dog shit I've ever seen compiled in a report. One lie and denunciation after another. It's an outrageous fabrication. Who scribbled this shit?"

Anabelle looks at him. "Since you haven't noticed my presence yet, good afternoon, Herr Glatzeck. I wrote this report after thorough investigation of facts and documenting them."

Herbert casts her a sideways glance. "Who's talking to you? Hacks like you are a dime a dozen. I'm here talking to the editor not some blatant liar who falsifies facts."

Anabelle's voice takes on a sharp tone that cuts through his attempt of talking to Alfons. "How would you know what's fact and what's fiction? Take your complaints about my report up with Carlos Cortés and Alexander Bonilla Durán, two Costa Rican environmentalists, journalists and published authors of several books. They know their country better than you know the contents of your pockets."

She tosses some of the photos of devastated landscapes on the desk in front of him. "Here's my evidence, Herr Glatzeck! Have a good look at the photos. I took them three days ago. You want more documented proof of what's really going on in your little dream paradise. Here it is!!"

Anabelle slams a copy of her clear-cutting licence and purchase of a rainforest in a wildlife habitat on the desk. "And don't you ever dare to call me liar or a hack, you pathetic little man!"

Herbert lifts his bony arse out of the chair and snarls, "Who in the devil's name do you think you are?"

He stares at Anabelle with his mouth open when she laughs at his ludicrous question and then snarls, "That's the kind of question one should expect from a mental midget. Most people know who they are and don't have think about it. You seem to have delusions of grandeur because you probably inherited a few million from your parents and think you have something to say for yourself. Your opinion about my report you can blow out your ass, buster!"

Herbert sinks into his chair, touches the documents in front of him with a shaking hand, gives the photos a scant look, and gets up. He leaves the office, points a thumb at Anabelle over his shoulder and caws, "I want her out of here! Today! Get rid of her!"

Alfons looks shaken up. As soon as Herbert has disappeared down the hallway, he says, "That was uncalled for, Anabelle."

"Is that so? But calling me a hack and a liar was called for?"

"No, it wasn't. But he will retaliate. He's a successful publisher of religious books in Germany and has an extensive readership."

"It figures. And how will he retaliate?"

"Giving you a bad name for a start."

"Let him. I'm not afraid. Soon we will receive news from Costa Rica that will vindicate my report and give him a heart attack."

"Really? What news is that?"

"I can tell you tomorrow. I'll receive it first and we'll have an exclusive you can sell to hundreds for thousands. Promise."

"That's nice. Let's talk about your report. It's very hard hitting and I'm afraid too harsh for us to publish."

"What? Not even in our nature magazine?"

"No, out of the question. We've never had such a hard-hitting report in our magazine."

"Then it's about time! Think of all the young people demanding action against environmental destruction and climate change. I can write my report in three other languages to publish it globally and put on the Internet. Imagine the impact it will have."

"Yes, I can see that. But how will we deal with the backlash of picking on such a small and poor country?"

"Small and poor country? That's the best reason to pick on it. That microcosm demonstrates day after day what our world would be like if its example was followed. Imagine all tropical and sub-tropical countries between the tropic of Cancer and the tropic of Capricorn suddenly chopping down eighty-five percent of their rainforests and turning over twenty percent of their land into uninhabitable dust bowl deserts. That would be the end of our world as we know it and make the entire planet uninhabitable. Nature doesn't need humans but humans need nature to survive."

Alfons picks up the documents. "Where did you get these?"

"Look at the top of each page."

"Yes, I see they are official government issued documents. But it says here the area was sold to Elisabeth Berndorf. Who is that?"

"Well, sometimes you have to pretend to be someone filthy rich to achieve your goals."

"I see. So, you obtained those documents by fraudulent means." Alfons takes a deep breath, ponders everything he heard from Anabelle, and says, "You've changed a lot in less than a week. You are very aggressive now, far too aggressive for a social news reporter. So, I'm afraid, I'll have to cancel your present contract."

Anabelle smiles from ear to ear. "I accept, Alfons."

He looks very surprised about her reaction. "You seem to be happy to have your contract cancelled. Why?"

Anabelle gathers her report and document copies as well as her photos and puts them in her folder. "Alfons, I am happy not to work any longer for an editor who needs to swallow a walking stick to have something resembling a spine. You prefer to publish inoffensive and essentially empty blather about the lives of the rich and powerful and a nature magazine that denies climate change and pretends that everything is beautiful and intact. As a social news reporter I accepted that. As an investigative reporter I cannot. You said I've changed a lot in the past week. That is correct thanks to some Costa Ricans who opened my eyes to what is really going on in this world and how it is systematically destroyed for the enrichment of a few unscrupulous criminals in business and high office. And you function as their henchman by promoting their lies, pretence and hypocrisy. That's why I am happy to leave. Get my severance paycheque ready and send it to me. Good bye, Alfons."

She picks up her dog's leash. "Come on, Zeus. Let's get outside before Glatzeck, the wrinkled Cerberus shows his face again."

Zeus gets up quick, stretches his legs and then pulls Anabelle with all his might out of the office.

Alfons gets up to say something. Seeing one his best reporters not looking back and walking away without having wished her good luck in all her endeavours or some similar empty phrase, he sits down again. He feels crushed and slaps his hands to his face.

In a mood somewhere between elation and trepidation, Anabelle is on her way home. On the one hand she feels free to pursue a new venture and on the other, she doesn't know what the future holds for her. It reminds her of the hot summer day when she stood on the shore of a lake she had never visited before, did not know the water's temperature or depth but dived in anyway. It was a very shallow lake and she got stuck with her face in the murky silt at the bottom. Giving up was out of the question. She washed off the silt, kept on swimming, and it turned into a wonderfully refreshing experience. She hopes her new venture, whatever it will be, also turns out to be such an experience.

She parks the car near the doggy park to let Zeus run around for having been a 'good boy'. But he doesn't run off on his usual bum sniffing tour of other dogs. Instead he stands close to where she sits on a bench, blinks at her and puts a paw on her thigh. He appears to understand the new situation Anabelle faces and seemingly wants to reassure her that he will be by her side no matter what happens. She strokes his head and they leave the park.

Next stop butcher shop. She wants to make her neighbour's family happy with a chunk of meat and gets a rib roast for them, a steak for herself and a bone with a bit of meat on it for Zeus.

Back in her apartment, she drops her packages on the kitchen table. Her purchase had cost so much it would require most people to take out a second mortgage to pay for it but her neighbour would be as happy as her dog who is busy with the beef knuckle. Checking her watch, she realised it was time to call Rico.

"Hello Rico. How are you and Martha? How's things?"

"Anabelle, it's good to hear your voice. Martha and I are fine although somebody took a shot at our house last night. I guess it was meant to be a warning in answer to a stunt I pulled in Alajuela. But there's more bad news that show how urgent it is to get your documents."

"Goodness! I'll send the documents off today. You should get them tomorrow. What's the bad news?"

"I got word this morning that Maria Villafuerte, a witness in the murder of Felipe Suárez, was victim of a hit and run by a big car in the village of San Jerónimo. It is alleged she walked in a drunken stupor across the street although she never had a drop of alcohol in her life. She will recover from her injuries a doctor assured me. But that wasn't the only thing. Something happened of concern to you."

"To me? How's that possible? I was deported yesterday."

"You were deported? How did that happen?"

"It was after Monty had said good-bye and I was checking into the flight when I was arrested by two guys in checker shirts and jeans, taken to a cell in the basement, strip searched by three guys, slapped and beaten when I told them all my films, the report and documents had been sent to Switzerland the day before. They showed me a picture of me, a screenshot from a security camera. That's how they had identified me as the woman who had pulled that caper with the forest purchase. When they dragged me away to the cell, I yelled, 'Run, Monty, run!' because I feared they had a photo of him as well and would go after him."

"They did, Anabelle. That's the other bad news. He was found at the bottom of a cliff along the Interamerican Highway. He was still alive and is now in intensive care but the doctors give him less than a ten percent chance to survive."

"Oh shit! Please, Rico, look after his family. I think they may be next. I'm sure the goons know that Monty's real name Juan Antonio Castro and where he and his family lives."

"Okay, but why should his family be in danger?"

"I feel so terribly guilty. We found an attaché case in that black sports car on the cemetery. I estimate there was more than two million dollars in it. I gave it to Monty. We bought cartons and clothes, distributed the money among eight packages addressed to his wife, kids, brothers and sisters and shipped the parcels by courier. I will never be able to live it down if something should happen to his wife and kids."

"That solves the attaché case mystery. Don't worry. I'll see to it that his family gets all the protection it needs. I'll make sure that a team of OIJ officers will accompany me to Bahía Potrero within the hour. These bad news show how important it is to receive your documents and put an end to the mayhem and murder.”

“I’ll go right away and send the documents by express courier. What’s Gus’ address?”

Rico gives her the address, tells her once more not to worry, wishes her all the best and ends the call.

Anabelle is now in panic. She shoves the meat packages into the fridge, rushes around in search of an envelope, finds one, writes Gus’ address on it, folds the original documents and puts them into the envelope. It is 15:30 o’clock. She decides to drive to the airport to assure the letter gets on a direct flight leaving today.
***

Rico’s police protection request for his wife is denied once more by his boss Ángel Gerardo Carrazo on the grounds that a suspended officer cannot expect protection from the squad he betrayed. Rico is enraged to be accused of betrayal but cannot do anything about it as long as his corrupt boss occupies the seat of commissioner.

So, he digs some more money out of his ‘private bank’ in the freezer, goes to the local police station, talks to the captain, negotiates a price, pays the bribe and two policemen follow him to provide protection for his wife. That little problem solved the traditional way, he calls Gus and explains the situation with Juan Antonio Castro alias Monty alias José Antonio Castillo Montalban de Gallego and his family. But Gus is reluctant to get involved in that situation.

“Rico, we can’t provide protection for a family. That isn’t our job. We investigate crimes that have been committed. Prevention and protection is the job of the local police.”

“Yes, Gus, but Monty’s wife should be interviewed to provide evidence about the stolen attaché case. It is another duck in the row to strike effectively and close the case.”

“Hmm... I don’t know. Practically all the ducks are in a row. Only documented evidence is missing.”

“Regarding the documents I have good news. They are on the way and should be in your hands by tomorrow. We should tie them to the stolen drug money and make the case watertight.”

“Okay, but how?”

“By interviewing Monty’s wife and finding evidence. You see, the money in the attaché case was drug money meaning it will have

242

traces of cocaine on it. If we find any of that money and provide proof of cocaine on it, you have all the evidence you need."

"Fair enough. I see your point. I'll get Omar to tag along and we can pick you up in about thirty minutes. See you then."

Rico ends the call and faces Martha and Olga. "What's the matter? You two look anxious."

"I wanted to take Olga on a shopping spree," says Martha. "Is it safe for us to go outside?"

"Yes, I organised your personal bodyguards. They are outside."

"Bring them in. They should know who they have to protect. But how do we get around? Four people in a taxi is not possible."

"No problem. Gus will pick me up. You can use our car. Okay?"

Problem solved. The two policemen are invited into the house and served coffee and some snacks while Rico gets busy on his computer. He types a brief message, 'From: Bruno - To: José Antonio Castillo Montalban' requesting his silence in return for the money contained in the parcel. He prints it out and tucks it into his shirt pocket. Expecting to encounter potential trouble in Bahía Potrero, he puts on his shoulder holster with his gun and pockets a spare magazine. Dressed in a suit, he wishes his wife and Olga fun going shopping and goes outside. When Gus and Omar turn up, he gets into the back of the car. Gus hands him the safe deposit box key before he steps on it to get out of the urban area and onto the highway to Guanacaste.

Gus is a hot-tempered driver who likes to go fast. A flashing blue light on top of the car and the red, white and blue pulsating light strip at the bottom of the windshield marks him and his passengers on official duty and prevents any police harassment for exceeding the speed limit. On the highway to Liberia he overtakes the familiar American cars of Argentinian manufacture three times and grumbles, "These bastards are out in full force. I wonder who will disappear this time. Must be someone important."

Before they get to Bahía Potrero, Gus takes down the blue light and switches off the light strip to stay inconspicuous. Since they don't know where Monty's house is located, Rico directs Gus to the cantina near the beach to have a chat with Chavez, who is well informed about everything going on in his locality.

He greets Chavez who is happy to see him. "How are you, Señor, and how is your wife? Have you heard anything of Monty and his latest conquest, that attractive foreign lady?"

"My wife and I are fine. Monty is in hospital. He had an accident. We need to inform his family. Could you direct us to his house?"

"That's funny. You are the second person to ask where his family lives. You see that bus churning up all that dust? The driver was here a minute ago and asked me the same question. He has several parcels to deliver. Just follow him."

"We'll do that. Thank you. We'll see you later."

Rico gets back into the car and tells Gus to follow the bus. They should get to it before the driver can deliver several parcels. Gus races along the dusty trail of dirt road and stops in front of the bus near a small dilapidated wooden house where three children play hopscotch near the front door.

Rico shows his OIJ badge to the driver and asks, "Are you delivering parcels for the residents of this house?"

"Yes, that's right," responds the driver. "I have five parcels of clothes to deliver here."

"All right. We would like to inspect them."

The driver opens the luggage hold and shows him five neatly wrapped parcels.

Rico looks at the addressees' names, identifies the one for Monty's wife, and whispers to Gus and Omar, "This parcel is off limits. I'll tell you why in a minute. Take the other four and put them in the trunk of the car. We need to inspect them."

He picks up the parcel he selected and turns to the woman with a little child on her arm stepping out of the house. He speaks very quietly when he addresses her. "Good afternoon, Señora Castro. I'm an OIJ officer. This parcel was sent by your husband."

She holds the door open and he steps into the impoverished looking interior. The entire house consists only of the combined bedroom-living room arrangement with space at the back for the kitchen where soup is simmering in a pot on a woodfired stove and a niche with an open shower and toilet. Monty's wife and her four children live in abject poverty.

Rico puts the parcel on the one big bed that serves the entire family and says, "Please, Señora, do not open this parcel until we have assured that you are safe. Should you find any money in the parcel, use it wisely and don't show it off to anyone. Do you understand? Your husband, my friend, had an accident and is in hospital in San José. I'll give you my phone number. You can call me any time you have questions. My name is Rico."

Monty's wife starts to cry silently and sits down on the bed. Rico finds a snippet of paper, jots down his phone number and hands it to her. The little boy cuddles up to his mother and holds her tight around the waist as far as his arms can reach.

Outside Rico talks to the driver. "I guess you want to get going. Do you want me to sign for the delivery of these parcels?"

The driver holds out a clipboard and points to spaces for the parcels. Rico signs, digs into his pocket and gives the driver a tip who expresses his thanks, gets into his bus and slowly drives a turn to pull away. The bus is not completely out of the way when a big car without license plates slowly lumbers towards the house. It stops about twenty meters away.

"Gus, Omar, look," says Rico pointing at the car. "We have unpleasant company and made it just in time. Get your guns ready."

Two burly guys in their 'uniforms' of checker shirt and jeans get out of the car, keep the engine idling, and slowly approach Rico, Gus and Omar. One of them holds up a plastic card.

While Omar ushers the three children into the house, Gus holds up his badge and shouts, "You don't need to flash your fake identity. We expected you. We are OIJ inspectors."

One of the guys asks, "OIJ? There's nothing for you to investigate. What the fuck are you doing here?"

Gus replies, "I can ask you the same question, although it's clear that you follow orders to liquidate the woman and her four kids who live here and let them disappear."

Rico shouts, "Where is your boat?"

"What boat?"

"The boat you need to let the five corpses disappear out at sea."

The two guys confer with each other and seem to want to return to their car. Rico gets out his gun and loads it through.

Gus and Omar follow his example and move to stand behind the car next to Rico. It is just in time to see the two guys turn on their heels, pull their guns from the small of their back and fire at them. Gus' car gets punctured by three bullets. Mad as hell, he aims carefully and kills one of them with two shots to the chest. The other one is missed running in a zigzag to get into the car and spin it around to escape. Rico steadies himself on the roof of Gus' car, takes aim and hits the car's rear tyres and petrol tank several times. It swerves into a ditch, flips over crashing on its roof, and bursts into flames.

"Son of a bitch," mutters Gus. "I don't have a fire extinguisher. Before we call the local police, let's inspect the parcels."

They tuck their guns away and quickly rip open the cartons in the trunk. Putting the money they find into an emptied carton, they heap the children's clothes and shoes in the remaining three.

Gus counts the bundles of banknotes. "That's about three hundred and fifty thousand. Where's the rest of the money?"

"I was told that Monty divided the money among a whole lot of packages he sent to brothers, sisters and friends," says Rico and tucks his note into the banknotes. "I have no idea where they live. Anyway, this amount is enough to prove our case. A drug sniffing canine only needs to confirm with his nose that it is drug money."

"Shouldn't we check the carton you took inside to the woman?" asks Omar.

"No!" is Rico's very firm response. "Let's take the kids' clothes into the house. I want you to have a look around and then I'll tell you why we should leave the woman's parcel alone."

Each guy takes one parcel of clothes, Gus shuts and locks the trunk, and they enter the house. Monty's wife sits with her four children on the bed legs pulled up to their chests looking scared. The cartons are put in front of the bed. Gus and Omar look around.

Rico pulls his colleagues to the side and says quietly, "This is what abject poverty looks like, friends. Would you want to deprive a woman, possibly a widow with four children of a little windfall?"

Omar is rankled by that assertion. "Any money in her parcel is the proceeds of a crime. The law requires us to confiscate it."

Rico nods. "You're right, the law requires us to do that. But do you know the difference between the law and justice? I appeal to your sense of fairness and let justice prevail. That woman has done nothing wrong or broken a law. She and her children deserve a break. So, let them enjoy whatever is in the carton."

Gus nods earnestly, takes Omar by the arm and pulls him outside. Rico sits down on the corner of the bed. One of the boys crawls over to him. "Where's my dad? Did you arrest him?"

"Your dad? He's my friend," says Rico and puts his arm around his shoulders. "I wouldn't arrest him. I arrest only bad boys."

"The two guys you shot, were they bad boys?"

"I don't know. They shot at us first and we defended ourselves."

He gets up, signals to Monty's wife to come outside. She follows him to the door, leans in the frame and watches him talking to his colleagues before they drive away.

246

Rico turns to the woman. "Señora, the police will be here soon. My colleagues and I will give statements and remain until the police leave. Do you have somewhere else to stay? Family or friends? You should leave this place for at least a few days."

She shakes her head and starts to cry again. "We can't leave. This is my children's home. I don't have enough money to stay in a hotel or rent a room somewhere."

"Oh, yes, you do. I'm sure of that. It's in the parcel. That's why I told you to use it wisely and not show it to anyone. Look, I will go to a nearby hotel or lodging and book a room for you. Is there any place in Bahía Potrero you prefer?"

"There are many new places. I know only the little beach hotel."

"That's okay. I've stayed there before and will talk to Pablo, the manager if he's not too drunk. If you stay there you're out of the way and still close to home. You better get ready."

Two police cars and Gus in his jalopy are approaching. They come to a stop in a thick cloud of dust. Four policemen and Gus and Omar get out to inspect the scene. Two cops go with Gus to the man he shot and Omar takes one to the burned-out car. The remaining cop asks Rico to identify himself. Presented with the OIJ card, he takes down the data and wants to know why he came to this place.

Rico explains his reason in the simplest terms possible. He states that the woman's husband is a key witness in a case against organised crime. So, they wanted to interview her to learn more about her husband's activity. The two men came and fired their pistols at them and they defended themselves. More he couldn't say because it was an open case investigated by the OIJ.

The other policemen return with Gus and Omar and one of them calls the station on the police radio requesting a hearse for two corpses and a tow truck. He is told it would take at least an hour for these requested vehicles to come from the city of Liberia.

Rico asks Gus if he may use his car to drive Monty's wife and her children to a nearby hotel. Car keys in hand, he beckons the mother and her kids to come outside with whatever they needed to take along and get into the car. Everybody safely seated with the cartons on their knees, Rico drives to the beach hotel.

Persuading Pablo to rent a room to a woman with four children takes some persuasion and Rico to vouch for them. When he returns, the tow truck is loading the wreck, and the corpses have been put into the hearse. It is time for the trio to get back home.

They visit Chavez's beach cantina upon Rico's recommendation for an early dinner. While they eat, they can hear the dull sound of an explosion. They turn and see Monty's house going up in flames in the distance.

Rico mumbles, "They never give up, do they?"

Gus nods. "It's time to clear up this entire mess of mayhem and murder. If we succeed, the Suárez murder may turn out to be a turning point in our country's history. Let's get to work, guys."

***

It is just after midnight in Alajuela when two cars turn into the side road and stop silently in front of Muñoz's mansion. Four guys in black overalls get out, look around to assure they are alone, put balaclavas and latex gloves on, and approach the house.

One of the men, the driver of the fake taxi, carries a length of thick rope slung over his shoulder. He looks at the locks of the front door, gets out a battery operated lockpick, inserts it silently and carefully unlocks three locks. The third lock switches off the burglar alarm and the four men enter the house unnoticed.

Quickly they spread out, orientate themselves and check every room downstairs. The guy with the rope goes up the stairs and attaches the rope with one end to the sturdy corner post of the banister and lets the end with a noose drop down.

He goes down to the vestibule where one of his companions gestures from the door to the large living room. He and the other two join him and they see Octavio Muñoz dressed in a red silk morning coat asleep in an easy chair with an empty bottle of Scotch and a full glass on a side table next to him.

They wake him up. Surrounded by four guys in black with balaclavas, Octavio wants to scream but the guy behind the chair clamps a hand over his mouth.

"We've come for the attaché case with the money," says the leader of the quartet quietly. "Cooperate and hand it over or else."

Octavio struggles to free himself but is held back by the grip around his mouth. He waves a hand and barely manages to shake his head. The guy behind him loosens his grip a bit to let him speak.

"I don't have the case," Octavio whimpers. "I gave it to Cholo with the instruction to hide in Ramírez's house."

"Cholo is dead and he didn't have the case, you bloody liar. Open your safe. We have to inspect it."

Octavio is in total panic and starts to whine. "There's no money or the case in my safe. Only papers of no interest to you."

"That's for us to judge. Open the safe and let us have a look."

Brutally he is pulled up by his morning coat. He lets out a brief scream before a hand is clamped over his mouth again.

One of the guys in black goes along the walls and checks the framed paintings by pushing them a bit. All of them move except one that is mounted on hinges. It flips open and reveals a wall safe.

"Give us the combination to your safe," the leader says quietly.

Octavio shakes his head. One man takes pruning scissors from his pocket, another one grabs Octavio's wrist and holds out his hand. The pruning scissors are placed on the little finger ready to amputate part of it. Octavio starts to cry and hastily says six numbers. He is told to repeat the numbers and the required turns slowly while one of the men follows the instruction. On the second try an audible click indicates the lock is open. A turn of the handle and the door opens. The contents of the safe are indeed just piles of paper and neither an attaché case nor bundles of banknotes can be seen. The papers are ripped out and flung to the floor.

"Where is the money?" the leader asks in a threatening tone.

"I told you I gave the attaché case to Cholo," shouts Octavio with tears streaming down his face.

"Why do you make life so difficult for yourself and us?" asks the leader. "We'll find the money. Rest assured."

Octavio pleads, "If it is only the money you want, I can get it for you in two days from my bank in the British Virgin Islands."

The leader shakes his head and gestures to take Octavio to the vestibule. At that moment a lisping woman is heard asking, "Bubba, do you have late night visitors again? Keep it quiet, please!"

One of the man pulls a cosh out of the long side pocket of his overalls and sprints upstairs. The other men can hear a brief scream of the woman followed by two blows and the clatter of the cosh. The man stays at the top of the stairs and jiggles the rope. One man brings two chairs from the dining room and places them to the left and right of the noose. The two men holding Octavio drag him under the noose, their leader places the noose around his neck and says, "Last chance, Señor Muñoz. Where is the case with the money?"

Octavio howls, "I don't have it!"

The leader gestures to lift Octavio. The two men get up on the chairs, lift Octavio by his arms about two meters into the air, the slack of the rope is taken up and secured firmly around the post.

The leader gestures to drop him. Octavio's neck breaks and he dangles with his feet almost touching the floor.

The leader shrugs and gestures to the men to start searching the entire house. The only items they find are six hundred dollars in one hundreds and an extensive collection of rare wine and expensive liquor in a wine cellar. They pack the bottles into two holdalls and go upstairs.

As they leave the house, the leader says, "No money but at least we can have a decent party back at the barracks."
***
In the morning Gus hears the news that a mailman found the front door of Octavio Muñoz's house ajar. When he stepped inside, he saw the Special Envoy for Nature Conservation dangling from a rope in the vestibule, an apparent case of suicide. He called the police who also found the mother of the man upstairs near the landing. She had been beaten to death with a cosh. Everything was left as it was found for further investigation by the OIJ.

Gus calls Rico and asks him if he would like to accompany him. Neither should he worry about his suspension nor fear any flak coming from the boss who was called to an urgent meeting with some top bureaucrats.

Rico weighs the pros and cons of being seen so soon in the guy's house after he cream-pied him. The barrage of questions from the media he may have to face about him being the catalyst to Muñoz committing suicide could create an awkward situation. But he agrees to accompany Gus and the OIJ forensic team.

Forty minutes later they meet in the Muñoz mansion. Gus and his men get to work looking for evidence to ascertain that it was what looks at first glance to be a case of murder-suicide or if it is something more sinister like a double murder.

Rico looks at the papers strewn on the living room floor. As he sifts through them, he starts to chuckle and after reading one of the documents, he calls Gus to come and have a look.

"What is it, Rico? We are extremely busy."

"Yes, of course but have a look at some of these secret and confidential papers. That's all you need to get arrest warrants for more than a dozen government officials and top bureaucrats."

Gus skims a few documents and raises his eyebrows. "Damn it, any judge presented with these documents will hand out arrest warrants with glee. It'll end the careers of many of the high and mighty."

"Including our boss. I'll put all the papers in a carton and have them sent to your office to sort them by name and date sequence. How are you coming along with your search?"

"The pathologist says that the victims died more or less at the same time around 01:00 o'clock plus minus an hour. We found no fingerprints on the cosh that was used to kill the woman but some small black fibres. Also, on Muñoz's upper arms were bruises that seem to indicate he was held by two persons, probably men who lifted him before he was dropped with the noose around his neck. It points to a case of double murder but..."

Gus' cell phone rings and interrupts him. "Hello? Yes, dear, what is it? A letter from Switzerland delivered by courier addressed to Detective Inspector Goicoechea? Yes, that's me... No! No, you will not send it to the OIJ. What's your problem? Just keep it on my desk. I'll pick it up in an hour or so. No! It wasn't a mistake! Okay?"

He ends the call and groans. "My wife! The most obedient devotee of rules and regulations and stubborn as a mule. You're so lucky, Rico, to have Martha. She's such an excellent collaborator. By the way, the media is gathering at the front door. Better you don't show your face. Get out the backdoor or wait until I've given a statement and the reporters leave."

"Good idea. In the meantime I'll scan this treasure trove of incriminating information for any reference to Felipe Suárez. I need to find a box or carton for all these papers."

"Have a look in the basement. Go down the stairs in the kitchen."

In the wine cellar, Rico is surprised to see the empty bottle racks. A list is attached to a shelf with the name of wines, the date of delivery and recommended duration of storage. None of the listed bottles are in their allocated slots. Somebody must have cleared out the wine cellar, he surmises and takes the list down. It may provide a clue about the thieves if a big booze-up taking place somewhere can be found. He picks up a couple of cartons from a wine merchant and goes back to his task upstairs.

He gathers the papers, scans some of them and puts them away until he comes across one with the letterhead of the OIJ. He reads the letter and mutters, "What a giveaway!"

He looks up at the ceiling with a big smile, kisses the page, folds it, and tucks it into his shirt pocket. A commotion can be heard coming from the front door. It is Gus saying very firmly to some people that they can't enter the house for some footage of the victims. Against loud protest he slams the door shut after the guys with morgue stretchers have entered.

Rico looks into the vestibule where Muñoz's remains are put in a body bag and carried outside. The other crew with the woman's remains comes downstairs and leaves the house as well. It is time for Gus to provide a press statements. He explains that by all evidence found at the scene of the crime the tragedy that took place in the house was not a case of murder-suicide but a double murder. The OIJ will follow every lead to find the perpetrators of this heinous crime.

In response to some overexcited question, he states that the attack on the male victim with a cream pie the previous day is not related to the murder but may be an indication of the motive for the crime. At this point he cannot provide any further details due to an ongoing broad investigation. He turns away and refuses to answer any more questions. The videographers and reporters pack up their equipment and leave rather disappointed to broadcast and print the breaking news of the day.

Rico signals to Gus to come and have a look at something of interest to him. He shows him the wine list and says that not one bottle was in the racks of the wine cellar. Perhaps he can find out where a big booze-up is taking place, probably in the barracks of the Rapid Reaction Force. But Gus doubts the RRF was involved. They would have removed the corpses and let them the disappear.

"No, I think they left the corpses on purpose," counters Rico. "They were looking for something specific. I suspect it may have been the attaché case with two million bucks. That's why the wall safe was open. When they didn't find it, they had to provide proof of having done their job to whoever gave them the order. Within the next hour when the breaking news are broadcast, the worms will come crawling out of the woodwork."

Gus considers Rico's argument cautiously and reads the OIJ letter held out by him. He chuckles and says, "I knew our boss had a couple of bats in his belfry but to put his name and title on these secret instructions and sign it is beyond belief. That's the evidence we need to have Ramos arrested. Will you do that?"

"With pleasure. I guess you will have a hectic weekend ahead sorting all the papers. First thing Monday morning you want to see a judge, present the evidence and request the issue of a vast number of arrest warrants. Aw, you'll have so much fun."

"Heh, hang on a minute. What do you mean you, you, you? As a senior detective inspector I'm lifting your suspension on the strength of the evidence in these two boxes and expect a full day's work from you today and on Sunday. Is that clear?"

"Can you do that, I mean, lifting my suspension?"

"Of course! Your suspension was issued orally and repeated on TV but was never confirmed in writing. That alone will lead to an enquiry. I expect to see you shortly in the office to help me with this tedium of sorting several hundred pages by name and date. Okay?"

***

Back home a pleasant surprise awaits Rico as soon as he has parked his car. Martha and Olga with the two policemen in tow come walking along the pavement. The women look content and wave to him. He asks, "What are you so smug about?"

"Smug?" asks Martha. "We are not smug but content to have got a real bargain. Olga can tell you all about it."

"Olga? What bargain was that? Did you get the pretty dress you're wearing for half price?"

"No, much better than that," replies Olga and can hardly contain her happiness. "I've decided it's time for some big changes in my life thanks to Martha's advice. I will go back to school to qualify for university. Then I will study criminology and hope to become your colleague in about five years. That means I won't go to Spain. I'm going to stay right here. You see that townhouse with the pretty pink window frames and the For-Sale sign? Martha and I talked to the owner and haggled him down to a fifteen percent price reduction if I pay in US dollars. I'll be your new neighbour and I'm so happy."

"Welcome to the neighbourhood, Olga," says Rico, "and I look forward to the day of welcoming you to the OIJ. It's just the right time for such a move. Yesterday and even early this morning I would have advised you strongly against it but latest developments have turned the tide in your and our favour." He addresses the two policemen, "And you will be relieved of looking after my wife and our friend come Monday afternoon. Let's go inside and watch the news. That'll explain a lot to you. Come on you guys, it's time to crack open a couple of cold brews! What do you say?"

They settle in the living room and switch on the TV set. Rico hands out beer to Olga and the cops and a lemonade for Martha. It takes a while before the late morning soap opera is interrupted with breaking news. They listen to the commentary announcing the murder of the recent appointee to the post of Special Envoy for Nature Conservation and his mother who were found dead in their home. Gus' statement of a broad investigation raises questions that remain unanswered.

Rico is surprised to see some shots of him carrying a box to Gus' car and hear speculative comments about a suspended OIJ inspector taking part in the scene of the crime investigation.

Rico chuckles. "That last bit will put more than just a couple of hornets up some people's trouser legs. I suspect the toilets in some government buildings will be fully occupied in a minute."

Martha, Olga and the two cops want to know what he is talking about with reference to government buildings. Rico tells them they have to be patient until Monday early afternoon and the breaking news that will be beamed out round about 15:00 o'clock. He gets up and says that he will have to go to work.

Martha is astonished. "But it is the weekend. I am going to make a really delicious lunch. You can't leave now and go to work."

"Oh, yes I can and have to go. Remember last Sunday when this chaos started? Gus promised it would take only two hours. They were the longest two hours in my life that lasted a whole week. Your delicious lunch will have takers. These two boys in light grey and blue will be happy to oblige. I'll see you at the latest on Monday afternoon."

Before he leaves the house, he turns to Olga and holds a key out to her. "I almost forgot. This was found in a wallet of Felipe's killer. It may be the key to Felipe's safe deposit box. At least I hope it is. I guess I will have some time on Monday. Then we can go together to the bank and open it."

Olga flushes emotionally, takes the key and holding it firmly in her hand presses it against her chest.
***

It takes Rico and a crew of OIJ inspectors all of Saturday and Sunday to sort the papers recovered in Muñoz's house. Before Gus got involved, he used all his trickery to inveigle himself and three assistants into the quarters of the Rapid Reaction Force barracks where a booze-up was taking place. Armed with the wine list Rico had found in the wine cellar, he identified the bottles taken, confiscated them, and arrested the four drunk members of the force for the double murder of Muñoz and his mother.

Back in the office sorting the papers by name of the senders and date turns out to be a major difficulty due to numerous cross references. It takes Rico to draw a diagram on a whiteboard with the names of twenty-four bureaucrats and high-ranking government officials to show all the links. It allows the team to identify who is involved in corruption, embezzlement, laundering of drug money, fraud, intimidation of land owners, and orders to liquidate antagonists. Late Sunday night their job is finally done by associating each of the culprits with specific crimes and having suggested charges attached to each pile of documents.

On Monday morning Gus calls a judge for an urgent review of the evidence with the request for issuing warrants for arrest. At 10:00 o'clock, after having been granted an audience, the judge is presented with the twenty-four piles of paper. She requests time to review the material and calls four hours later that she has issued the arrest warrants.

During this lull of activity, Rico receives a call from Monty. He is enormously pleased to hear from him and asks what his chances are for a complete recovery. Monty explains that he underwent surgery to remove one squashed kidney and will undergo more operations in the next few days to fix or remove damaged organs. He does not provide more details about his overall state of health but wants to know if his family is all right. Rico assures him of his family's safety and explains that he persuaded his wife to stay with their children in the beach hotel of Bahía Potrero. He can call there and speak to his wife. Finally, he promises to drive him home once he is released from hospital.

He remembers to call home and speaks to Olga about taking a trip to the bank and find out if the key fits. He assures her of taking along some documents that will allow them to access the box in case the key doesn't fit.

He picks up Olga and they drive to the bank branch in San Pedro. All he needs to show is his OIJ badge and Felipe's death certificate for them to be permitted to enter the vault room with the safe deposit boxes. The bank employee inserts one key and Olga follows suit with the one Rico gave her once she overcomes her jitters and excitement. The key fits, the door is opened and the box is pulled out. The bank employee leaves and the great moment of finding out what the box contains has arrived.

On top of a lot of bundled letters and banknotes is a notebook. Rico asks Olga's permission to open it and see what notes Felipe had taken. Page after page details columns of dates, the sender and recipient of his courier deliveries and the amount of money received for copying and delivering the confidential and secret documents.

The notebook turns out to be a bombshell of revelations. It confirms Felipe's activity of more than four years of supplying a heretofore unknown recipient with the copies of secret government and business documents and appears to clearly outline the purpose of this clandestine operation. It was Muñoz's intended power grab prepared in advance over many years.

Rico says, "Olga, I have to confiscate this notebook. It may be a crucial item of evidence in any of the upcoming trials of the people we accuse of fraud and having ordered the elimination of their antagonists."

"Oh dear," responds Olga looking shocked. "You mean to say that Felipe knew of the elimination, the killing of people and didn't inform the authorities about it? That's horrible."

"No, Olga, Felipe didn't know about it. The fraud and ordering the killing of people is a conclusion I can draw based on the evidence found in Octavio Muñoz's house. Felipe was used by a nasty character who intended to usurp the government. I will keep the notebook and provide it as evidence when the trials demand it. How much money is in the box? Have you counted it?"

"No, but it's thousands and thousands of dollars. I have found his last will and testament. It's almost as if he anticipated to die soon because he made me the sole inheritor of all his worldly goods including his house in San Antonio."

"Well, you can sell the house unless you want to live there."

"No! I could never live there. It would be a nightmare for me."

"Yes, I understand. But you better hold on to all the money you still have because you will be hit by a massive inheritance tax. Put whatever money of the lot I gave you and don't need in the box. Here it'll be safe. Take the testament and let's close up. You still have to have the safe deposit box transferred to your name and I have to get back to the OIJ."

She closes the box, shoves it back into its slot, locks the door, and they are on their way.

At 14:30 o'clock the warrants for the arrest of the twenty-four people are issued and picked up by Gus. He hands them out to twelve OIJ inspectors, calls the media to announce the upcoming action and tells all his colleagues to swarm out at once.

It is Rico's great pleasure to go straight into the OIJ commissioner's office and ignore the order to get out.

"Good afternoon, Ramos," sounds like a friendly but deadly opening salvo coming from Rico that gives Ángel Carrazo de Gallego almost a heart attack. He knows the game is up and does not need to listen when he is presented with the arrest warrant for the planning and cover-up of government officials' orders for the liquidation of alleged antagonists

It is a very satisfying moment for Rico to put the shiny metal handcuffs on his boss' wrists, drag him through the antechamber past the shocked secretary and deliver him to the cells of the OIJ Prison Section. A couple of reporters and a TV crew watch his every step along the way. Their questions remain unanswered except a statement that a warrant for Carrazo's arrest was issued by a judge.

The arrests of Manuel Cardenas, Roberto Chaverry, Roberto Zuñiga, and the Minister for Public Security are the focal points for the media. Shortly after 15:00 o'clock, as predicted by Rico, all TV and radio stations start to broadcast the breaking news.

Before he goes home, he goes to the airport and enquires with the migration officials about the deportation of the journalist Anabelle Bouchard. At first it is denied that it took place and also a search of the *Libro Grande*, the 'Big Book' and computer files containing the names of anyone wanted for crimes or barred from entering the country yields no results. Despite the late hour in Switzerland, Rico calls Anabelle and gets her out of bed with the request for her passport nationality and number, her full name and date of birth. He explains the situation of having to find proof of her deportation and her being declared a 'persona non grata' barred from entering Costa Rica. He tells her to stay on the phone while he enters her data into a migration computer terminal at the airport. The moment he hits the 'Enter' button, her deportation record shows up on the screen and a long list of her alleged crimes, but the crucial entry of an accuser is blank. In his capacity of OIJ detective inspector he demands the record and all other references to her name to be erased. He states that this visitor was crucial to the discovery of crimes committed by twenty-four government officials, bureaucrats and businessmen. Anabelle Bouchard was falsely accused in the attempt of covering up these crimes. Based on the breaking news, the migration official in charge has to agree to have her records erased. Rico tells Anabelle that she will be welcome to visit Costa Rica any time as long as she gets a new passport.

Anabelle sheds some tears of joy and wants to tell him her story about the rejection of her report. But he ends the call when he thanks her for the prompt delivery of her caper documents that were crucial for the arrest warrants for Cardenas, Chaverry and Zuñiga. These three and twenty-one other culprits are safely locked up and are due for their first court hearing in the course of the week.

Rico gets home in the early evening to watch a live statement by the President of the Republic who expresses his deep regret that so many people in the service of the country were involved in criminal activities for their personal enrichment. He promises a major review of the government's environmental policy, a reshuffling of his cabinet of ministers, the restructuring of the public and national security forces, and heaps glory, laud, and honour on the officers of the OIJ for showing the whole world that Costa Rica is a country of law and order.

Rico is not impressed. He says to Martha and Olga that he will believe these lofty declarations and promises once he sees actual change taking place.

The discussion of the day's events with Martha and Olga go on until late in the night. He explains how the murder of Felipe Suárez was the crucible of investigations leading to the arrest of crooks and criminals in high office. Upon hearing this, Olga declares she will go to San Antonio, see Felipe's grave and order a monumental gravestone with an inscription and a big white angel on top for everybody to see and remember what a wonderful man he was.

Shortly before midnight the telephone rings. It is Anabelle calling. She thanks Rico profusely for his intervention to clear her name and calls at this hour because she could not go back to sleep after receiving the fantastic news. He switches the phone to speaker for Martha and Olga to listen in.

They are dismayed to learn that her report will not be published in the nature magazine although she assures them that it is positive change. She is very busy putting her report and photos in a magazine format. It will include a eulogy to Don Oduber Madrigal's effort of protecting his forest with an extensive selection of her best photos. After contacting several environmental organisations with excerpts of her report, she has received invitations for a speaking tour to present her findings to audiences in several European countries where her publication, issued in four languages, will go on sale for a nominal price. Also, a news magazine in Germany has expressed interest in her report and will publish it.

She leaves her three listeners speechless with what she says next. "It is my aim to contribute to the end of pretence, hypocrisy and lies that mar environmental protection on a global scale to this day. If the deforestation is not stopped entirely then all the efforts of battling climate change and preserving our biodiversity will be for naught. Reforestation as it is done nowadays is not going to counteract or neutralise the effects of deforestation because none of the endemic plants that were destroyed can be recreated. Planting massive monocultures does little if anything to provide the environment for the wildlife that needs the rainforests most to survive and thrive. The Central American squirrel monkey, for example, has been categorised as threatened with extinction unless the environment that threatens its survival and reproduction is improved.

"Costa Rica's much lauded effort of having reforested 150,000 hectares of barren land amounts to little more than a bad joke when you consider that over eighty percent or 2,657,200 hectares of its forests were razed to the ground and that some 50,000 hectares of forests are still cut down year after year. No rainforest is grown and its original biodiversity is not restored by planting monocultures or a man-made mix of plants. A rainforest has to be nurtured without human intervention and given time to grow again. It takes more than a century for 150,000 hectares of rainforest to grow naturally and it can only regrow from within the parcels of existing rainforest to expand slowly at its own pace. If Costa Rica and all other tropical countries doubled the land area around the remaining rainforest and cloudforest, declared it to be absolutely protected land where any human activity is prohibited, except to study and observe it, we could see a regrowth over the next one hundred years. Such action would contribute to reducing climate change and saving our planet Earth from making it uninhabitable for all creatures, our species included, although it may already be too late. That applies only to the land area. Similar protective measures would have to be undertaken for the oceans."

A moment of stunned silence follows Anabelle's lengthy plea until Martha finds her voice. "That is amazing, Anabelle. You've changed a lot since we first met. Remember when Monty called you a social news junkie? He wouldn't do that now. You've become an investigative journalist and an environmental warrior. Such a change amounts to a metamorphosis."

"Thank you, Martha. I agree to have undergone something of a metamorphosis. For many years, I crawled around like a maggot in search of social news that has no real purpose. My eyes were opened to what is really important in life thanks to you and Monty and especially Don Oduber Madrigal as well as the sting operation he had suggested and instigated. It's the survival and preservation of our planet's environment and biodiversity that's at stake."

"Yes," says Rico, "and I have to thank you once more for sending the documents of the sting. We have finally emptied a huge barrel of effluent, as my colleague Gus Goicoechea calls it. That operation started with the investigation of a murder, drew wider and wider circles and concluded with the death of the killer and the arrest of twenty-four corrupt government officials, bureaucrats and businessmen who gave the order for the murder. Your documents are the crucial evidence to send several of these criminals to prison. Our president responded to the successful conclusion of our investigation by regretting that so many people in the service of the country were involved in criminal activities for their personal enrichment. He didn't express anger, outrage or fury, no, just regret, and promised a review of our environmental policy, which means in plain text that nothing is going to change.

"When you come back to Costa Rica, and I hope you will come back soon, you shouldn't only give your lecture to a crowd of university students but also to a full house of the legislative assembly in parliament with our president in the front row to listen, learn and have his eyes opened. The president may even pretend to have listened and thank you profusely for your nice speech. But politicians, as you know, do not listen, will not learn and are loathe to take decisive and drastic action to save the environment of our planet. Such action should start with our country, but it won't. So, nothing is going to change. That's the reason why Costa Rica is known in all Spanish speaking countries as Costa Risa." [1]

---

[1] Costa Rica (the Rich Coast)
Costa Risa (the Laughable Coast)

260

Some Final Notes

The reports and the book mentioned in the latter part of the chapter 'The Sting' are real. They were written and published in Costa Rica by Costa Rican journalists and writers. Excerpts of the reports are presented here as background material of this novel. The dates show that not very much, if anything at all has changed in the course of well over thirty years. Yet, there is hope that it will.

The Paradise Dies *

Rumbo, Carlos Cortés, San José, Costa Rica, 21st November 1989

Few Costa Ricans know that our country ranks first in the world in the deforestation rate per capita, that we only have a quarter of our forests left and many consider that these will be exhausted in a few years, before the end of the next decade.

It is likely that there are also few who know that the 12% of the national territory, which is the protected area of national parks, reserves, and refuges is proportionally the largest in the world dedicated to conservation.

On 0.04% of the globe's surface - the land area of Costa Rica - one of the regions with the greatest biological diversity in the tropics, the following number of different species are found: 8,000 vascular plants (trees, shrubs, and herbs), 2,000 orchids, 1,239 butterflies, 205 mammals and 850 birds.

It contrasts with the reality of Costa Rica annually losing between 3.6% and 3.9% of its forests - the deforestation rate is 50,000 hectares - in addition to the loss of 680 million metric tons of soil due to erosion caused by the forest massacre. Thus, it is estimated that 17% of the country is extremely and a further 24% is moderately eroded. This is very serious when you think that it takes from one to four centuries to restore 10mm (1cm = 3/8") of soil.

The "beautiful Costa Rica" - touristic, paradisical, tropical - contrasts with the more than 1,000 metric tons of faecal matter that are flushed daily into the rivers and hydrographic basins of the Central Valley without any treatment, and with the 800 tons of garbage of the 1,650 tons that are produced daily and are left uncollected and "thrown away in any lot".

It contrasts with more than 11,500 metric tons of pesticides that are used in the country each year with little control. It causes "pollution of water, food poisoning and death. Here in the region products are used which, due to their high toxic power, have already been severely restricted or prohibited in other countries", warns Alexander Bonilla Durán in his book Ecological Crisis in Central America. It is the biggest pollution problem facing our nation.

These are the two Costa Rica: the one with the "beautiful ecology" with the national parks, a living laboratory of greatest interest in the tropical world, and that of the other, the "ugly ecology" of dead forests, toxic waste, excessive energy waste, rivers of excrement, poisoning pesticides, beaches turned into garbage dumps, and that of polluted seas.

Corruption at the Highest Office *

Calderón Fournier sentenced for receiving illegal commissions

Ernesto Rivera, La Nación, Tuesday, 6th October 2009

Yesterday, a court unanimously convicted former President Rafael Ángel Calderón Fournier of crimes of embezzlement to the detriment of the Costa Rican State and sentenced him to 5 years in prison. After ten months of oral and public debate, Calderón Fournier became the first former president in the history of Costa Rica to be convicted of a corruption case.

Update

On 11th May 2011 Calderón Fournier's appeal was rejected by the Third Chamber [Court]. The judges confirmed the previous sentence. However, they reduced the prison term from five years to three. According to Costa Rican law, he can be expected not to serve this time in prison.

In 2017 Costa Rica's Attorney General office indicted former president Oscar Arías for the Crucitas case, where former Environment Minister Roberto Dobles and Arías signed a 2008 decree ceding control over a protected area known as Crucitas near the Nicaraguan border for gold mining to the Canadian company Infinito Gold and declaring it "national interest", something that the Prosecution argued was illegal as protected areas can't be granted for exploitation of any kind.

Drug Trafficking Police *

Two convicted of drug trafficking - Ten years prison for each one

Rodrigo Peralta G., La Nación, 19th May 1989

Edwin Viales Rodríguez, former police commander of the rural police in Santa Cruz, Guanacaste, and Carlos Eduardo Zapparolli Zecca of Liberia were sentenced yesterday to ten years in prison each, by the Superior Criminal Court of Liberia, after being found guilty of the crime of international cocaine trafficking.

The prosecutors Guido Jiménez and Liliana Zamora concluded that the illicit actions of transferring about 4,000 kilos of cocaine to the United States was conducted by using our country as a bridge.

*   Translated from Spanish by the author of this book

Index

9 780968 771198